SAVING TOBY

Interior Format

saving TOBY

A Novel By

SUZANNE McKENNA LINK

Also By
Suzanne McKenna Link

❧

KEEPING CLAUDIA
(Toby & Claudia Book 2)

Acknowledgements

WRITING IS A FAIRLY SOLITARY job, and writers are often oblivious to the world around them during the creative process. So, I'd like to take the time to let a few people know that their encouragement and support means the world to me.

Thanks and appreciation to my editors, Enrica Jang and Veronica Jorden. Enrica, my first tough critic, spent countless hours helping a wannabe debut author understand what it takes to create a good story and set me on the road to sharpen my craft. (And much love to my wonderful big brother, Mark McKenna, for his support and for introducing us). To Veronica, your immediate love for Toby and Claudia's journey breathed new life into this book. You've made revisiting this story a thrill for me … again. I'm grateful we found each other, and I hope we make many more beautiful books together.

To my dear friends, you are a never-ending well of encouragement.

To my family, you are the lights and laughter that replenish my soul.

To my husband, Brian, thank you for your nutritional support and enduring patience throughout my mid-life career change. It is your love and steady support that allows me to stand on my toes and reach for the stars.

"It always seems impossible until it is done."

~ Nelson Mandela

Prologue

"GOOD LORD! WHAT HAPPENED?"

Julia's eyes went wide when Al and I burst into the kitchen. She stopped putting birthday candles on the cake and tightened the belt on her bathrobe.

My face was bleeding.

Al threw a roll of paper towels at me and then turned to our mother.

"He cracked his chin open on the coffee table."

I wadded a dozen sheets and pressed them to the gushing wound. My jaw ached—there wasn't a spot on my body that didn't—but I just shrugged.

"I'm fine."

"There's so much blood." Julia came closer, but I could tell she didn't want to look. She hadn't been feeling well, and the sight of the blood seemed only to make her more squeamish. She glanced back at Al. "You look at it. Tell me how deep it is."

Annoyed, Al came over and yanked the towels away. He pushed my chin up to inspect the gash with his big hands, and a new stream of blood flowed down my neck.

Julia turned away. I knew she'd seen the cut anyway.

"He'll need stitches," she said. "Take him to the emergency room, Al."

Al grunted. "What's the matter with you? Why can't you take him?"

"I'm not feeling well," was all she said.

Al wouldn't stop. "Maybe while you're at the hospital, the doctors can finally figure out what's wrong with you."

I stepped forward. "Leave her alone. I don't need stitches."

"Yes, you do," Julia insisted. "Let me get dressed. I'll take you."

"I'll take him," Al barked, snagging his car keys from the hook near the back door. "Get in the car, you pussy."

"Fuck off," I snarled.

Dwarfed between us, Julia held up her hands and pleaded, "Boys, please stop fighting." She turned a distressed grimace on me. "And Toby, your profanity upsets me."

I lowered my head. "Sorry, Ma. I'll go with Al. Just relax."

Like yesterday, Julia was having a 'bad' day. Today, trying her best to be upbeat, she'd roused herself out of bed. Still, she hadn't managed to get dressed.

She rubbed my arm. "When you get back, we'll have your cake."

Fourteen stitches for my sixteenth birthday—and a scar I'd probably have the rest of my life. As Al drove me back from the hospital, I got a call from Dev.

"We're hanging out in town. Come down, we'll celebrate your birthday," Dev said.

I told Al to drop me off in front of the donut shop on Main Street.

He pulled the car alongside the curb. "Mom wanted you home for cake."

"I'll be home later," I said and got out. Leaning back in, I saw that his right cheek was swollen. At least I'd gotten in a few good shots before he'd taken me down.

"Hey, thanks for the birthday present." I patted my bandaged chin.

Al didn't reply. Before I had a chance to shut the door, he floored the gas pedal. I jumped backwards before the car's heavy door slammed shut, narrowly avoiding being decapitated.

"Asshole!" I gave him the one-finger salute as he drove off.

From outside the donut shop window I could see Ed, one of the local beat cops, at the counter. He eyed me through the plate glass, his stare fixed on my ridiculous bandage. I glared back.

"Get your donut and get out of here," I muttered under my breath.

Rounding the corner to the back, I saw Dev in the shop's small parking lot behind Main Street. He was with Ray—the two of them mostly concealed by a large commercial dumpster.

Just then, three younger elementary school kids rode by on their bikes, skirting the edge of the walkway doing wheelies and slide tricks over the curb. Dev shot out from behind the dumpster, growling savagely as he gave chase. The unsuspecting boys shrieked and took off down the block, pedaling as fast as they could. Winded, Dev picked up a handful of pebbles from the ground and chucked them in the kids' direction.

Near the donut shop entrance, four freshmen girls from my class sipped overpriced iced coffees and babbled incessantly. Only mildly interested in Dev's idiotic performance, their attention latched onto me as I drifted towards my friends. I scanned them, hoping to see the familiar shape of this one girl I'd been dying to tag. She wasn't among the crowd.

I'd been lighting up a Marlboro when the cute, dark-skinned girl from my Earth Science class, April, sidled up to me and smiled.

"What happened to your chin?"

I took a drag and said, "Skiing accident in Utah. Bad fall out of the helicopter."

She laughed and I immediately liked that she had a sense of humor.

"Hey, how come I haven't seen your friend around school?"

She sighed, loud and dramatic. "Claudia? Her parents sent her to St. John's. Can you believe that?"

"Bummer." Though I hadn't been close to making anything happen with her, I was disappointed with the news. Tucked away in private school, there was little chance anything ever would.

"Want me to tell her you said 'hi'?" April offered.

I squinted at her, wondering if she was yanking my chain, but she seemed sincere.

"Okay," I shrugged.

Right away, walking back to her friends, she began tapping on her cell phone, relaying the message. I didn't kid myself that anything would come of it, though.

Dev stepped up to me, looking over my shoulder at the girls.

"Think they'd hang out with us?"

I didn't even bother considering it. "No."

"Even if we tell 'em we got some ganja?"

"No."

Alone, I might've been able to hang with those girls. Unlike most of my classmates, I wasn't plagued by acne, and I'd grown two inches in the past year. An unexpected bonus to the constant battles with my brother was the way my once weedy body was morphing into a powerful fighting machine. I liked the change in my appearance—and girls seemed to like it, too.

Alongside scrawny Ray, who could barely string two words together, and Dev, built like a massive tugboat and prone to doing stupid shit like chasing down defenseless little kids on bikes, our collective odds were ridiculous. Getting with any of the girls here tonight would require a whole lot of clever chitchat and persistence. Normally, I wouldn't pass up the opportunity, but I was still wound up after the throw-down with my brother.

I was itching for a good fight and if there was anyone who could find one, it was Devlin Van Sloot. He was as predictably reactive as a lit stick of dynamite. Even without a fight, we could always get lit. Ray's house was stocked, and his mom was generous with her booze.

Chapter 1

~CLAUDIA~

"THIS IS AN EXTRAORDINARY LIST of service credits." Bill Ramsey, the managing director of Sterling Senior Care, looked over my recently updated résumé. Listed were all the organizations and service clubs I'd been a part of over the years, as well as the titles I'd held within each association. There was not one paid position.

From the corridor windows, the flowering March daffodils had been only a yellow blur in my dash to the director's office from the activities room. I had just finished getting my butt whooped in two straight hands of gin rummy by the adorable Mr. Ricci, one of the senior residents. In anticipation of discussing a new opening with Bill, I'd rushed the length of the building to his office with my résumé tucked under my arm, protected in a manila envelope. I was excited about the possibility of taking on a real job.

"The position is a home companion of sorts for a cancer patient, a woman in her fifties. Part-time, three nights a week," Bill explained.

"But I'm not licensed for that sort of work."

"You don't need to be licensed for it, and as wonderful as this is," Bill said with an apologetic smile, passing my résumé back to me, "they probably won't ask to see it either. They want someone to be home with the woman and maybe do some odds and ends around the house. I assured them you were reliable and would be a perfect fit for their needs." He handed me another sheet of paper from atop his desk.

"Joan Reitman, 563 Roosevelt Avenue," I read. The local address was familiar, but not the name.

"Yes, a family right in town, so your father should approve," he said.

I was used to these kinds of remarks regarding my father. Dad was a decorated Suffolk County police officer. Though my weekend position as junior coordinator of activities at Sterling was only voluntary, Bill had to meet my father's rigorous stamp of approval before I had been permitted to work at Sterling.

"I believe it's only for a few months, just until she gets back on her feet. Which made me think it would fit in nicely with your schedule. Probably finish up just before you leave for Los Angeles." His expression softened. Bill knew I was planning on transferring to the University of Southern California in the fall.

"Any news from USC yet?"

"Just that they have the application."

"So, I guess it would be pointless to ask if you'd made any headway with your father?" he said.

I shook my head.

"I hope you told him that the Davis School of Gerontology is one of the finest programs in the country."

I appreciated his interest in seeing me get into the program.

"Across the country is not an easy sell. Unless I can drive there in under forty minutes, it's practically useless to talk to him about it. I only hope when my acceptance comes in, I can figure out a way to get him on board."

"I'll keep my fingers crossed for you," Bill smiled.

"Thanks," I sighed, knowing I would need more than crossed fingers.

I hated going behind my father's back. After the divorce, my mother had followed a job to California and my dad and I had become a team. We'd weathered three years without her, still in the house I'd grown up in, about a half-mile from the Great South Bay on the South Shore of Long Island in the small town of Sayville.

My dad had always been my hero, chasing away monsters from under my bed and kissing my scraped knees. Even though I didn't need him to baby me like that anymore, to my ever-growing exasperation, he was insistent on being a part of my every decision. He wasn't buying into California. It was too far away for him to keep an eye on me.

I suspected that the bigger issue, the one that made him practically foam at the mouth, was that I'd be much closer to my mother. Dad had never forgiven her for leaving.

I put aside thoughts of sunny L.A. that Monday as I drove down Roosevelt Avenue, a few minutes before my five o'clock appointment with Mrs. Reitman. The neighborhood was just over a mile northwest of my house. The streets ran north of the railroad tracks and apartments, near the soccer fields where I, and just about everyone I knew, played as a kid. The houses were closer together and on smaller lots, some well cared for, some not.

I pulled up in front of house number 563. Two compact cars sat in the driveway beside the faded red-shingled house. A rusty, chain-link fence ran the perimeter of the property. The two-story house appeared exhausted, as though it had lost the fight against time and the elements.

I'd never actually been there before, but something about the house was familiar.

And then I remembered.

I had only a little time, but I fumbled for my cell and hit the first person on my contact list.

"Hey, chica," my friend April said, in her usual cheery greeting.

"You won't believe where I am."

"Outside my salon in a stretch limo with piña coladas and two first-class tickets to the Caribbean, where we'll dance the nights away under the stars?"

"Not quite," I laughed, looking out my windshield at the overgrown bushes and a weedy, dead lawn. "I'm interviewing for a job at the Fayes' house."

"The Fayes? You're kidding!"

The things that happened to the Faye family were the kinds of things folks in small towns loved to gossip about. As the daughter of Police Officer Donato Chiametti, I had the scoop on most of the town buzz. Back when I was in middle school, Mrs. Faye became a widow after her husband drove his pickup truck into oncoming traffic, killing himself and the two people in the other car. There was a lot of local controversy and anger over the accident, mostly because Mr. Faye had been drunk. After his death, Mrs. Faye quietly retreated, vanishing from all community involvement.

"Did Mrs. Faye remarry?" I asked April.

"I don't know. I haven't heard anything about her since Al Junior was convicted of killing that guy last year."

Al Junior, the older of the Fayes' two boys, was a rough character four or five classes ahead of me. I remembered him as a schoolyard bully. He'd grown up into a big, beefy guy with a temper. That he'd killed someone with his bare hands during a barroom brawl shocked the town, but most weren't surprised that Al was capable of it. Last I'd heard he was serving out a long prison sentence upstate somewhere.

"And Toby?"

Though the youngest Faye was a year older than April and I, he'd been in the same grade. Toby had gotten into his share of trouble, but wasn't known to have the same angry, intimidating personality as his brother.

After eighth grade, my parents had me transferred to a private high school. April, though, had gone to Sayville High School with Toby, and from what I remember her saying, he seemed fairly well liked by the other kids at school.

"I haven't seen him since graduation," April said.

I glanced at my dashboard clock and inhaled sharply.

"I have to go in. I don't want to be late."

"Good luck. Let me know how you make out."

Promising to call her back tomorrow, I said goodbye and scrambled out of my car. I walked through an opening in the fence where a gate should have been and up the pitted cement walk to the front door. The antiquated black scrollwork on the porch steps was peeling and rusted dry in more places than not.

A moment after I knocked on the dark wooden door, a slender, serious-faced older woman answered. She was not Mrs. Faye.

"Mrs. Reitman?"

"Yes?"

"I'm here about the job. We spoke on the phone."

"You're Claudia?" She pursed her thin lips when I nodded. "You're so young. I thought the residence would send over someone a little more mature." She stepped back, her manner almost patrician, as she allowed me to enter.

I was a little deflated by the quick judgment, but tried to turn it back. "I'm pursuing a career in health care. And I take my work very seriously."

She blinked at me before her face settled into a gentler expression.

"I'm sorry, please forgive me. Mr. Ramsey did speak highly of you," she said, and signaled me to follow her.

To the left of the doorway, a large bay window in the living room flooded the foyer with natural light.

She led me through the quiet house, down a wide hallway. We passed a tidy den and a staircase with faded mauve carpet. Her stride was quick and sure, and she didn't look sick, so I asked, "I'd be your assistant?"

"Me?" She glanced back with furrowed brows. "No, I'm as healthy as a horse."

We stopped inside a tired, old kitchen at the back of the house. The scent of woodsy cleaner intermingled with the spice of freshly brewed herbal tea.

On the far wall, the hazy late afternoon sun shone through the glass sliders, illuminating little floating dust motes. The kitchen had mismatched appliances, Formica countertops rubbed thin in spots, and a tan threadbare braided foot rug in front of the sink. But it was clean and certainly functional.

A slight, pale-faced woman sat at a rectangular, cloth-covered kitchen table. Her back was bolstered with a bed pillow. At the sight of us, she self-consciously patted her teal patterned silk headscarf.

"You'd be taking care of my sister," Mrs. Reitman said, motioning to the woman. She spoke across the room. "Julia, this is Claudia."

I stepped forward and held out my hand. "Mrs. Faye."

Her smile was slow, as if it took effort, but recognition lit her eyes. She gently grasped my proffered hand with cool, fragile fingers.

"Claudia Chiametti," she said, sounding surprised, but pleasantly so. "You've grown into such a beautiful young lady."

"Thank you," I said. "It's nice to see you again."

When I was younger, Mrs. Faye taught catechism, and back then it was rare not to see her at church functions, selling raffle tickets or organizing bake sales. Although I'd always known her to be petite, she now appeared painfully frail. Illness had taken its toll. Her milky-white complexion and sharp, angular face was similar to that of some of the older Sterling residents, but I knew she had to be at least twenty to thirty years younger.

Bill Ramsey had taught me that nothing was worse for a sickly person than seeing their sad condition mirrored in someone else's eyes. I forced myself to smile.

"I hear you can use some help. Tell me what you need," I said. Mrs. Faye's appreciative smile softened her features.

The ladies asked me to sit, and we started to discuss the job. Light cleaning, some cooking, and assisting Mrs. Faye when needed.

"Someone is here every day until my nephew gets home," Mrs. Reitman said. "He gets in around five o'clock. But he needs time to get out and unwind."

"You remember Toby, don't you?" Mrs. Faye asked.

"Of course," I replied, quickly doing the math in my head. Four years of high school and two of college. "It's been at least six years, though. I'm sure I wouldn't even recognize him if I saw him."

"That's right. You went to Catholic high school." Mrs. Faye nodded approvingly.

Mrs. Reitman pulled us back to task. "Julia needs wholesome, cooked meals. Can you cook?"

"I love to cook," I said, anxious to show them I was flexible. "I'll even find some healthy recipes for you!"

"This is going to work out better than I thought." Mrs. Faye sounded delighted.

The front door creaked on its hinges, and then we heard the sound of heavy footsteps entering the house.

"That's probably my nephew." Mrs. Reitman motioned over her shoulder and stood. "Since you'll be seeing him around the house, we might as well re-introduce the two of you now."

On a mission, the brusque woman left the kitchen. Mrs. Faye finished the tea she'd been drinking and, with effort, pushed the cup aside.

"He'll be in, in just a minute." Mrs. Reitman bustled back into the kitchen.

"Toby works at that appliance and electronics store in town. You know, the one on Main Street?" Mrs. Faye asked.

Wanting to demonstrate my initiative, I rose from my chair and picked up her empty teacup. "Yes, I know the place," I said, keeping eye contact with her as I moved toward the sink. In my peripheral vision, I became aware of motion, but too late to stop myself, I bumped into a solid wall of body.

"Oh!" I gasped, surprised as I hit a warm, immoveable mass with my shoulder and bounced off. A pair of masculine hands caught me around the waist and kept me from tumbling over. The teacup rattled in the saucer, but somehow I managed to avoid dropping it.

"Excuse me," I mumbled, looking up into a pair of almond-shaped, blue-gray eyes. Windswept, tawny brown hair streaked with multi-hued highlights softly framed a tan, handsome face.

He seemed just as stunned by our impact. We stood there, staring at each other for what seemed like an eternity while the warmth of his hands on me spread like a blaze up my torso and flamed my face. The spell was broken when his full lips parted and he said, "Claudia?"

That he knew my name set off alarms in my head. I struggled to reassemble my disjointed thoughts, and it took a moment to put it back together—where I was, who I was with.

This was Toby Faye.

Embarrassed at my inane reaction, I quickly regained my balance and retreated several steps.

"Oh, hi. Sorry about that."

"No problem," he said, and seeming to recover from our run-in with little effort, he turned to his mother.

"Hey, Ma. What's going on here?"

Mrs. Faye's face brightened as her son moved towards her. "Hi, honey. I guess you remember Claudia. She's going to help out with my care."

At a safe distance, I looked him over. I hadn't given Toby Faye a moment's thought in many years and had absolutely no expectations about him, but he was clearly no longer that lanky kid from middle school I remembered. In fact, he didn't look anything like I remembered. His chin was shadowed with a few days' growth of manly facial hair. He was much taller and had filled out. In well-fitted gray workpants and a plain white undershirt, I could see he had a hard, flat stomach that tapered down into a narrow waist. But it was his arms that drew my attention. Tight with substantial musculature, they were bronze with the deep tan of someone who worked out-of-doors.

He moved behind his mother's chair and rested both hands on her sloped shoulders. "I remember Claudia," he replied. Once again, he turned those eyes on me.

His weighted stare felt familiar. Uneasy, I was reminded how, years ago, I'd felt his gaze every time I passed him in the school halls.

"I didn't think you still lived around here," he said.

Though his comment sounded casual, I heard the insinuation. I turned and put the teacup in the sink. "Yes, well, I have to say, I didn't think you'd still be around here, either."

"I try not to be." He dropped his chin, but his eyes never left me.

"We'd like to have Claudia help out on Monday, Wednesday, and Friday evenings, from five to ten," Mrs. Reitman said, and I silently thanked her for not sitting idle while her nephew stared me down. "Toby, do you have anything to add or any questions you'd like to ask before we make our decision?"

Toby crossed his arms, seeming to give the question serious thought.

Finally, he said, "One."

I sat stiffly, worried. My interview had been going exceedingly well until he showed up. I prayed his one question wouldn't undermine it.

"Mets or Yankees?"

I blinked and glanced at the two ladies. Mrs. Faye looked amused. Mrs. Reitman sighed.

"Yankees?"

Toby squinted at me. "Are you asking or telling?"

I sat a little straighter.

"Yankees," I said, with more conviction. "Understand, my dad is a huge Mets fan. He considers my liking the Yankees a terrible disloyalty."

"A girl willing to betray her dad over baseball, and for the Bombers, no less. Now that's hot." He grinned. "You're hired."

Mrs. Faye laughed. Her laugh made me laugh.

Mrs. Reitman snorted. "Will this work for you, Julia?" she asked her sister.

Mrs. Faye answered with a nod, her eyes bright. Then the older woman turned to me. "You'll start Wednesday."

"Sure," I agreed readily.

"Good. Now that we have that settled, Julia, you should rest," Mrs. Reitman said sternly. "You look tired."

"Come on, Ma," Toby urged. "Let's get you upstairs."

Mrs. Faye and Toby said goodbye and, together, moved out of the kitchen. Mrs. Reitman folded her hands and waited until their voices became faint before speaking to me.

"My sister has Stage 4 non-Hodgkin's lymphoma. Normally this type of cancer is very treatable, but Julia's health wasn't so good going into it." The older woman glanced down at her hands and stood up, exhaling a weighty sigh. "I'd take care of her myself, but I lost my husband three years ago. Now I'm the sole caretaker for my elderly mother-in-law."

"I'm sorry," I murmured.

She looked at me. Frown and worry creases depressed the skin around her eyes. "You seem like a nice girl. And a strong one. I think your being here will help Julia regain her strength."

It made me feel good that she thought I would make a difference. I hoped to. Understanding the gravity of the situation, I intended to do all I could to help.

Chapter 2

~TOBY~

MY NEW UNIFORM FELT A little itchy, but I was whistling as I pulled inventory from the stockroom to load the small delivery truck that belonged to AB's Appliance and Electronics.

"What are you so chipper about this morning, Mr. Faye?"

Abraham Bernbaum, the owner, stood next to me, checking over my list. He was dressed in his own 'uniform' of creased khakis, plaid button-up, and despite the warming temperatures, a sweater vest. I looked down at his gray, balding head and figured him to be about five feet, five inches. Similar in height to Claudia Chiametti.

"Possibilities," I replied, not able to keep the smile from my face.

"Regarding?" he prompted.

"A girl I used to know." Sort of, in the loosest of definitions.

"One of the young ladies in here last week?"

He was talking about two old girlfriends that had stopped by when they heard I was in town. They'd left me their numbers. I wanted to tell Abe, "been there, done that," but I knew the old codger would only 'tsk-tsk' me with the disapproving face I'd already seen more times than I cared to count.

"No. Someone different," I said. Changing the subject, I reminded him about my schedule next week.

"Yes, yes, you have to leave early for a doctor's appointment on Tuesday. How is your mother doing, by the way?"

Canned reply. "Julia is good."

He made the face, put off by my use of Julia's name.

"Give your mother my regards," he said. Finally, he left me to continue alone.

It had been only a month ago since I'd come into the store look-

ing for work. Abe sized me up with a calculated eye and offered
me the position. I could tell he saw a sturdy guy, six-foot-one and
strong enough to move the large, heavy boxes that the delivery job
required. It was only minimum wage plus tips, but Abe had agreed
to be flexible about me coming in late or leaving early whenever
Julia had treatments or doctor visits because he'd heard of my
mother's hardships. I didn't ask what he'd heard. I didn't want to
know.

Until yesterday, I'd considered coming back home only an
obligation, something I needed to do because I was all Julia had.
Sentenced to life behind bars, my brother would be no help.

Taking care of Julia was not something new. Coming home,
I assumed I'd just fall back into routine. The rotating flock of
churchwomen volunteering for care shifts during the week was
unexpected. There was even talk about hiring someone from the
local adult home to cover a few nights so I could go out, too. I
pictured having to move around some mom-type lady in shapeless
scrubs and told Julia it wasn't necessary. Major League Baseball
season had started, and as long as I had Internet connection and
a decent TV to watch, I didn't really need to leave the house. But
she knew me well—knew I'd lose my mind if I stayed holed up
for too long.

I had driven home, dreading the return to my former existence,
and tried to come up with a few positives about being back, like
the weather this time of year being so much cooler on Long Island
than it'd been in Florida. After busting my ass the last eighteen
months taking whatever jobs that would keep me afloat—most
of which involved hard, sweaty labor intensified by the Sunshine
State's blistering heat and mind-altering humidity—the milder
weather here was a definite plus.

After yesterday though, the relief of a cross island breeze paled in
comparison to the glory that was Claudia Chiametti.

She used to sit in the front row of every class and raise her hand
to answer the teachers' questions. I used to stare at the back of her
head, at the shiny brown hair that poured down her back like dark
liquid. Sometimes she twirled it around her fingers and the teacher's voice would fade away. In the hallways, I kept my eyes peeled
for even a glimpse of her, hoping a smile would float my way, even

if it was only in my general direction. My body responded to the curve of her lips, tensing in a way that left me almost unable to walk.

Once, in seventh grade, I dropped my science folder in class. Red pen-slashed tests and class notes scattered in every direction. I was furious, but noticing, Claudia laughed and helped me chase down every last page. When she moved closer to hand me the papers, I intended to say something funny to make her laugh again, but her nearness made me lose my nerve. Not visible from our usual distance, up close, I could see a trail of freckles across her nose, and her creamy caramel skin looked so smooth. I could almost imagine touching it. Even though her smile was friendly, I was intimidated by her eyes. Clear and bright blue, like a cloudless sky, I'd been afraid that just by looking, she would see all that I tried to hide—the shame and embarrassment I felt about my family, the most common subject of the town gossip back then.

Claudia was never caught up in that obnoxious pecking order that was so much a part of life in the school halls. She was friendly—quick to lend notes or a pencil, to me or anyone else in need. Although she was nice to me, I never felt like I had any right to like her. She was one of the 'smart girls,' and I was a backwards, skinny kid with bruises all over. She was too perfect.

Even back then, small and starting to develop, it was obvious she would be a beauty. She was beautiful, in that classic kind of way. The pretty girl next door, but now, the little girl body was curvy in all the right places. Just the way I liked it.

To come home and practically have her fall into my arms was a fucking dream. My imagination was already working overtime envisioning all the things I'd like to do to her—stuff I guarantee she'd never in a million years considered doing with me.

Claudia was a major plus to being back. The mother lode. Not to mention she'd be on my turf, which gave me home-field advantage.

After the hard physical labor of installing pools in Florida, I was in good shape. Even fueled that Claudia was seeing me at my best, I had to admit I was still sort of intimidated by her. She seemed as close to perfect as any girl I'd ever known.

Out behind the store, I loaded the truck for my first round of deliveries, the whole time considering how best to approach

Claudia. I knew I could get with her because hooking up with girls was something I was good at.

A loud noise echoed through the cargo hold and startled me out of my musings. Something had smacked the outside of the truck. I looked up from my clipboard to see a familiar face grinning up at me from below the loading dock.

"Fuck me. I thought that was you, motherfucker!" Devlin Van Sloot yelled inside.

"Hey, dirt bag!" I called out to him. Without invitation, he climbed aboard. Big and strong as a heavyweight boxer when we graduated, Dev was thicker, but had somehow managed to maintain his fighter's build.

"When did you get back in town?" he asked, whacking me solidly on the back. The long scar over his right eye glowed white against the ruddiness of his fair skin. A broken bottle smashed on his forehead during a late-night fight, years ago, had left its mark.

I hadn't seen him in over a year, so I filled him in on my return and Julia's condition.

"Abe gave you a job, huh? That Jew never even trusted me in the store." His eyes scanned the contents of the truck, and a hand came to rest on the box of a GE washing machine. "Any chance this thing could fall off the truck?"

I laughed and shook my head. "Fuck, no. Abe double-checks everything, and I need this job."

He shrugged, but continued to survey the appliances. "We should go out. You, me and Ray. Take your mind off your mom's thing. What d'ya say?"

"Yeah. Wednesday after work is good," I said.

"I'll come by and get you." He threw a jab at my shoulder and hopped down off the truck bed.

I leapt down to see him off just as guys from Dean's Landscaping pulled up next to us and the usual four crewmembers piled out of their big red truck, heading for the coffee shop next door. As was becoming our routine, they waved to me, and I returned the gesture.

"Where's fucking immigration when you need it?," Dev grumbled as the Latino men walked by.

He hadn't changed one bit.

"You still hate everybody?"

Dev grinned. "Yeah, but I'm no hypocrite. I hate everyone equally." The comment was exactly what I remembered about him, and I laughed. He pointed at me. "I'll see you Wednesday. It'll be like old times."

"Old times? Hell no," I raised an eyebrow. "You'd better bring a new game."

"I might just do that," he said.

"Now get away from my truck." I waved him off to start my round of deliveries.

Chapter 3

~CLAUDIA~

DAD WAS MAKING DINNER WHEN I got home the next night. The savory aroma of simmering tomato and basil alighted my senses. My mother used to say my father was a good-looking man, but she thought he was handsomest in the kitchen. He was a sight—tall, solidly built, with full head of black hair graying at the temples. He kept his mustache bushy and thick so that his upper lip disappeared under it. Completely confident in his surroundings, he stood before the stove with one of my mother's old aprons tied around his waist. The flowery apron, however, didn't make my father any less intimidating.

"*Bella faccia*, baby girl." He kissed the top of my head when I came over to peek in the pot. "Chicken cacciatore."

"Smells good," I said, and gave him a quick hug. He was in an amicable mood, so I figured I might as well throw it out there.

"I went on a job interview yesterday."

His dark brows came together. "What kind of job? What about your schoolwork and Sterling?"

"It won't interfere with either," I said, picking up a slice of bread from the kitchen table and lifting the lid off the pot.

He shook his wooden spoon at me. "You'll get bread in my gravy."

Ignoring him, I waited until the bread absorbed the zesty sauce, saying, "It's an aide job, three nights a week at a private home. I start tomorrow night." I folded the whole piece into my mouth. The taste was as delicious as the smell.

"Where is this job?"

Chewing slowly, I leaned my hip against the counter.

"Remember the Fayes? On Roosevelt Avenue?"

Without pause, my father said, "You are not working for Al Faye."

I rolled my eyes. "Dad, the man's dead, and Mrs. Faye is very sick."

"Well, that's a shame." Dad pointed. "Set the table. If I remember correctly, there were two boys. One's a convicted felon. Where's the other one?"

"Toby is still home." I busied myself getting the dinner dishes and glasses from the cabinets.

"What's his story? He's been in trouble?"

"I don't think so. You'd know, wouldn't you?"

"Ah, probably just a matter of time before we arrest him for something." Dad added some salt to the sauce and tasted it.

"That's not a nice thing to say," I chided him.

"Maybe not nice, but the truth. The residual effects of a parent's weakness always spiral down to the kids. The older boy was ruined, and, mark my words, if there is trouble to be found, the younger boy is going to find it, too."

I remembered the way Toby greeted his mother that day, unexpectedly tender and attentive. Even if he did find trouble, I was convinced he wouldn't bring it home.

"I'll only be doing some cooking and cleaning three nights a week. How much trouble can I find?" I folded napkins and tucked them next to our plates.

Dad laid down a trivet and set the pot on the table. "Why do you need a job?"

My father's upbringing was steeped in tradition. My grandparents came to this country, off the boat from Italy. Like all the men in his family, my father was upright, moral, and fiercely protective of what belonged to him. Timeless, admirable traits perhaps, but the tradition of male dominance over the home was a throwback to the Old Country that should've stayed there. My German mother was fifth-generation American—liberal and open minded. She raised me to be independent. Being an obedient wife was not something she ever aspired to. How they ever got together, I never understood.

With my father, I learned early on that it was easier to do as I was told. But I'd also figured out that if I really wanted something, I had to dig my heels in and be stubborn, more so than him.

"Please, Dad. At Sterling, I don't actually get to do anything but play games with the residents." For good measure, I laid a hand on his arm. "With this job, I'll be hands-on. I'll be helping Mrs. Faye do so much. It's great career training."

He stroked his thick, dark mustache thoughtfully.

Finally, he said, "I'm going to call Mrs. Faye and get the details."

I hated that he felt it necessary to check up on me, but it was a small price to pay for the toehold.

After dinner, I called April.

"I don't get it. Why do you want to work?" she asked. "If my parents gave me gas, clothes and going-out money, you wouldn't find me working."

April had gone right from getting her hairdresser's license to working full-time in a salon. Her large Cuban family expected her to support herself and pitch in on finances.

I tried to explain. "If I'm lucky enough to get him to go along with USC, I don't want to push it by hitting him up for cash while I'm there," I said. "Besides, it's about time I start making my own decisions. I'm tired of being a marionette."

"You're like Pinocchio-ette," she teased. "You just want to be a real girl."

April had a way of twisting things to make me laugh at myself. It was good. I needed to lighten up sometimes.

"I saw Toby," I told her.

"You did?" April's voice went up an octave. "How's he doing? And how does he look? I bet he's even better looking now than he was in high school."

"He's doing okay, I guess. We didn't get a chance to talk much."

"And?"

I didn't want to give her ammo, but I also knew she wouldn't let it go until I spilled it.

"He's very good-looking," I grudgingly confessed.

"Ohh, you and a hot guy under the same roof," she purred. "This job could prove interesting. I mean, you haven't been out with a guy since Fast Phil."

I groaned at the mention of the name. Phil was a guy I'd dated briefly my freshman year in college. It ended before it had really started because the guy was all hands.

Despite my long dating hiatus, April's speculation about Toby

Faye did not thrill me.

"He might be good-looking, but we have absolutely zilch in common. And, really, I'm far too busy with school and my volunteer work to entertain your crazy pair-ups."

"Chica, why you always have to spoil my fun?"

On Wednesday, I headed over to the Fayes' for my first evening of work. Mrs. Reitman was there to greet me and show me around the house. Leaving me with a list, she departed for the night.

While Mrs. Faye slept, I decided to start with some cleaning in the kitchen. The refrigerator was full of plastic- and foil-wrapped food dishes, compliments of the church ladies, I suspected. I pulled everything out to the kitchen table, chucked a few suspicious items, and began scrubbing the inside of the refrigerator.

"What's going on in here?"

I jumped at the sound of Toby's deep voice.

Shielded from his view by the refrigerator door, I leaned back to peer around it and saw him grinning at me.

He eyed the table and turned back to me. "Someone's awfully hungry."

"I can never resist the urge to raid an overstocked refrigerator," I joked.

"Cool. I like a girl with a good appetite," he said, as he began lifting foil covers to inspect the contents before he leaned back against the counter and faced me.

Avoiding his gaze, I turned back to wiping down the inside of the fridge.

"So, what do you think of all this?" he asked.

Brushing hair from my face, I said, "I think the amount of food in here is obscene."

Toby just laughed and shook his head. "I mean, I haven't seen you since middle school, and now you're here in my house, cleaning the refrigerator." He crossed his arms and eyed me. "Kind of strange, no?"

Flushing, I scrambled to reply. "I guess. But I'm glad I can help your mom. She's really sweet."

"Yeah. She is." He nodded. "So, what have you been up to? Going to college?"

"Yes, I'm at Stony Brook right now, but I just applied to transfer."

"Not happy over at the Brook?"

"SBU is great, but I'd like to try someplace new," I said, not sure why I suddenly had loose lips about the transfer I'd mostly kept on the down low—and with him of all people.

He opened his mouth to reply, but we were startled by a loud bang at the front of the house, followed by the crashing sound of the front door opening and slamming against the wall.

"Yo, Faye. Where you at?" The loud booming voice seemed to shake the house.

"Shit." Toby's eyes widened, and he bolted from the kitchen. I followed.

"Hey, man." A big stocky guy with blond hair leaned heavily against the door, as if he needed it to remain standing.

"Dev, man, you can't come crashing into my house like that," Toby said, his voice tight and low. "Julia is resting."

"Whoops, sorry." The friend laughed, but lowered his voice. "Are you ready?"

Toby shook his head. "I didn't even have a chance to eat or change out of my work clothes yet."

"Hey, who we got here?" The big guy perked up, his attention shifted to me, standing in the kitchen doorway.

He had trouble written all over him, the kind my father warned me about. The kind I always avoided.

I ducked back into the kitchen and overheard Toby tell him, "She works here."

"Got her doing hands-on stuff, huh?" The guy snickered. "Nice, dog."

I stopped listening and got back to work. Scrubbing finished, I started to put the food back into the refrigerator, trying not to listen to them mumble to each other. The door opened and shut. Toby reappeared in the kitchen.

"That was Devlin. He's a little crazy, but he's okay."

He seemed to want to talk more, but I had finished with the refrigerator and closed the door.

"I'm going to check on your mother," I said, using the excuse to escape the kitchen. That was the most I'd ever spoken to Toby. Though he seemed nice enough, his friend Devlin was a reminder that we didn't have much in common socially.

I ignored Toby's presence in the house as I concentrated on getting Mrs. Faye settled into a large easy chair in her bedroom and served her dinner. I would be glad when he was out of the house and I could spend the rest of my shift with her.

We talked as she ate, but soon rowdy voices and the distinct pungent odor of marijuana wafted up through the narrowly open bedroom window overlooking the backyard. I glanced out and saw Devlin and another questionable looking guy sitting on the outdoor table set. They were passing a joint and joking around, some of their crude comments loud enough for me to hear.

"Oh, dear." Mrs. Faye frowned. "Smells like Toby's old high school friends are here."

It was awkward, but I didn't respond. Instead, I straightened the pill bottle collection on her night table, reminding myself that Mrs. Faye was the sole reason I'd put up with whatever those boys were doing.

Toby came into the room, hair wet and outfit changed from work clothes to loose-fitting jeans and a T-shirt. With a slight swagger in his step, he smiled at me as he passed by. His cologne mingled with the smell of shampoo and tickled my nose.

I hadn't quite reconciled this new version of Toby with the boy I remembered. The way he held himself, his shoulders back and chest out, he appeared to be much more self-assured. No doubt, many girls found him appealing, but honestly, if I hadn't been so startled by his transformation, I wouldn't have given him a second look. Just like his friends in the yard, he had street attitude written all over him.

"Hey, Mama Bear," he said, running his hand over her shoulder. "You're not ready? I thought we were going out dancing tonight."

"Don't be ridiculous." She waved a hand, her laughter making her sound like a young girl.

His lips curled around a smirk. He was entertaining her—and enjoying it.

"You better watch this one." He motioned to me, making me a participant in his show. "She has one helluva appetite. Cleaned out our entire refrigerator."

Way corny, but I chuckled despite myself.

"Claudia, honey, you're welcome to whatever you want when

you're here," Mrs. Faye reassured me, oblivious to the teasing.

"Am I included in that 'whatever'?" He winked at me.

"Don't be fresh," Mrs. Faye warned.

"Hey, look at her, she's beautiful." He gestured to me as if I were a work of art hung upon the wall. "You can't blame a guy for trying."

Unaware of how his attention embarrassed me, he kissed his mother on the cheek and told her he'd be home by ten.

"Wait. I need to talk to you," Mrs. Faye called to Toby as he started to leave. He halted waiting for her to go on, but she looked to me. "Honey, could you give us a moment alone?"

"Of course." I nodded, left the room, and pulled the door closed behind me. I didn't mean to listen in on their conversation, but the door was thin.

"Those boys," Mrs. Faye said. I imagined her shaking her head. "Promise me things will be different while you're home this time."

This time? Had he been away? At the sound of Mrs. Faye's pleading voice, I felt fiercely protective of her. I wouldn't tolerate him upsetting her.

Toby chuckled. "Okay, Mom. I promise, I promise. I'll keep it on the down low, Scout's honor."

I rolled my eyes at the thought of Toby as a Scout and jumped back when the door swung open, catching me by surprise.

"I've been properly chastised, so you can come back in now." Making a show to be formal, he held the door for me. "But be careful. She takes no prisoners." He finished the warning with a slicing motion across his neck.

"Oh, go on, get out of here," Mrs. Faye laughed, apparently in a better mood. "And behave yourself!"

"Yes, ma'am." He saluted her and turned to me. "See ya later," he said, and very casually flicked a lock of my hair as he walked by.

Stunned by his boldness, I stared after him as he proceeded to shuffle down the stairs, whistling.

Chapter 4

~TOBY~

RAY RUDACK HAD ALWAYS BEEN a small kid, smaller than most the boys at school, and much smaller than Dev and me. But it was his stutter, the halting, jumbled spray of words that stumbled off his tongue when he was nervous, that kept him from making other friends. I liked him though, and he easily fit in as the sidekick, our comic relief. Dev and I pushed him around, teased him, as tight friends do, and he took our crap without complaint. Looking at him now, I could see he was still a freaking mess. Hair hung in his eyes, his breath stank, and the nasty sweatpants he had on looked like he'd been wearing them for days. He'd set sail on a cruise to nowhere and sadly, seemed ignorant of it.

Through most of high school, I'd spent a lot of time at the Rudacks' house, mostly to avoid home. And Al Junior. It was a place where no one cared what you smoked, how long you stayed, or if your family was messed up.

We were hanging out in Ray's kitchen, the same now as then, having a few beers. Leaning against the sink, I looked around. The wall above the stove was yellow with oily residue, the sink had a few dirty dishes in it, and trash overflowed the container. Ray and Dev pushed aside a cheap-looking, plastic flower basket and sat at the table with their stash and rolling papers spread out on the pitted surface. The scent of a burning blunt blew in from the den. Ray's younger brother and a few friends were hanging out much like we had a few years ago.

Nothing ever changed.

We heard a crash from the other room, followed by laughter. Ray leapt out of his chair to investigate, yelling, "Little shit, you'd b-b-better fix that!"

"Ah, the familiar sounds of brotherly love," I drawled.

Dev snorted.

The back door opened, and Mrs. Rudack came in. Despite the cool night, she had on a tight, open-neck shirt that made it hard not to notice her perky, surgically enhanced boobs. She was clearly coming in from her own little party out back.

"Tobeee," she crooned, pulling me into a hug. "I've missed you."

Dev and I both agreed. She was a MILF. Her body was tight for her age, though her face was wrecked from years of drinking and hard-core partying—she made us guys look like amateurs.

"Hello, Mrs. Rudack." The hug lasted a few awkward moments longer than it should have. I drew away from her.

"Please call me Diane—I'm not married anymore." She wagged a finger and smiled at me. "'Mrs.' makes me sound so old. If you guys don't have plans, my girlfriends and I are having drinks out back around the fire pit. You can join us if you want." She might have meant the invitation for all of us, but her eyes were only on me.

"No, thanks, Mom," Ray jumped in. "We're going into town."

"Oh, okay. Maybe some other time." She batted her eyes at me.

When she left the room, Dev let out a low catcall.

"What'd you think of that rack? She took out a loan for those puppies."

"Impressive," I said and looked out the back door.

Diane and her two friends were drinking and laughing around a small, steel-bowled fire pit set up on the beaten-down lawn. I eyed the prospects.

"I don't know, guys. There are three experienced cougars out there all primed to pounce—one for each of us, but I call dibs on your mother, Ray. I think she's hot for me."

"Shit, with the way she was all up on you, you could definitely get her." Dev nodded and grinned. "In fact, you'd be my mother-fucking hero if you did."

"G-guys, come on, that's m-my mother," Ray protested weakly, more concerned with rolling and lighting the next joint.

"Come on, Rudy. I haven't gotten laid since Florida," I continued, just to bust his chops. "If I hook up with your mom, you can call me 'Daddy.'"

Fingers halted, eyes darted to me. I finally got Ray's attention. "Screw you, Faye!"

His reaction broke Dev and I up, but after we settled down, Dev eyed me with a smirk.

"Seriously, dude, you're not hitting that hot little number hanging out in your kitchen?"

"I told you she works at the house with Julia. Leave it alone." I leaned against the counter, refusing to talk about Claudia with these knuckleheads.

Dev slanted forward. "If you're not interested, I'd like a crack at her."

"Man, you are delusional if you think you have a shot with her." I shook my head and took a sip of my beer.

"Not delusional. Not with these." Dev smiled and pulled out a baggie with a couple of pills in it. "I'll mix her a cocktail that will ensure a night of sizzling interaction."

I choked on a mouthful of beer, and it dribbled down my chin. "You're fucking crazy if you think I'd let you slip any of those to her." I swiped my face with the back of my hand and glared at him. Just the thought of him touching her pissed me off.

Dev gritted his teeth and squinted at me. Just as quickly as it came, the anger slipped away, and he leaned back coolly and smiled.

"Ah, you just want her for yourself." Dev threw his hands in the air. "And you'll probably get her, too. Girls like you. Shit, Ray's mom was practically ready to blow you."

"Goddamn it, Dev!" Ray was suddenly on his feet. "Don't talk about my mother like that!" Totally out of character, with his face twisted in anger, he punched Devlin in the arm.

We all became quiet. Dev's eyes flashed. I considered intervening. Provoking Van Sloot was a death wish. Understanding that he'd overstepped, big time, Ray dropped his arms limply at his sides as his face went blank. Without another word, he sat back down.

Dev's nose twitched, followed by tight moment of uncertainty. He seemed to calm down … and then he lunged towards Ray, quick as a shot. I thought he might hit the kid after all.

Instead, he reached forward with a giant hand and swiped the joint Ray was holding. He took a hit and held it out to me. I waved it off.

Dev slowly exhaled a stream of heady smoke. "Come on, let's get stewed and rip up the town like we used to."

"Not me, man. I told you I'm not interested in repeating that stuff. Besides, I can't get wrecked, not while Julia's sick." The smoke wafting around the room was already creeping into my mind. "But we can still get out of here for a while."

"Ye-yeah, let's go to Murphy's. They have the Yankee-Red Sox p-pre-season game on the big screen. And free wings during the g-game," Ray said.

"I'm not going anywhere with you unless you freaking put on a clean pair of pants and brush your teeth," I snapped.

"Shut the hell up, Faye," he grumbled, but he disappeared and came back with different pants on.

Dev offered to drive. There was no question I'd be up front with Dev, which put Ray in the backseat of the fully refurbished black Cutlass.

As I climbed in, my shoe caught on a large canvas bag on the floor of the passenger seat.

"Just throw that in the back," Dev said.

"What is it?" I lifted the bag, intending to hand it to Ray, but then I saw envelopes inside. "Working for the post office?"

"Yeah, undercover," Dev laughed. He turned the key, and the engine roared to life. "It's from my job. You know, looking for cashable checks. I hit a good bag last week, but I can't take any-more after this one. They'll get suspicious."

"Glad to see you raised your crime standards from petty to fed-eral," I said, needling him.

"God, what the hell is up with you, Faye? Stop getting all over me. You ain't so fucking clean either."

"You know man, I don't do crap like this anymore." I shook the bag. "And I'm not cool driving around with it. Either you leave it at Ray's or I'll take my Jeep."

Dev shook his head but twisted around to Ray. "Rudy, throw that bag in the house, will you?"

Ray grabbed the bag and hopped out. Dev's scrutiny returned to me.

"You sold out."

"What the hell are you talking about? Working a legit job is selling out?" I chuffed.

"Yeah. Come on, not getting high, and working that nine-to-five every day? Bet you're breaking your fucking back. And for what? How much is old Abe paying you?"

"It doesn't matter. It's a job," I ground out, not wanting to talk about the crappy money I was making. "As soon as Julia's in remission, I'm outta here."

Chapter 5

~CLAUDIA~

IT WAS EASY TO WORK with Mrs. Faye. Within the first few weeks, I became familiar with her preferences—she took honey with her tea, her food heavily salted, and drinking water at room temperature. She liked to play rummy and watch game shows. She read a passage in her bible every night before she went to sleep, and I was never ever allowed to see her without her head kerchief on.

"I didn't see your car out in the driveway." Propped up in her bed, bible open in her lap, Mrs. Faye looked older than her fifty-three years.

As I did each night, I put her hot tea on the night table and sat in the upholstered chair bedside her bed. "My father dropped me off. Car troubles. The mechanic thinks it's my starter. He's keeping it overnight. Thank God it's a nice night for a walk home."

This was fast becoming my favorite part of my time with Mrs. Faye, the end of the night, just before Toby came home, when I sat down with her and we talked. She told about what was happening in the lives of her church friends, and we discussed our favorite shows, what I was studying in school. Just about any subject could pop up. She had a clear, soft voice that hinted at insight and clarity. I'd never met someone like her, and I was intrigued.

"You don't have to walk. It's too far. Toby can drive you," she said.

"No, it's really not far. Only about a mile. I used to play a lot of tennis in high school, but with my current schedule, I don't get much exercise. The walk and fresh air will do me good."

"It's just you and your father then? I heard someone mention your mother was in California. Is that right?" Mrs. Faye asked.

"That's right. She's a real estate agent in San Diego," I said, sorting the evening's medications and handing them to her.

She accepted the pills and met my eyes. "That must be difficult having her so far away."

I shrugged. "Sure, but my parents can't be around each other. They just fight. But, I see my mother as much as I can, and I'm planning to transfer in the fall, to a school not far from her."

"In California?"

"She's always trying to get me to come out there." I stood and started to tidy up around her. "Thought this would be a good way for us to spend more time together. I'm waiting on my acceptance, crossing my fingers and my toes that everything goes through. And that my dad goes along with it."

"He doesn't approve?" Eyebrows arched over her bright blue eyes.

"Dad's old-fashioned. He'd much rather I settle down and pop out a brood of kids. But kids and a husband? Not me, not yet." I made quick work of folding a blanket at the foot of the bed. "I don't want his conventional life. I like school. And USC is amazing. I visited last time I was in California. That's when I decided I was going to make it happen."

She patted my hand. "I love that you're following your dream. That kind of enthusiasm is contagious."

I assisted in turning her onto her side and tucked the sheet and blanket around her. "It means I'll be gone for most of the year, but I'll try to come visit."

"Please do. It'll be wonderful to hear all about it," she told me, then smiled. "I never went to college. Maybe I can live it vicariously through you."

"Great, then we'll make plans to get together whenever I'm home so I can tell you everything," I said, pleased to think I'd made a lifelong friend in Mrs. Faye.

Just then, the front door creaked, announcing Toby's arrival and the end of my shift. With Mrs. Faye settled, I wished her a goodnight and went downstairs to leave.

Toby was rummaging through the refrigerator and came out with three beers. Though I was at the house a few times a week, I was usually busy cooking and cleaning and we didn't interact much. Still, I felt reasonably at ease around him.

"Hey," he said holding one of the bottles out to me. "Want one?"

"Thanks, no." I shook my head. "Your mother is all set for the night. See you Wednesday."

He nodded, and I headed out the door.

It was a nice night—spring was in the air—and I didn't mind that I had to walk. Outside the Fayes' front door, two guys leaned against Toby's red Jeep Wrangler. I recognized his friend, Devlin, from the other night. The second guy was smaller and raggedy-looking, with messy, dark brown hair. I caught their attention as I started down the steps.

"Hey there, beautiful." Devlin pushed off the car and came forward.

His hulking size and overfriendly smile did more to intimidate me than make me want to talk to him. I kept walking, but to be polite, I acknowledged him with a nod and a brief smile. Behind us, Toby came out onto the front steps.

"Wait, look." Devlin's fingers brushed the sleeve of my jacket. "It's cocktail hour. Stay for a drink."

"No, thanks." I angled away from him and kept walking, but the smaller guy got in step with me.

"Y-y-your pretty," he said, affording me a glimpse of overlapping front teeth as he grinned.

The unexpected compliment sat awkward on my shoulders. As I opened my mouth to respond—a thank you for his kind words— his hand cupped my backside. "Got a na-na-nice ass, too!"

Anger rose up, hardening inside me, and with a feline hiss, I lashed out and solidly whacked the offending hand. The little creep yowled and jumped back, but I stepped forward and jabbed a finger at him. "Ever touch me again and you'll lose that hand."

Despite my boiling anger, a cold sweat dampened my armpits and crept down my back. The creep raised his hands in mock surrender and backed away. Devlin and Toby, with front row seats to the show, rolled with fits of laughter. I eyed the two of them, my glare sharpening on Toby.

I'd figured because of his mother, we were on the same team. What a foolish thought. He'd betrayed me, for the sake of his friends. There was no one I could trust in this group. With the knowledge weighing me down, I ran—through the darkened neighborhood, flying as fast as my feet would carry me, houses a blur—until my lungs protested and I had to lean over, hands on my knees, to catch my breath.

And that's when I heard them—running footsteps coming from behind me.

"Claudia!" Toby called. "Wait up."

"Asshole," I hissed under my breath.

I righted myself and intended to run again, but could only manage a hurried walk. It took only seconds before he caught up with me.

"Hey," he said, slightly winded. "Are you okay?"

"Perfect. I'm always glad to provide amusement for a couple of rowdy jerks," I growled, and kept walking. "I'll be back again next week, and we can really yuck it up."

"'Yuck it up?'" A dubious smile flitted across his face.

I whirled around to face him. "Shut up!" I was furious that he'd somehow made me feel self-conscious. "Did you follow me just to make fun of me?"

"No." He backed up a step and put his hands in his pockets. "I just wanted to tell you I'm sorry and that I shouldn't have laughed."

His apology was too late, but I bit my tongue, turned away from him, and stomped on.

He began walking also, continuing his lame explanation. "Ray's a bonehead. Neither of those guys knows how to behave around a beautiful girl like you."

"Your friend harassed me, and you laughed." I kept my head down, arms tight to my sides, and refused to look at him. "Don't try to flatter me now. Go away and leave me alone!"

Without warning, he took a large step and positioned himself in front of me. I almost crashed into him. "What are you doing?" I snapped.

He tilted his head to look into my eyes. "Hey. I mean it, I'm sorry." He had the decency to look ashamed. "It will never happen again, okay?"

"Oh, it won't because I'll … "

He put a tentative hand on my shoulder, his expression serious. "If anyone even thinks about touching you again, I will kick their ass up and down the street."

"Great. That's very comforting." I couldn't hide my sarcasm. "Now get out of my way. I want to go home." Thankfully, he stepped aside.

"Where's your car?" he asked, falling into step with me again.

I sighed and mumbled, "Auto shop."

"I would have given you a ride."

I stopped and faced him. "I don't need a ride. I can get home just fine all by myself. Go home. I'd actually feel safer without you."

"Ouch. That hurts," he said, but although he claimed to be injured, the corners of his mouth tweaked up in a smile. "Come on, I feel bad about what happened. Let me walk you home. If it makes you feel better, I can walk behind you, like a shadow. You won't even have to look at me."

Sighing again, I put a hand over my face, and, despite it all, I laughed. "You're a special type of ridiculous."

"Yeah, the cute kind, right?" He cocked his head to one side and grinned.

I shook my head at his arrogance, and too tired to fight anymore, I let him walk me home.

Chapter 6

~CLAUDIA~

MONDAY I HAD TWO LONG lab sessions, and afterwards, I had just enough time to make myself a quick sandwich before heading over to the Fayes' house.

I was glad when Mrs. Faye told me that Toby was running some errands and I wouldn't see him until later. He had done his best to make amends on the walk home, but I still had mixed feelings about our interaction after that last unpleasant night.

I had to coax Mrs. Faye to eat. She managed a little, and when she couldn't eat anymore, I straightened up her bedroom while she flipped on the TV.

"Wow, a new television," I said, admiring the small, sleek, flat-screen set attached to the wall on the other side of her bedroom.

"Toby says everything in this house is so old and tired. I guess he's right. I haven't had any interest in improving things around here for a long time. Too long," she admitted with a sigh. "Toby got the TV at work. Said Mr. Bernbaum gave him a decent employee discount."

Everyone knew AB's. The store had been around forever. I was surprised Mr. Bernbaum had hired Toby. I'd heard he was very selective about employees.

"How long has he been working there?" I dusted her dresser, mildly interested.

"He's only been home about a month—since he found out I was sick," she said, lowering the TV volume. "He was in Florida for the last year and a half."

"Oh? What was he doing for work while he was there?"

"Let's see, first, there was building houses." She began ticking off a list on her fingers. "Then landscape work and finally pool installations. He hasn't quite found his niche yet. A few months ago, he said he might talk to a recruiter about enlisting."

"The military?" Boot camp would be perfect for an aimless guy like him.

Mrs. Faye raised her thin shoulders in a shrug. "He hasn't brought it up since I told him about the re-diagnosis, and honestly, I'm glad."

"Re-diagnosis? You've had cancer before?"

"I've been in remission for a few years. But these things happen. It's just a setback. I'll be fine." She waved her hand in nonchalance. "I didn't even want to ask Toby to come home."

"You shouldn't have had to ask," I blustered.

"I didn't. He came home on his own."

Embarrassed by my gaffe, I murmured. "That's good."

"Yes, it is. But though I'd like him to stay, he won't. Being here only seems to make him restless. Too many bad memories, I suppose."

"You mean Mr. Faye's death?"

"Mostly. Despite what everyone seems to think about my husband, he loved his boys, but the relationship between him and my oldest son, Al Junior, was terribly strained." Mrs. Faye fingered the remote distractedly. "Al Junior was such a handful when he was little. We could never get him to sit still. We never had him tested, but looking back, I'm sure he had one of those attention disorders. To make matters worse, I was anemic when I was pregnant with Toby. I didn't have the energy to deal with a busy toddler. My husband didn't tolerate misbehavior. He was tough on our oldest, but it was because that's all he knew. His own father was a stiff physical disciplinarian. Thank God for Toby. He was a much easier child, such an easy disposition."

She smiled when she spoke of him. "He and his father had a less complicated relationship. But you can't treat your children so differently without them noticing. It makes siblings angry and resentful towards each other."

"Do the boys not get along?" I forgot about cleaning, giving her my full attention.

"No, not really. When my husband died—" She stopped to inhale. "Well, when my husband died, things got bad. I let so many things slide. The boys fought. A lot."

I'd never really thought about what Toby was going through back when I knew him in school, but now his quiet moodiness fit into place like a missing puzzle piece.

"Al Junior has been doing a great deal of reflecting since he was sent away, and I can see he's changing. It's my hope that one day my boys will get along, but there's a lot to do to get them there. That's why I refuse to let this cancer defeat me. I have work to finish." For the first time, Mrs. Faye's sounded strong, firm. "Toby is a much gentler and more compassionate soul than his brother, but he holds onto bitterness like a hungry dog with a big, meaty bone."

The Toby I had been around for the last few weeks appeared quite comfortable in his skin, haughty with self-confidence. Not in the least like the bitter person his mother was describing.

"With all that Toby's been through, I would've understood if he hadn't come home, but he did, so that means there is hope." She sniffled and reached for a tissue at her bedside. "But I know the moment I'm feeling better, he'll take off, looking for something to make him happy, something he'll never find out there."

Whatever it was that Toby was looking for, Mrs. Faye seemed to believe it was here, right under his nose. Seeing how much Toby's being home meant to her, my frustration with her son began to ebb.

"Oh, dear, Claudia, honey. I'm sorry. You must think I'm crazy to rattle on this way!" She blotted her eyes.

The story had moved me, and I sort of felt like I needed to do something to help her resolve the dilemma, though I didn't know exactly what. I sat on the edge of the seat across from her bed.

"It's fine, Mrs. Faye. If there's anything I can do to help the situation, just ask."

"You're such a doll." She patted my hand affectionately. "And so easy to talk to."

I smiled. People often told me that.

When it was close to ten o'clock, I went down to the kitchen. I was writing a grocery list at the kitchen table when Toby came in.

"Hey." He approached cautiously. "We still okay?"

He acted as awkward as I felt.

"Well, that night certainly left an impression," I said and got up to tack the list on the refrigerator.

He blew out a loud breath. "Come on. Don't hold that against me. Despite a moment or two of bad judgment, I'm not a bad guy."

I faced him and crossed my arms. "Keep your creepy friends away from me, and I'll let it go."

"I can do that," he said and stepped closer. "Is Julia sleeping?"

His closeness alarmed me, but it would seem cowardly to move away.

"Yes," I answered, standing my ground. "Why do you call your mother by her first name?"

"'Cause mommies and daddies take care of their families. Around the Faye house, we don't subscribe to traditional family shit. That's much too ordinary." He shrugged and looked away.

I heard the bitterness his mother had spoken of earlier.

"I suppose not. Your mother gave me a quick overview of your family tonight."

"And you haven't run for the hills yet?" Toby snorted. "What did my dear mother say about our lovely family?"

"The truth, that things were rocky between your father and your brother. And you and your brother, too." We caught each other's eye. He looked away again. Poor guy. There was no doubt the topic made him uncomfortable.

"Hmm, yeah. Surprising, but we survived," he said and began tracing a knot in the wood molding with his finger. "Julia's had to deal with a lot more crap than she deserves."

"You've had it rough, too," I said. "I didn't realize until tonight that this was the second go-round with your mother's cancer. Dealing with it can't be easy for you, either."

"Nothing about this is easy." Noticeably frazzled, he ran his hand across the top of his head. "Being home again, watching her wasting away while she goes through chemotherapy and radiation. It's hell."

His words softened me, and I felt the need to reach out to touch him. But I resisted.

"If it's any consolation, it means a lot to her that you're home," I said.

He shifted his feet restlessly. "I need to be here. I just wish there was more that I could do. With my aunt, you, and the church women doing stuff for her, I feel useless."

Without his normal confidence and joking banter, this tough guy looked lost—more like the boy I remembered. Fully acknowledging the situation of what he was dealing with, there was no way I could continue to be distant.

"You're not useless. You support her in many ways, and more importantly, you make her smile." I laid a hand on his shoulder, fighting the urge to shake some sense into him. "Your mom is an amazing person and much stronger than you think."

"Yeah, she's a tough one. But I don't know. This time around the cancer seems to be kicking her ass." The last few words came out with a crushing weight. He blew out a shaken breath and quickly turned his face away.

Oh no. Nothing affected me quite like a person breaking apart in front of me. But a tough guy? My need to offer comfort spiraled off the charts. I swayed toward him, arms twitching, but I couldn't bring myself to do it. He was like a mountain lion, and getting that close to a big cat scared me.

In the end, it was he who leaned in those last few inches, a silent appeal, and I automatically responded by putting my arms around him. My cheek met his hard, warm shoulder, and his face rested against the crook of my neck. His breath fanned my skin, and musky aftershave invaded my nostrils. I tentatively patted his back in attempt to comfort him, but the intoxicating scent coupled with our contact made my body respond in a vexing way. I released him from the embrace and forced myself to look at him while trying to conceal my body's muddled reaction.

"You'll both get through this."

He was quiet for a few moments before he let his eyes meet mine.

"Sorry," he said. "I didn't mean to dump my problems on you."

"It's totally fine," I said. "I always find talking to someone helps."

"Thanks, but it's not my M.O. to air my dirty laundry." He cleared his throat and ran a hand through his hair again. "Anyway, I should go say goodnight to the old lady. I'll see you Wednesday?" He gave me a half-hearted, lopsided grin.

My stomach fluttered. "Yes. Wednesday."

Chapter 7

~TOBY~

ON WEDNESDAY, I HAD TO deliver a refrigerator to an older couple's house. While hauling out their ancient one, some slimy water spilled on me. The smell was so foul I nearly hurled.

Abe Bernbaum just shrugged when he heard.

"That's the job. If you want to do something different, use your brains."

Pissed off, I couldn't wait to get home and into the shower to scrub the nasty off me.

Freshly showered and dressed, I slipped in across the hall to check on Julia. She was sitting up, reading in bed when I came in. I was relieved to see that she looked rested.

"What's on the agenda tonight, Ma? Strip poker, male dancers, and Jell-O shots?"

She laughed. "Oh, no, something even more exciting. Claudia's making me soup!"

"Soup! I love soup. Maybe I should stay home, too."

Her laughter was strong. "No, no. Go out and have some fun. Give me a hug and then get out of here. I'm in good hands."

My stomach growled when I smelled the sautéed onions and garlic in the kitchen. At the table, Claudia was busy chopping carrots. I stopped in the doorway, my palms on either side of the opening. I had stepped up my weight training, and I knew my arms looked powerful. Flexing, I leaned forward into the room.

"What are you making?" I asked, willing her to look at me.

"I found a recipe for this soup loaded with cancer-fighting antioxidants." Claudia glanced up, but only briefly. "It's going to kick your mother's immune system into high gear." This made her smile and, in turn, made me smile.

Focused on her chopping, she appeared uninterested in my presence. I don't know how she managed to be so sexy and so damn cute while making Julia 'cancer-fighting' soup, but she was.

I wanted to keep talking to her.

"Listen, a guy who graduated with me, Jim Ryan, is having a party this Saturday," I said.

"My friend April mentioned it," she replied.

"April DeOro?"

"You remember April?"

"Sure. We were good friends in high school."

"Good friends?" she asked doubtfully.

"After Ray and Dev, I understand your shock."

"I'm not shocked. She just never mentioned you two were friends."

"Well, ask her. We had some good times together." I leaned against the doorway. "She still with Dario?"

"Yes. In fact, he and I go to Stony Brook together."

"I should give him a call," I said.

"You should. He's a good guy."

"Unlike my other friends."

Claudia simply smiled.

"So." I crossed my arms over my chest and flexed again. "You going?"

"Maybe. If April wants to." She shrugged. "Are you?"

"Oh yeah. It wouldn't be much of a party without me."

"Too much." She giggled and shook her head. "I guess I'll see you there."

"Definitely." I hoped the party would be an opportunity to impress her. So far, she wasn't giving me much to work with.

I spent another night looking for a quick thrill with Dev and Ray. I took a few pulls from the bottle Ray offered, but it wasn't long before I was feeling out of sorts. I wanted to go home and try to make a little more headway with Claudia.

Dev pulled into an unbranded gas station the next town over. I planned on cutting out when the gas station attendant came out to pump the gas. The Hispanic attendant's English was limited, his speech broken and choppy.

Dev lasered in. "Yo, speaka da English, man."

It was sort of funny and at first, I laughed. But then Ray joined in, rolling his window down. Both of them started hassling the guy.

"Hey, you," Ray called out. "Go back to M-m-mexico."

I grunted loudly. The guy didn't even look Mexican. He was too dark.

"Where's your legalization papers, *Paco?*" Dev cackled.

The guy was smart enough to ignore them, but I could tell he was uncomfortable and probably intimidated by us.

I bowed my head and avoided looking at him. "You sound like assholes," I grumbled.

"If he lives here, he should speak the fucking language," Dev shot back.

Another attendant came out. He must have been watching from the kiosk.

"Listen, guys, we don't want any problems. I'll finish taking care of your gas, and if you need anything else, you deal with me."

He took over the transaction, filling Dev's gas tank, and wrapping up the exchange quickly.

Dev took his cash change, but instead of turning back toward town, he pulled into a dark lot across the street and parked the car with the lights off.

"What are you doing? Let's get out of here," I said.

"I told you my old man got laid off from the roofing company last year. Those wetbacks are the reason he can't find any work. He says, 'Ain't nobody want to pay an American a decent wage when he can get three illegals for the same price.' Now he sits in his damn recliner, chain-smoking two packs a day."

I turned to Dev. "You have no idea if the guy's here legally or not. Just because his English sucks doesn't automatically mean he's illegal."

"Ah, your d-d-dad's better off staying home collecting unemployment," Ray threw in.

"Shut up, Rudy," Dev snapped, then eyed me. "There is no way that guy is legal. Immigrants like him are stealing all our jobs and getting the benefits of our taxes for free. Who do you think pays for that guy's hospital stay or his little *enchiladas'* education?" Dev sounded just like his old man. "My father is a miserable bastard since he got laid off—yells at me as soon as I walk in the door. I'm so fucking done with it."

The gas station's lights blinked, then went dark. We watched as the two attendants left, the manager in a car and the other guy on foot.

Dev got out of the car and crossed the street.

Some shit was about to go down. A quick rush of excitement began to uncurl inside me as I watched from the car.

Dev approached the attendant from behind and, even from a distance, we could hear him mouthing off. Rushing ahead, farther down the street, Dev got in the guy's face. The little dude seemed to be doing everything he could to avoid a fight, but Van Sloot wouldn't be ignored. He shoved his shoulder into the guy as he tried to get past. Before long, Dev had the guy cornered against the brick wall of a closed shop.

Ray and I looked at each other and hustled out of the car to catch up with Dev.

As Ray and I came upon the scene, the dark-skinned attendant was clearly anxious. Baring his teeth like a feral dog, he weaved side to side looking for a route past Dev.

Dev was too quick. He blocked every path to escape. Out of the corner of my eye, I saw a quick flash of metal. The attendant had pulled a knife and was clutching it in his fist.

Given the growing hostility from locals against immigrants' right to work, it didn't surprise me that this guy would be prepared to defend himself. None of us made to leave, but we backed up a step. The attendant tried to take advantage of our hesitation by charging past us, but Dev twisted and hit him with high kick to the stomach. The little Hispanic careened backwards against the brick.

The road next to us was quiet, and no cars were coming, but I still looked around, trying to figure out what the hell to do.

"Come on, man. I know some girls," I threw out, trying to persuade Dev to cool it and leave the guy alone. I didn't want to get into a scrap with the pint-sized gas attendant, but even as I thought it, I instinctively clenched and unclenched my fists.

Dev glanced over his shoulder at me. At the same moment, the guy sprung forward and jabbed the knife in his direction.

"Ah, shit!" Dev clutched his side.

The guy shrank backwards holding out the bloodied knife, seeming almost as shocked as we were.

"Son of a bitch!" Darkness took over, and I stepped up to the guy. Seeing me, his eyes went wide with fear. He dropped the knife just as I grabbed him and hit him in the stomach. He grunted and crumbled to the ground as if a wrecking ball hit him. Satisfied, I turned back to Dev. He was gritting his teeth as Ray inspected the wound.

"It's not that bad," Ray said. "But we need something to stop the bleeding."

I yanked off my shirt and handed it to Ray, who bunched it up and pressed it to Dev's wound.

"Shit. He's getting away!" Dev swore.

I looked over my shoulder and watched the terrified guy scamper away as fast as he could.

"Forget him!" I snapped. "We have to get you back to the house and see how bad this is."

"Fuck that." Dev shoved Ray's hand away. He stooped to pick up the knife, gave it the once over, and stuck it in his pocket. "Let's get the car. He can't get too far before we catch up with him."

It had been close to eight-thirty when we'd first hopped out of the car. I was torn. The darkness inside me howled to go on the chase with the guys, but I knew I needed to let this go. To keep my promise to Julia.

I made a decision.

"I'm not going."

"Are you shitting me?" Dev snapped, and without waiting for me to answer, he yelled, "Find another way home. I gotta get this guy." Grunting and holding his side, he hurried to his car. Ray glanced back at me, but followed Dev. Ray barely shut the passenger door before Dev gunned the engine, and the car shot off. I stood alone, panting in the dark.

I started the walk home, taking Middle Road towards town. The two-lane road wound through the south side of town and had very little traffic. I wasn't bothered by the cold as much as I was worried that I looked like a shiftless loser walking around shirtless, at night.

As I got closer to town, I passed streets with big, pricey homes and wondered what the people inside were doing.

Up ahead, a thin old man was walking a little, fluffy white dog on a leash. I gave him a wide berth, intending to walk by him quietly, but then he looked up at me. Too late, I realized I knew him.

"Mr. Faye?" he called, and I turned to face Abe Bernbaum. I could hardly meet his eyes. "What are you doing here?"

"Walking home."

"Where's your shirt?"

Felt like I was on trial, but still, I answered. "My friend needed to borrow it."

"Where is this friend?" Abe looked past me, in the direction I'd come from.

The dog jumped up on my leg and licked my hand.

"He had to leave." I shrugged and reached down to pat the dog's head.

Abe eyed my tattooed shoulder, then snapped the leash, pulling his dog off me. "You kids today, running around looking the way you look and getting your bodies branded and pierced." His mouth turned down, which made his face look like it was made of clay. He hastily waved a hand at me. "Ah, don't get me started."

I stood there looking at him. He'd not said anything that I could add to, so I asked, "You live around here?"

Abe didn't answer right away. Instead, he looked me over as he'd done the day he hired me. I was sure he was considering why I'd want that information.

"Yes," he finally said. "Around the corner." He didn't point or suggest which corner, and I knew then, he didn't trust me to know.

It was clear that he, in his expensive loafers, and I, shirtless like a thug in the hood, lived on opposite sides of town. Whatever. He was my boss; I needed the job. There was nothing nice I could say, except, "I'll see you tomorrow."

"Yes, don't be late," he said, then called to his dog.

At work the next morning, I wheeled air conditioners on a rolling cart to the delivery truck. Devlin pulled up in the back parking lot across from the truck. Holding his side, he slowly got out.

"Crazy night," he said. "We found the guy."

I kept working. "Yeah, what happened?"

"Messed him up a little. The little bastard deserved it after sticking me. My side is fucking killing me."

Squinting in the sun, I turned to eye him. "How bad?"

"Not deep, but probably should've had stitches," he said, lifting his shirt to show me his bandaged stomach.

"No. How bad did you hurt him?"

"Ah, he'll live. But maybe now he'll know not to mess with the working man."

He reached behind him and withdrew an item from his back pocket.

"Check this out," he said, tossing it to me. He snickered when I caught it, and I realized it was because I was holding the gas attendant's knife in my hands, the blade folded away.

I depressed the release button on the black handle. The switchblade popped open, dried blood on the blade. It was a serious weapon.

"Why the hell are you carrying this around?" I folded the blade down and tossed it back to him.

"It makes me feel bad-ass. And it's a cool souvenir of the evening's festivities," he said, tucking the knife in his pocket. "We on for that party Saturday night?"

I shook my head in disbelief. "Asshole, you left me standing at that goddamned gas station last night."

"Don't be so fucking sensitive, man."

"Dude, you're a psycho," I said. "You're all over the place. Spitting fire one moment, planning parties the next."

"You'd be bored with any other friend." He smiled. "I keep it exciting."

I looked at my unpredictable friend and realized he was right. During high school, Van Sloot could twist even the smallest event into all out chaos—and I had eaten it up with a spoon because it made me forget the shit happening at home.

He slapped my back. "I'll make it up to you at the party."

"Don't do me any favors," I said. "Now get the hell out of here. Some of us have to work."

Chapter 8

~TOBY~

IT WAS RAINING WHEN I got home from work Friday. The vinegar scent of window cleaner hit me when I walked in the door. Claudia was in the living room wiping down the front bay window. Sheeting rain poured down the other side of the glass, obscuring the neighborhood from view. Loud thumps of pelting rain hit the window and muffled our greeting. She smiled as she worked, and I wondered, what would it be like to live a day in her positive little world?

I'd just pulled on a clean shirt after my shower when I heard the squeal of brakes out front. Checking out my bedroom window, I caught a glimpse of a police cruiser stopped in front of the house. For a quick moment, I thought maybe Claudia's father was stopping over until two cops in bright rain slickers got out.

I didn't hear them knock, but I heard the muffled sound of Claudia talking to them at the door. I opened the bedroom door to listen.

"Claudia, I didn't expect to find you here," one of the officers said, sounding surprised.

"I work here," she answered. "What brings you here, Officer Perelli?"

"We're looking for Tobias Faye," the other officer said. "Is he here?"

"Yes, yes he is. Come in."

Damn, she let them inside. I smacked the molding. I had to get down there and head this off before Julia found out. Passing her room, I saw that she was napping and pulled her door shut.

All sets of eyes locked on me as I came down the staircase. I braced myself.

"What's going on?"

"I'm Officer Perelli, and this is Officer Cassidy. We need you to come down to the station to answer some questions and look at some photos in regards to an incident that occurred Wednesday night."

Perelli was dark-haired and serious looking. The other, Cassidy, looked as bloated as a cream-filled donut. The dude was fat.

Cassidy's police radio bleared loudly.

"Hey, can you turn that down?" I growled. "My sick mother is upstairs resting."

Both policemen regarded me warily as Cassidy adjusted the knob on the radio.

"Can we expect your cooperation?" Perelli asked, clearly expecting nothing but my cooperation.

"Whatever," I muttered and turned away from them to face Claudia. "Julia doesn't need to worry about this. Okay?" I waited for her to confirm that she understood we were keeping this between us.

She nodded, and I added, "If for some reason I'm not back when you have to leave, you call my aunt. Make up some excuse if you need to."

"Don't worry about anything here," she assured me. She tried to look tough, but I saw her hands shake.

I looked at her face a final time before I followed the cops out the door. I hoped I was coming back. It was obvious that Dev must have done more than just mess around with the guy. It wouldn't be the first time he'd gone too far.

When we got to the precinct, I was put into an interrogation room and told a gas station attendant, a man named Ricardo Velerio, had been stabbed and left on the road. Someone found him hours later, but the knife had nicked an organ. The guy was in intensive care. His condition listed as serious.

Velerio was unconscious and unable to identify his attackers. Information from his co-worker, the other gas station attendant, is what brought the cops to my door. He'd gotten a good look at Ray, Devlin, and I, and along with descriptions of the three of us, he had noted the car make, model, and license plate. He told the cops we'd harassed Velerio earlier that night, before the attack.

A couple of detectives questioned me. I told them I had been out, but because of my sick mother, I was home well before ten o'clock. Claudia would be able to confirm that. They wanted to know my whereabouts prior to arriving home, and where Dev and Ray were going when we parted ways.

I offered very little, and since they had nothing they could charge me with, they had to let me go. When they dropped me back at the house, they told me that if I 'remembered' anything more about that night I should call the detective in charge.

I puffed a cigarette outside the house, pacing and swearing silently. I dipped out of this town to get a fresh start away from the mess. And I had never looked back. Until Julia got sick. I was here only to take care of her, so what the hell was I doing wasting my time with Dev Van Sloot again?

Listening to him boast about his shady accomplishments the other night was enough to make me sick. But now, after this? I was so done with Dev.

Claudia came into the kitchen as I was getting a beer out of the refrigerator.

"You're home," she breathed out. "Are you all right?"

I twisted the top off the bottle. It would be great to unload some of the burden, but I couldn't do that to her.

Instead, I said, "Just some confusion about the other night. But it's fine. Is Julia awake?"

"Yes, but she doesn't know anything." Claudia stepped closer. "Do you want to talk about it?"

I snapped the bottle top between my fingers and sent it flying across the room before I turned to face her. I wished I could pull her close like the other night. I would tell her how glad I was that she was here, mostly for taking care of Julia, but for being concerned about me, too—but that would be too much too soon.

"Thanks, but it's nothing to worry about," I said, shaking the hair out of my eyes.

She watched me pensively and bit her bottom lip. The stress of the situation seemed to unite us for a moment, like a gravitational force pulling us toward each other. I admired her mouth and felt myself growing warm as I imagined how it would feel to kiss her, but I turned away and forced the thought from my head. It would be a bad time to make a move on her.

"Why don't you go? I'm not going anywhere else tonight," I said, pretending to be interested in the pile of mail on the table.

"Are you sure?"

When I looked up, she was standing in exactly the same spot, staring at me. Around her, I didn't trust the thin control I had over my tongue. She seemed to have a knack for making me reveal stuff.

"Yeah, go," I said. Though I really wanted her to stay.

Chapter 9

~CLAUDIA~

I WENT STRAIGHT UP THE STAIRS to my bedroom when I got home. I needed privacy to talk to April about what had happened.

"The police took Toby to the station," I said. "We decided not to mention it to Mrs. Faye. We didn't want to upset her. I'm dying to know, but he wouldn't tell me either."

"I hope it doesn't have something to do with those trouble-making burnouts he used to hang out with," April grumbled. "I wouldn't trust them if my life depended on it."

"But you trust *him*?"

"Yes, chica, I do. Despite what we all know about his family, and that he was somewhat of a brawling legend in high school, Toby is a good guy." She continued, "He has a good relationship with his mother. I think taking care of her kept him grounded, especially when everything with his father and brother was so messed up."

"Mrs. Faye is a good person," I acknowledged.

"My mother said women from church go over there regularly and help out. That true?"

Thinking of the revolving presence of church ladies at the Faye house, I smiled. "Yes, they're surrounded by lots of bighearted people."

"It's nice to know she has help," April said. "And since Toby came home, he obviously wasn't charged. No need to worry her about it."

"I suppose," I answered. "Hey, how come I didn't know you and Toby were friends in high school?"

"I distinctly remember telling you some years ago that he asked about you. I was surprised that he remembered you, but I guess, like most guys, he was a nonentity to you. You, my dear, were far too busy with your Saint John's friends, raising awareness of the atrocities in Darfur or fundraising for a cure to the AIDS epidemic in Africa to care about cute guys showing interest in you." April laughed. "I, on the other hand, was busy flirting with all sorts of cute guys over caramel macchiatos."

"You did support local business."

She laughed again. "Chica, you can put a positive spin on almost anything."

"Put a positive spin on Toby, 'cause I'll need a line of defense when my dad hears what happened."

"He's actually quite sweet and always easy to talk to," she said. Suddenly, she giggled. "Oh, my God, I just remembered that he and I were voted Best Eyes in the senior class! He has those eyes that made the girls in school fall over themselves whenever he looked in their direction."

"I'm sure my dad will be impressed with that."

"Forget your dad. Aren't you?" she asked. "Mmm, kind of hard to ignore boys with pretty eyes and broad shoulders. And who are good to their mothers. Means they treat their women well—"

"Stop trying to sell him to me," I groaned. "If you think he's so wonderful, how come you never had any romantic interest in him yourself?"

"Oh, please." She sighed dramatically. "Toby is cute and all, but you know I never had a thing for pale-skinned guys."

"Yes, I know, my beautiful, mocha-skinned friend. No pasties."

We both laughed.

"That party is tomorrow night," April reminded me. "Do you know if he's going?"

"He said he was, but after what happened with the police, who knows?"

"Well, either way, we should go. The Ryans have crazy money, and I heard Jim hired a live band. It's going to be absolutely amazing."

"Okay," I agreed. "I'll go."

"Good. Dario has to work, but he said he'd meet us there. We'll wear our new dresses, and I'll come over early and do your hair."

It came in handy having a hairstylist for a best friend.

When I hung up, my father still wasn't home. Short reprieve. I lay in bed wondering what happened with Toby and the police until I heard the car in the driveway. I held my breath.

"Claudia!" My father bellowed from the bottom of the steps. "Come down here."

I crept down the stairs. My father was a formidable figure in his dark blue officer's uniform. His belt was loaded with gadgets worthy of any crime-fighting superhero.

"There was an attack on a Dominican man a couple of days ago." The key ring attached to the belt loop of his uniform jingled as he moved into the kitchen.

"Wednesday night?"

"Yes. Between ten and eleven p.m."

"Oh. That's terrible," I mumbled.

"They brought that Faye kid in for questioning as well as two others, Van Sloot and Rudack, known friends of his."

No wonder Toby didn't want his mother to know. Thinking he might have been involved in this would devastate her. I looked at my father. "Pete Perelli came to their house while I was there."

Dad wasn't surprised. "The victim is in bad shape. They could be charged with aggravated assault or ethnic intimidation. That means jail time." Dad shook his head, aggravated. "This is a serious crime. I don't want you at that house anymore."

My mouth dropped open. "But, Dad, Toby wasn't charged. And personally, I don't think he had anything to do with it. He came home early that night."

"What time was that?"

I thought back to that night, trying to remember exactly when I'd noticed he was home. He'd come inside the house without me hearing him, but I'd seen his bedroom light on. "It must have been just after nine o'clock because he came into the kitchen and kept me company for at least a half hour before I left. I finished at ten."

"Did he look like he'd been fighting? Cuts, scrapes, swollen areas?"

I couldn't recall any telltale signs.

"No, he was fine."

Dad shrugged. "That doesn't mean he didn't do it."

"What happened to innocent until proven guilty?" I harrumphed.

"Watch your tone with me, young lady."

"Dad, please. You can't seriously expect me to quit. Mrs. Faye needs me." I tried to reason more demurely. "Besides, would all those church ladies go over there if it was dangerous?"

"I'll only let you keep that job if you agree to check in with me regularly whenever you're over there," he said.

Resigned, I agreed.

April came over after I got home from Sterling Saturday night. I didn't dare tell her that after the last few days, I didn't feel much like going to Jim Ryan's party. April loved parties. Instead, I was fidgety and cranky as she twisted my long brown hair into ringlets.

"What's up with you?" she asked, as she sprayed my hair into place.

I yawned. "My dad is tightening the noose because of this stuff with Toby and the cops. I'm worried about keeping my job, not to mention what it will do to Mrs. Faye if it turns out Toby's somehow involved in all of this."

"The Toby I know wouldn't do that." She handed me my new white dress, the one we'd shopped for last week. "Stop worrying or else you'll have wrinkles before you even hit thirty. Everything will be fine."

"I hope so. I really like Mrs. Faye. She's so sweet." I slipped into the dress, and April zipped me up.

She stepped back to admire her work in the mirror. "Forget about all that for now. Look at us. We look fan-tas-tic."

April looked gorgeous, as usual, with her black hair pinned in a loose knot and her yellow dress setting off her darker skin tone. She had worked her magic with my hair, making it curl softly around my face and shoulders. My white dress with the sheer sleeves accented my light olive complexion and made my eyes look bluer. We did look pretty fabulous.

Cars lined both sides of the road as April parked her car in front of Jim Ryan's house. The street was buzzing with throngs of kids walking to the party.

"We'll have to keep an eye out for Dario and Toby," April said, stepping next to me.

"Dario and Toby are coming together?"

"Yeah. It's strange, but Toby called Dario out of the blue. He's picking Dario up. I told them we'd meet them here." She hooked her arm through mine and led me through the backyard gate. "Maybe you guys will get together. Then we can double date."

I stopped her just inside the yard. "I already told you, I'm not interested."

"Fine." She patted my arm gently like she was calming a cranky spinster. "I'm sure there'll be a lot of guys here. We'll find someone for you."

"No, thank you. I don't need anyone."

"*Mami*, we got to get you to kiss a few frogs so you can find your prince."

I rolled my eyes. "You're such a romantic."

I hadn't seen Jim Ryan in several years, but I remembered his dad was a lawyer with a major firm in Manhattan. This bash would be no typical keg party. The Ryans believed in nothing but the best, and the size of their backyard was no surprise. It was big, wide and thoughtfully landscaped. Several manicured gardens with perfectly scalloped edges and pruned bushes created a winding walkway into the yard. The path opened up into a poolside oasis. A curved, in-ground pool was set into a stone tile area just off the back of the mini mansion the Ryans called home. It was too cool to swim, but I was sure the pool was heated.

Many of the partygoers converged into groups around the pool, sipping from red plastic cups. Past the pool, under a white canopy on the other side of the yard, a small band was playing live as a large group of people danced nearby. We stopped on the bricked patio and scanned the crowd for familiar faces.

Someone grabbed April into a hug. She introduced me, but I couldn't hear what they were saying. As they continued talking, I saw Toby's burly friend from the other night. We caught each other's eye, and he made a beeline for me.

"Hey, it's you."

Up close, Devlin dwarfed me. There was nothing slight about him. He had a big, square head with a thick neck, a wide nose with nostrils so large, I could see up them. His tightly cropped hair made the expanse of his scarred white forehead appear infinite.

"I'm real sorry about the other night." He sounded clogged-up, congested.

I cleared my own throat, as if that would help his.

"I'd rather forget it."

"Sure, I understand. I'd never do that. But Ray, he can be a dick. Guy's got no manners." He was quick to throw his friend under a bus. With one beefy hand wrapped around a plastic beer cup, he held out the other to me. "We never formally met. I'm Devlin."

I glanced up at his face trying to judge his sincerity. He had apologized for what happened in front of Toby's house, and he was trying hard to be friendly. I couldn't see any real reason to be rude.

"Claudia," I said, putting my hand into his expecting to shake. Instead, he put it up to his lips and kissed my knuckles. I pretended to be flattered, but when he released my hand, I covertly wiped my knuckles on the back of my dress.

"Nice to finally meet you, Claudia." His smile was slightly askew, and gummy, like his teeth were too small for the size of his mouth.

He cleared his throat and shuffled uneasily. Feeling kind of sorry for him, I offered another subject.

"Did you graduate with Toby?"

He tilted his head. "Yeah, but you didn't. I'd remember someone as pretty as you."

I chose to ignore the compliment. "I went to Saint John the Baptist."

"Oh, Catholic school. Does that mean you're too uptight to have fun?"

Odd question. "No, just like most people, I like to have fun."

"Good. I happen to have a nice fatty in my pocket." He patted his shirt. "Want to get high?"

"Gee. Tempting, but no." I shook my head. Hanging out with a recreational drug user was clearly not my scene. Looking for a reason to move on, I glanced over my shoulder and searched the party for the sight of anyone familiar.

"Have you seen Toby tonight?"

Devlin's eyes narrowed. "I knew it. You're hooking up with him, aren't you?"

"No, I'm not." Like a reflex, I answered fast.

"Cool." With a rapacious stare, he paused and held up his cup. "I need a refill. Can I get you a beer?"

"No, I don't drink."

"Okay, a soda then," he offered, and before I could decline again, he walked away.

I didn't plan on waiting for him to come back. I grabbed April's arm and pulled her from her conversation. Wrinkling her nose, she watched Devlin walk away.

"Trust me, Van Sloot will never be anything more than an ugly toad. Let's get lost in the crowd."

We darted into a group of people and mingled. It was nice catching up with old friends, but it wasn't long before Devlin returned. He was carrying two red plastic cups when he found us.

"Here you go, ladies. I got one for you, too, April." He offered her a cup, but April shook her head. He shrugged and turned to me. "Claudia?"

He grinned at me hopefully, and I honestly felt bad for him. I reached out my hand for the cup, but he suddenly pitched forward, stumbling, and soda sloshed over the cups onto his sneakers. April and I backed up.

"Ah, shit!" He spun around to see who was responsible for bumping into him.

From out of nowhere, Toby appeared. I smiled for a split second until I saw the angry expression on his face. Without a word, Toby reached forward and, with a quick swipe, sent our drinks tumbling from his friend's hand. The liquid splashed up when the cups hit the ground. April and I shrieked as it showered our shoes and calves.

"Faye, what the hell?" Devlin eyed Toby.

Toby made a growling noise and inserted himself between Devlin and me.

"Stay away from her, Van Sloot."

"Toby, it's okay." I touched his arm, unsure why he felt the need to protect me. "We were just talking. He got me a drink. That's all."

Twisting, he acknowledged me with a stony glance. He let out a breath, and his expression softened a bit. "That's not all. That's just the beginning."

Devlin's eyes narrowed. "What the fuck are you doing, man?"

Toby whirled back to Devlin. "What, am I ruining your game tonight?"

"You are, and it's starting to piss me off." His fingers curled into fists. "Pissing me off is always a mistake."

"If you don't want to get pissed on, leave."

"You going to make me?" Dev's face warped into a sinister mask as he leaned closer, just inches from Toby. "'Cause, I'd really like to see you fucking try."

Time froze for me. This was not like two boys fighting in the schoolyard. No teacher would come and break it up, and they both appeared fierce enough to do some real damage to each other.

"Come on, tough guy." Devlin shoved Toby with open hands. Toby stumbled back, but quickly regained his balance and swung a balled fist. We all heard the crack as it connected with Devlin's jaw. A group nearby jeered in excitement, egging the guys to keep fighting. Devlin, bent over, wiped his bloodied mouth. He appeared shocked for a moment before an even darker expression slid over his face. Before he could fully recover, though, Toby had him by the back of the neck and put him in a headlock.

A crowd instantly formed in a circle around us. Alarmed, I grabbed April's arm. Devlin thrashed about trying to break free, but Toby didn't let him loose. His strength was frightening.

"Come on, you—" Through gritted teeth, Devlin rattled off a string of vicious curses.

Toby twisted back hard, and we all watched as he flung Devlin away. The momentum carried the mammoth guy into the pool several feet away. He hit the water with a loud splash. Cheers and whistles erupted from the party crowd.

Devlin came up sputtering.

"You're going to be fucking sorry for this, motherfucker!" Devlin hoisted himself out of the pool. Dripping wet, he spit onto the brick patio and eyed Toby, the menacing look unmistakable, before he pushed roughly through the crowd. People applauded his exit.

Toby stood there, his tall form tense and ready to spring as he watched Devlin leave. It wasn't until then I realized Dario Manolo, April's longtime boyfriend, was standing with us. With a grim face, Dario pulled April and me to his side. At five-foot-eight, he was several inches shorter than Toby and not quite as muscular, but Dario, who was more likely to elicit laughs than start a fight, looked after me like a brother. Normally, it was very hard to ruffle April's stylish main squeeze—it might have been the first time I'd seen his dark, handsome features marred with such an angry scowl.

"Did that baboon touch you girls?" Dario asked, giving us the once over.

"As if I'd let him," April replied with a snort.

I shook my head, but my eyes were on Toby. With Devlin gone, the anger left him, and his whole demeanor transformed to one of concern.

"You didn't drink anything he gave you, did you?"

"No, I didn't." I pulled away from Dario. "What did you mean by 'that's only the beginning?'"

Toby looked troubled as April and Dario exchanged knowing looks. I felt like a small child, out of the adult conversation.

"Toby, take Claudia and go sit down over there." April pointed towards a few chairs off the patio. "Dario and I will get drinks."

Before they walked away, April leaned into Toby and kissed his cheek.

"Always one to make an entrance."

Chapter 10

~CLAUDIA~

APRIL AND DARIO WENT INTO the Ryans' house to get drinks, and the crowded circle of people loosened. A few guys slapped Toby's back, congratulating him on the fight, before they moved away.

Toby twisted his head from side to side stretching the muscles in his neck.

We sat in the chairs April had suggested, and I faced off with him.

"Are you going to tell me what that was all about?"

He leaned forward in his seat, putting his head in his hands and rubbing his forehead. "I'm pretty sure he spiked your drink."

"Once I tasted it, I would have known right away."

"I'm not talking about alcohol."

"You mean..." My chest felt tight. "Oh, no. That can't be right."

"You don't believe me?"

"No, it's just...I don't understand," I stammered. "Why would he do that?"

"Would you have gone somewhere to be alone with him tonight?"

"No, of course not." I shook my head vehemently.

"That's why. He knew he didn't have a chance with you. He's been talking about you since he saw you at my house. All he had to do was be nice enough so you'd accept a drink from him. After that, he would wait a little while, then take you somewhere."

He didn't need to say more.

Nauseated, I covered my face for a moment.

"I was totally unsuspecting," I groused. "Really, quite the perfect victim. My father would have a canary if he knew."

"There are lots of screwed up guys out there," he went on. "You shouldn't take drinks from people you don't know and never let your drink leave your sight."

A father-like speech, but I was grateful.

I nudged his shoulder and said, "Thank you. I really appreciate that you were looking out for me."

"Sure."

I felt a chill tingle up my arms and remembered I'd left my sweater in April's car.

"Cold?"

"Probably just nerves, but yes, a little." I nodded. He took off his black zip-up sweatshirt and put it over my shoulders. The sweatshirt, still warm from his body heat, smelled musky with his cologne.

"Thanks."

"Let me just grab my cigarettes." He hesitated before reaching over and putting his hand in the pocket. I felt his hand at my rib cage. I held my breath as he pulled out the pack.

"I didn't know you smoked."

"I don't smoke in the house, around Julia." He shook the pack and pulled one out. "Want one?"

I shook my head. "I don't smoke."

Strobe lights came on, and the music pumped up. A sizeable crowd was dancing when Dario and April came back with our drinks. They were laughing as they offered us beer and water. Holding the unlit cigarette in his mouth, Toby took the bottled water from Dario, twisted the top off, and handed it me.

April touched my shoulder. "You okay, chica?"

I nodded. "I'm fine."

"The band is amazing." April moved her hips, swaying to the beat. "We need to dance. It'll put us in a better mood."

Dario held out his hand to her. "I'm ready, mama. Let's boogie."

April took his hand and waved to us. "Come on, Toby. Claudia loves to dance."

Toby didn't move. "I make it a habit to never dance in public. It's not pretty," he said and turned to me. "But you go. I'm okay by myself."

I pushed back into my chair. "No, I'm not in the mood."

April made a pouty face at me before following Dario into the crowd near the band. I watched as they started grinding along with other dancers. They were a well-matched couple.

"So did you fight with your friend because of me or is something else going on?" I asked.

He lit his cigarette. "What do you mean 'something else'? Isn't trying to drug you enough of a reason to kick someone's ass?"

"But I thought he was your friend. A friend would have tried to talk to him."

He held the cigarette at an angle, watching it burn, and shrugged.

"There's no talking to Devlin Van Sloot. He's fucked up. Does what he wants. I just realized I've had enough of it. I'm out."

"But this isn't just about what happened tonight, is it?" I paused to look at him. "He was brought in for questioning on the assault case, just like you were."

A look of surprise came over his face and, just as quickly, disappeared.

"Should've figured you'd find out with your father being a cop and all. I was only questioned, not charged."

I nodded, wanting him to continue. "What happened that night?"

For a long moment, he just smoked his cigarette. Finally, shifting in his seat, he said, "Not much. Some Hispanic guy we talked to was found stabbed later that night."

"No one has been charged?"

"Guess there's not enough evidence."

He was too nonchalant. "You know something, don't you?" I asked.

Tossing his cigarette down to the ground, he stomped on it. "Can we just drop it? I don't want to talk about it." He gulped down the rest of his beer and stashed the bottle under his chair.

But I persisted. "It's your moral obligation to tell if you do."

"My 'moral obligation'?" Toby laughed. "You make me feel like I'm on trial. Are you studying criminal justice or something?"

"No. Gerontology."

"Doesn't that have something to do with old people?"

"I'm surprised you know that."

He raised an eyebrow at me. "I'm a lot smarter than I look."

"I didn't," I started to say and changed my mind. "Yes, I'll be working with the elderly."

"Poor old folks. I can see you cracking the whip, making them do a dozen laps with their walkers before you'll allow them to sit and play Bingo."

I sat up and crossed my arms. "You don't have to be mean."

Smiling ruefully at me, he touched my knee. "Sorry. The whole police thing is a sore subject and, well, you're just … so intense." His fingers were warm on my bare skin.

I tried not to appear offended by the casual, familiar contact. "My father believes the attack was racially provoked." I shifted purposefully, and his hand fell away. "People of all skin colors and nationalities deserve justice."

"Jesus. This has nothing to do with anyone's skin color. I don't judge people like that." Clearly annoyed that I continued to bother him about the subject, he stirred in his seat impatiently. "You think I had something to do with the stabbing, don't you?"

"No!" I answered quickly. "Not at all."

He tilted towards me. "I'm glad you think so, but how can you be sure? You did just see me fighting with someone."

He was daring me to believe him. I studied his face for a moment and became conscious that unlike a few weeks ago, I was not afraid of him.

"Tonight was different. You were protecting me. I don't think you'd hurt someone just for the sport of it," I concluded. "But after what you've told me, it doesn't seem like such a stretch for Devlin to have pointlessly hurt someone."

Leaning back in his chair, he shrugged. "Maybe, but you don't really know him. Or me, for that matter."

"I have eyes. I see how you are with your mother," I said. "And besides, April thinks you're a decent guy."

His interest peaked. "You guys were talking about me?"

"Don't let it go to your head. The conversation was very brief," I replied coolly, despite the flush that rose in my cheeks. "I trust her judgment."

"Now that's a girl with mighty fine judgment," he drawled in a mocking voice and then winked at me.

Thankfully, Dario and April made their way back to us before more could be said. With a mischievous grin, April collapsed into the chair next to mine and grabbed my hand.

"April, don't do it." I knew the look on her face, knew the teasing that was coming.

Ignoring me, April said, "What do you think of my little chica, here, Toby? She's going to make a really terrific girlfriend for the right guy." She smiled at him. "Do you know anyone we can fix her up with?"

"I might know a decent guy for her," he replied.

April elbowed me. I gritted my teeth.

"Lots of prospects here tonight." Dario winked. "The fight brought you a lot of attention. Everyone is talking about you."

I cringed, my crankiness from earlier returning. "I want to go home."

"No! We just got here," April huffed.

"April, I don't want to be here anymore. I'll be a drag the rest of the night."

"Oh, *mamí*." She hugged me. "Just hang out a little more, and if you really want to go, I'll take you home."

Toby checked his watch and rolled to his feet. "I'll take you. I have to get going anyway." His keys jingled as he pulled them from his pocket. "My aunt is with Julia, and I told her I wouldn't be too late."

I nodded, grateful for a way out.

Toby hugged April and casually shook Dario's hand.

As we walked away, Dario called out, "Don't be such a stranger, man. Call me."

I quietly followed Toby to his Jeep, but as soon as I saw what big tires it had, I realized it would be difficult for me to get up into it.

"Oh!" I gasped as, without asking, Toby pinned me to his side and my feet left the ground. He lifted me into the doorless passenger side and gently dropped me into the bucket seat. With my pulse racing, he leaned over me and secured my safety buckle. I was too intimidated to say anything.

He tested the strap with a tug and leaned back. His blue-gray eyes caught me staring at him.

"Your hair looks really nice tonight," he murmured, reaching up to touch a loose strand.

"Thank you," I said, hoping he didn't catch the hitch in my voice.

Toby considered his Jeep for a moment. The top was down, and the vehicle open to the night. "The ride will probably mess it up."

I wasn't deterred. "After almost being drugged and watching a fistfight up close, what's a little wind in my hair?"

Not missing the hard edge to my comment, he put a hand over mine. "You're safe with me, okay?"

His words were protective, like my father's, but the vibe coming from him was most definitely not paternal. It took a moment before I could answer, but smiling meekly, I nodded.

"Yes, okay."

Toby drove fast, shifting gears manually with skill. I wasn't afraid. In fact, with the cool night air blowing in our faces, the ride was exhilarating. We both laughed as my hair blew up and whirled around my head. It felt silly, but for the moment, I didn't mind. He took the turns quickly, each time reaching over to hold my arm and keep me in my seat.

He pulled up to the curb in front of my house, cut the engine, and turned to me. "Can you hang for a few minutes?"

"I thought you had to get home." Uneasiness fluttered in my chest.

"Nah, I wanted to get out of there, too," he said.

I tried to settle myself. "All right, but just for a few minutes."

As he reached towards the stereo to turn on some rock music, the sleeve of his T-shirt slid up, revealing the edge of a tattoo design on his upper arm.

"You have a tattoo," I said, more as an observation than an opinion. He nodded, and, before I knew what he was doing, he whipped off his T-shirt. My mouth hung open loosely at the sight of his bare torso.

"See." He presented his shoulder to me. "I'm actually a cyborg robot."

I heard the words, but all I really noticed was that he had great shoulders. While his skin looked smooth, the breadth of him was a multitude of carved dips and peaks—mountain ranges of tight muscle. Heat seemed to radiate from his bare skin, warming my face. I tried to ignore how confined it suddenly felt in the car and concentrate on what looked like a realistic-looking metal plate with rivets carved in to his upper arm and extending up, onto his shoulder. The art made it look as though his skin was peeling away, revealing metal just beneath the surface.

I studied it, secretly wanting to touch it, but I kept my hands in my lap.

"Did it hurt?"

"Cried like a baby."

"Really?"

He laughed. "Do you really think I would tell you that?"

"No, I don't." I laughed at myself.

"It wasn't too bad. Thinking of getting one?" He put his shirt back on, and I was relieved.

"I could never. My father would disown me if I ever came home with a tattoo."

"Do you do everything your dad tells you to?"

"My dad has lots of expectations," I said. "I'm trying to figure out which ones are worth challenging. Tattoos are not so important."

"Hang out with me. That'll be a challenge," he said with a smile.

I chuckled. "Oh, yes. You and I hanging out, that would not go over well. I could just see his face." Catching myself, I covered my mouth. "I'm sorry, that sounds terrible. It's just that in his line of work, he assesses people quickly."

"You don't have to explain. I understand." He sighed and drummed his fingers on the steering wheel. I could tell it bothered him more than he let on.

Looking to change the subject straight away, I asked him about what musical groups he listened to, but as we chatted about our likes, it became obvious that there was nothing remotely similar in our tastes.

He leaned back against the seat, and he rolled his head to look at me. "Did you know I had a wicked crush on you years ago?"

"Oh, boy," I sighed loudly. "I wondered if this would come up."

"I was that obvious, huh?"

"Ah, yeah. You drew that picture for me in Mrs. Richard's second-grade class."

"Guess I should probably remember since I repeated that grade, but I don't."

"Then let me refresh your memory," I proposed. "Remember 'Star of the Week'? Whoever was the star got their name up on the bulletin board and everyone had to draw a picture of themselves interacting with the 'Star' student. When it was my week, you got up in front of the class with your drawing of us holding hands and proceeded to tell everyone that it was us getting married."

"I did?" He put a hand to his chest and laughed loudly. It was such a hearty laugh that I giggled, too. "Wow, I didn't know I was such a young Romeo."

"Yeah, but having a boy say something like that in second grade—jeez, *seriously scandalous*. Second-grade girls are merciless. I was totally embarrassed over it." I shook my head remembering. "I cried because I thought it meant I had to marry you. But when I got home, my mother said I didn't have to."

"Dodged a bullet." He grinned. "Do you still have the drawing?"

"Nope. When I got home that day, I tore it up."

"Ouch. You obliterated my marriage proposal! Way to hurt a guy." He feigned an expression of pain that had me giggling again.

"Can't be good when the girl you pined for laughs at your prepubescent crush on her." He added a melodramatic sigh which only made me laugh more. "I might have gotten up the nerve to ask you out in high school if you hadn't gone off to Saint John's." He turned to face me. "If I had, would you have at least considered going out with me?"

Just like that, the conversation turned uncomfortable. I itched to get out of his car. "I didn't date in high school."

"What about now?" Slanting towards me, he reached into the sweatshirt pocket, his hand brushing against my hip, to grab his cigarette pack again. We caught each other's eyes for a moment before he busied himself with the pack.

"I … date sometimes."

"No, I mean, would you go out with me now?" He rested back in his seat. "The way I see it, you owe me a date."

"How's that?"

"You dashed all my little-boy dreams."

"I'm pretty sure the statute of limitations has run out on that," I remarked, smartly. "And even if it hadn't, I wouldn't go out with you anyway."

"Why? Not your type of guy?" He put a cigarette between his lips.

"You seem like a nice guy, but we're very different."

"In what way?"

"For one, that." I pointed at his cigarette. "I think smoking is disgusting. I hate the way it smells. That alone would keep me from going out with you."

He took the cigarette from his mouth and tossed it on the dashboard. "Easy, I'll quit."

"Yeah, right."

"I will."

I swallowed hard. "Then there's the fact that I work at your house."

"That's nothing. It's not like some corporation that prohibits dating among the staff."

"Honestly, we don't have any similar interests."

"And what are my interests?"

The question stopped me. "I guess, I don't know, but I'm pursuing a master's degree and I'm extremely focused on school."

"Got me there. That is definitely not in my realm of interests." Unfazed, he tugged at the sleeve of the hoodie trying to pull me closer. "Come here."

A pulse of nervous excitement coiled inside me. I resisted.

"Why?"

"So I can kiss you and see if we have any chemistry."

My face warmed at the thought. Still, I laughed as I pushed at his chest to keep him from getting nearer.

"I don't think so, stud."

"Chicken," he said, releasing his hold on my sleeve. "All right, I'm out of ideas."

"If it's any consolation, by defending me from your creepy friend, you succeeded in turning my opinion of you around. And, besides that, I think you're funny. I'd like it if we could be friends."

"Friends." He twisted his mouth as if the word tasted bad. "Guess after tonight, I need a new one."

After he helped me from the jeep, he told me I could hang onto his sweatshirt until I saw him next week. I started up the walkway to the house, feeling his eyes on me as I walked.

"Hey," he called out, and I turned back. "Just so you know for sure, I really didn't have anything to do with what happened to that guy the other night."

"I know," I replied.

He was smiling as I unlocked the front door and didn't leave until I shut it behind me.

Chapter 11

~CLAUDIA~

SUNDAY MORNING, AS USUAL, BEFORE church, I made breakfast for Dad. He sat at the kitchen table in our sunny kitchen reading the newspaper, while I cut fresh cantaloupe and poached eggs.

I'd come in the night before and found my father sitting upright on the couch, snoring away.

"You know, you don't need to wait up for me anymore."

"I can't sleep until I'm sure you're safe," he replied. "I heard a car, but it didn't sound like April's Chevy. Didn't she bring you home?"

"No, I got another ride."

"With?" He glanced up from the paper, his reading glasses perched on the tip of his nose.

"Toby Faye." He let out an exasperated sigh and I quickly added, "We only hung out for a little while."

I focused on my eggs. Slipping them into a dish, I set them on the table in front of him before realizing he was staring at me, rigid in his seat.

"I'm not thrilled that you're working at his house, but now you're spending your free time with him, too?" He laid the paper down and gave me his full attention.

"We just happened to meet up. And good thing, too," I said.

"Why is that?"

"That guy, Devlin Van Sloot, was there."

Dad leaned heavily on the table. My orange juice rippled. "You had a problem with him?"

"It was nothing, really," I said quickly. I couldn't tell him the details. He would flip. I dodged instead. "But he was, um, well, annoying. And Toby made him leave the party."

Dad leaned back and stroked his mustache. "Divided they fall. I imagine it won't be long 'till someone caves and runs his mouth off."

"Well, don't worry about Toby. He told me he didn't have anything to do with that stabbing incident last week."

"Oh, baby, you're a sweet kid. Always believing the best in everyone." Dad shook his head. It irked me. "But realistically, do you actually think he would tell you if he did?"

"Call it gut instinct or whatever, but I would bet my life that he didn't," I bristled.

"As far as I'm concerned, it doesn't matter if he isn't actually responsible. He hangs out with a rough crowd. I checked their records at the precinct. Van Sloot was brought up on petty larceny charges, and the other guy, Rudack, was picked up for possession of drugs a few years back."

"He quit hanging out with them," I said defensively. "April, Dario, and I are his friends now."

"There are much better choices of young men for you to keep company with," he said. "Like that guy, Phil. He was a nice young man. What ever happened to him?"

Fast Phil. If only my father knew why Phil was no longer around.

"Dad, that was almost a year ago."

"All I'm going to say is that nothing good will come from time spent with that Faye kid."

"You know nothing about him," I said, losing my patience. "Why can't you trust me to make my own judgments?"

"Because I see guys like him come through the precinct all the time. They're trouble. And, the ones your age, they're a big mess of raging hormones. You know what that means, don't you?"

I rolled my eyes. "Yes, Dad. I've studied hormones, and I know how the whole reproductive system works, too. But we're just friends."

"Friends or not, I don't trust him, Claudia. Watch yourself around him." He waved a righteous finger at me. "And, no more of those parties. Any parent that allows them has got a screw loose."

I jammed some bread in the toaster. "Okay, Dad. Whatever."

I brought Toby's sweatshirt with me to work on Monday. I went to lay it over the railing in the entryway and caught Toby's scent on it again. I lifted it to my nose and inhaled one last time. The musky aftershave tingled in the back of my throat. I hated to admit it, but Toby always smelled really good.

I followed the voices coming from the rear of the house to the backyard. Out behind the house, the Fayes' small lot consisted of a simple wooden deck that overlooked a very dry and weedy lawn. Mrs. Faye, a lavender silk scarf wrapped around her head, was in a semi-reclined position in a faded chaise lounge. She seemed to be listening politely to a very short, round, elderly woman, seated to her right. The woman wore a large pair of eyeglasses too big for her kindly, crinkled face. I was amused at how she waved her hands about dramatically as she talked.

"Hi," I said, and they both turned to me as I greeted them.

The sunlight exaggerated the sharp lines of Mrs. Faye's angular face. I could see she was tired.

"Claudia," Mrs. Faye breathed out my name, as if gasping for some much-needed air, and reached for my hand. "Marie, this is who I was telling you about. This is *my Claudia*." I warmed at the introduction. "Claudia, this is Marie, one of my dearest friends from St. Lawrence. Marie spent the day with me and even has dinner set up for us—her delicious pot roast."

Marie smiled proudly at her friend's compliment, lingered a little bit longer, and then said her goodbyes.

When Marie left, Mrs. Faye sagged in the lounger. "I love Marie, but she is quite a wash woman, spreading everybody's business." Mrs. Faye gestured to me to take Marie's vacated chair. "Now, sit and tell me about your weekend. I heard you and Toby were at the same party and that you looked very pretty."

"He said that?" I was surprised, and a little bit flattered, that he had talked to his mother about me. I pulled the chair closer to her and sat.

"Yes." She smiled. "He seems quite fond of you."

Remembering how he had asked me to make out with him, I said, "Your son is a character."

"Yes. Out of both the boys, Toby reminds me so much of his father when we first met. Al was charismatic—handsome and funny, too," she said wistfully, and with more brevity, she went on.

"His drinking and the way he handled the boys was frustrating, but he was quite wonderful in many ways. There are still times when I can't believe he's gone. I would have forgiven him … if only he had let me." Her own words seemed to catch her off guard. With a flush, she pressed her knuckles to her lips and grew quiet. I was shocked at her undiluted sadness, still mourning Mr. Faye after all these years.

I touched her arm. "Are you all right?"

Her smile returned immediately, and she patted my hand. "Of course, I am. But would you look at my disastrous garden! I wish I had the energy to get out there and clean them up."

I wanted her to continue, to tell me how she fell in love with the man whose life had such a tragic end. Instead, I looked over the neglected flowerbeds lining the perimeter of the yard. A few clusters of wild primrose randomly poked through the tangle of fallen leaves and branches that had come down with the ravishing winds of the past few seasons.

"I love planting things and watching them grow. If I was stronger, I'd be knee-deep in the dirt now." She smiled despite her obvious longing. "I guess there are some things that you just have to let go."

We were talking about gardening and our favorite types of flowers when, from inside the house, I heard the front door open and shut.

Toby appeared at the sliding glass door. "Hey, sunshine," he called to his mother and the corners of her eyes crinkled. "Is it time to get you inside?"

"Yes, honey. I'm tired. Help me upstairs." Mrs. Faye's deep blue eyes were glazed with fatigue. She turned to him and extended her arm.

"Hey, Claude," Toby said, and we smiled at each other before he walked over to his mother, helped her to her feet and into the house.

I stayed behind, looking out over the yard, trying to imagine it green and filled with flowers the way Mrs. Faye had said she'd kept it. I thought, too, it would be nice if she could sit outside and not be reminded of what she couldn't do.

Inspiration hit. I would plant some flowers for her.

To the right of the house, where the driveway ended, there was a red, barn-style garage. I went over to it, lifted the door latch and stepped inside. It was warm and musty with an earthy odor. Several large windows on each side let in lots of natural light. It was a great space—on one side, a gardener's dream—a wall lined with shovels and rakes of all sizes and a few corded power tools. I saw a wooden worktop with a large slop sink centered on the wall, the perfect potting area, and a wooden sign hung over it with painted cursive words that read, "Between the weeds, flowers grow." I smiled, thinking how typical the quote was of Mrs. Faye. I stepped closer and admired all the planting supplies. Everything I needed was basically here, except for a few bags of topsoil and the flowers.

I turned to inspect the other side of the garage, the one closest to me—a large area devoted to an impressive craftsman's workshop. Another wooden worktop spanned the long wall, only above this one there was a collection of hand tools hanging neatly from a pegboard. Everything was coated in a thick layer of dust from years of disuse. A spindle-back chair lay upside down on a table saw, the unfinished piece spun heavily with spider webs. Someone in the family was a carpenter. Part of my weekly cleanings involved polishing the unique coffee table in the Fayes' living room. I had admired its beautiful stained wood, beveled edges and sculptured legs. I wondered if it had been crafted in here.

"There you are." Toby's voice made me jump. As he stood in the doorway, the sunlight shone over his back, outlining his shoulders, making him glow. "What are you doing?"

"Thinking," I said.

"That could be dangerous."

"Ha, ha. Funny," I rolled my eyes. "But really, I want to plant a garden for your mom. All the yard tools I'd need are in here. In fact, there are so many tools in here."

"Don't remind me. Julia's been pestering me with a list of projects." He stayed in the doorway as if some force prevented him from coming inside.

I looked at the pegboard. "Are you a carpenter?"

His gaze followed mine. "The old man was."

"The coffee table in the den?"

"He made it."

"It's really nice."

"The one thing he was good at."

"What's this?" I asked, picking up an odd-looking device. It was about a foot long and narrow. It resembled a miniature sleigh, but with a knob on one end and a handle on the other.

"It's a wood planer. It smooths out wood," Toby said, and taking it from me, he turned it over to show me the flat-bladed bottom before he placed it back in its place, reverently. "My old man is probably rolling over in his grave. He never liked us touching his stuff."

Knowing it was an area to tread lightly, I just bit my lip and nodded.

"So," I said and stepped past him out into the yard. "I was thinking to start there, close to the deck so your mother can see the garden from the lounge chair." I pointed and looked up at him. "I'll do it on my own time. What do you think?"

"I think that you are way too good to be true. And if you keep this up, Julia's going to replace my picture on her night table with yours."

"So why don't you help me? Then maybe she'll just put my picture next to yours?"

"Yeah, all right. But I know you really just want to use me as your grunt for the heavy lifting." His comment made me laugh. I was looking forward to getting started.

On Tuesday, Toby and I met at the home garden center during his lunch break. He followed me around the center, lifting the heavy bags of topsoil and peat moss as I pointed to them. We planned that I would head to his house after my classes and a quick stop home to change, and Toby would join me when he got home from work.

It was a beautiful spring day, a perfect day to start the garden. Wearing old jeans and sneakers and my hair up in a ponytail, I went over to the Fayes', prepared to get dirty.

Marie, the church friend that I'd met the previous day, was at the back door when I walked around the house to the backyard. She must have taken a double shift tending to Mrs. Faye this week. We waved at each other.

Toby had the bags of topsoil and peat moss stacked near the deck. He also laid out a few different shovels near the bags. The dry yard needed rejuvenating if any of the flowers were to survive.

I went right to work, sectioning off a patch of lawn to begin pulling up the dead grass. It was sweaty work, but I felt happy as I dug
into the earth.

The back door opened, and Marie waddled out, bottled water
in hand, looking somewhat arthritic. "I brought you some cold
water."

Although breathless from her short walk, she smiled. Her short
silver coif was shellacked into perfect curls, reminding me of my
grandmother.

I leaned on my tall shovel handle and accepted the water from
her. "Thank you," I said. "How is Mrs. Faye doing?"

"She's finally feeling better after her last round of chemo. But
then she'll have to start radiation."

Though Mrs. Faye never complained about her treatments, I
could see her strength waver after she received them. Right now,
she was on the upward swing; each day was better than the day
before.

"The cure for this disease is poison." Marie clucked her tongue.
"What a terrible strain to add to her weak heart."

I was startled by this. "Wait. She has a heart condition, too? Is it
serious?"

"As serious as heart conditions get." Marie put her hands on her
hips, seeming ready to settle into a lengthy conversation about it.
"Well, certainly the cancer is the bigger threat. Julia's doctors are
most concerned about getting it contained. They're optimistic that
she'll be strong enough to continue the entire course of treatments
and bring the disease into remission once again." Marie shook her
head. "She's such a lovely woman. It's sad that she has been plagued
with such heavy burdens—with her illnesses, to the difficult and
untimely demise of her husband, to that troubled eldest boy. At
least she's fortunate to have the youngest. He's a good boy, and
helpful to her."

Like she was telling me a secret, Marie leaned in and whispered,
"And not to mention, he's quite easy on the eyes."

Her naughty admission made me grin.

"I'd love to stay and chat, but I need to tend my charge. One
cannot question the Good Lord's ways, but do our best to comfort
a friend in need. I'll be here for another hour if you need me."
As Marie began to walk away, she left me with a final sentiment.

"What you're doing is lovely, dear."

She stepped inside, and I got back to shoveling. I thought about Mrs. Faye's heart condition, another of a growing list of crosses to bear. She was truly an amazing woman. I felt thankful for the opportunity to work with and for her. I prayed that she soon recovered her health.

I kept working until I saw Toby come into the yard. Wearing a white undershirt and the appliance store's gray uniform pants, his work shirt thrown over his shoulder, he stopped and eyed me.

"Nice view."

With a sigh, I raised my eyes. "Friends don't say that sort of thing to one another."

He came over and purposely bumped my shoulder with his. "Who said I was talking about you? I mean, look at this yard." With his hand, he made a sweeping gesture over the sad space. "It's a paradise."

When he turned to look at me, the blue of his irises had turned an unusual color. In the sunlight, they were so pale they appeared almost iridescent.

"You have pretty eyes."

The compliment rolled off my tongue without any thought. It seemed to catch him off guard, too.

"You like my eyes?" he asked, a definite rise of interest.

The back of my neck prickled with unease. I couldn't let this get weird between us. I bowed my head and returned to my digging. "Yes, they're nice. Now, how about grabbing a shovel and helping me?"

Toby ignored the other shovel, though, and started moving towards the deck steps. "I will, but first, me and pretty eyes are going inside to check in with the lieutenant up in command central."

"Please tell the lieutenant I'll stop in to say hello before I leave," I said.

He saluted me. "Will do."

A little while later, he came back wearing faded jeans ripped at the knees and a black tee shirt. With a toothpick in his mouth, he traded me a new bottle of cold water for the shovel. Taking over, he began to dig.

I watched for a few moments before I said, "I just found out about your mother's heart condition. Is it serious?"

"Who'd you hear that from? Mrs. Doubtfire?" Seeming unconcerned, he continued shoveling.

"Mrs. Doubtfire?" I eyed him. "Marie told me."

"Yeah, her. Euphegenia Doubtfire. Doesn't Marie look like Robin Williams in a wig to you?" Toby perfectly mimicked the famous, "Hellooo!"

"Oh, my God, yes!" I giggled.

"But to answer your question," he said, and stopped digging. "You have to understand something. Julia is defective … maybe the result of poor wiring, some faulty chromosomes, or something irreparable. She's always sick—anemia, low blood sugar, poor circulation … She's been afflicted with just about every ailment under the sun. Pretty much her whole life."

"I had no idea."

"Yeah, well, the heart thing is just another one of her background conditions. It's all about the cancer right now. If she survives this, she'll probably outlive us all."

"Oh," I mumbled. "Marie made it sound like..."

"Marie's a busybody. Likes to hear herself talk." Toby said the words without anger, despite the dig at Marie.

"Seems she also likes you." I tried to lighten the mood. "Said you were easy on the eyes."

"Hey, we need the help, so I do what I can to keep those women coming back. I'm always polite, but I got them figured out," Toby said, with an air of knowing. "Mrs. D and the rest of those church ladies are all about the eye-candy. Every so often, I walk around without my shirt on."

About to pick up a shovel, I burst out laughing.

"You are a real piece of work."

He grinned and said, "Thanks."

I had a feeling Toby would keep me amused all week.

"Euphegenia. What a name," I mused, tickled that he remembered it.

"I'll score a copy of the movie so we can watch it together sometime." The offer was casual.

"Sure. Sounds like fun," I replied, certain it would never happen.

Our project continued the next day much like the first. Toby came home, changed clothes, and met me in the yard with a bottle of water in hand. He gnawed a toothpick as he worked.

Ripping open a bag of peat moss, he asked, "Where do you want this, Claude?"

"Here," I pointed at my feet. "And I prefer to be called Clauddia."

"Okay, Claude." When I sighed, he just smiled and emptied the bag, before picking up his shovel again. "You are so serious. You're allowed to have some fun, you know."

"I am having fun. I'm always happy when I plan something and accomplish it."

He chuckled and rested his hands on the handle. "Wow, such a life of purpose."

I stopped shoveling. Self-conscious, I raised my eyes to his face. "Does that make me seem weird?"

He shrugged. "Nah. Just focused, I suppose."

"What about you? What kind of things do you want to accomplish?"

"Gonna climb Mount Everest, but only after I learn to speak Mandarin and recite the alphabet backwards twenty times in under one minute." He smiled. "World record on that last one."

"You're insane." I shook my head. "Seriously, you're not going back to Florida, are you?"

He stopped and eyed me before answering. "Julia told you I was in Florida?"

I nodded.

"Nah, I'm not going back there. Too hot. But as soon I can, I'm getting the hell out of here." He stomped heavily on the butt of the shovel blade, and it disappeared into the dirt.

"Why?" I watched him maneuver a heavy load of soil with ease.

"'Cause unlike you, I don't have a plan."

"You could take a few liberal arts classes at Suffolk Community," I offered, thinking I could help Mrs. Faye out by touting the benefits of staying home. "Maybe you'll find something that interests you. How about criminal justice?"

"School has never been my thing." He shook his head. "And the law, even less."

"There are lots of career offerings. You need to explore the options," I insisted.

"I am exploring the options. In other cities. In other states."

He dropped the shovel, ripped open the last bag of topsoil, and dumped it. "What about you? You said you applied for a transfer. Where did you apply to?"

"I'm pretty much set to go to University of Southern California."

He blew a low whistle. "Maybe we're not so different after all. Even you want to get far away from this place."

"I picked USC because my mother is in San Diego. I'm not trying to get away from Sayville. I love it here."

"What could you possibly love about this place? Around here, we're all labeled, classified in one of two groups. Group one is the bunch that makes the big bucks, like Jim Ryan's family—people with six-figure incomes. If you're unfortunate enough to be in group two, you're pretty much invisible."

"I think you're generalizing. I never felt invisible."

"That's because *you're in* group one, Claude. Your dad is a Suffolk County cop."

Dad was well paid, but not wanting to get into a financial discussion, I digressed. "But still, there's a great sense of community here. People actually envy me when I tell them where I live."

"If you love it so much, why do you want to leave?"

"I need to put space between my father and me," I said, bending to incorporate the new soil into the garden.

"Officer Chiametti isn't an easy guy to live with?"

I nodded. It was no secret. Anyone who knew my father knew he was intense. "I admire him and all, but I can't breathe without him wanting to know the details. He is suspicious of everybody. He didn't even want me to work here, for your mom. You'd think I was coming to work for a hardened criminal," I said.

Toby didn't respond right away. He pushed around the dirt without any real effort and said, "My brother is as 'hardened' a criminal as they come. He killed someone. It makes sense that your dad would be concerned."

"Yes, I guess you're right." Embarrassed by my slip, I kept talking to move past it. "But his concern is always over the top. He knows there's no real danger here anymore, but he never trusts anyone or anything. Living with him sometimes feels like walking a tightrope—watching every little step, trying to avoid fallout. I'm sure that's why my parents got divorced."

"I didn't know your parents divorced," he said.

"They split just before I turned seventeen," I said. "Supposedly, my father wanted more kids, but my mom only miscarried after me. She played house and held the marriage together, probably longer than she should have. She was never cut out for the role of a housewife my father tried to mold her into. She wanted a career. I don't blame her for getting out. I won't let him bully me like that, either."

He seemed to think a bit on what I'd said before he responded. "Don't seem like he learned any lesson from your mom leaving. Now that you're old enough, you're about ready to kick him to the curb and abandon ship, too."

Abandon. The word hit me with unexpected force and burned like acid in my heart. For a brief moment, my mouth twitched, and I was unsure if I should growl or cry. I let the shovel fall to the ground and drifted over to the deck steps.

"Whoa. Touchy subject." Toby followed as I folded myself down onto the bottom step and pressed my forehead to my knees. A moment later, he sat down next to me.

I kept my eyes cast down. "I know it may not sound like it, but my mom didn't abandon him. Or me. And me going away is because I want this and not because I want to hurt my father," I said, feeling a need to explain it to him.

"Sorry, it was a stupid thing to say." Toby rubbed a knuckle, the only clean part of his hand, up my arm.

He couldn't have known how talking about this would affect me—he didn't know how I battled with this very thing. "It's not your fault. I just don't want to feel guilty about going to California."

"Then don't. Don't feel guilty."

"That's easy for you to say. Your mother willingly let you go when you wanted to leave."

"She really didn't have a choice," he said. "Don't let your dad hold you here. Do what you want to do. Go."

I raised my head and looked at him. Even though I didn't feel as sure as I would have liked to, I said, "I will."

Our eyes held for a long moment, and a swirl of current passed between us. It made my toes curl. He leaned towards me. I had a feeling he was going to kiss me. Though I suspected it would feel

nice, I swallowed hard and quickly looked away.
"Let's finish up here."

Chapter 12

~CLAUDIA~

I WENT TO THE GARDEN CENTER again after classes on Thursday, this time to select flowers, and headed over the Fayes' house. I stopped inside to visit with Mrs. Faye before getting dirty.

She was in the den, sitting on the couch looking over a catalog with her sister. The scene was so ordinary, but not something I'd seen her do before, and it cheered me.

"How's the project going? Has Toby been helpful?" Mrs. Faye asked.

"It's going great, and Toby has been terrific," I said. "Couldn't have done it without him."

"For someone who's never shown any interest before, I've never seen him so anxious to get out in that yard," Mrs. Faye bubbled with delight. Her laughter was a happy sound, like the ringing of tiny bells.

"You know what Momma used to say, Julia. 'The twist of a woman's hair...' A pretty girl can get boys to do many things he wouldn't normally do."

The sisters exchanged knowing looks, and my cheeks flushed at the insinuation.

When I got back outside, Toby was already in the yard, raking out one of the older flowerbeds, clearing it of the snarls of leaves that impeded the perennials planted there. At the sound of the sliding door, he looked up and smiled. Before he could speak, his phone rang. He eyed the caller ID with a frown and held up a finger to signal me to hold on.

I crouched down and began planting the flowers, watching him. His face was already tanned, but now it had a new glow from our few days in the sun. He absently paced the yard while talking, which presented a nice opportunity to admire him from different angles.

Over the last few days with Toby, I had become an avid fan of his quirky, conceited humor. As exasperating as he was when he challenged my opinions, I enjoyed the teasing. I'd laughed so much during the time we spent together. I liked, too, that he had a warm, sincere side. His compassion during my meltdown tugged at my heart and even if it were, as his Aunt Joan said, a 'twist of my hair,' his dedication to my gardening project impressed me.

I only wished he were a different kind of guy—one with a more deliberate focus and less cynical outlook on life.

A few minutes later, Toby finished his call and got down on his hands and knees next to me to help finish planting the rest of the flowers.

"Bad news?" I asked about the phone call.

He shrugged. "It was Dev. He's been trying to kiss and make up with me. I guess cracking his head didn't get my message across."

"And?"

"And nothing," Toby replied, aloof. "I told you, I'm done with him."

"Good," I said with a firm nod.

"I'm glad you think so, cause now you're stuck with me." He stood and gathered the shovels to take them back into the barn. "You're officially my new best friend."

"Lucky me," I mocked, goading him to a humorous scowl.

He went to the barn and came back carrying a coiled watering hose. Unrolling it, he handed me the end. I pulled the trigger on the rusted old nozzle. It worked. And leaked. A steady stream rained down on my sneakers.

"Great! I'm getting my feet watered, too."

"After this, we'll both need to be hosed down." He showed me his blackened hands. His T-shirt and face were smudged with dirt stains, too.

I smiled. "I can help with that." Aiming the hose, I soaked the whole front of his shirt.

"Hey!" He laughed, covering his face. Taking the full blast of the spray, he closed the distance between us and easily pulled the hose from my hands. I yelped and ran away, but not before he wet down the top of my head and the back of my shirt with icy cold water. When he finally turned off the spray, we were both sopping wet and breathless with laughter.

"So, now that we're done," Toby said, sitting on the deck steps and yanking off his muddy work boots, "can I bring Julia out?"

"Oh, yes!" I nodded, eager for her to see our efforts.

Minutes later, Toby held his mother's hand as he steered her outside. Stooping forward, Mrs. Faye stepped out onto the deck. "You're done already?"

"Yep." Toby used his free arm to motion to the flowerbed. "Your paradise, madam."

I stepped behind her to see the yard from her point of view. The emerging green perennials in the outlying beds could now be clearly seen where Toby had raked them, further complementing our new, colorful flowerbed.

"Oh, my." Mrs. Faye took my hand and clutched it to her while she leaned forward to admire the new plantings. "The yard looks so beautiful." She turned to face us, her watery eyes large in her thin face. "You don't know what this means to me. God bless you both." As weak as she was, her smile was so beautiful, my chest felt like it just might burst.

Toby walked his mother back into the house and returned several minutes later, having washed up and put on a clean T-shirt.

"Sorry if Julia's gushing was a little much." He leaned against the deck rail.

"No, not at all." I shook my head. "I love your mom."

"Yeah, and it's clear she thinks you're 'all that.' You got a framed five-by-seven of yourself for her night table?" he asked, crossing his arms.

"Oh, I wouldn't dream of making you share that spot with me. I'll give her an eight-by-ten for her dresser."

"Whoa, a whole lot of 'tude' to go with the sweetness. That's pretty hot." Chuckling, he walked over to the barbecue grill near the back of the house and lifted the hood. "How about something to eat? Julia said I should feed you."

"The question is, can you feed me?" I eyed him skeptically.

"What?" Toby feigned surprise. "You doubt my culinary skills?"

"Well, frankly, yes. You don't seem like the cooking type."

"Stick around, I will amaze you." He gave me a positively smug grin and then, wire brush in hand, began scrubbing the metal grill.

"Amaze away, Master Chef Faye. Meanwhile, I need to wash up and call home."

"You know where the bathroom is. I left a clean shirt on the counter in case you want to change."

"Thanks." I liked that he'd thought to offer me one of his shirts. I went inside and took it off the counter. In the bathroom, I sniffed it, trying to catch that familiar musky scent.

No trace.

I washed my face and did the best I could to get the dirt out from under my nails. Toby's shirt was a lightweight button-up and hung loosely on me. I buttoned the first three buttons, and tied the shirttails. When I left the bathroom and reentered the kitchen, I had to step back as Toby bustled about, cutting onions and sprinkling spices.

"Here," he said, taking each of my arms and rolling the sleeves to fit. I stood patiently, resisting the urge to lean forward and try to smell him. He looked me over approvingly and then pulled two dishes from a cabinet and handed them to me.

"Next time, I'll take you out for dinner."

"Friends night out?" I asked. "We can ask Dario and April to come."

"No friends. You. Me. Date."

I shook my head. "We've been over this."

"But we have more in common now." He paused to pick up a package of hamburger rolls. "We're not only both Yankee fans, but gardeners. And Mrs. Doubtfire fans."

I laughed. "I'm sorry, but I stand firm on the no dating thing."

He exhaled at my rejection. "Oh, Claude, you're killing my ego."

I set the outdoor table while Toby was busy at the barbecue, and then stepped away to call my father. I told him Mrs. Faye had insisted on feeding me, though I didn't mention that she wasn't eating with us. I promised not to be too late as I had some studying to do anyway.

Our dinner was simple, but good. Burgers, grilled asparagus, and a pasta salad Toby swore he made, but I knew Marie had brought over.

We sat, we ate, and he continued to make me laugh over and over again. When we were finished, we cleaned up together and went back outside to admire our garden. As the sun made its last appearance in the sky, we talked for a while about our plans for the summer.

He'd been mostly a gentleman the last few days. Though I remained rigid about controlling our interactions, Toby managed to edge past my objections and mellow my guard. I liked being in this comfortable place with him.

When it was time to leave, Toby walked me to the door. He leaned against the jam, chewing on a toothpick, while I fished my keys out of my pocketbook.

"The garden was a cool idea. It made Julia pretty happy," he said.

"I'm so glad. Maybe we can tackle the front yard next. Something needs to be done with those bushes."

"You're a slave driver, Chiametti. I'll think about it." He flicked his toothpick from one side of his mouth to the other.

I pointed at the little wooden stick. "What's up with your sudden toothpick obsession? Seriously, I'm going to start calling you Farmer Joe."

He laughed, his eyes bright. "I quit smoking."

It wasn't until he said this that I realized I hadn't seen him with a cigarette all of the last week.

"Wow, I am extremely impressed."

"Good," he said. "I quit for you."

"Really? Why for me?"

He shrugged. "You said you don't like the smell of cigarettes."

"That's very considerate."

He tipped his head to one side and smiled playfully. "Would you still think it was considerate if I told you what I really had in mind was to get my mouth on you, that I want to know what you taste like?"

I froze.

After a moment, not sure what to make of his comment, I decided to play it off as another one of his nutty lines. I even managed to smile.

"Very funny."

"Oh, Claudia Chiametti, I am so not joking. I really, really want to kiss you. I can't think of anything I want more right now."

Toby moved in close and ran two fingers up my arm. The light touch flickered inside me like a gentle tickle. Gooseflesh arose on my skin.

"My satisfaction rate is very high. Aren't you the least bit interested?" His gaze dropped from my eyes to my mouth.

Despite a growing warmness, I responded without hesitation. "No."

He seemed to enjoy my unsettled state. "Everything inside tells me you want to kiss me. I bet you've even imagined it."

"Then your radar is way off because there's not an iota of me interested in you in any other way than as a friend."

Undaunted, he suddenly pitched forward, positioning his arms on either side of me and trapping me in the doorway. "I know a quick way to find out for sure."

Biting my bottom lip, I glanced around for some space to get away from what was coming at me. I felt his soft breath caress my face as he lowered his mouth towards mine.

I squeezed my eyes shut and thought, all right, all right, let's get this over with. We'd have this one kiss—then he'd see I was not in the least interested.

I was not mentally prepared for his gentleness, the way his hands cradled my face as he pressed his lips to the corner of my mouth. Not prepared for his lips to be as soft and tempting as they were, far more than I could imagine. As I stood still, he worked his way to center our mouths, his motion deliberate and slow. His efforts grew more persistent, forcing my lips to mold against his, and once the bond was complete, he emitted a soft sigh. The sound infused me with a wavering heat, and my brain felt scrambled. My resistance slackened and, as I swayed into him, my bag plunked to the floor. I didn't resist as his arms slid down, around my waist, and he pulled me up against him.

I tried to muster up the strength to move away, but his lips continued their intimate exploration, nipping and teasing mine. His tongue slid along the seam of my lips, feathering me with a promise of more to come. I found myself wanting to open my mouth and let him kiss me deeper, but instead, I twisted my head away.

"Stop." Despite my demand, I held onto him, fearing my legs would give out, and I would melt at his feet.

Sighing, he rested his forehead against mine, a smile teasing the corners of his mouth. "I knew it."

I closed my eyes for a moment to collect my scattered thoughts.

"I wish you hadn't done that."

I tried to step away, but his arm tightened around me.

"That kiss was only the beginning, the fireworks before the show. Let me loose on you and I'll make you sing." With haughty confidence, he leaned in to kiss me again.

"Don't." I turned my face to my shoulder.

"Come on, admit it. That was amazing." The whisper near my ear sent more chills up my spine. "Maybe the best first kiss I've ever had."

It was hands down *the* best kiss I'd ever had and the brief taste of him made me want more. A relationship with him was almost guaranteed to be exciting, but it would never be anything more than short-term. And that was not my thing. Especially not with guys like him.

"It was a nice kiss," I admitted. "Our first, and our last. I'm sorry, I'm just not interested."

"Yes, you are," he gently insisted, nuzzling my cheek. "You were checking me out all week."

The hair on the back of my neck stood up. I'd looked too much, too long.

Feeling sick, I pushed away from him and straightened my shoulders. "The point is, we don't mesh. Our lives are on two totally different planes."

"I wouldn't mind floating around in your space for a while."

"Yeah, that's the problem—you're a floating spaceman and I like gravity."

"Don't knock me because I haven't landed yet. I'm exploring." He leaned against the doorway, crossing his arms, and let a slow grin wind its way across his lips. Even the slight, casual move was somehow sexually disturbing, and that annoyed me.

"Some girls really dig guys who have that edgy, searching-for-the-meaning-of-life thing going," he said, slipping the toothpick back between his lips.

"I don't find that to be a good quality in a boyfriend. At least not in someone I'd consider dating. I prefer someone who has an idea of what they want out of life. So whatever you're imagining might happen between us, it won't."

"Ouch." He leaned back for a beat. "Okay, Claude. I get it. You have big plans, and I'm not part of them."

Rattled, I sighed. "I didn't mean to come off sounding so condescending, but I'm leaving for college in a few months. Getting involved with someone now wouldn't make sense."

"Who needs to be involved? Friends with benefits works for me."

"Okay, now you're just being an ass."

His smile told me he wasn't taking this seriously at all. "I should kiss you again. I have a feeling I can change your mind."

"No!" My breath caught, and I held out my hand in case he tried to come any closer.

Instead, he leaned back, crossed his long legs, and sighed. "Whatever. I know a shitload of other available girls who definitely wouldn't say no to me."

My heart twisted. I was the one snuffing the fire, so I shouldn't have been affronted by the taunt.

But still.

"Glad to see I didn't damage your ego!" Stooping, I quickly reclaimed my bag from the floor.

"That's the good thing about getting thrown around most of your life. You learn how to take a knock."

I frowned at his comment. "I'm not trying to knock you. I'm just drawing a line."

"Line acknowledged." His clipped tone ended the conversation.

Chapter 13

~TOBY~

I GOT HOME FROM WORK A few minutes earlier than normal Friday afternoon and waited for Claudia in the foyer. I decided to ignore the balk she played last night. Our kiss had leveled our playing field, and the only game I wanted to keep playing was to make her want to kiss me again.

I watched as Claudia made her way up the steps and how she immediately halted as she came through the door. I positioned myself in the doorway with my arm out so she couldn't pass. Her eyes flicked to mine, and, clearly annoyed, she sighed.

Her hair was down, not up in the usual ponytail. I liked it that way, and I wondered if she wore it like that for me. The trail of freckles across her nose drew my attention, and I itched to trace them with my finger. I let my eyes wander over her face to her long, appealing neck and back to her mouth. I saw her lips part on a breath, and my mouth went dry.

"Back for more?"

Her eyes flashed, and she put a hand on her hip. "Why don't you go find one of your other 'available girls' tonight and leave me alone?"

Ohh, jealousy. Home run.

I leaned in close and whispered, "I'm not used to having to try this hard, but the chase is kind of exciting."

"I'm here to work. Please, get out of my way," she glowered.

"Toby." Julia's warning voice came from the other room. "Leave the poor girl alone."

"Ah, saved by your mother." Claudia pushed my arm away, smug with satisfaction. Turning stiffly, she walked towards the back of the house.

I was embarrassed that Julia might have overheard what I was saying, but I didn't let on. "There's always later," I called to her, and she waved an irritated hand at me. Whistling, I left the house.

I had to let her do her thing with Julia, so I planned on keeping myself busy for a few hours, hanging out over at Ray's. I called to let him know I was coming over after I went to the store. Without Dev there, it would be an uneventful night. Suited me fine.

On my way to Ray's, Dario called and asked about hanging out. We made plans to meet back at my house later. I told him to bring April. I wanted Claudia to stay, and April, my secret ally, would ensure that.

I couldn't stop thinking about Claudia. She was really quite the challenge. Our little sparring felt like a tie score in the deciding game of the World Series. Just like a worthy opponent, she was pushing me to concentrate and play hard.

But I was saving up my fastball, sure I'd take the win. I wanted it so bad, I could taste it.

When I got to Ray's, no one answered the door. I found both Ray and his mother stretched out in lawn chairs on their sagging back deck. They were both lit, passing a roach back and forth.

Diane smiled when she saw me and told me to join them. She offered the clip to me, but I shook my head and sat down. Next to me, Ray was completely and thoroughly cooked.

"Is he okay?" I asked his mother.

"Yeah," Diane said. "When he's on his meds, the weed makes him even more sleepy."

The antidepressants Ray took were supposed to help his stutter—and some of his other issues. When he was on them, he never drank more than a beer or two, but weed was another thing. It was his poison.

"Got anything to drink around here?" I asked.

"Beers are in the fridge. Help yourself," she said, her smoke-addled voice particularly harsh.

I entered the house through the back door and found a half case of cheap canned beer in the refrigerator. I pulled a can out just as the back door opened and Diane slinked in.

I hadn't noticed how she was dressed before, but now I couldn't help it. Skintight jeans and a thin blouse left open a few buttons too low.

"Grab me one, would ya?" she asked.

I took out a second can, popped both open and held one out to her.

Rather than take the beer, she moved closer. "Thanks," she said.

With my height advantage, I had a clear view down the front of her shirt. Her black lace bra seemed to be suffering under extreme duress, barely holding onto those radically modified mammaries, the material begging for mercy. A quick flick of the straps would set them free. For a brief moment, I wondered if they felt real.

Playful, she walked her fingers up my chest, "Want to fool around?"

I laughed. "Wow, you're really stoned, aren't you?"

"No. I'm really horny."

Holy shit.

I pushed her hand away. "I don't think that's a good idea."

With a man-eating smile, she arched her shoulders back, pushing her rack into my airspace. "You're not a little boy. We're both consenting adults."

I couldn't help but look down at what she was offering me. I exhaled sharply.

"You're not afraid of an older woman, are you?"

"Afraid?" I laughed darkly. "No, I've been with older women before. Just not my friend's mother." I let my eyes drop again, openly admiring her jugs before I looked back at her face and said, "If it weren't for that, we wouldn't be talking right now."

"Oh, my," she cooed. Pulling at the hem of my T-shirt, she smiled. "It's really too bad you and Ray are such good friends. But then, you were always a better friend to Ray than that other one."

As if on cue, I heard a distinct loud engine out front. Dev's Cutlass. Moments later, he stalked into the house, shouting for Ray, his heavy footsteps echoing through the Rudacks' small, one-story house. He filled the kitchen doorway and eyed Diane and me. Diane moved away.

"And speak of the Devil," she said under her breath. "Hi, Dev. Ray's out in the yard," she told him, all sweetness. Before she left, she looked at me and lifted an eyebrow. "If you change your mind, I'll be around."

She left us alone in the kitchen and went out back.

"Fuck me. What was that?" Dev reached forward and clapped my shoulder. "Women are just throwing their panties at you. You are my goddamn idol, man."

"It was nothing," I insisted. This was our first face-to-face since the fight at the party.

"Yeah, right. I'm just glad to see you, you piece of shit. I missed you, bro."

I ignored him and started towards the door.

"What? You still not talking to me?" Dev moved fast and stood in my way. I tried to go around him, but he blocked me.

Steeling myself, I looked straight ahead. "I'm leaving. Get out of my way."

The backdoor opened, and Ray shuffled in. Dev turned to look, and I used the distraction to pass by and head out the front door.

Dev followed me outside, Ray not far behind.

"Tell me this is not over that girl at the party, your mom's helper," he demanded.

I hesitated to answer just a split second, but he caught it. "Holy shit. It is."

"Shut up," I snapped. "This is not about her."

"Then what?"

I halted, took a breath, and swung around to face him. "It's the way you went after that guy that night. It was fucking unprovoked, man. I can't be a part of that kind of shit anymore."

"Ah, stop being a fucking girl," Dev chuckled. "You used to love nothing better than a good fight. That's all it was. Forget about it," he said, reaching out to shake my shoulder again.

"Stop," I warned him, but he smacked me upside the head in a gruff jokey way, aggravating the shit out of me. I raised my fists in front of me. "Leave me the fuck alone."

"What the hell is up with you? The Faye I used to know never gave a shit about laws, screwing with a girl, or busting a guy up. What happened to him?"

Ever since I'd been home, I'd allowed myself to be sucked back in. I didn't want this.

"Last time I hung out with you, I got hauled into a police interrogation. Christ, stabbing someone—that's serious shit." I gritted my teeth. "And honestly, man, I have enough to deal with. I don't want to hang with you anymore."

Dev sucked in deeply and spit out a thick loogie. "You're afraid."

He was so pathetic, his big, slow brain didn't get it. I found it kind of funny and laughed.

"You laughing at me?"

"Yeah, I am."

"Fuck you," he barked. Leaning forward, he spat down at my feet. A large glob of his disgusting dribble landed perfectly on top of my left sneaker.

Before I let myself react, I tried to remember that was exactly what he wanted. I wasn't about to give it to him.

"Whatever. Just leave me out of your fucking stupid, ass-backward shit." And then I made a mistake; I turned my back on him.

The next thing I knew, my head was bouncing off the wheel well of my Jeep, and I was on my ass in the dirt driveway.

"That's for last Saturday. And just a little reminder that I can take you down whenever, and if ever, I fucking want to." Dev's upper lip curled with a sneer.

I laughed again even as I felt my brow beginning to swell. The trickle of blood tickled my face.

"Why the hell are you laughing?" Dev turned to Ray, who just stood there, stoned and staring. "Can you believe this fucking asshole? He just lost his best friend, and he's laughing his mother-fucking ass off."

I couldn't hear anything else Dev said as he walked away. I only stopped laughing when I heard his car engine rev, and I knew he was gone.

Claudia was waiting in the living room ready to leave when I got in. Prepared to make a quick escape, no doubt. Not far behind me, Dario and April were just coming up the driveway as I wobbled into the house. The two of them were probably wondering what had happened to me.

"Hey." I waved to Claudia. Ignoring her startled stare at the bloody rag I held to my forehead, I went to the kitchen to clean myself up. Her keys jangled as she dropped them on the coffee table and followed, hot on my heels.

"You're bleeding! What happened?"

"Got clocked by my own Jeep," I told her, pretending to be embarrassed.

"Dude, you tripping? Like, for real?" Dario asked, coming into the house. Out of the corner of my eye, I saw April go to Claude and give her a hug.

"Yeah. Two left feet."

"I'd say it looks like you were in a fight," Claudia eyed me.

I looked away knowing I was just confirming it. She muttered "liar" under her breath and slipped in next to me at the sink, both of us blotting at the cut.

"Do you think you'll need stitches?" she asked.

"I don't think so. It's just bleeding like a bitch."

"Let me take a look." She pulled a chair out from under the table and motioned for me to sit.

She wanted to play doctor. I sat. As she prodded my puffy right brow, her warm breath fanned my face. I closed my eyes and tried to reign in the urge to touch her.

"It's a clean slit over your eyebrow. I think if we pinch it together with a bandage and ice it, you should be okay," she said. "Do you have a first aid kit or something?"

Not waiting for an answer, she went into the bathroom in search of bandages and antiseptic.

"Hey, now that we know the guy's going to live, how about April and I go get pizza and a six pack?" Dario asked.

"Fine with me. Just make sure you get bottles. None of that canned shit," I said, and looked to Claude as she reentered the kitchen.

"I'm getting an iced coffee," April said. "You want one, chica?"

"Yes, that sounds good." Claudia nodded. My plan worked—she was staying.

"Cool. Be right back then," Dario said. The two left the house.

Claudia prepped a triage area. "Another fight, huh?" When I didn't answer, she shook her head. "Aren't you getting too old for that?"

"Nah. I'm just getting good at it." I smirked.

"My father thinks you're just another young guy with raging hormones. Maybe he's right." She doused some gauze with peroxide and held it to the cut.

It burned like a blowtorch. I tensed and then slouched down in the seat, sliding my legs straight out in front of me, one leg between hers. I nudged her knee with mine. "I'm surprised he allows you to be in the same house with me."

"Believe me, he'd rather I not be." She picked up a bandage and hovered over me. "The only reason he agreed is because I'm helping your mother."

After the fight and Diane's proposition, I was feeling hyped up and reckless. I looked up at her as she leaned over me. So close, I could smell her and feel her skin radiating heat. Even if she wasn't aware of it, her body was calling me.

"You smell good," I murmured, and I slid my hand around the back of her knee, feeling the warmth of her leg.

She slapped it away like an annoying mosquito. "I'm not wearing any perfume."

It was true. She didn't smell of flowers, vanilla, or any other nameable scents, but that didn't mean she didn't still get to me. I had an urge to taste the smell of her skin.

"I guess I just like the way you naturally smell." I admired her body, letting my eyes travel slowly upwards, my gaze hanging on each curve. I put my hand back on her leg and caressed her thigh. Our exchange suddenly became less like a ballgame and more of a hunt.

"Don't start this again." Grumbling impatiently, she pushed the offending hand away. "We're just friends, remember?"

"Right, the 'F' word," I quipped.

Ignoring me, she leaned forward to apply the bandage. I tried to snatch it from her. "I got this."

"Just let me finish," she said, refusing to give up the bandage.

"You're too close." I sat up, continuing the tug-of-war. "My hormones are *raging*."

"Oh, come on." She scoffed. "Seriously?"

I patted my lap. "Sit right here and see for yourself." Her eyes darted downwards. Releasing the bandage like the thing had just grown legs, she practically hopped away. All I could do was laugh.

Keeping her distance, Claudia followed me to the bathroom and watched as I faced the mirror and applied the bandage. When I finished, I rested my hands on the basin. The cut wasn't too bad, but the area was swollen. I'd have to come up with something to tell Julia.

What a night. I closed my eyes and took a slow breath.

"God, I really want a cigarette," I grumbled aloud. Turning to look at her, I raised my eyebrows hopefully. "Since I gave up smoking for you, I think you should kiss me and help me forget about wanting one."

She covered her mouth with her knuckles and shook her head, but not before I saw her hide a coy smile. I didn't expect her to agree, but the flirty refusal only stoked the fire.

I made a grab for her, but she quickly stepped back away from me. Reaching into her back pocket, she pulled out a pack of gum.

"I've heard chewing gum helps with cravings."

Chewing hard and fast on two pieces of gum, I went up to check on Julia while Claudia called to check in with her father. Julia was sleeping. I ducked into my bedroom to put on a clean shirt and some cologne and then brushed my teeth.

Staring at my reflection, I gave myself a pep talk. Tonight was the night. Before Claudia left, she would agree to go out with me. I wasn't taking no for an answer.

In the kitchen again, I filled a baggie with ice and pressed it to my forehead. Dario and April returned a few minutes later with the food and drinks. We served up the pizza in the kitchen and then moved to the living room.

The night slipped by easily. Dario and April were longtime friends of both Claudia and me. The girls were relaxed and laughed at all my jokes. Like a good wingman, Dario mentioned my guitar, doing his best to impress Claudia with my abilities.

"Bet you didn't know this guy was one of the main attractions at high school band nights," Dario said, selling me like an up-and-coming talent to an agent.

"The same guy who doesn't like to dance in public performed at band night?" Claudia eyed me doubtfully.

I nodded.

"Interesting. What other talents do you have?"

I smiled slowly. "I'll show you later."

She rolled her eyes, and everyone laughed.

I flipped on the television to catch the Yankees' score. This time everyone groaned. Down by three runs in the sixth against Boston.

"Ah, they cannot let the Sox take it. I bet a guy at work on this game." As I complained, I casually slipped my arm behind Claudia's shoulders and pressed my leg against hers. She inhaled sharply, and both of the girls grew quiet. When I glanced over at them,

Claudia looked away, but April smiled knowingly at me.

Claudia slid away, out from under my arm, closer to the end of the couch.

I laughed at her retreat. "The heat getting to you?"

"What heat?"

Dario and April just watched as I slid close again, cornering her against the end of the couch.

"Stop." She batted my hand away, but she was also laughing.

I ignored her attempt to stop me and pulled her close. Grinning triumphantly, I held her snug against my side. "Is your skin burning off yet?"

Cheeks flushed, she lifted her chin, defiantly. "That would be no."

"Relax. Even with all this undeniable heat between us, touching me doesn't hurt. It's all good."

"Yeah, well, sorry to tell you, but I don't feel *the heat*." She pushed me away. "And I absolutely do not plan on touching you."

"What if I plan on touching you?"

"That's called sexual harassment, and it's against the law."

The air was still. Even as her eyes warned me, I was too keyed up with her this close.

"We should get going, Dar." April stood up trying hard not to smile, but Dario laughed out loud.

"Yeah, me too." Claudia jumped to her feet, clearly getting ready to bolt.

April gave Claudia a hug, then leaned over her shoulder, and blew me a kiss. "Goodnight, sweet frog!" Giggling, she took Dario's hand and slipped out the door.

"Sweet frog?" I asked, watching them leave. "What's that mean?"

"I don't know. Anyway, goodnight." She rushed the screen door, racing to catch up to April.

Nice try. I followed her outside.

Claudia stood next to April by the door of her car. I pinned her with my eyes. "Come over tomorrow night. We'll watch a movie or something."

"I don't think so." Her eyes lowered to the collar of my shirt.

"It's the bandage, isn't it? I look like hell."

She let out a tiny laugh. "You do look a bit like a roughed-up gang member."

I jutted my chin out and leaned close. "But my lips are in perfect working order. Not a scratch."

Claudia's mouth twitched, and she glanced at April for a way out. Like a little girl, she snatched at one of April's hands in a schoolyard attempt to keep me away, but I moved in anyway. She put up her other hand trying to stop me, but I grabbed it and used my whole body to press her against the car.

"Come on, April," Dario called from across the lawn. "Let's make tracks."

"I'm trying, Dar, but the girl's got a death grip on my hand. And woo wee!" April began to fan herself. "It sure is getting hot over here!"

I smiled at April's comment but didn't take my eyes from Claudia. I held her there, against the car, letting the heat build between us. Both of our breaths came in shallow gasps. It was hot. Spontaneous combustion came to mind.

"Get off me," she commanded, but there was no force behind the words.

"Stop playing hard to get and just admit that you like me." I dipped my head closer. "Come over tomorrow night. You won't be sorry."

When she shook her head no, I reached up to hold her chin with my free hand. She eyed me nervously just before I ran my tongue over her lips, deftly licking the entire length of her mouth. Her eyes went large with surprise and letting go of April's hand, she pressed her knuckles to her mouth.

"Tomorrow," I repeated before releasing her and walking back towards the house.

"Wow," I heard April laugh behind me. "That's one *rana caliente!*"

"A what?" Claudia asked.

"That's one hot frog."

Chapter 14

~CLAUDIA~

I WENT TO BED STILL RATTLED from Toby's overtures. Normally, when guys came on too strong, I only had to make it clear nothing would happen for them to leave me alone. But nothing I said or did seemed to dissuade Toby. Most upsetting was that, despite my resolve to remain uninterested, whenever he came near, I couldn't do it. I found myself anticipating his closeness, almost desiring it.

This was completely uncharted territory for me.

I slept badly and my sleepless night took its toll on my day. I struggled to get through my shift at Sterling. At the end of it, I dragged myself through the door, just happy to get home.

The relief was short-lived.

My father stood in full uniform in the kitchen, as though I'd caught him on his way to work. His face was grim.

"Dad? What's wrong?"

"Care to explain all this?" His hand fanned across some paperwork on the counter.

There, lined across the counter like drug paraphernalia in a court case, laid the evidence of my secret pursuit—my stack of college brochures and application receipt letter. I felt the color drain out of my face and then return as a burning flush.

"You went through my room!"

"I'm your father. I have a right to know what you're up to."

I was flabbergasted. "But you violated my privacy!"

"Too bad!" Dad smacked the counter with his open palm and made me flinch. "I shouldn't have to go through your things to find what you're up to. *This*," Dad poked at the college paperwork, "is inexcusable."

"Calm down," I snapped. "This is exactly the reason I didn't tell you."

He put his hands on his hips and shook his head. "Oh, you have no idea how much you sound like your mother."

"And what's so bad about that?"

"Your mother wanted things we never agreed to. And when she didn't get them, she left." Angling his chin down, he eyed me. I imagined the fear he put in the people he interrogated. "Is that what you're doing?"

"Dad, I just want to go away to school. It's only two years. Not forever!"

He remained silent and seemed to consider this. I was almost hopeful, until he asked, "Are there other things you're hiding from me?"

"Yeah. I'm pregnant." I punctuated the wild declaration with a glib snort.

Dad's jaw tightened. "I don't find that amusing."

Circumspect, I pulled back. "There's nothing else."

"Claudia, I'm disappointed in you. You've damaged my trust, and I don't take that lightly." His tone was quiet and controlled, effectively paralyzing me with guilt. "You listen and understand this: I won't finance USC or any college that I do not approve of."

I felt my bottom lip begin to quake. "But what if I get accepted?"

"No point in debating that." He reached into the pile and pulled out a flat, white envelope imprinted with the USC logo—one that had already been opened. "You'll be staying home."

My heart dropped into my stomach. Snatching the envelope from him, I turned and ran out the front door.

I could hear him calling after me, but I got in my car, revved the engine, and threw it into reverse. Someone honked, but, ignoring them, I sped down the road. I needed to get away—from the house, from him. Immediately. I smacked the envelope down in the car seat next to me and watched it out of the corner of my eye as though it was an unpredictable passenger who might grab the steering wheel and drive me off the road.

Around the corner and down the block, I raced to the bay. Careening into a parking spot in the empty lot at our little town beach, I turned off the engine and stared at the envelope. It was addressed to me! It was mine! He had no right to open it! Seizing it, I yanked out the letter, ripping it in the process.

Thank you for your interest... blah, blah, blah... The Davis School of Gerontology ... unprecedented amount of applicants for this specialized program ... currently, enrollment has reached its limitation ... regretfully your application will be placed on our pending list...

Wait-listed! I crumbled the letter into a ball and chucked it against the door. Folding my arms over the steering wheel, I pressed my face down onto them and let the tears come. My dreams were trashed, ripped out from under me. I had nothing now. Nothing! I was doomed to stay in Sayville, living under my father's thumb, attending the school of *his choosing* and doing *his bidding*. I would never have a life of my own.

The sun had hit the horizon when I finally stopped crying, too tired to continue. I watched the sunset, feeling anesthetized. Somewhere deep inside, I knew I should be sensible and start thinking of a Plan B, an alternate goal, but I couldn't. Not yet. I was too numb.

I picked up my phone to call April, but then I remembered she had a family party tonight. I knew she would tell me to come. I usually enjoyed her large, boisterous family gatherings, but tonight I couldn't see myself enduring it. I scrolled through my contacts and saw Toby's number.

For a moment, I felt a flood of warmth as I thought about his mouth on mine, his arms holding me. I leaned back and sighed wearily.

"Hey, Claude," the deep, familiar voice came from my lap.

I jerked and stared down at the call screen. I had accidentally hit the call button.

Tentatively, I put the phone to my ear.

"Hi," I said and attempted a laugh. "I butt dialed you."

"Oh, good, I thought you were calling to cancel on me."

"Cancel? We don't have plans."

"Yes, we do. You're coming over here to watch a movie with me," he said.

"Oh, that."

"Come on, Claude. Don't make me beg," he begged. "I even got a copy of 'Mrs. Doubtfire' to watch."

"I'm sorry. I can't." I meant to say it without any emotion, but my misery churned inside me like molten lava and a tiny sob leaked out.

"Are you okay?" When I didn't answer, he became more direct. "Where are you?"

"Town beach," I mumbled.

"I'm coming down there."

The phone went silent.

I got out of my car and went out onto the sand, walking the few feet of the narrow beach to the water's edge. It was only minutes before I heard tires crunching over the gritty pavement of the beach's tiny parking lot. Through the blur of my tears, I saw the red Jeep, heard the door shut. And then he was there, the sand kicking up behind him as he came closer. He looked tough and strong, and though I was not sure exactly why, the fact that he was the one who came to me now, at this particular time, felt completely right.

I watched the wind whip at his T-shirt, making it cling to his muscular chest. Each step stripped away a piece of my composure, and when he was finally there, standing inches from me, I had no resistance left. I pushed myself into his arms and rose up on my toes to kiss him. He held me tightly and kissed me back. When my tears began to flow too heavily, he pressed my face to his chest and held me as the wind tangled our hair and the sky grew dark.

Finally, with his arm around my shoulders he asked, "Jesus, Claude. What's going on?"

"I got wait-listed for USC," I said and reflexively curled into him.

"But doesn't that mean you'll get in if a spot opens up?"

With my face buried in his shirt, I shook my head. "It's a specialized program. If something opened up, I wouldn't necessarily be the first one they offered it to."

"Ah, shit. I'm sorry." He rubbed my arm.

"I had a big fight with my father over it. He threatened to cut off my college funds."

"He's just angry. He'll cool off. It'll be fine," he said, trying so hard to say the right thing.

I shook my head. "None of it matters now. I didn't get in."

"But aren't there, like, a million more colleges you can go to?" He stroked my hair, soothing me. "You'll find another school."

I sniffled. "I don't want to find another school. And I don't have it in me to start the whole application process over again. I'm stuck here."

"Hey, if it makes you feel any better, until Julia's better, I'm stuck here, too." He rubbed my arm again. "We can be stuck together."

Though the idea that he wanted to be 'stuck' with me sounded sweet, I didn't understand why he'd want to. As I looked up at him, our eyes held, and I wondered out loud, "Why me?"

He swept a lock of hair from my face. "Why not you?"

At that moment, it seemed like a perfectly acceptable answer— and when he leaned down to kiss me, I turned my face up to him and kissed him back.

Still holding me, he whispered, "Come back to the house for a while."

Emotionally, I was exhausted, but I got in my car and followed him back to Roosevelt Avenue.

At the house, I followed Toby through the front door, but in the foyer, he stopped me.

"What?" I asked.

He pointed to the stairs. "Go see Julia. I know it'll make you feel better. She's good with stuff like this."

At that moment, I thought he might be the sweetest guy I'd ever met. "You did pretty good yourself," I said, and he smiled.

"I'll be waiting for you to come down," he whispered and twirled a piece of my hair around his finger. Our eyes met, and for a moment, I couldn't breathe. Breaking our gaze, he turned me in the direction of the stairs and gave me a little push.

I crept up the stairs to Mrs. Faye's bedroom door. It was slightly open, and a dim light shone through the gap. I knocked softly and called to her.

"Hi, honey." Mrs. Faye was sitting up in her bedside chair. Her smile was motherly and sweet as I came through the door. "Is everything okay?"

I thought I was all cried out, but as soon as she asked, I felt my lips begin to quiver and knew my face was a dead giveaway. Still, I attempted to be brave.

"It's fine."

"You just missed your father. He was looking for you," she said. I sucked in a breath and waited for the bad news. She touched my arm. "He was worried. Said you ran out of the house upset."

"USC," I choked out. "It's not happening."

"I know, honey, and I'm so sorry about that." Her expression was sympathetic. "How are you holding up?"

"I guess I'll survive," I said.

"You will, you will." She patted my hand.

"I'm sorry my father bothered you." Dad had a banner day, first intruding on me, and now Mrs. Faye.

"It was no problem at all. You should call him and let him know you're here," she said.

Wanting to dismiss him and move on, I nodded.

Glancing at the book in her lap, I saw it was a photo album, but then I realized she was dressed—white slacks and a pretty blue blouse, and shoes instead of slippers. To see her in day clothes was unusual.

"You look as if you've been out," I commented.

"Yes, Toby and I took a drive up to visit with Al this afternoon."

Mrs. Faye swiftly drew me into the day's events, complete with details: the car ride, the dopey guard who checked her pocketbook twice, and the nice lunch she and Toby had on the way home. She prattled on, and it was not hard to see she was intentionally distracting me. It was working.

"And then, I came home and pulled out some old photos. Here, look." She opened the book and turned it towards me. "My boys, so precious on Al's communion day. Look at the expression on Toby's face." I glanced down at a page of images. Mrs. Faye pointed to one, a dated photo of two impish, handsomely dressed little boys on the steps of our church downtown. The older boy was looking straight at the camera; the younger one, Toby, stared at his big brother with open admiration, trying to mimic his brother's exact stance.

Toby hadn't mentioned the visit. Not a surprise. My crisis had been front and center.

"Did Toby and Al talk?"

Mrs. Faye lowered her chin and shook her head. "I couldn't convince Toby to come inside. Al was disappointed. He gave me a letter to give to Toby. Toby told me to throw it away, but I saved it—along with all the others." She said pointing to her night table. "There, in my drawer, waiting to be opened."

I marveled at a drawer full of unopened letters from Al Junior to his estranged brother. Were they letters of anger or resentment? Of apology or grief?

"I'll see if I can talk Toby into reading it," I offered.

"It's kind of you to consider it. Both of my boys are just so hard-headed." She closed the photo album and reached for my hand. Her thin fingers closed over mine. "Claudia, you're such a good girl, and I'm so pleased that the two of you are friends. Toby needs to be around more positive influences like you."

I felt a little embarrassed and pressed my lips together. I had been nothing but cranky and resentful all day. Toby had been the upbeat one this go-round.

"He's been a positive influence on me, too," I said.

Mrs. Faye tilted her head, and a great big smile lit up her face. For a second, I wondered if I'd revealed something that I hadn't meant to, but I couldn't think of anything.

"Would you like to watch a movie with us?" I asked.

"Oh, no, honey. You kids have fun." She shook her head. "I have my television shows. And after being out all afternoon, I probably won't last." As I edged out the door, she said, "Don't forget to call your father."

"I won't," I promised.

I felt much more upbeat after my Mrs. Faye fix. As promised, I pounded out a text message to my dad informing him of my whereabouts, and then I silenced my phone and headed down the stairs.

I sat on the couch, curling my legs under me. Toby plopped down next to me.

"Did you see my father when he came over?" I asked him.

Toby's expression was guarded. "He was here? When?"

"You must have passed him on the way to the beach. He spoke with your mother," I said.

"What did he say?"

I was surprised at this line of questioning. "He was looking for me," I answered, and it dawned on me why he was so put off. "You never told your mother about the investigation, did you?"

"No," he said. "And I don't plan to. It's still an open case."

"I didn't get the impression that the subject came up," I said and bit my lip. "But, she was upset over something."

"What?"

"That you didn't go in to see your brother at the prison today."

"Oh, Jesus," he groaned. "She got to you."

"I don't see what the big deal is. Why can't you just stop in and hear what the guy has to say? Or, at the very least, read the letters he wrote? Your mother said she has a whole pile of them up in her room."

Toby wrapped his arms around his head and leaned forward as if he were trying to block out the words. "You don't understand. What my mother, *and now you*, fail to realize is my brother and I hate each other."

The photographs Mrs. Faye had shown me looked like that of any young family celebrating the milestones in life, but I knew there was much they didn't reveal.

Boys fought. When my young cousins, Paul and Frank, weren't eating or playing video games, they were always knocking each other around. But unlike my cousins, I sensed a barren emptiness between the Faye brothers. Toby never talked about Al Junior. Apart from when Mrs. Faye talked about him, it was as if the older brother didn't exist. I suspected their fights had been laced with enmity.

I touched Toby's arm tentatively. "I don't understand, not completely. But I want to. Explain it to me."

He blew out a breath. "You want to hear the gory details?"

"You don't have to tell me if you'd rather not."

"It's fine," he shrugged. "I'm sure you know my father liked his alcohol. For a guy that drank regularly, he was weirdly strict about details. Julia claims I was his favorite, but that's probably because I pretty much did as I was told. But my brother, man, he never did anything without a fight. And holy crap, when he was a teenager, my he and my father used to really go at it."

I could visualize the scene, right there in the living room. Biting words, hits that bruised.

"Didn't your mom try to stop it?"

"She always tried, but with two big guys fisting it out, there wasn't much she could do. When the fighting was really bad, she would take me into another room and ask me to pray with her." His eyes strayed across the room. "Then, God answered our prayers."

"How so?"

"My father died."

Shocked, I said, "God doesn't answer prayers like that."

His eyes shifted back to my face. "How do you know? I didn't necessarily wish him dead, but I wanted him gone."

"But you didn't really mean it," I countered.

"I meant it," he said without blinking. "My house was like a war zone. Al was always mouthing off and getting into trouble. As far as I'm concerned, he deserved the pummeling he got, but Big Al was a hard guy. As a kid, I was afraid of him. When you go through something like that, seeing your family battling all the time and your mom crying, you want it to end. I prayed for a divorce."

"How old were you when your father died?"

"I was twelve, Al was sixteen. I thought things would be … quieter, I guess, without my father around. But, it wasn't easy—he was so stinking drunk he drove his truck into that couple's car and killed them. Damn."

Toby leaned forward and clasped his hands together. "It felt like people hated us for what he did. After that, things got really bad with Al. We never got along, but without my father around, he beat on me like he wanted to kill me."

Red crept up Toby's neck, and after a heavy moment of silence, he rushed into an explanation. "This is old news, and it's not like he could hurt me anymore. I'm a lot stronger than I was then. I'm just telling you so you'll understand why I don't want to see my brother. We have a bad history."

"You were so young. Why didn't your mother intervene or call social services?"

"My mother was a sickly, grieving widow, and I didn't know about that stuff. I just tried to stay out of his way." Toby shrugged. "Then I met Devlin and Ray. Ray's parents divorced, and his mother didn't care who hung out at the house. She even bought us alcohol and got stewed with us."

"Stewed?"

"Yeah, cooked, blazed, high. Whatever you want to call it."

"His mother got high with you?" I scrunched my face in distaste. "That's so irresponsible."

"Maybe, but escaping to Ray's was the way I got through those years."

"Do you still do things like that?"

He shook his head. "Not really. It messes my head up too much."

"Well, that's good. I don't like that stuff," I said. "And I don't like to think about you hanging out in a place like that."

He snorted. "Sorry, Claude. I'm no pillar of the community."

"But you're better than people like that."

"Thanks. I take that as high praise coming from you," he said.

"Good, 'cause I mean it. If you haven't noticed, I'm pretty picky about who I hang out with," I said, and he smiled. "So with you out of the house, things got better with Al?"

"We managed to get along just enough to take care of Julia during her first bout of cancer. After she went into remission, I left. We didn't see each other much after that. The shithead went and got his girlfriend pregnant. Then one night he was in a bar, and some guy pissed him off. I'm sure you've heard the rest of the story."

"There's a baby?"

"Yeah. In Florida. After Al was sentenced, Felicia moved in with her sister in Tampa. While I was living in Cape Coral, I looked her up," he said. "I got to see him once, before I came home."

"A boy?"

"Yeah, and he's so cool. His name is Dylan." By the way Toby smiled, it was obvious he had a soft spot for his nephew. "I want to get Julia down there to meet him."

My mouth dropped open. "She hasn't seen him yet?"

"Felicia took off as soon as Al got moved upstate to Otisville. She was still pregnant. I don't blame her. Al will never be any kind of father to that kid," he said. "But as soon as Julia's finished her last treatment, I'll get her down there."

"Please don't make your mother wait. Let's ask Felicia to come visit. Right away."

He looked at me for a serious moment. I knew he was considering what the implication of waiting meant—maybe there wasn't time. He ran his hand through his hair.

"I guess it can't hurt to ask. I'll email Felicia. We'll make it happen."

Eager to get Mrs. Faye and her grandson together for the first time, I reached for his hand. "Let's do," I said, "That'll be amazing and something I'd like to see."

"Okay. But just because it's my brother's kid, doesn't mean this is in any way about him."

I would have to let this go, for now at least. I swallowed the lump in my throat and nodded.

"Now, I want to talk about what happened down at the beach." Leaning back on the couch, he smiled at me. "You kissed me."

My mouth dropped open. "But you kissed me, too."

"But you kissed me first. In fact, you threw yourself into my arms, and then you kissed me."

I blushed and closed my eyes. I wasn't used to discussing this kind of stuff.

"Yes, I did," I confessed.

"I kind of think you like kissing me." He leaned closer, his lips inches from my face.

I don't know why it felt so painful to admit what was obviously the truth. Like it gave him power over me. It's okay, I told myself. Get over it, and maybe he'll kiss you again.

"I do," I finally whispered.

He smiled, his grin wide and smug. "How about that? Claudia Chiametti likes kissing me."

"All right, so I admitted it. But what does this mean for us— what are we now?"

Without answering, Toby leaned back against the couch and slowly stretched his arms over his head like a big, proud tomcat. Sinking deeply into the cushions, he lifted his long legs to rest on the coffee table before he turned his eyes on me. "What do you think we are now?"

"Dating?"

"Hmm." A smile touched the corners of his mouth. He picked up my hand and ran a thumb over my knuckles. "Are you saying you want to be my girlfriend, Claude?"

I was intimidated by the conversation. He seemed to be purposely making this painful. I glanced at him, nervous. "Isn't that what you want?"

While I sat on the edge of my seat wondering if I was making a fool of myself, he concentrated on our hands, aligning my hand to his and slowly, one by one, intertwining our fingers. Finally, he shrugged. "Yeah, that'd be okay."

"Wow. That is hardly the enthusiasm I was expecting." I tried to pull my hand away, but he held tight and rolled his head in my direction.

"I don't want to get too excited until we make it official."

"Official? And just how do we do that?" Suspicious, I eyed him.

"First, you have to understand, if we're *official*, all purchases are final—there's no returns or exchanges. You cool with that?"

"I don't know."

"Maybe you need a little persuading," he murmured. He leaned into nuzzle the crook of my neck. His breath was hot on my skin as his tongue traced my collarbone. He nipped up the length of my neck gently with his teeth. The area tingled under his attention, and I felt it down to my toes.

"Okay, okay," I pushed at his shoulders. "You're very convincing."

"Good," he said, rolling back to put his arm around my shoulders. "Now we just have to seal the deal with a kiss."

"This is some kooky ceremony," I muttered, but I leaned into him to press a quick kiss on his mouth anyway. Once my mouth touched his, though, he caught me and held me to him. His lips moved over mine in a soft, but thorough kiss.

Leaning back, he held up our intertwined fingers in triumph. "Opa! Congratulations, you are now my girlfriend!"

I giggled. Toby made laughing feel like breathing. It just happened. After the traumatic day, being with him was exactly where I wanted to be.

He picked up the television remote. "So what do you say? Want to watch 'Mrs. Doubtfire?'"

He switched off the lamp on the side table, putting us in almost complete darkness. The television screen illuminated the far corner of the room. He stretched his long length out on the couch, his feet extending over the arm at one end, and patted the cushion in front of him.

"Come lay down next to me. I want to give my new girlfriend a little TLC after her tough day."

"That sounds nice," I said, sidling closer.

The irony of the situation, however, was not lost upon me. Over the last few days, I had boasted about my plans and taken pains to hammer home how different we were. I had my lofty dreams with my wonderful plans while he had this awful history and a sick mother lying upstairs. Now, here he was, comforting me. I was ashamed at how distraught I had been over my insignificant problems. I would not whine about them again.

He lifted his arm so I could position myself next to him. Once I moved back against his chest, he used the remote to start the movie, and he wrapped his arms around me.

We watched the movie quietly for a little while, but Toby kept nuzzling my neck and stroking my hip. As funny as Robin Williams was in drag, Toby's "TLC" was distracting, and I simply could not concentrate on the movie.

Trying to derail the growing sexual tension, I asked, "So, would you consider signing up for a college class?"

"Huh?" He stopped nuzzling my neck. "Please tell me you aren't talking about me going to school, again?"

"We talked so briefly about it the other day. If you found something you were interested in, you'd feel more grounded, and maybe, happier here."

"There's no way I could be happier than I am right now." I could hear the smile in his words. I rolled onto my back so I could see him better. His eyes swept across my face as he reached over to trace a finger across the bridge of my nose. Then he took a deep breath and looked into my eyes.

"You're so beautiful."

The expression of awe in his eyes was so unrestrained, so raw, it did weird things to me. I couldn't take my eyes from his. My heartbeat began to accelerate. Damn, I'm in way over my head with this guy.

I tilted my face up and boldly raised my mouth to his. With the invitation, Toby took no time launching a lethal attack, our connection propelling him into action. Wrapping his arms around me, he eased his weight over me as his mouth fully covered mine. His whole being exerted hot energy, and under him, my body melted.

Our lips moved over each other's, this time with more lingering intensity than at the beach. He splayed a hand on my side, pressing and kneading my hip. The effect was unexpected—a radiating heat shot through my pelvis. I was feeling breathless and needy when he suddenly shifted tightly up against me, his excitement blatantly obvious. I froze, trying my best not to move against him in any way.

Breaking off our kiss, he put his mouth near my ear. "So, how long do you usually wait?" he asked, his voice lilted and husky.

"Wait for what?" I asked, hoping he wasn't asking what I thought he was asking. Knowing he was.

Pulling back, he looked at me. "Your internet connection," he said wryly. "Come on, Claude. It doesn't have to be carved in stone, just an estimate." He must have mistaken my expression to mean I didn't understand the question. He rephrased, "Tell me how long you want to wait before we can, you know, get tight."

Oh, God. How do I answer this? "I don't know. I never thought about it in terms of time."

"If it feels right, you just do it?"

He didn't get it, but I was distracted. A specific male body part was pressed against me, and I could barely manage a complete thought, let alone talk. I shook my head.

"No?" he asked. He stopped touching me and tilted his head in confusion. "I don't understand."

Our mismatch was rearing its ugly head. It was all so ridiculous—my complete overwhelmed state, his expression, and our bumbling miscommunication.

At the same time, I couldn't help but find it humorous. I giggled and bit my lip trying to suppress the embarrassment. "I can't say."

"You can't or you won't?"

I took his confusion as an opportunity to sit up and shift so I could see his face. I wanted to observe his expression when I clarified my answer.

"As you probably know, I've always been very focused on school," I said, carefully picking through my words. He waited patiently, so I continued. "In high school, dating took a back seat to schoolwork. And now, with my heavy course load of health classes, it's been even less important to me. So," I took a breath and willed myself to finish it up, "as you might imagine, I don't have a lot of experience racked up in my *sexual repertoire*."

His eyes did a little whirligig thing, spinning around. "You're a … *virgin?*"

He spoke as if we were talking about a mythical entity like Big Foot or the Loch Ness monster.

I looked down at my fingers, puckered my lips, and nodded.

"Holy shit!" He pressed his hands atop his head as if I'd told him the most insane news. My face, I'm sure, was crimson.

And then he had the nerve to laugh.

I shoved his arm. "It's not funny!"

He rubbed his hand over his face and blinked his eyes. "I'm sorry. I don't actually think it's funny, but it never occurred to me that you'd never been with someone. You—you're too old to have not done it. I suppose that's nice…"

"Old? Nice?" I snapped. "It's called being discerning, selective. Moral."

Toby blew out and slowly sat up next to me, his manner suddenly subdued. "Does that mean you straight-out won't have sex?"

Letting me consider my answer, he remained quiet. Negotiating sex. Way, way, way out of my comfort zone. I didn't expect to have to deal with this so soon. Was this the 'customary talk' he had with all his girlfriends? Ugh, I was so out of my league.

"So," he prompted. "What is it?"

I didn't know. The answer didn't seem so clear cut. Without responding, I threw my hands up in the air. "This isn't going to work."

Humiliated, I stood and pulled out my car keys. The faster I got out of there, the better.

"Hold up." Toby snagged a belt loop on my jeans, and unfolding himself from the couch, he hauled me against him. I held myself stiffly in his arms. "Hey," he said, raising my chin so I would look at him. "I didn't think you'd be someone who gave up so easily."

"Because you expect me to be different than I am," I challenged.

His eyes traveled over my face. "I did. But you are way more than I expected. Virginal you—you who laughs at all my jokes, makes me quit smoking, forces me think about college classes, and for the first time, makes me happy to be home. Claudia Chiametti. You. Are. Perfect."

"Yeah, right. Virginity is a dirty word to you."

He shook his head. "No, I actually like that no one has ever touched you before. I'm not saying we have to get busy, like, tomorrow or anything. I only want to know you'll consider doing it. With me." Lowering his chin, he gave me a hopeful look.

Leaning away, I crossed my arms. "What if I say no?"

"I won't lie, I'll be disappointed." He tugged at my arms until I allowed him to place them around his neck. "But I'd try very, very hard to make you change your mind."

I nervously curled my fingers under his shirt collar. "Being like that with someone would be a big deal to me."

He lowered his mouth to my ear. "Just say that it's a possibility, if it feels right." His whispered words tickled my ear.

Sex was probably something he excelled at. With his slow kisses and practiced touch, I was sure that if I wasn't careful, I might be persuaded into something I'd later regret.

I would need to keep my head.

"A 'maybe' will have to suffice," I said, at last. "But you'd better not push it."

He rubbed slow circles over my lower back. "When the time comes, I won't need to."

"You are so unbelievably sure of yourself."

"Trust me, with sex," he murmured, "confidence makes a difference."

"You sure talk about it a lot."

"And you keep listening."

I flushed. "Yeah, well, I'm not sure why."

"Because you're interested, as you're supposed to be. It's only natural." He looked into my eyes, all serious. "Since this is new to you, anytime you feel like grabbing me and experimenting, you go right ahead."

I snorted. "You offering to be my tutor?"

"Yeah." He grinned. "I'll show you everything you need to know. My body can be your learning tool."

"How charitable of you." I rolled my eyes for the thousandth time, hardly believing I, of all people, was having a conversation about sex. I laughed at the absurdity of it.

"We're going to be good together, Claude," he said. "I make the serious girl laugh, and you make the bad boy behave."

"Oh, yes, we're quite the quintessential, complementary couple," I teased, but then, on a more serious note, I added, "You know, you'll have to meet my dad. You prepared for that?"

He groaned. "Do I have to?"

"Of course. This girl comes with her own personal security service, and if you want to continue seeing her, such formalities apply."

"Is that in the virgin girlfriend handbook?"

"Virgin humor, not funny."

"Okay," his expression gentled. "How about I work something out with my aunt so I can take you out next Saturday. I'll pick you up and meet your dad. Do the date thing."

"That would be terrific," I said. And I really meant it.

Chapter 15

~CLAUDIA~

THE NEXT DAY, I SLEPT later than normal. I was sure Dad had gone to church without me, but when I did finally make it downstairs to the kitchen, he was sitting with his coffee and the Sunday paper at the kitchen table.

I poured myself a cup and leaned against the counter. He peered over the edge of the newspaper. We were at ground zero.

"So you were over the Fayes' last night?" he asked.

He already knew the answer, but I nodded anyway.

"Mrs. Faye told me you came over looking for me. I wish you hadn't done that."

"I was concerned for you."

"Dad, I'm one of the most responsible twenty-year-olds you'll ever know. I don't go around doing crazy things."

"You don't? Explain this whole USC debacle to me then."

I flinched at his choice of adjectives. "I want to go to USC." I bowed my head. "I mean, it was my hope to go."

"To be with your mother?" he accused.

"That's part of it. But mostly I want to go away to school, to live somewhere else." I found a cuticle on my middle finger and began rubbing at it with my thumb, anxious to bite it off. "Mom and I figured USC was a good choice because it's so close to her."

"You know, it was her decision to leave New York. You shouldn't be so quick to run off and satisfy her need to make up for it," he said sharply.

And here we go again.

"Dad, this is not a war. No one is against anyone. Mom insisted that I talk to you about this, but …"

"You didn't," he finished, with a little more anger in his voice.

"Is it any wonder? You always react like this."

"That's no excuse, Claudia," he said. "If you're not mature enough to face a difficult conversation with me, how can you think you can manage life on your own?"

That stung, but he was right. Like a baby, tears filled my eyes. I couldn't even finish the conversation without crying. I wiped furiously at my tears, vowing to work on toughening myself up.

"You have two more years. You'll graduate from Stony Brook." From his tone, it was clear I was not to defy him.

"I don't know if I can wait that long." More than ever, I wanted out, and I was tempted to say I didn't care what he said, but his scowl, the one that had long intimidated me, appeared on cue.

"One day you'll be married, and you'll be free to do as you please. For now, while you're under my roof, you'll do as I tell you."

Though my legs wobbled underneath me, I straightened up. "I'll get financial aid if I have to, but I'm going to keep applying to other colleges."

"I see. You be sure to let me know how that works out for you." He snapped his newspaper open and went back to reading.

Don't you cry! I chastised myself. I turned on heel and flew up to my room.

God, my father was insufferable. How was I supposed to bring Toby into the house to meet him? I considered possible ways around it for a few moments. Finally, I thought, no, I was going to do this right. Even though it might not bring me any closer to proving to my father that I was well-informed and mature enough to make sensible choices, it would prove that I wasn't afraid. If even just to myself.

I logged onto my computer and typed gerontology majors into the search field. I would find another college that would fit my needs. One away from here.

Far away.

Chapter 16

~TOBY~

OH, FUCK! HE HAS MY arms pinned to my sides. I kick to get away, but he's too strong. I can't escape.

"No!" I yell, but the pain explodes through me. It's so hot. I'm burning up. Every nerve in my body screams, but I grit my teeth. *You won't make me cry.* You won't. Suddenly, I am free and I am running, running, running. Ripping shards of pain pulse through my shoulder, but still, I run.

I bolted upright, my heart pumping hard, ready to burst out of my ribcage. Goddammit! It was just a stupid nightmare. I pressed the heels of my palms into my eyes and groaned. Slowly, I dragged myself out of bed and went into Al's old room.

It hadn't changed much since the day he'd last been here or the day I'd dreamt about, many years back. His furniture and most of his clothes were still here.

Back when I was about eleven years old, if anyone had asked me, I would have said, without any hesitation, that I was going to play pro ball one day. Baseball had been everything to me, but I had decided one day that I didn't want to play anymore. Julia never understood why.

I never told her it was because of what happened when my father bought me a new mitt that season. It wasn't my birthday or anything, but he came home and handed it to me. He even came outside and had a catch with me. For that one day he was a regular dad, just like everyone else's.

The folks had me registered in Little League, and, just before practice one day, I couldn't find the mitt. I was freaking out, tossing my room when Big Al came in. I remember telling him, my voice shaking, that my mitt was gone. I was afraid he was going to punish me, but he just spun around and marched off to my brother's room. I heard him yelling, and then, a scuffle with some grunts and thuds. Moments later, he came back and tossed the mitt to me.

"Go play," he ordered.

I passed Al's room on the way out, daring to look at him. His eyes were so dark with hate; I could still remember them. I knew he was pissed that he'd been beaten for taking the mitt. I remember feeling bad about the way my father had come down on him, but the mitt was mine. He had stolen it. I slunk out and went to play ball.

When I came home later, I found the shoebox I kept my baseball cards in, on my bed. I hadn't left it out, so I knew immediately something was wrong. I rushed to open the box, fearing the worst.

Eight cards, my most valued ones—the Yankees' starting lineup—ripped in two. I had traded, bought, and spent all my money to complete that year's Yankee team, and now the hardest ones to get were destroyed.

I ran to Al's room with the box. He was sitting on his bed, smoking a cigarette. He laughed in my face, so I threw the box at him as hard as I could. Cards flew everywhere.

He jumped up and grabbed me into a headlock.

"Fucker, let go of me," I growled. He only exhaled a plume of smoke and lowered his cigarette to my shoulder. It's hard to forget the feel of my skin melting. I gritted through the pain even as tears came to my eyes. When he was done, he shoved me outside his room.

I ran. From the house, down the block, to the wooded area south of the soccer fields. Lots of derelicts and stews hung out there, including Devlin Van Sloot. I don't know how it started, but we got into a fistfight. He bloodied my nose. I was aching afterwards, but I felt better, calmer. Later that night, I covered the painful circular welt on my shoulder and told my parents I wanted to quit Little League.

I reached up to touch the scar on my shoulder, now many years old, camouflaged with the tattoo. I admired the art in the dresser mirror. The tat artist had done a good job masking it. No one would ever be able to tell that the one wrinkly bolt in my realistic armor tattoo was a cigarette burn.

On my way out of the room, I saw a picture of Felicia on the dresser. After my talk with Claudia, I'd kept my promise to email Felicia about bringing little Dylan up to meet Julia. I was more than a little surprised when she readily agreed. I headed downstairs planning to check my email, to see if she had decided on a date.

I was psyched to find that Julia was not only up, but she was dressed and insisted on coming down the stairs herself.

In the kitchen, I set about making her my famous, 'garbage pail' omelet—anything I could find in the refrigerator that could conceivably be mixed with eggs.

When I sat down to eat it with her, she reached up to look at the cut on my forehead.

"It looks better today, but you should be more careful."

I gently nudged her hand away. Yesterday I'd told her I'd hit my head at work. She believed me. She always did.

Her appetite was decent, another positive sign. She'd finished her chemo and had just one more round of radiation to get through.

"How did your movie night go?" Julia asked.

"Pretty great. Except for the part where Claudia got on me about Al Junior."

Julia smiled guiltily. "I'm sorry. She looked so defeated about not going to USC, I decided she needed something else to concentrate on," she said. "I thought maybe she could talk some sense into that thick head of yours."

I wanted to tell her it was only thick from all the bashings I'd taken. But I'd never told her the half of it. I probably never would. What would be the point?

"Listen," I said instead, moving past it, "I sent Felicia a message about coming up with Dylan to visit with us. She said yes, and we're trying to figure out a date."

"Really? Oh, honey, that's wonderful!" Julia clapped her hands like a little girl.

"I'd like to take the credit, but it was Claudia's idea."

"I never thought to ask. I didn't think she'd come," Julia said. "Maybe she agreed because you asked. You and Felicia always got along well."

"Whatever the reason, she wants you to meet Dylan. We all do."

"Thank you. I'm so excited," Julia said, and grabbed hold of my hand. "Maybe she'll visit your brother, too."

"Mom, stop pushing. It might set some people off," I warned.

"Your brother made mistakes, but that doesn't mean he's not to be forgiven," she said. "He's changed. Things are different for him now."

"Oh, I imagine they are." Being surrounded by violent psychopaths who literally wanted your ass probably made things very different.

I redirected our conversation and dangled a different topic before her. "Hey, in case you're interested in knowing, Claudia and I hooked up."

She took the bait. "What?"

"Yeah, she's in love with me. She's all, 'Oh, Toby, I want you to be my baby daddy,' but I told her I'm not that kind of guy. I want my kids to be legit. So we're gonna fly to Vegas and get married by an Elvis impersonator."

Julia burst out laughing. "Wow, and this all came about last night?"

"What can I say? The girl digs me."

"Well, I love Elvis, and my schedule is free. When do we leave?"

I laughed. She was feeling better. "All right, there's no Elvis... or wedding, but I guess you're okay if I go out with Claudia?"

"If I had to pick someone for you, well, I think she's a wonderful girl. She's sweet, she's got her act together, and I simply adore her," Julia gushed.

"You forgot to mention, she's beautiful and smart."

Julia sat forward. "Are you going to ask her out?"

"It's a done deal. We're going out next Saturday."

Her eyes opened wider. "Oh! Take her someplace nice."

"I was thinking that café place on Main Street," I said.

"That's a good place. Oh, Marie mentioned there's going to be a concert in the park that night. You should look into it," she added. "Try to make a good impression—wear something nice. No jeans and absolutely no T-shirts." She wagged her finger at me. "And bring her some flowers. She likes flowers."

I laughed. "Have you been stockpiling tips in hopes we'd hit it off?"

"I got the impression, quite early on, that you liked our Claudia. I only hoped she felt the same."

What could I say? I couldn't hide anything from her.

When I didn't respond, Julia tilted her head. "Well, look at you! You're speechless. You must like her a lot."

My neck felt prickly, and I tugged at my shirt collar.

"I don't know where this is going to go. I'm probably in over my head." I played with the spoon next to my mug, suddenly not able to be still. "I have to go over and meet her father before I take her out Saturday. More than likely, I'll mess that up."

Julia's lips tightened. Claudia had said he'd been to see her. For a tense moment, I wondered if Mr. Chiametti had said something to her, but then, I realized she was worried about me meeting him, too. My mother knew this wasn't going to be easy for me.

"Mr. Chiametti is a stern man, but only because he wants the best for Claudia. You'll be fine. Remember, be polite. Shake his hand. Call him sir."

"He's going to hate me. I mean, I'm not bringing much to the table. She's the one who has it all together," I unleashed my biggest fear to Julia. "I'm not sure I can pull this off."

"Toby, you can do this, and you will," she said firmly, and she touched my face. "Life is throwing you an opportunity with a special young lady. You need to reach out and grab onto it, with both hands." Leaning back, she pointed a finger at me. "That said, you treat her like a lady and be respectful. Then her father will see what a good boy you are." She beamed, and her voice softened. "No. He'll see the good man you are."

Her faith amazed me. I shook my head and got up to stack the breakfast dishes.

"Thanks, Ma," I said and smiled. "But I am not going to her house carrying flowers."

"All right," she said. "How about balloons or candy?"

I raised my eyebrows at her. "You're kidding, right?"

"What?" she asked. "Is that frowned upon these days?"

"In this century, all we bring on a date is a cell phone, credit card, and condoms."

"Tobias Michael Faye! You're not too old to be spanked."

I couldn't breathe I was laughing so hard. She swatted my leg, and though it didn't hurt, I said, "Ouch," just to satisfy her.

"Behave yourself," she warned, but her stern face kept slipping. A smile lay underneath.

"Yes, Mother," I said, leaning over to give her a hug. She touched my hair and pressed her head against mine.

"I love you," she whispered.

Closing my eyes, I nodded. "I know."

Releasing her, I brought the dishes to the sink. Julia was being all pushy about this date. She only got like that when she really wanted something for me. I didn't usually talk to Julia about girls; I could see she really wanted Claudia and me to work out.

So did I.

To break the tension, I said, "I'm going to try to do something with the hedges out in front of the house. They look bad."

Her face brightened.

I pulled out the hedge trimmer and some yard tools and thought about meeting Claudia's father for the first time.

Part of me wished Claudia was like other girls who didn't need to have me meet their parents. She was different, so principled about stuff. Strange, but I kind of liked that about her.

Talk about principled! Still a virgin. Christ, I'd been dreaming of getting into a body tangle with her for half my twenty-one years. No need for Trojans on our dates. At least for now. But, I was sure of one thing: I would be her first. Until then, there were many other, interesting things we could do.

As I trimmed the hedges, I imagined how happy Claudia would be when she saw it. Then, I laughed at myself. All for a girl. It was as if she had punched holes in my world, and all the bad stuff that had happened and the crap that I'd done in the past were being filtered out. I already felt different. I was on a new path. Maybe she was what I'd been searching for—the piece that would finally make it all come together for me.

Chapter 17

~CLAUDIA~

I TOOK THE LAST OF MY final exams, and with classes over I could give my attention to other things.

Like what I was going to wear on my date out with Toby.

April and I planned a post-exam celebratory shopping expedition to the mall.

It had been a long, stressful week, but thankfully Mrs. Faye had been doing well and had been fine with me taking both Monday and Wednesday off to study. She said she was feeling so good; in fact, I could take Friday off, too.

April and I drove up to the Smith Haven Mall, on the North Shore. As we browsed outfits for me to wear Saturday night, I brought her up-to-date on my college drama.

"I found several other colleges with my gerontology major, but deciphering financial aid requirements is mind-boggling. Apparently, while I live as a dependent, I'm not eligible for much. My parents' income bracket puts me out of any need-based funding." I scanned a rack of brightly colored dresses. "Basically, if I want to go away to finish my degree, I either have to declare myself an independent or cough up a load of dough."

"Sorry, fresh out of loads of dough," April said, and held up a red-sequined mini dress.

"Trashy." I shook my head.

"I don't think it's that bad." April shrugged and put it back on the rack.

"So, I don't have much other choice than to stay put. I just hope my father and I can come to some sort of agreement. He has to back off."

"Chica, some dads have a hard time letting their little girls grow up. Insist on some compromises. You can totally handle another two years with your dad," she said very simply and nodded towards the back of the store. "Come on. I have a bunch of dresses for you to try on."

I followed her into the fitting rooms. As I tried on the assortment of outfits, she commented on them—that's okay, I like the neckline on that one, but the color is yuck... until I put on a fitted, chocolate halter-dress.

Her eyes lit up, and she shouted, "That's the one!"

Pulled taut, the bodice hugged my curves and was gathered underneath the bust line, held in place by a large wood ring embellishment.

April stood next to me and looked at my reflection in the mirror. "It's so flirty and sexy. And, look at the girls, up high and proud," she gushed. The way the halter top was fashioned, it pushed everything up while at the same time the low-cut neckline allowed a generous amount of cleavage to show.

"I love this dress," I said, turning this way and that to admire it from different angles. The free-flowing skirt ended just above the knee and gently swished back and forth with my movement. The soft cotton mix caressed my legs. It was a simple summer dress I was sure most girls wouldn't worry about wearing. But it was not my typical style.

Doubts began to creep in. "I can't buy it."

"You have to! Toby won't be able to take his eyes off of you." For April, the decision was made.

"It's his hands I'm more concerned with," I sighed, and unhooked the strap from behind my neck. "It's too sexy for a first date."

"Wear the dress. It'll be a good way to gauge how Toby feels about you." April pushed my hands away to refasten the strap. "If no matter what you say, he's all hands, you drop him in a hot minute. But if he looks at you and you can see all the nasty, delicious things he wants to do to you in his eyes, and he's able to keep his hands to himself, it means he's a keeper."

"You mean, if I choose to keep him," I added.

"You got that right." She smiled.

"Who would have thought one little dress could wield so much power?" I laughed. I admired my reflection once more. "As much as I like this dress, I'm afraid I'll feel self-conscious all night. And my dad, he'll hate it."

"Wait a sec," April said and left the dressing room. She came back moments later with a silkscreened scarf in several shades of cream and taupe and wrapped it around my neck. She arranged it over my exposed cleavage, making the outfit tastefully modest.

"After the lickfest the other night, I can't guarantee your safety once you remove it, but your father shouldn't have any complaints."

When I got home, I hung my new dress where I could see it from my bed. I was nervous, but I hoped to show Dad that despite what he knew about people's history, it didn't necessarily predict their destiny. That regardless of what had happened with his father and his brother, Toby was not going to end up like them.

I wanted Dad to see Toby as I saw him: funny and kind. The good Faye.

My father was doing paperwork in his office when I got home from my normal Saturday shift at Sterling.

Over the course of the day, I reflected that USC, or any away-college for that matter, might be beyond reach, but I still needed to assert my independence in other ways. Tonight it would be about what I did with my time and who I dated, but after this, there were other areas of contention I would get to, all in good time.

Even though we'd barely spoken all week, I charged right in.

"Dad, I'm going out with someone tonight, and I asked him to come over to meet you."

I resisted biting on a cuticle while I waited for him to respond.

He put down his pen and leaned back in his seat as if he were preparing himself for bad news.

"So I'm finally going to meet the younger Faye kid?"

"How'd you know?"

"It's a reasonable conclusion considering how much time you've been spending at that house." He shuffled through some papers before looking back up at me. "With your attitude lately, I suppose I should be grateful that you're telling me about this at all."

"It's been a tough few days with all my finals. I just want to go out and have some fun. Will you meet him?"

"By all means. I look forward to it," Dad commented, suspiciously upbeat.

I had to get ready, so there was no time to hash out whether or not he really meant it. Given my father's obvious disdain for any male Faye, and Toby's aversion to authority, as much as I tried, I couldn't imagine the two getting along.

I finished my makeup and hair and strategically adjusted the scarf the way April had done in the store. When Toby's Jeep pulled up out front, I rushed downstairs to answer the door before he rang the doorbell. I wanted to greet him before my dad got at him.

"So this is what *casa de Chiametti* looks like. Nice place," he said, glancing around the spacious front room and modern kitchen. "I opted out of a bulletproof vest, but I hope I look presentable enough to meet the old man."

He was dressed in a pair of stylish black slacks and a soft short-sleeved, white collared shirt that set off his tan and contrasted with his blue-gray eyes. Almost clean-shaven, his facial hair was trimmed down to a goatee that outlined his mouth. The look and the scent of shaving cream that lingered on his skin were very appealing.

God, he smelled great.

"Whether he's impressed or not, I approve." I touched his smooth cheek. It felt like silk.

"You like?" Toby pressed his hand over mine. "I went to the barber and got a hot shave with a straight razor—just for you."

We eyed each other. A flutter rippled through my stomach. Toby leaned forward to kiss me, but at the sound of footsteps, he stepped back. Dad sauntered in looking like a gunslinger out of a Western movie.

He silently appraised my dress, and I was glad for the scarf. Then, his scrutiny shifted to Toby.

I introduced them, and they respectfully shook hands. I glanced from one to the other assessing them. My father, with his disciplined, military background and police training, stood ramrod straight while Toby stood with a casual stance, his hands pushed deep into his pants pockets, his gaze lowered. This was awkward for him, but he'd done it anyway—for me.

Dad said, "Before I let you take my daughter out tonight, I'd like to speak to you, alone in my office."

"Dad, no."

"If he wants to take you out, he'll spend a couple of minutes with me." Dad held up a hand to me and turned to Toby. "All right?"

Toby nodded and followed my father. I watched, helpless and uneasy as the door shut behind them.

I waited several minutes, drumming my fingers nervously on the counter. The door finally opened, and Toby came out followed by my father. He smiled tightly as he came to my side.

"Ready?" he asked quietly.

I nodded and picked up my bag, prepared to leave.

"One last thing, Toby." Dad's words stopped us. "I see you're driving a Jeep. My daughter is in a dress. Perhaps it would be best to take her car tonight."

"I'm fine," I started to say.

"The car will be easier for you," Toby said calmly, agreeing with my father.

"Okay, fine." I pulled out my keys.

My father seemed satisfied. "You two have a nice time tonight and not too late."

Toby nodded, and I kissed my father's cheek before we left the house.

"I didn't know he was going to do that," I said, as we made our way to my reliable silver Camry. The weather was warm and muggy, but being outside was still a relief.

"Can I still drive?" Toby asked. I handed him my car keys, and he walked to the passenger door to open it for me. I paused, and he just shook his head. "That was a first."

"Was it bad?" I hesitated before getting in the car, trying to get a read on his mood.

"No, it was great. We had a few beers, a couple of laughs. He's quite the joker."

"Yeah, right." With a huff, I slid into the seat. He shut the door and went around to the driver's seat. He had to adjust everything, the seat, mirrors and steering wheel to fit his long legs.

"Seriously, what did he say?"

"He asked me if I was involved in that attack," he said, navigating his way out of my neighborhood. Worry was etched in his grimace, and I searched his profile for some kind of clue of what he was thinking.

"And you're not," I said carefully. "But you know something

about it. I see how it upsets you. You know, my dad could actually help with something like that."

He braked for the traffic light to turn left on Main Street and shook his head. "Your dad would help me right into a pair of handcuffs."

"Come on, my father isn't that bad."

"Maybe, but he's not a fan of mine," Toby said, his tone markedly cool. "But then again, we never expected him to be."

I lived so close to town, it was only a few moments before Toby pulled my car into a parking spot along Main Street. He got out and came around to my door. I swiveled in my seat, showing a little more leg than I'd intended.

A wolf whistle pierced the air. Toby and I both turned to see, about thirty feet away, Devlin and Ray staring at us.

With his hands cupped around his mouth, Devlin yelled, "Hey, beautiful, why don't you come over here and let me show you what a real man has to offer?" and then, he grabbed himself between the legs.

"He's disgusting." I cringed.

Toby's face tightened, and his nostrils flared. Putting his back to me, he subtly arched his shoulders as if he were preparing to do battle.

I lurched forward, grabbed his hand, and pulled hard. Toby snapped around and squinted at me, his whole stance emanating menace.

"If you respond to that, this date is over," I warned.

I saw the conflict play out on his face. Quickly looking for a way to pull him back, I fingered the knot on my scarf.

"And, I'm really insulted." Taking a breath, I slowly pulled the scarf off. "I bought this dress for our date, and you haven't even mentioned it."

His eyes darted down at my cleavage, and the moment became so charged, I don't think either of us drew a breath. He sagged against my car, the tension visibly leaving him. Slowly, he turned his attention back to me, and I made myself stay still as he openly admired the generous allotment of skin the dress left exposed.

"Whoa," he murmured.

Reaching for my hand, the corners of his mouth tipped up. "I'm sorry. You look absolutely smoking hot in that dress, and there's not a chance this date is ending before it's actually started."

Exactly the response I wanted. I caught him throw one last glance over his shoulder before he put an arm around my waist and drew me towards the restaurant.

Chapter 18

~TOBY~

I TOOK CLAUDIA TO DINNER AT Café Raphael. It was the same restaurant that I took Julia to on her birthday each year. My mother liked the old-world decor, that the wait staff wore matching black vests over crisp white shirts, and that they piped in soft, classical music overhead. It was one of the more upscale places on Main Street—a place a girl like Claudia Chiametti should be taken on a first date.

She sat across the candlelit table from me looking killer in a dress that showed off a whole lot more than I'd ever seen of her. She blushed when I hurried the busboy away from the table. He'd been eyeing her as he refilled our water glasses for the twentieth time. I just wanted to be alone with her, but once we were, it took effort to keep my own eyes from drifting downwards.

"I'm sorry," I apologized again. "I can't believe I didn't tell you at the house how amazing you look."

"Forget it," she said with a wave of her hand. "Who could think of anything else but my father?"

I reached across the table for her hand. "He's not here and all I'm thinking of is how beautiful you are."

I would never tell her just how much her giant, mustachioed father had a hard on for me. Inside his office, he'd told me to take a seat while he sat behind his enormous wood desk like a scripted, formal job interview.

He ticked off questions: Do you go to school? Are you working? What happened to your eye?

I joked that I'd been clumsy and split it open on a fall, but he didn't crack a smile.

He leaned forward on his elbows and asked, "Were you involved with the Velerio stabbing?"

"No, sir."

He had paused for a long time. Then he'd come right out and said, "You know she's too good for you." He sneered like he wanted to put me out in the trash. "Let me make myself clear. I don't accept any bullshit when it comes to my daughter. If I find out you hurt her, or that you're doing anything that might hurt her, I will make your life miserable. Got me?"

Message loud and clear—old pops was prepared to throw me in lockdown if I stepped out of line with his daughter.

If it weren't for the fact that I'd been forever jonesing for her, I might have pursued Claudia just out of spite. But, I wanted this. I wanted to make Claudia mine. If it pissed old pops off, well, call it a bonus.

When dinner was over, I paid the bill, and we headed out. I'd told her in advance that we were going to sit in the park and listen to music. We stopped at the car to pick up the blanket she'd stowed in the backseat, and, leaving her car parked on Main Street, we crossed the road to the south side.

She had loved the park idea. "How great is it that our town has these free concerts?" We strolled the short distance to Rotary Park.

No matter what her father thought, Claudia seemed just as happy holding my hand as I did hers. I didn't get the impression she thought I wasn't good enough for her.

The concert was decent, a really great Beatles cover band. It turned out that Claudia and I both liked the Beatles. I joked that we had so much in common, soon people wouldn't be able to tell us apart.

She laughed and leaned into me, and I pressed my face into her hair. When the band struck the first chords of "Something," I stood up and asked her to dance with me.

"I thought you didn't dance." She rose up next to me and twined her soft, bare arms around my neck.

"Don't tell anyone," I whispered. "I'm making an exception for you."

The song was slow, and I only had to hold her to me and sway. The heat of her body against mine boxed my mind off. There was only me and her.

I sung the words of the song to Claudia as I pressed my nose into her neck. The sweet smell of her skin and hair elevated my high. Being with her felt amazing. Better than all my dreams.

Chapter 19

~CLAUDIA~

THE CONCERT ENDED, AND BACK in my car, Toby drove south, towards the water, and my neighborhood.

"Are you taking me home already?" I asked.

He shook his head. "If you think I'm settling for a kiss on your doorstep, you've got the wrong guy."

"No, I'm pretty sure you're the guy my father always warned me about," I teased.

Taking my hand in his, he interlaced our fingers and rested our hands on my thigh. "And you still went out with me?" He raised an eyebrow at me and grinned. "Well, now you're about to find out why he said that."

"Oh, boy," I said, trying my best to appear indifferent while my stomach curled into a tight bundle of anticipation.

He laughed as he pulled my car into the Land's End parking lot. The large paved area had a spectacular view of the water and of the jetty lining the Brown's Creek inlet. Fifty or so yards off the jetty, a Fire Island ferry was churning up a wake as it began its journey across the bay.

Now that dusk had settled in, the regulars who usually came down to fish, or simply to admire the view, were gone for the day. Only a few other parked cars dotted the open lot. Local kids, I guessed, just like us. "Parking."

Toby turned off the engine and twisted in the seat to face me. The warmth in his eyes made me tingle all over.

"Remember, I have limits," I warned.

"I'm not going to push you anywhere you don't want to go. But you didn't wear that dress just to engage in conversation all night."

"That's not exactly true," I demurred, playing coy. "I like talking to you."

"I like talking to you, too, but I spent most of our date thinking about getting you alone."

He held my hand, slowly rubbing each finger gently between his before kissing my open palm. All the while, his eyes danced with wicked intention. "Does that make you nervous?"

In the swelling heat of awareness, I struggled to allay a quiver of excitement, and I lied.

"No."

"Good," he said and brazenly stared at my chest. "Because I'm ready for skin to skin contact."

My face grew hot, and I let out a tinny laugh. "Are you this aggressive and explicit with all girls?"

"With you, I think I need to be. You're always so cool and collected. But I know something's bubbling hot underneath that self-control."

His assumption amused me. "And you know this, how?"

"You react every time I come near you. Even right now, you're practically squirming in your seat. And I feel it all over me, especially here," he held my hand over his heart. Our eyes held as his heartbeat drummed under my palm. "And here," he lowered my hand. Before I realized what he was doing, my fingers brushed his groin.

I yanked my hand away. "Oh, my God! You're such a caveman," I huffed, shocked at his audacity.

He just cocked an eyebrow at me. "But I bet you're sitting in a puddle over there."

"Jeez!" I groaned. My pulse was racing. Other than a brief cuddle at the park, we hadn't kissed all evening. Despite all his innuendos—or maybe because of them—I was eager to get close to him.

His smile grew wider. "Prepare to defend yourself," he said and slipped out of the car. With nervous thrill, I watched as he strode around to my side and opened my door. "Slide over."

"Where?" I asked as he pushed himself into the seat with me. I was wedged against the center console until he pulled me onto his lap. He dropped his right hand between the seat and the door, and yanked the seat lever. The seat dropped back, and we were instantly fully reclined—me prone atop him, breathless and fidgeting with the thought of what was about to come.

"That's more like it," he said, putting his hands around my waist. "This car is pretty comfortable. Make out in here much?"

"No. I generally just use it for driving," I felt his hands move warmly over my back. "You'd be my first."

"Mmm," he murmured, and drew my face towards him. We kissed, slowly, with just our lips. It was sweet, nice, not anything like the bold taunts he'd made. I settled comfortably into the crook of his arm, and, breaking off the kiss, I admired the flawless symmetry of his face in the dusky light. I laid a fingertip on his cheek and got caught up in tracing the straightness of his perfect nose down to the flared tip, to the fullness of his bottom lip as it curved with his grin. I continued languidly exploring his face, tracing the angle of his jaw and sliding my hand over his perfectly groomed chin until my finger settled into a small groove. I stopped, traced it again, and inspected it closer. It was a thin, jagged, white indentation made by scar tissue.

"What's this from?"

"Close encounter with my brother and the coffee table." Toby reached up to thumb the ripple on his chin and then shrugged. "Just one of many."

I laid my head on his chest and stroked the scar, trying to soothe the old hurt. "I get that your brother was awful to you, but aren't you in the least bit curious to see if he's trying to apologize in those letters he wrote?"

"Nope. I'm not interested in an apology or anything he has to say. If you're so curious, you read them."

Excited, I rolled back on top of him. "Really? You'd let me read the letters?"

He shifted my weight, centering me over him, but with a look of uncertainty, he stilled. "Um, maybe. I don't know. Please don't make me think about it while you're lying on top of me like this!" he groaned, a hitch in his voice. "My brother and your body cannot coexist in my head."

He looked down at my cleavage. I was mashed up against his chest, and because of the open neckline, the girls were popping out all over the place. I blushed profusely.

"I've been praying for a wardrobe malfunction all night." He grinned, and suddenly his hands were cupping me through the material, his large palms making a circular motion over my breasts. My breath caught in my throat.

The next kiss was hot. With our mouths fused together, I forgot any objection as I sank down into him. As his hands pressed and kneaded me into a heightened arousal, he began to trail kisses down my throat, intermingling them with a flick of his tongue. I sighed with pleasure. He unequivocally knew how to stir things up with his mouth.

Sliding his hands to my hips, he gripped me tightly and our bodies created a hot friction as he slid me forward over him. All the while, he continued his trail of licks and kisses right down into the hollow of my cleavage. He held me above him, and all I could do was clutch onto his shoulders as his mouth began to travel places no other's had ever been. The dress strap stretched, the fabric gently rubbing against my sensitized skin as he pushed it aside, exposing my left breast. I heard his murmur of pleasure, and then his lips were on my breast encircling my nipple.

He enticed the peak into a hardened nub with his tongue, and my whole body ached sweetly in response. One hand possessively cupped my breast while the other pressed me to him, molding my body to his. His sensual attack was heady and unremitting, and it made my body burn with a need long ignored. With a fervent sigh, I arched forward, pushing myself at him, and filling his mouth.

A soft rumbling growl rolled low in his throat and he tangled a hand in my hair. Each stroke of his tongue ratcheted up the tension in my body, and I felt myself beginning to toe a line I was not ready to cross. With trembling hands, I captured his face and pulled his mouth from me.

"Please," I begged.

"Please, what?" he asked in a low, husky voice. "What do you want, baby?"

"I want you to stop."

"No, you don't," he said, and as if to prove his point, he flicked his tongue over me. Hot sensation shot down through my belly, and I practically folded under it.

It took more willpower than expected, but I rolled off of him, and found myself wedged snugly between his body and the console. I covered my breast with my hand, embarrassed by the swollen state of my nipple. "Did you forget we're in a public parking lot?

Anyone could pull up alongside and see us."

"They're too busy having sex in their own cars to care what we're doing. Except maybe the pervs who come down to watch."

"Pervs?" My eyes darted to the windows.

His smirk mirrored the devil-may-care look in his eyes. "I'm kidding. Don't worry. I guarantee you no one's looking. If someone pulls up next to us, we'll hear them. Now, where were we?"

Coyly, he attempted to peel away my hand from my breast to replace it with his.

I redirected the wayward hand.

"Even if that's so, it's only our first date. It's too much, too soon."

With a sigh, he watched me adjust the dress to cover myself. "I'm almost afraid to ask, but what do you consider acceptable?"

I twirled my necklace around my finger. "Kissing and some touching, over our clothes."

He cocked his head in surprise. "That's all?" When I nodded, he lowered his face into the crook of my neck and mumbled, "Damn, this is going to be tough."

"You make it sound like such a test. Do you honestly have to try that hard?"

He leaned back to look at me. "Claude, sex feels good," he said, stroking my upper arm with his fingertips. The gentle touch sent little tingles down my back. "And unlike you, most girls don't feel the need to hold off."

"Are you telling me you had sex with every girlfriend you've had?"

"No, not every one."

"Did you love them?"

"Maybe no one told you, but you don't have to be in love to have sex."

"I'm well aware of that. I just want to know if you loved any of them." Though I wondered how many girls he'd been with, I was more curious about his emotional intimacies than his physical ones.

Toby shrugged. "I liked them all, and some I liked a lot, but it's never been more than that."

His inexperience with love seemed to even us out somewhat.

"I believe people should be in love before they reach that level of intimacy," I said.

He traced my bottom lip with his index finger. "So I have to make you fall in love with me if I want to get anywhere with you?"

"No, you don't have to do anything," I clarified. "But when I get, as you call it, tight with someone, I plan on being in love first."

"All right," he said. "Got it."

"Good." I took his hand. "Can we go easy tonight? Maybe lay here and just kiss a little more?"

He shifted himself from under me so now I was on the seat and he was over me. Pressing a kiss on my mouth, he smiled. "Okay, but be warned, my hands are addictive. It won't take long before you'll be begging me to put them all over you. And definitely under your clothes."

"If you say so," I replied, mocking his confidence.

"I do say," he curled an arm around my waist. "Now be quiet so I can kiss you. We don't have a lot of time left."

"Why's that?"

"I have orders to bring you back to my house. I think Julia wants to make sure I haven't made our whole date up."

"Why would she think that?"

"Because she's met some of my other girlfriends. You're very different—smart, good—the whole package. I'm sure Julia's home doing a happy dance."

Laughing, I put my arms around his neck. "Your mom is so cute. I would love to go back and see her before you take me home."

And then, I pulled his face down to mine.

Walking to Toby's front door, I noticed that the bushes along the front of the house were trimmed, and some of them were gone altogether. The house still needed a lot more work, but the difference was noticeable.

Aunt Joan and Mrs. Faye were doing a large jigsaw puzzle at the kitchen table, and we joined them for a while. Mrs. Faye was practically giddy over us ending our date with her. I caught her watching us as Toby put his arm around me. Unlike at home, the atmosphere with Mrs. Faye was relaxed. Toby and I were accepted without question.

"Did Toby tell you that I'm going to finally see my grandson?" she beamed.

"No." I turned to Toby in surprise. "You didn't tell me you'd spoken to Felicia already."

"Hey, I was getting my date on," he smiled.

"Felicia is bringing Dylan up for a visit the second week in July," Mrs. Faye filled me in.

I grinned. "You must be so excited."

"Oh, yes! She emailed us some pictures, too." With a smile a mile wide, she pushed some computer printed images towards me. "He's such a beautiful baby."

We stayed for about an hour before Toby drove me back to my house. Before we got out of the car, we exchanged a couple of quick kisses, and he asked, "Did you have fun tonight?"

I thought back to our evening's dramatic start, the concert, to parking by the water, and finally to the calm end with his mother.

"Yes, I had a really nice time," I said and glanced up at him. "I just hope it's not going to be a problem for you to go slow with me."

"It's not a problem," he answered without pause. "I won't stop trying to touch you, but if you think I'm coming on too strong, tell me. I'll back off." He ran a hand through my hair and brought it around to touch my face.

I warmed at the sweet gesture. "Thank you," I whispered.

Lifting his eyes to mine, he asked, "Claudia, can you see yourself falling for a guy like me?"

His tone was unusually serious, and, for a moment, I was startled, almost paralyzed over the topic—he wanted to know if I thought it possible to fall in love with him. And then I remembered our earlier conversation.

"God, you are really hung up on the sex thing."

He leaned away from me and sighed. "It's not that," he said quietly, and I waited for him to go on. He fidgeted with my car keys and avoided looking my way. "I just want to know if you think that I'm, I don't know … good enough for that to happen."

I blinked. I didn't expect such an insecure question from him.

I tried to be truthful. "When we first met, I didn't think we had anything in common, but on some strange, unpredictable level, we connect. But," I said, "I have never thought I was too good for you, Toby."

We stayed quietly locked in a long gaze until he leaned forward and kissed my cheek. It was a soft, undemanding kiss, like a thank you.

We got out of the car, and he handed me my keys.

"So, despite my dad and my need to take things slow, I get the impression that you really like me."

With a grin, he swiped his chin with the back of his hand. "Damn. Am I drooling again?"

Chuckling, I tugged playfully at his shirt. "The fact that you are deciding to hang around, be patient and put up with a lot more 'issues' than you normally would with other girls ... well, it kind of gives you away."

"You're so smart. You've got me all figured out." He stroked my cheek and then pressed a soft kiss on my mouth. "Yes, Claudia Chiametti. I really like you. I like your laugh, the way you say my name, and even the way you squirm when you're excited. Too many things to name. I'll just say, I like everything about you and leave it at that."

I all but floated through my front door. I even smiled at my father who was sitting in the living room, waiting up for me.

He eyed me strangely.

"Is that the same dress you were wearing when you left the house?" he asked.

I touched my chest. Oops.

"Um, yes," I replied, deciding I would not feel guilty about it.

"Don't wear it again. It's far too revealing."

Insulted, I put my hands on my hips. "What does it reveal? That I'm a full-grown woman? I feel beautiful in it, and if I want to, I will wear it again."

By his expression, I could see Dad was disappointed. "I don't know my own daughter anymore," he said stiffly, and then got up and went to bed.

Dad's words upset me, as he knew they would, and I went up to my room with a little less bounce in my step. Yet, despite my father's disapproval, the date had gone well. Even the run-in with Toby's friends hadn't detracted from it. I loved that he had asked me to dance. Had sung in my ear. I would never hear that song again without thinking of Toby and this night.

Somewhere, nagging in the back of my mind, I knew we still

weren't a perfect fit, but I was way too far gone to care. For maybe the first time in my tediously planned life, I wanted something that didn't make complete sense.

I admired myself in the dress one more time. I never even thought I knew how to do sexy. Turning and studying my profile in my dresser mirror, I remembered Toby's eyes on me.

For the first time, I was acutely conscious of my femininity. Toby was the first guy who dared to touch me so sexually. His unflagging interest in physical exploits should have scared me, but instead, being the object of his desire left me feeling powerful. I could barely wait to be with him again.

My father was just going to have to realize his baby was not such a baby after all.

Chapter 20

~CLAUDIA~

SURPRISINGLY, AFTER MY FIRST DATE with Toby, our lives fell together seamlessly. With Mrs. Faye's health at the forefront of both of our concerns, we teamed up, keeping her company, doing jigsaw puzzles on the kitchen table, watching television, and barbecuing out on the back deck.

In the beginning of June, I switched my hours around at Sterling, working a few weekdays and freeing the weekends. I carefully divided my time between seeing Toby and April. But Dario and April often popped over to hang out with us, making it easy for me to do both. On a rare occasion, we actually got out of the house to spend a few hours at the beach or at the multiplex theater, watching the latest blockbuster.

Mrs. Faye was on the upswing after her last radiation treatment, and she swore that soon we would not have to babysit her anymore. I assured her I was happy to be there. Being at the Faye house was like having a home away from home—it was comfortable and I always felt welcome.

It didn't hurt that the gorgeous guy who lived there had a thing for me.

Stopping by on a Sunday afternoon, I found Toby and Mrs. Faye sunning out on the back deck. Toby was shirtless and barefoot, wearing only a faded pair of light blue board shorts that hung low on his hips. He had a guitar on his lap, and played and sang while Mrs. Faye lay on her chaise lounge, her eyes closed and a contented look on her face.

Unnoticed, I stayed behind the closed screen door for a few moments to admire the view and listen to him play. My boyfriend was an impressive sight sitting there, half-naked, soaking up the sun. To look at him, there was nothing that said 'urbane.' But he was kind and thoughtful—a combination of gentleness, charisma and brawn that was all so very appealing.

Even now, his tanned, muscular shoulders and chest charged my senses. I drank him in, knowing how warm and hard to the touch his sun-warmed chest would be. Over the last few weeks, our relationship became more sure-footed, our kisses more heated and our touches more bold. I'd had moments of unrestrained pleasure, touching and feeling those muscles with both my hands and mouth.

I had never been in love before, but I was beginning to understand how it happened to people. When Toby came home after work, I grew flustered by just the sound of his work boots inside the house. He would be excited, too. I could tell. His mouth tipped upwards in that cute, mischievous way it did. An undeniable magnetism drew us together, and we would press into each other to hug and touch until our mouths joined. Our kisses were addicting, neither of us wanting to stop, but each time, struggling to pull away, he begged me to let him go so he could shower and get clean for me. Eventually, I would release him and wait impatiently for him to come back to me.

There were times when all I wanted to do was to watch him. But, oh, the never-ending need to touch him, even just casually, was particularly distracting. I was dumbstruck to think I was having my first true romance with Toby Faye. How could I ever have known I would feel this way?

Head bent, Toby concentrated, his capable fingers strumming the chords and creating beautiful music. He sang along with the melody, his singing voice in perfect pitch with the unfamiliar song. The piece was slow, and it appeared that he was singing his mother a love song. I was moved by the scene before me.

Once Toby saw me though, he stopped playing.

"Get that cute butt out here, and give me a kiss," he said, smiling.

Cover blown, I stepped out onto the back deck. Mrs. Faye lifted a hand to wave at me.

Guitar pick in his hand, Toby reached over, snagged a belt loop on my jean shorts and drew me to him. I laid my hands upon his shoulders to steady myself, and reveled in the heat of his skin, as hot as I had imagined. He planted a quick kiss on my lips and released me. I enjoyed the natural ease in which he kissed me in front of his mother. I settled down next to Mrs. Faye on the lounge chair and began playing with her yellow headscarf. Though her hair was growing back in, it was thin. She still needed to protect her scalp from the sun.

"That was pretty. Did you write it?" I asked him.

"No. John Lennon did," he said. "He wrote it for his mother."

"I like that," Mrs. Faye said. "I like when I hear about celebrities honoring their mothers. Because, really, where would anyone be without their mother?"

Toby shrugged. "Unborn?"

I giggled while Mrs. Faye pretended to disapprove of his sarcasm. Then she asked him to play something else.

Toby bowed his head over the guitar, and I heard the familiar sweet notes of "Something." Our song now. With a voice deep and sure, he smiled his alluring grin at me and sang.

After a month of his sexy, sometimes sly and often comical innuendos, I was still learning how to handle them without turning three shades of red. I smiled demurely at him, making sure he knew I appreciated his choice of song.

Toby started to gripe about his job at the electronics store more and more each week. His boss, Abe Bernbaum, seemed to be pushing Toby's buttons. We talked about other ways he could make a living. He seemed to have a natural gift for playing guitar, and I had suggested that he could give lessons. Although it might be good as a side job, it wouldn't be a viable source of primary income. He needed benefits, insurance and all.

After some needling from both his mother and me, Toby met with a career counselor at Suffolk County Community College and signed up for the first part of a series of computer classes. The classes, which began in the fall, would result in a certification.

It was a step in the right direction. Everyone needed a goal, and I was determined to help Toby establish one. And to get serious about it.

I had my own goals to worry about, too. At home, I remained respectful. I came in at my usual midnight curfew and did my chores without complaint, but conversations between Dad and me trickled to a cursory give-and-take of information. We ate dinner and went to church together, but we barely talked about things other than those pertaining to household matters. I was insulted and more than a little hurt that he continued to begrudge Toby, but since he had quieted down considerably, I wasn't about to rock the boat.

If my family discord wasn't upsetting enough, I appeared to still be on USC's mailing list. Weekly, informational letters and emails effectively taunted me with details on orientation and start dates for the upcoming fall semester. As I glumly tossed another letter into the recycling bin, I was sure at that very minute, somewhere on the USC campus, someone was applying a sticky label with my address to yet another envelope. I contemplated calling the registrar to inform them of the terrible reality—I would not be attending USC.

Chapter 21

~TOBY~

I TOOK THE TURN INTO THE driveway too fast, and the Jeep bounced roughly to a halt. I threw it into park and yanked the keys from the ignition. I wanted a cigarette, but would settle for a beer and the possibility that I could coax Claude somewhere private to help me forget about work. I didn't know how much longer I would be able to last with Abe Bernbaum, the little troll.

It was perfect timing that Claudia happened to be in the kitchen when I came in. I forgot about the beer and went for her first. I pushed her back against the counter and kissed her hungrily. She opened her mouth, easily accepting and meeting my tongue with hers. The edginess of the day began to fall away; everything inside me brought to a standstill. As our kisses heated up, my hands edged over her hips, and my gears began to click and turn in a whole new direction.

She dragged her mouth from mine. "Easy, Romeo. You're all fired up."

"I had another shitty day," I sighed, and pulled back.

"What did Abe do now?"

I let her go and went to the fridge for a brew. "He double checked my delivery this morning, and when I offered to lock up tonight, he wouldn't give me a key. This job is not nuclear science. I'm capable. Really, I'm over-fucking-qualified, but he doesn't trust me. Cocksucker."

She winced at my language. I popped the top off my bottle and took a swig of beer.

"Maybe it has something to do with the robbery a few years ago," she said.

"What robbery?"

"Some kids broke into the store. My father said besides stealing the cash from the register, they roughed Abe up pretty bad."

"Well, he needs to get over it."

"I'm sure he'd like to," she said, meeting my eyes. "But sometimes people have a really hard time facing what scares them the most."

"Yeah," I agreed, though I was distracted by her mouth again. I moved in closer to her, putting my beer on the counter behind her. Without actually touching her, I leaned in and whispered in her ear. "What'd ya say we go up to my room for a little one-on-one?"

Claude twitched and let out a little nervous laughter. It wasn't the reaction I'd hoped for, and I pulled back to look at her face.

"I have something I want to talk to you about." She pointed to the kitchen table, and I looked over my shoulder. Lying there was a creased piece of loose-leaf paper, and I grabbed it. I recognized the block-styled handwriting.

Gritting my teeth, I waved it in her face. "What the fuck is this?"

She lowered her chin and eyed me cautiously. "It's one of your brother's letters."

"Yeah, it is. Why do you have it?"

"I was helping your mother clean her room out. We came across the letters …"

I wasn't listening anymore. I charged toward the stairs. "Where the hell are the rest?"

Julia was standing outside her room, and I thundered up the steps taking them two at time to get to her. "Ma, where are the rest of those letters?"

"Honey, calm down. We only opened the one." Julia tried to touch me, but I pushed her hands away.

"The two of you have some goddamn nerve. Give me the rest of them. I want them. Now!"

With a tight face, Julia scrutinized me before she turned away. Returning with the small stack of letters, she held them back, out of my reach.

"Toby, I'll give them to you, but I want you to read them. Please."

"When I agreed to take you up for those visits, you promised you wouldn't do this! You promised!" I yelled, and punched the hallway wall. The sheetrock dimpled under my fist. I reached forward and snapped the letters from her clutch. "Al's no longer a part of my life. And he's never going to be a part of it again. Ever!"

I spun around and almost bulldozed over Claudia behind me. She jumped out of my way.

"What are you going to do?" she asked, as I stormed down the hall to Al's room.

I didn't answer. Darkness slipped over me and snarled for release—it had a life of its own and now that it was awake, I had no control over it. Yanking Al's old dresser away from the wall, I pitched it off balance. Wood splintered as it toppled over, crashing loudly to the floor. And still Darkness wasn't satisfied, so I sent other objects flying after it.

I could hear Julia and Claudia yammering in the hall. Their conversation floated around me as if I wasn't actually there.

"Oh, my God! What should we do?"

"Leave him, it'll be all right. It'll blow over."

Darkness did not retreat until Al's room looked like a tsunami hit it.

Winded, bruised and achy, I collapsed on the floor among the debris.

"Holy cow," Claude gasped by the door. She and Julia had been watching me the whole time. Claude's eyes jumped around nervously, but Julia, noticeably pale, only shook her head at me and disappeared down the hallway.

"What a fucking mess," I mumbled to myself, staring at the ceiling.

Claudia glanced around the room at my trail of destruction.

"Just a tad extreme," she snipped. "I mean, seriously, it was only a letter."

I was too spent to exert any more energy. I leaned back against Al's bed frame.

"I meant it when I told you two I didn't want anything to do with Al."

"And that's your excuse for this mess?" She raised a perfectly shaped eyebrow at me. "Your reaction was over-the-top, bordering on crazy."

She turned on her heel and left me in that detonated minefield.

I felt so stupid, humiliated by my own behavior and embarrassed that she'd witnessed it.

Julia came in after I had most of the furniture back in place. Stepping inside, she picked up Al's old alarm clock and an almost empty bottle of cologne and placed them on the dresser.

"Stop. I'll do it," I told her.

"I'm used to your temper, but others aren't," she said. "It can scare people."

"Claude's not scared. She's pissed," I said.

She moved to the doorway. "You need to learn how to calm yourself down before things get out of hand. Maybe you should go back to church. Ask God to help guide you."

I snorted. "Ma, if you'd just let the Al thing go, this would have never happened."

"Is it so wrong to want my boys to get along? Is it wrong to forgive him just because you fought years ago?"

I closed my eyes and willed myself not to let her stir me up, again. It was probably my own fault for keeping it from her—for never telling her how bad it was at times or just how cruel Al could be.

When I didn't answer, she said, "Well, at the very least, you should go talk to Claudia. Apologize for behaving this way."

"Go back to your Bible and stay out of my business," I snapped.

Finally, Julia walked away. I set a now-cracked framed photo of Al and Felicia back on the dresser and headed for the stairs.

"Hey," I said, as I entered the kitchen where Claudia was cutting up some vegetables over the table. Continuing her task, she ignored me.

"I had a bad day. I let my mood get the best of me."

Finally, she let her eyes meet mine. "It upset me to see you caught up in so much anger. It was frightening."

I leaned my head back and blew out. "Claude, I'm sorry. It's just that this thing with my brother… it's a mess. It'll never be right," my voice cracked and floated away.

"I'm sorry you and your brother don't get along, but really it's no excuse."

I went behind her and wrapped my arms around her waist.

"Don't." Obviously still upset, she tried to shrug me off.

"It won't happen again, and besides, I'm not the only one at fault here. You opened that letter without my permission."

Frowning, she turned around to look up at me. "That's true, but you suggested that I could read them on our first date."

"That was the night you wore that dress. I was in a weakened state," I said. "I probably would have agreed to cut my arm off."

She tried to hold back a smile. "I should have asked. I'm sorry I didn't."

"If I promise to control my temper and behave, can we call a cease-and-desist?"

Claudia's look was so intense it felt like she was studying me, trying to decipher the many gray areas.

I closed my eyes. "Stop looking at me like that."

"Like what?"

"Like you can see inside me. It makes me all twisted up."

She sighed, "Okay, I cease and desist."

When I opened my eyes, a tiny smile had cracked her stern expression. Relieved at the sight of it, I raised my hands to her face.

"I don't want you ever to be frightened of me. I would never hurt you," I whispered. Pressing my mouth to hers, I felt the tension leave her body as she answered my kiss with her own.

After a few moments, she pulled back and bit her lip.

"Just so you know, in the letter, your brother said he wants to see you."

I took a breath and calmed myself. "See," I said. "This is me controlling my anger."

Chapter 22

~CLAUDIA~

ONE AFTERNOON, IN THE LAST week of June, just as I was finishing up at the senior home, my cell phone rang. I didn't recognize the area code.

"Hi, this is Claudia," I answered.

"Hello, Claudia. This is Caroline Watson. I'm with the admissions office at the University of Southern California. I have your application for our Davis School of Gerontology here in front of me. I see it was put on hold, and, well, we called to see if you were still interested."

I froze. "Yes," I answered on a delayed exhale.

"Then I think it might make you happy to know we've had a spot open up, and it's yours if you want it."

I hadn't yet left the Sterling grounds. Astounded by the news, I dropped down onto one of the wooden benches by the front doors.

"Oh, wow. This is seriously fabulous!"

Caroline Watson laughed. "From your transcript, it looks like you've maintained excellent grades, and with all your activities, you'd be an asset to the school. Transfer student orientation is the second week in July. I have your email address here. I'm going to forward you a packet with entrance instructions. Get it back to us as soon as you can. Okay?"

"Sure, yes, absolutely!"

"Welcome to USC, Claudia."

I immediately called my mother with the news. She promised to talk to my father about hashing out the financial details. This was going to happen!

I drove straight from Sterling to the Fayes' house. I couldn't wait to share my news with them. It was after six o'clock, and Toby was already home.

Mrs. Faye was sitting on the living room couch reading an inspirational magazine, one the church ladies seemed to share with each other.

"Hi! I got some fantastic news." I smiled and glanced around. "Where's Toby?"

Mrs. Faye lowered her magazine. "Finally fixing that molding in the bathroom."

"Be right back," I told her, and went to find him.

Toby stood in the doorway of the small downstairs bathroom, his hands raised up over his head. His T-shirt was pulled taut over his arms as he held a hammer poised to hit the head of a nail.

I eyed the tool belt and the extra nail he held between his lips. "Aren't you just the cutest handyman ever?"

"Handyman? Ugh." He took the nail from his mouth and smiled. "Boy, you sure have a shit-eating grin on your face. What's going on?"

"I got a call today. A good one." I pressed a kiss on his mouth and took his hand. "Come into the living room. I want to tell both you and your mom."

Toby stood idly next to the living room couch where Mrs. Faye sat. With both of them looking on in anticipation, I blurted out, "USC called me. I'm in!"

"That's wonderful! Congratulations," Mrs. Faye exclaimed, rising off the couch and lifting her arms in a hug. She embraced me, but over her shoulder Toby didn't exactly seem enthused about my news.

"Your dad is okay with this?" he asked.

Mrs. Faye and I both stared at him. I put my hands on my hips. "Hey, whose side are you on here?"

"Yours," he said. "But I thought going away to school was off the table."

"My mother and father are working out the details as we speak," I said. "You're not happy for me?"

He ran a hand over his face. "No, I am. It's what you wanted," he said, and then smiled. "Claude, it's great news." He pulled me into a hug and kissed the top of my head.

"Thank you," I beamed.

He held up his hammer and started to back away. "I want to finish up this molding tonight. I'll talk to you when I'm done."

A moment later, the banging of the hammer echoed through the house. Mrs. Faye patted the couch next to her. "Come sit down and tell me all about it."

I settled down and told her about the call and the immediate things I had to do to get ready for my orientation in two weeks.

"I had really given up hope that this would ever happen." I confided in her how strained things were at home since my father had found out about the application. "I haven't seen my father since I learned about the acceptance. I'm nervous about talking to him."

Toby walked back through the room. He gave me a quick smile as he passed by into the kitchen. We heard the back sliding door open and snap shut. Mrs. Faye sighed.

"What?" I asked, wondering what she was seeing that I didn't.

"He's not going to do well with this," she murmured. "You should go talk to him."

"Why? It's not like anything is going to change," I said.

"You have two men in your life, both are afraid to lose you. One tries to control you, the other gets quiet and retreats," she said.

I glanced up towards the back of the house where Toby had 'quietly retreated.'

My euphoria over the news had eclipsed any thoughts of how hard leaving would be. Months ago, before I'd stepped foot in this house, I hadn't had much to leave behind. Starting out fresh and reinventing myself in California sounded exciting, and for two years, I had dreamt of nothing else.

But now, everything was different. Now there was Toby and Mrs. Faye.

"The call was such a surprise. I haven't really had time to consider how it will change things," I said. "You and Toby are my life right now. If I go, I'll only see you every few months—for the next two years."

Mrs. Faye pulled me into her arms and hugged me. Though thin and frail, her embrace was strong. "I'm going to miss you terribly myself. You're practically like family now." She stroked my hair. Her embrace and words brought tears to my eyes. "But when you love someone, sometimes letting them go is the only way to show them how much."

She pulled back and smiled at me. "My dear girl, you've brought so much happiness to this house. I love you for it. And, more than anything, I want to see you happy, too."

Tears rolled down my face. Mrs. Faye offered me tissues, and, embarrassed, I mopped them up.

"If I go, do you think Toby and I will be okay?" I looked at her hoping for some kind of intuitive insight she could share.

Mrs. Faye smiled and shook her head. "I'm not going to say anything but that God has a plan for each of us. You are obviously being led towards yours. As for Toby, I think he chooses different paths than the ones God opens up to him. You might be the only gift God has planted in front of him that he hasn't ignored. I'm thankful for that. His life has been messy and difficult, but I know once he chooses to have faith, he will find his joy. Hopefully, while you're away at school, he can focus on completing those classes he's signed up for and land himself a better job. Then when you're finished, you'll both be prepared to move forward, and maybe, think about making a commitment to each other."

I covered my mouth to hide my shock. "Mrs. Faye, Toby and I are a really long way off from any formal kind of commitment."

She smiled and patted my hand. "Forgive me. I'm an old romantic. I dream of having a daughter-in-law just like you, someone who'll bring steadiness to our family. And babies. Lots of babies."

I giggled because she was sweet. I didn't bother to tell her I wasn't getting married anytime in the near, or not-so-near, future—if ever. Why squash her dreams?

I gave her another hug and kissed her cheek. "I already feel like family."

"You're a doll." She smiled, and clutched my hand. "Honey, if this is important to you, don't let anyone hold you back."

"I won't," I promised. "Do you need help going up?"

"No, I'm good," Mrs. Faye reached out and touched my cheek. "I'll see you tomorrow."

I watched her climb the steps. Alone now, the house was quiet. I thought about what Mrs. Faye had said about Toby and me making a commitment to each other. Why would she have brought that up? Could she tell I was falling in love with her son? Had he said something to her about his feelings for me?

From outside in the yard, I heard a dull thump followed by a cracking noise. After what his mother said about him not taking my good news well, I wondered if instead of building something, Toby was out back destroying something. I took a deep breath and went to find out.

Chapter 23

~TOBY~

THE LIGHT IN THE GARAGE was broken, and it was getting too dark to do anymore work after I cut the last piece of molding. The barn had all the tools I needed to repair the bathroom molding, but I hated being inside it. It reminded me of Big Al.

Pulling off his old carpenter belt, I slung it over the workbench and picked up the bottle of beer I'd been nursing. I thought about how my day was turning into a complete pileup of shit and how much I wanted a goddamn cigarette.

Frustrated, I picked up an adjustable wrench and chucked it across the space. It hit the textured plywood wall with a loud thud and fell to the floor with a metallic clink. It didn't create nearly enough damage to make me feel any better. Gulping down the beer, I gripped the bottleneck and flung it tomahawk style. In the fading sunlight, I watched it spin in full circles as if it were in slow motion until it exploded against the garage wall, the glass shards spraying the floor.

Neither Claudia nor Julia had any idea that not an hour earlier, Van Sloot had made an appearance.

I was making myself a sandwich in the kitchen when he barged in the front door as he'd done hundreds of times throughout high school.

Without a greeting or any explanation, he hurled some heavy information at me.

"That illegal developed some kind of serious infection and died. The fucker died!"

We stood on opposite sides of the room staring at each other. I hadn't known what to say.

"The cops have been following me around," he continued, his eyes wild. "And when I asked them what the hell they were doing, they said they'd gotten a tip—'a source' willing to testify against me," he snarled. "I can't believe you would do that to me."

"Whoa!" I held up a hand. "I have nothing to gain by testifying against you. Come on, man, this is typical cop M.O. When they don't have any evidence, they buzz around and stir things up. They're waiting for someone to slip or crack up. And anyway, if I had tipped the cops off, you'd already be in jail."

"I don't trust you anymore," he said, jaw tight. "I'm warning you, man, if you so much as hint to those fuckers that I had anything to do with this, you'll go down with me."

"Down with you? Yeah, right. I wasn't even there, asshole."

"Doesn't matter," he lobbed at me. "Remember that knife? Well, now it's a murder weapon. And, it has your fingerprints all over it."

"What the hell are you talking about?"

He grinned. "I paid you a little visit at work the next day. I tossed it to you. Boy, your expression was priceless. You sure thought that knife was the shit."

A sickening chill ran up my back.

"Ahh, now you remember," he jeered. "Believe me, it won't take much to get you arrested along with me. If the cops come for me, I'll hand over the knife and tell them how I tried to stop you."

I grabbed the kitchen chair in front of me and threw it across the room. It smashed against the cabinet, the harsh sound vibrating through the house. Dev twitched, but stood his ground, staring at me through narrowed eyes, as the chair, with a final, defeated clatter, fell over.

"Go to hell." My bitter words further blackened the air.

His lips rolled back from his teeth. "Maybe I'm on my way there, but I swear, I'll take you with me." Glancing down, he swiped the yellow sweater Claudia had left on the back of a chair and flung it at me. "And maybe someone you care about, too."

Darkness was roused. I'd tossed the sweater aside and stepped only inches from him. I flexed my arms, ready to trash him as we eyed each other—both waiting for the other to make the first move. My fist itched to make contact with his face. I knew if I went there, it would be a fight to end all fights.

But, Julia was right up the stairs.

"If you go anywhere near her, I'll kill you," I bit out. "Now get the fuck out of here."

He stared at me for a tense moment, before stepping back and wiping his mouth with the back of his hand. He left finally, slamming the door behind him.

I wanted to call his bullshit, but I couldn't be sure. I didn't want to chance facing murder charges to find out.

When Julia had asked what the commotion was downstairs, I'd told her I was working on the bathroom molding, a job I'd promised to do months ago. Once I said it though, I actually had to do it.

Claudia's 'happy' news had just added to the pile. I was a hands-on guy—I didn't do long distance relationships. Going a day without being with her was hard enough. I would go insane if I had to go weeks, or months even, without being able to touch her.

Everything was such a mess, and Darkness was sneering, howling at the injustice of it all.

I picked up another tool, a mallet, and imagined the damage its weighted end could do to the wall.

"Toby?" I heard Claudia's voice from the backyard. "Are you in the garage?"

"I'm just finishing up in here." I dropped the mallet and moved towards the sound of her voice.

I saw her and was struck by how beautiful she was, even just wearing her typical volunteer-day clothes, a white polo shirt and a tan skirt that came about mid-thigh. Snug enough that you could tell she had a good body, but without flaunting it. Here she was, my grade school crush, all grown up. Her tan legs were bare, and as she walked, I admired them. I imagined the old geezers at the home working one up over her, wishing they were younger. Wishing they were me.

We met in the doorway, and I reached for her. As soon as my arms went around her waist, she pressed into me, and the steam left me. It was replaced by a crushing weight of worry. I wanted to forget she was excited to go to a school that would take her away from me, wanted to forget about the dead Dominican, to forget the threats cast by my old friend, now my enemy. Closing my eyes, I fought to block it all out and concentrate only on the way her soft curves yielded to me. I wanted to bury myself in the sweet scent of her body.

"Hey," she whispered. "Your mom thinks you didn't take the news about USC as well as you appeared to. Are you upset?"

"Depends," I shrugged. "Are you planning on breaking up with me before you go?"

"No, of course not." She frowned. "I really want to go, but I also want you to be okay with it."

"What do you want me to say, Claude? You're going to be like twenty-five hundred miles away." I shook my head. "That's not a good thing."

"You know how much I wanted this. Don't you remember how devastated I was when I got the letter?"

"How could I forget? It was the day you kissed me at the beach."

Our eyes locked, and, as I stared at her standing there with her mouth slightly parted, her eyes reflecting the last trace of sun, something unraveled inside me. I felt unbalanced and my heart too tight inside my chest.

"This won't change us," she said, and rose up on her toes to press a kiss on my mouth.

Her smell, the warmth of her breath on my lips—it mesmerized me. She went to end the kiss, but I held her tightly and moved my mouth over hers until she wound her arms around my neck and started to kiss me back. I needed this. I needed her.

Pressing her back against the workbench, I ground my hips into her. Devouring her mouth, I yanked her shirt out of her skirt and pushed my hands inside her bra to squeeze her soft tits. I sensed her willingness and dropping to my knees, I tried to tug her down with me. She resisted.

"Wh-what're you doing?" Dazed, she blinked at me.

"Shhh. Just feel," I whispered, rubbing my face against the fabric of her skirt at the apex of her legs. I inhaled deeply and blew out a long hot breath against her pelvis.

Her legs went soft, and she folded down against me. Her face was flush with excitement as I pressed her back onto the foot rug that lay over the cement floor. I wrapped a hand around her thigh and slid it up under her skirt, to stroke her between her legs. Her sighs grew louder. Soon her hands flew into a flurry of movement, grabbing at my hair and pulling my mouth more tightly against hers.

"Claudia," I moaned her name, before guiding her hand under the waistband of my pants. I wrapped her fingers around me, and she gently squeezed me. I closed my eyes and pushed into her hand, imagining how amazing it would feel to be inside her.

I licked my fingers and launched them under her panties. She gasped as I began to pet her, teasing her with my fingers. Writhing under me, her shoulders rounded, pushing against me—pushing away even as she held me, stroking me and tried desperately to keep her mouth on mine. She was panting, arching up into my hand, and I felt the give, the pliancy that told me she was ready. I sunk two fingers deep inside. Her response was instantaneous. As her sex tightened around my fingers, her eyes practically rolled back in her head. With a breathy moan, her body jerked under me.

Insane with need, I whispered into her ear, "Baby, I want to fuck you so bad." I pushed her skirt up higher and snagging the elastic of her panties, I dragged them down over her one hip.

"Toby, no," she grabbed at my hand.

"Relax," I took both her wrists in my one hand and held them over her head. "We're almost there. This is going to feel so good."

Chapter 24

~CLAUDIA~

TOBY LIE ATOP ME, THE cold, hard floor under my back. One large hand anchored both my wrists above my head while the other played between my legs, stroking me mindless. His mouth moved over my neck, my chest, my face, his tongue soothing what his teeth nipped. My body burned for him and betrayed me by responding to his sexual onslaught without my mind's consent.

"Toby, stop." My plea was not much more than a whimper. Despite it, he didn't slow down.

"Come on, baby. I need you." The heat of his tone was fused with determination.

He pushed the front of his shorts down and pressed his erection against my leg. It felt hot and hard against my thigh, and I was tempted by an innate sense—one that made me understand the unimaginable pleasure I derive from having him inside me—if only it weren't for that one missing element. Love. I saw no trace of it in his eyes, only a single-minded need. The absence of emotion shattered the last of my excitement and brought me crashing down. This was too rushed, too coarse, and nothing like the loving embrace I imagined it would be.

With his weight heavy on top of me, I steeled myself, becoming absolutely rigid.

"Is this how you want me to remember my first time?" I asked.

He was silent for a heavy moment, a profusion of emotions rolling over his face.

"Oh, fuck," he muttered. Letting go of my wrists, he pushed off me and rolled to his back on the floor next to me, banging his arm on the edge of the workbench. He let out a feral hiss. As I adjusted my underwear and skirt back into their rightful place, he rubbed at his elbow.

My heart was pounding.

"You were being so rough."

"You seemed to like it."

"You think I want to lose my virginity with a forced, quick, rough romp?"

He slammed his fist on the leg of the worktable and I flinched. "I've never forced myself on a girl. Never!"

"What the hell is wrong with you then? Why are you suddenly so impatient?" I snipped.

"Jesus, we've been dating for almost two months. How long are you going to make me wait?"

"I'll make you wait as long as it takes me to feel ready. And besides," I said, eyeing our surroundings, "my first time will not be next to a tool bench, on the dirty floor of an old garage."

Toby raised himself up onto his elbow and leisurely watched me as I got up and dusted myself off. "If all you need is a bed, then I'll take you to the motel up on the highway, the one with hourly rates."

His cavalier attitude was infuriating. "It takes more than a bed, you asshole." I felt my composure start to crumple. "I thought I wanted to be with you," I said, blinking back tears. "But after this, I don't want you to ever touch me again."

"Huh?" His expression finally registered some emotion. It looked akin to fear.

I didn't take any joy in being able to get him to react because the whole ordeal had sent me over the edge. Even as my tears began to fall, I felt an angry determination to get away from him. Focusing on that, I ran for the door. Behind me, I heard Toby scrambling to his feet. "Claude, wait," he called after me.

I bolted through the door but didn't manage to get out of the backyard before he caught my arm and spun me around.

We were breathing hard, and I thought I might just hate him right then.

"I'm sorry," he said as he tried to get closer and touch my face.

I shoved his hand away. "Leave me alone!"

"That's part of the problem. I can't seem to do that."

I was shaking, but my voice remained static. "Maybe your other girlfriends let you treat them like that, but I won't."

"I know. I'm sorry, baby." He wrapped his arms around me and drew me to him. I stood stiffly at first, but it took too much effort to stay away from him when what I really wanted was for him to comfort me—to make me feel as if being with him wasn't all a big mistake.

He pressed his face into my hair. "You didn't deserve that. You're right. I am an asshole. I don't know why you put up with me sometimes."

Holding me tight, he rubbed my back, slow and gentle. I closed my eyes and accepted his penitent caresses.

"You've never been so aggressive with me before."

"I'm sorry—so, so sorry, baby. I was in a crappy mood. Touching you like that took my mind off of it. I got worked up—I forgot about the virginity thing." He stroked my hair. "Some girls get off having their hands restrained."

I made a disparaging noise. "Please tell me you aren't using your sexual escapades with other girls as a way to apologize."

"I... no." He looked momentarily rattled, but then took a breath and restarted. "What I mean is, even though I wasn't being gentle, I swear I wasn't trying to force myself on you. Holy Christ, if you weren't so inexperienced, I would have absolutely made you lose your mind." His hands on my waist rocked my hips suggestively.

I exhaled a groan-like breath. I had never met a guy like him. His manners were erotic, explicit. And physically distracting. Although, around me, he had curbed himself, I knew from the first time I'd met him that this was how he expressed himself. The callous motel remark was inexcusable, but his suggestive words—a hint at a pleasure I wasn't yet acquainted with—affected me. As the air conditioner unit in Mrs. Faye's bedroom window above us hummed, so did my body.

"Maybe I will like that kind of rough stuff someday, but," I said, grabbing two fistfuls of the front of his black T-shirt and twisting it taut. "If you ever treat me so disrespectfully again, it'll be the last time. Understand me?"

"Yes! *Comprendo*," he said biting back a smile, his head bobbing with an exaggerated nod. "Are you going to hurt me? 'Cause I'm kind of afraid of you right now."

I let out a pent-up laugh and released him. "God, what am I

going to do with you?"

His arms tightened around me. "Be with me."

"Toby—" I started to object.

"Claudia, all I want is to get closer to you. If you just trust me, we could connect on a whole other level," he said softly.

I knew his words were not meant to hustle me into bed. Toby genuinely believed sex would unite us as nothing else would. I sensed he was right. The emotional side of our relationship had grown, and the physical side was speeding alongside it. Increasingly, the unsatisfying end even frustrated me.

I rested my head on his shoulder. "I know it's not easy for you to be so patient and wait for me. I want to be with you, too, but it's going to be more planned out. I don't want it to be rushed or just a release of frustration." I touched his face. "I want it to be out of love."

"That's right. That was part of the deal." He tipped his head against mine and rubbed my arms up and down. "Don't expect me to use that word, but I hope you know, I'm pretty crazy about you, Chiametti." He kissed my neck, and very quietly he asked, "Forgive me?"

I wrapped my arms around his neck and sighed. "Yes," I said and almost added that despite it all, I loved him. But I held it back. After the night's drama, it hardly seemed like the right time.

"How about we go inside and relax for a while?" I asked.

"Can't," he said drawing away from me. "You should go home. I have a few things I need to do."

He walked me to my car. At the curb, I hugged him goodnight. "We never even got to talk about USC," I said.

"Another night. Okay?"

I nodded, knowing it would be best, and pulled out my keys. But something wasn't right. The car had an odd 'settled' appearance. Then I noticed it, the back tire flared out on the pavement as if it had melted. Flat.

"You got a flat," Toby said, squatting to examine a front tire. "Open the trunk. I'll change it."

I walked around to the driver's side, and, unbelievably, they too were both flat. I shook my head in confusion. "Toby, they're all flat."

"All of them?" He came around to look for himself.

He muttered a string of curses and stepped into the middle of the road. With me behind him, we looked up the street, scanning for signs of other disturbances in the neighborhood.

It came from behind us—a car engine gunning loudly. We both jerked around in surprise to see two headlights speeding at us. I screamed and Toby pushed me back and away. I stumbled and fell in front of my car. As the vehicle careened towards him, Toby sprang onto the roof of the Camry.

It sped by narrowly missing him. The car tires squealed on the pavement as it spun in a perfect one-hundred-eighty-degree turn and skidded to a halt. Now in the middle of the road, facing the way it had come, it sat idling. The tinted driver's window was up, and we couldn't make out the driver, but it was Devlin's car.

"What's he doing?" I asked, stunned, shaken, and a little more than scared.

Toby slid off the hood of my Camry and cautiously approached Devlin's car, but as soon as he got within a few feet, the engine revved, and the car lurched forward. It raced down the road, and out of sight until, finally, the street was dark and quiet again.

I stared down the road, afraid he might return. "Why did he do that?"

"He's a lunatic." Toby took my hand and pulled me to my feet. "Are you okay?"

"I scraped my hands on the fall. Are you okay?" I didn't wait for him to answer to begin checking him over.

"I'm fine." He pushed my searching hands away.

"I'll call the police and report him." I went for my cell. "My father will make sure he doesn't get away with this."

Toby grabbed my wrist. "Claude, you can't tell your father about this. Tell him someone gave you flats, but he can't know what Dev just did."

"Why?"

"Just because. I need you to trust me on this," he said and then added, "Please."

My father was on shift and came within minutes of my call. He arrived by cruiser with emergency lights flashing, and when he stepped out onto the street, I could tell by his stance he was in full authority mode. With the briefest of glances at Toby and me, he snapped on his department-issued flashlight and bent to inspect the tires. Mortified at the display of theatrics over mere flattened tires, I wondered if calling him had been the right thing to do.

"Your tires were slashed," he noted as he examined them and the road around the car. He scribbled down some information and came back to us at the curb. "Neither of you heard or saw anything?"

We shook our heads. I didn't dare open my mouth.

My father asked Toby, "Where's your mother?"

Toby shrugged. "Probably sleeping."

"You don't know if she's sleeping?"

"I haven't been up to her room for a while, but she's usually asleep by now."

"Is that right?" Dad hooked his thumbs in his belt loops and eyed the two of us. "So where have you been?"

I'm sure he noticed my disheveled clothes and was at that very moment forming an opinion on what Toby and I had been doing while my tires were being flattened. Though I couldn't tell him we'd nearly been clipped by a speeding car, I was anxious to put him back on track.

"Dad, my car's been vandalized," I said, crossing my arms. "Are you here to help with this or investigate us?"

Dad's answering scowl might've scared others, but I kept my eyes on him until he stepped a few feet away and spoke into his police radio. He listened through a static-garbled reply, barked a few more commands, and then came back to us.

"I don't suppose you've heard the latest about Ricardo Velerio?" He aimed the question at Toby.

I knew the name—the Dominican immigrant—and I looked from my father to Toby. Toby tipped his head, hiding his eyes, leaving me to believe whatever it was, he knew.

I didn't, though, and asked. "What happened to him?"

My father's answer came sharp and immediate. "He died this morning. The charges have been increased to manslaughter."

I gasped and covered my mouth, instinctively aware that Devlin's actions were in some way related to this.

My father motioned to my car. "This doesn't look like a random act. There are several other cars on the block, and none of them appear to be damaged. Maybe someone is trying to send Toby here a message?" He paused, brows furrowed over his perfected cop-piercing stare. "Maybe you know something or did something that might cause someone to strike out at you?"

Toby met his eyes, shook his head, but said nothing. My father was clearly not convinced.

"Just to give you a head's up, son. With Velerio's death, this will get worse before it gets better. I guarantee it."

Toby looked so uncomfortable, I reached for his hand. Seeing this, my father narrowed his eyes and set himself squarely before Toby.

"With your family's history, I don't have a lot of confidence that you'll handle this properly. If it was my choice, and I could talk some sense into Claudia, I'd keep her far away from you. I don't like this situation, and since you've decided to keep your mouth shut, I can only assume you are more involved in this than you let on." Despite his obvious anger, my father's voice remained trained and even. "I wouldn't normally care what the hell you're doing, but you're keeping company with my daughter and I'll be damned if any of this bullshit puts her safety at risk. If anything happens to her, I swear I'll put your ass in prison, right next to your brother. Do you understand me?"

"Dad!" I fumed, unable to believe he'd go that low.

Toby eyed him, his hand clammy in mine. The tenseness in his body was palpable—my father's words had hit their intended mark.

"Yes, sir. I would never let anything bad happen to Claudia," Toby said. There was no missing the hard edge of resentment in his tone.

My father turned to me. "Claudia, get in the cruiser. I'm taking you home. We'll have to call a flatbed to tow the car."

"I need a minute, to speak with Toby," I said.

"A minute," my father repeated. With a stiff nod, he got into his squad car. I didn't look back, but I felt his eyes on me, watching me with Toby through the windshield.

I faced Toby, my mind spinning with worry.

"This news about Velerio, that's why Devlin came after us tonight, isn't it?"

"He's not after us. We had a falling out—stupid high school drama." Toby glanced towards the cruiser and back at me. "Relax. It's over. I'll talk to him."

"Okay." I rubbed my temples. "Listen, I'm sorry about what my father said."

Toby shrugged, emotionless. "It's nothing new to me."

"It's new to me, and I don't like it." I squeezed his hand firmly, but then let it go. "We'll talk about it, but right now, I have to go."

I turned, but he caught my arm and drew me back to him. "Hey, kiss me good-bye."

"Oh." More than aware that my father was watching us, I pushed up on tiptoe, cheeks heated, to give him a chaste kiss. Toby had other ideas, though. His arms tightened around me, crushing me against him, and his lips moved over mine, firm and possessive, for a long few seconds—until the blearing sound of the cruiser's horn made me jump back.

Having successfully provoked my father, Toby smirked. "That cop sure doesn't like me kissing you. You'd think he didn't like me or something."

"Have your fun," I said, exasperated. "I'm sure I'll get an earful about you in the car."

"Yeah. I'll bet. Sorry, baby." He raised his hands in apology, but, as I turned to leave, he swatted my butt. I gasped and spun around to find a dark smile teasing his lips. "Be sure to put in a few good words for me."

He had the audacity to wink at me.

"Oh, Toby Faye," I said, stifling the urge to smile. "After that, there are not going to be words to redeem you."

He merely shrugged. "Were there ever?"

The urge to smile faded.

The first few moments of the drive home were awful; my father and I drove in complete silence. Finally, he spoke.

"I can't begin to tell you how disappointed I am that you're still dating that guy."

He kept his eyes on the road, his voice low.

"I seem to keep disappointing you," I said, and looked out the window.

"Claudia, you're a bright young woman dating a guy who has absolutely no direction in life—and that's before you add in his involvement with this murder investigation. What could you possibly see in him?"

"I really hate that you keep insisting that my boyfriend is involved with killing someone," I seethed. "I could never be with someone capable of that."

Dad scoffed loudly. "Claudia, his father was a lousy, angry drunk who killed two people. His brother killed someone, too. Believe me, he has it in him to be dangerous."

Toby did have a temper. I'd seen that first hand. But other than tonight's steamy prelude into the world of rough sex, which I decided was far more erotic than dangerous, and altogether a different matter than what my father was suggesting, I'd never felt personally threatened.

"You've got him all wrong. Toby cares about me, and he's always been gentle with me."

We pulled up in front of the house, and my father turned off the engine.

"You know I've arrested guys who beat up their girlfriends. One was even killed."

"Holy cow, Dad. Just stop it." I was appalled, but I shouldn't have been so surprised. This was a typical scare tactic of my father's. Over the years, he'd told me stories—terrible things—many involving young girls getting kidnapped and/or taken advantage of, to warn me to be careful, to stay close by.

"I worry about your safety!" His squawk startled me. I sat back in my seat and closed my eyes. "What does he want with a girl like you? You two have nothing in common. He's not likely to settle down and make a good husband."

"Husband?" I almost laughed. "I don't want to get married!"

"Good thing because I'm sure marriage is the last thing on his mind. Guys like that always want the benefits of marriage without the commitment."

"And what if he does, Dad?" My cheeks burned in irritation. "Maybe I want to have those benefits, too."

He was speechless. I had shocked him into silence.

"Maybe I already enjoy those benefits," I continued to taunt him. "So what? I don't see how that affects you. It's my life."

"Claudia, you're a good girl. You can't be telling me…"

I sighed and turned to face him. "What I'm telling you is, I'm not a teenager anymore. You've raised me well enough that I know right from wrong. You need to let me take care of myself and make my own mistakes." I took a breath. "If you love me, you need to give me room to grow."

"You won't grow while you're with him."

"Dad!" I was unable to believe he wouldn't, couldn't let this go. "Back. Off. I've been a good daughter, done everything you've asked of me, but it's clear that will never be enough. I need out." I grabbed the door handle. "I know Mom called and spoke to you about USC. She said I could use my college savings for whatever school I wanted. Getting away from here is what I want."

My father scowled in the darkness of the cruiser. "So you've already decided to go?"

"Yes. Orientation is in two weeks." I eyed him waiting for his reaction. When he didn't respond, I threw open the door. "I'm sorry about the car. I'll get it fixed," I snapped, and got out.

Chapter 25

~CLAUDIA~

I CALLED TOBY FROM HOME, LYING in bed, that night.
"Your dad is a real hard-ass," he griped.

"He and I are no longer speaking to each other, but you were defended." I flopped down on my pillow. "You knew that man died, didn't you?"

Toby was silent for a moment, and, sighing, he finally said, "My bad mood was because Dev came to the house earlier to tell me. Claudia, he killed Velerio." In a disheartened murmur, he repeated, "Dev killed the guy."

In my gut, I'd known this all along, but hearing it confirmed was more unsettling. "How much do you know? What did you see?"

"Ray saw it all go down. But I swear to you, I wasn't there. I wasn't interested in chasing the guy, so Dev made me walk home."

"God, I am so glad you had the sense not to go along with them." I closed my eyes and let that bit of gratefulness settle over me.

"Dev says if I talk, he'll tell the police I was involved. We almost went at it in the kitchen."

"He has no evidence to do that." My eyes shot open and I sat up with a start. "Tell Ray to come forward. He'll be able to say what happened. He'll tell them you weren't there."

He hesitated. "It isn't that simple, but I'm working on it. 'Till then, you can't say anything to your father or anyone else about all of this. If Dev finds out I talked, scaring us with his car will only be the first of many things he'll do. I know how he is—he'll just get more insane. I can't take that kind of risk, not now when Julia still needs me," he said.

For the first time, I agreed with him.

In the following days, Toby spent a lot of time with Ray. I was proud of him for handling the situation with the attention and urgency it called for. I didn't get to see him much in those two weeks prior to my orientation. I had my own projects to work on too, getting things squared away for California: plane reservations, hours of entrance paperwork, and online forms.

As much as I wanted to go to California, Toby's situation with Devlin worried me, and I felt torn about leaving him. Stuff at my own house wasn't much better. Things between Dad and me got worse. An animosity sat heavily between us, a battle of who could be more stubborn. I hated to admit it, but I did stubborn well. With the situation as it was, for the first time since Mom left, I felt completely disconnected from home.

Despite the swirling dark moods, two days before their arrival, everyone's attention was diverted to getting the Fayes' house ready for Felicia and baby Dylan's visit. I readied the extra bedroom and made sure all the floors were scrubbed and clean enough for a baby to crawl around on, and Toby drove around to various church ladies' houses to pick up loaner baby supplies. The kitchen was outfitted with a high chair, the den with a playpen, and the spare bedroom with a portable crib. The colorful additions to each room, in anticipation of the newest little Faye, seemed to breathe new life into the outdated house. Mrs. Faye's health continued to improve dramatically. Dylan's visit seemed to inspire the surge. She would be fine without my help when I left for the West Coast.

The day of the arrival, Toby made the short drive up to MacArthur Airport. I waited with Mrs. Faye at the house and helped her wrap some gifts she'd purchased for her grandson.

"Remember, you need to rest while they're here. Toby and Felicia can do for themselves. And, don't lift the baby too much," I reminded her.

Mrs. Faye pressed a hand on my knee. "You'll be such a good mother someday."

Oh, good God. First the commitment comment, and now this?

Hearing the Jeep drive up, we went to the door. Felicia, a petite, slender platinum blond in white pants and a sleeveless yellow blouse, stepped from the car. Dangling earrings peeked out from her long and wavy hair. She reached back to the baby seat, unbuckled an adorable, sleepy blonde baby, and lifted him up.

While Toby unloaded luggage from the back of his car, Felicia came up the walkway in a pair of fashionable white heels. They were ridiculously high, and I wondered how she kept herself balanced with the six-month-old on her hip, but when she came through the door and saw Mrs. Faye, a genuine smile lit up her face.

"Here he is!" Felicia placed the baby in Mrs. Faye's awaiting arms. Little Dylan, his head covered with soft, baby-fine hair, appeared to have just woken up. His small face was ruddy and eyes still held the signs of sleep. But even so, he didn't fuss when Felicia released him to his grandmother's embrace.

Mrs. Faye held him, studying him, in complete rapture. "Who is this sweet, handsome little boy?" she cooed, tears welling in her eyes.

Dylan appeared uneasy and turned in search of his mother. He found Toby instead.

"It's okay Dylan. This is Grandma Julia." Toby squatted in front of his mother and patted her shoulder. Toby's words seemed to settle the baby, and he turned to study the new woman in front of him. He lifted a tentative hand to her cheek, seemingly fascinated by the crease lines of her illness-weathered face. Mrs. Faye leaned forward whispering sweetly to him, and his chubby little hand captured her nose.

The room grew quiet as we watched her face wrinkle with a smile, followed by tears. "He's absolutely precious." Her voice cracked with emotion, and she looked up at Felicia. "Thank you for bringing him to see me. You can't know what this means to me."

I just finished assembling a veggie platter and snacks when Felicia came into the kitchen. She flicked her long, blond hair over her shoulder, and I got the whiff of her perfume, sweet and flowery, like gardenias.

"Can I get some water? I'm parched."

"Water pitcher's in there," I pointed to the refrigerator as I grabbed a glass from the cabinet and handed it to her.

"You're Claudia, the girl who works here, right?"

I nodded.

"How is she?" Felicia nodded her head towards the other room.

"She looks so thin since I last saw her."

"It was really scary for a while, but she's doing much better," I said. "I think the anticipation of your visit really made a difference."

Felicia stood with the refrigerator open, her hand on the filtered water container. "That's a nice thing to say. I guess I never really thought about Dylan being her only grandchild. Now I wish we'd come sooner."

She filled the glass, took a sip, and left the pitcher on the counter. "But this family is so screwed up—I just needed to get out of here," she said by way of explanation. "Poor Mrs. Faye. Her boys are both such head cases." She twirled an index finger around the side of her head. "Al's in prison and Toby—I can't see that sexy mess doing the family thing, with kids and in-laws."

Felicia chuckled at her own comment and took another sip, staring out at the scene in the living room.

"But, I'll say this, Toby is good with Dylan. The two of them are so cute together."

I peeked over her shoulder. Toby and his mother were sitting side by side on the couch with Dylan on Toby's lap. My boyfriend was obviously enchanted with his little nephew, and, as Mrs. Faye looked on, he made silly faces and cooed at Dylan. I agreed with Felicia; they were sweet together. Watching them made me feel kind of silly-happy.

Without another word, Felicia went back to the other room to join them. She sat down next to Toby, closer than necessary.

"Why look at you! You're such a natural with a baby." With her arm around his back, Felicia leaned over and kissed Toby's cheek leaving a lipstick smudge. Then she made a fuss about wiping it off.

Watching Toby's reaction guardedly, I noticed his eyes stayed on Dylan as he spoke with her. "I can't believe how big he got since the last time I saw him."

"Well, it has been five months since you visited," Felicia said with a pout in her tone.

"They change so much in the first year," Mrs. Faye said, seeming reflective.

Felicia hit Toby's shoulder with a soft punch. "I expected to see you again before you came back here."

"I should've made time." Toby was enjoying Dylan's giggles as he bumped the baby up and down on his knee. I suspected there was more than 'sister-in-law-ly' intent behind Felicia's attention to him, but he didn't seem more than mildly responsive to her disapproval.

The baby let out a burp, and the three of them laughed.

"I want to take some pictures. Where's Claudia?" I saw Mrs. Faye glance around, and I busied myself with the snack platter, scraping the last of some hummus dip into a serving bowl.

Toby appeared in the kitchen with Dylan on his hip. "Hey, why are you hiding out in here?"

"I'm not hiding. I didn't want to intrude on your family reunion." I shrugged, about to lick some hummus off my fingers.

Snatching my hand before it reached my mouth, he said, "Don't be silly. You're not working today." He popped my fingers into his own mouth and licked them clean. "Now come out for pictures."

My face felt flushed when we stepped into the living room. Toby put his arm around my waist and drew me close. I saw Felicia's eyes narrow, but at that exact moment, baby Dylan reached out to me and threw his little body forward. I had no choice but to catch him.

"Look at this little lady-killer." Toby tickled Dylan's belly. "You trying to make time with my girl?"

Dylan's throaty chortle was musical, and I couldn't help laughing at its endearing sound. Smiling, I stroked his soft hair and inhaled his sweet baby smell. His eyes were so blue and skin so fair, it was almost translucent. Enthralled, I watched him as he grabbed the necklace around my neck and put my gold cross in his mouth. When I smiled, he smiled back, and a long string of drool slid out of the corner of his mouth onto my chest.

Toby leaned towards my ear. "He even drools over you just like I do."

We grinned at each other, and a flash went off. Mrs. Faye had taken our picture. She smiled as she looked at us, and I know she was lost in the moment, watching Toby interact with this beautiful baby, cooing and stroking his head in such a loving way. Despite motherhood not being part of my plans, I had to admit seeing my guy like this did strange things to me, too. This soft, gentle side of him was incredibly alluring, and a powerfully strong yearning for him raced through me. He was my sexy mess.

After lowering Dylan onto his mother's lap and taking a few photos, Toby glanced back at me. He always oozed such raw sexuality, but for some reason—perhaps my hormones were in an uproar or I was ovulating—my libido took a direct hit. I almost forgot to breath.

He came over to me and slid his hand loosely over my hip. I immediately felt our connection.

"You okay?" he asked. His eyes dropped down to my mouth, and I bit my lip.

Embarrassed by my state of arousal, I mumbled, "I … I need some water," and leaving Felicia and Mrs. Faye in conversation about Dylan's sleeping and eating habits, I headed back into the kitchen. Toby followed me, watching as I filled a glass with filtered water from the pitcher Felicia had left on the counter. I warmed under his gaze.

Taking the pitcher from my shaking hands, he put it on the counter next to me and touched my face.

"Claudia." He whispered my name as if he knew what I was thinking. I pressed my face into his hand, but I couldn't meet his eyes.

"Look at me," he commanded, and, very slowly, I raised my eyes to his.

I felt the force of our attraction run through me, every little pore in my body electrified. His irises grew darker, and his grasp on my hip tightened. He leaned in and kissed me, his lips soft but persistent. Wrapping my arms around his neck, I tugged him tight to me and met his kiss with my own eagerness, wanting desperately to feel his body against mine.

Toby dragged his mouth from mine, appearing as affected as I felt.

"If we don't stop, I'm going to nail you right here in the kitchen," he promised, his voice low and sultry. "And with the way you're acting, I have a feeling we'd be way too noisy to go unnoticed."

I smiled and touched my palm to his now flushed face. "What have you done to me? All I can think about is how much I want to be alone with you."

"Woman, you have freaking lousy timing. With Felicia and the baby here, swinging alone time today will be next to impossible," he said, his hand moving in slow, distracting circles over my rear end. "But maybe I can work something out."

I took a deep steadying breath and shook my head.

"No. I don't want to take you away from this." I motioned to the other room. "This time is so important to your mom and for you, too."

"But I want to be with you," he whispered, skimming his lips over my jaw.

"I know," I said. "But it can wait."

I left the Faye's and headed home to focus on the final detail of my trip: packing. At midnight, burning off anxious energy, I was absorbed in the task of pairing and laying out outfits. I hadn't heard from Toby, so I wasn't completely surprised when my cell jangled with a call from him just as I zipped up my luggage.

"Sorry to call so late," he apologized. "But I saw your light was still on and..."

"You're outside my house?" I flew to the window and pulled back the curtain. His shadowed figure waved to me from the driveway, and my heart began to race. "My dad would freak if he knew you were here."

"Claude, I really need to see you. Just come out here for a little while," he pleaded.

Of course, I knew I would. "Give me two minutes, then meet me at the east side gate," I told him. I ran around quickly collecting a few items and went down to the yard.

He was at the gate, impatiently trying to open it when I got there. I undid the locking latch and pulled the gate open. Toby stood for a moment and stared at me. I had piled my hair into a simple twist atop my head and slipped into a pink sleeveless summer nightie—the silky soft chemise was short, feminine and showed off my legs. The way he looked at me made me feel as though I were wearing the most erotic lingerie.

"Jesus, Claude," he hissed, and pushed me roughly up against the side of the house. As his hard body pressed against me, we gasped in unison.

Our warm bodies molded together in the shadows of my house. His lips found mine, and my heart beat at a maddening pace, every part of me attuned to his touch. I was fired up, spurred on by emotion only he seemed able to bring out in me.

As his mouth moved over my face, to my throat, I stroked the hardness of his chest, slowly moving my hands downward, over his tight stomach to his hips. I didn't stop until I encountered the solid ridge in his pants. I palmed him, and, as I knew he would, he groaned low and appreciative in my ear.

With a smile, I pushed him back and reached for his hand. "Come with me," I whispered, and led him into the yard.

Chapter 26

~TOBY~

MY LUNGS WERE SPAZZING, AND we were both panting as Claudia led me down a stone pathway into the darkened yard. I was so wrecked, I would have followed her anywhere.

Twice that summer, I had been in the yard to go swimming with Claudia. Her dad kept the house and the grounds cosmetically perfect. The backyard had the same clean lines and orderliness as their house, with precisely trimmed bushes and a big-ass grill on the patio. Just beyond the in-ground pool, giant column-like evergreens lined the edges, secluding the yard from the neighbors.

The night was alive around us. The chorus of crickets and cicadas were doing its best to drown out music from a party next door. A light, salty breeze rolled off the bay water nearby and stung my nose, but the breeze did little to cool the humid air.

Fumbling for her again, I scooped an arm around Claudia's shoulders and pulled her back against me. Pressing my face into her hair, I reached down to slide my hand over the silky smoothness of her thigh. My need to touch her slowed our progress, but she continued moving forward, hauling me along with her.

She moved past the pool toward a metal-framed, screened gazebo. She pulled back the black mosquito netting and motioned me inside. A low candle flickered in the dark from atop a patio table that has been pushed off to one side. A cushioned poolside lounger, as big as my bed at home, was covered with a sheet.

"Where's your dad?" I asked, craning my neck towards the house, looking for any signs of movement inside.

"He's a nervous wreck whenever I travel. He took a pill to help him rest. He's out."

Claudia zipped the netting closed, and we were cocooned in our own little space, away from the outside world. I sat down on the lounger and pulled her to me. As she kissed the top of my head and stroked my hair, I lifted her nightgown to press my face into her stomach and inhale the tantalizing scent of her skin. Running my hands up over her hips, I continued up her ribcage until my hands cupped her breasts, unhampered by a bra. A moan of pure, unadulterated pleasure fell out of my mouth, and I looked to see her smiling down at me. As I stared at her, I felt like her prisoner, caught up and held captive by all that she was.

She drew a finger across my bottom lip, and she slid her hands slowly down my neck, over my shoulders, and down my chest. Her touch was deliberate and unhurried, and I felt it all over. When she wrestled to lift my shirt, I tugged it off and tossed it the ground. Leaning back on my arms, I gave her full access. Holding my shoulders, she put a knee on either side of my hips and straddled me.

With her eyes on mine, she murmured, "Mmm, I love your shoulders," and gently swirled her palms over my feverish skin. Dipping her mouth downwards, she traced the outline of my tattoo, following her fingers with her lips.

I closed my eyes and let my head drop back. It was an indescribable feeling, light and sexy at the same time. I wasn't able to stay still for long as a fire raged inside me. Wrapping an arm around her hips, I began to grind my hardness against her. Separated by only thin layers of cotton, the friction was wicked, and we both reacted to the sensation.

I pulled her close and pressed my mouth to hers.

"Claudia, I want you so bad," I whispered, breathless against her lips.

She rested her forehead on mine, and in a serious tone, she said what I'd been waiting to hear. "I want you, too. I want to make love with you, tonight."

"You're sure?" I wasn't looking to change her mind, but after how I'd behaved a few weeks ago, I needed to be certain she wanted this to happen.

Lowering her eyes as if she were embarrassed, she reached behind me to the table and grabbed something. Picking up my hand, she pressed a small packet into my palm. Without looking at it, I felt the plastic square with the circular ridge and knew it was a rubber. I exhaled slowly and smiled. She'd thought about this. She came prepared.

With our mouths locked together in a fiery kiss, I drew her down onto the oversized, cushioned lounger with me. Draping my body over hers, I molded my lips to the warm, soft skin of her neck. She tasted like the salty night air. Slowly, I planted heavy, wet kisses along the column of her throat working my way back up to her lips again. Our kisses and touches were slow, blissfully agonizing, but each movement had an unspoken intent and purpose. This time, we both knew where it was going.

I teased her, sliding my hands over her curves, drawing soft gasps from her lips. Her response only excited me more. I tried to tug her panties down, but she got skittish and grabbed for my hands.

"I can work around these," I whispered, letting her hold my hands still for a second. Slipping a finger under the band of her sexy panties, I snapped the elastic against her hip. "But it would be easier if they came off."

She bit her lip. "I'm a little scared."

"Trust me?"

Her face turned serious as she stared into my eyes. "Yes. With everything I have."

My heart did an almost painful somersault in my chest. I didn't know how we'd come this far, how she had such faith in me, but I would take care of her as long as she let me.

"I won't hurt you. I promise."

Claudia released her grip on my hands and allowed me to peel her underwear off. I tossed them to the ground next to my shirt and kneeled between her thighs. Nuzzling her belly, I slowly kissed her, moving downwards, aiming to get between her legs and taste her. As my mouth neared her hips, her body tightened, and she fisted my hair.

"No, no," she pleaded. "I'm not ready for that."

"Okay, okay," I replied calmly. I knew she'd like it, but we'd hold off on that until next time. Tonight, I would not overwhelm her.

We kissed and touched until we were both shaking. I grabbed the condom package and ripped it open with my teeth. Picking up her hand, I pressed it into her palm. Shifting so I was next to her, I whispered, "Put it on me."

She concentrated on rolling the rubber down over me. "Like this?"

"Yeah," I breathed raggedly. Her hands touching me with such intent felt so good.

"Mmm, I just installed my first condom." With a sexy, charged expression, she lay back down.

I gazed down over her and shook my head. "Claude, do you have any idea how freaking beautiful you are?"

"No, tell me."

"Oh, baby, you're gorgeous. Your hair, your face, and damn, your body... A dream. My dream."

With my insides in a complete twist, I pressed the length of my hardness against her sex and rubbed along her slickness. The feeling was incredible, and we both moaned. As the friction grew more intense, she clambered underneath me. Not able to hold off any longer, I began to push inside her.

She drew a sharp intake of breath and gripped my shoulders tightly. Fighting off my impatience to move more deeply into her, I made myself stay still so she could adjust to the feel of me inside her. Our bond momentarily sapped my energy, and I squeezed my eyes shut. Holy shit. Nirvana.

I held myself up on my forearms, straining to keep my head as her visceral white hot heat continued to blissfully sear me.

"You okay?"

"I think so, yes." She blinked, her eyes burning into mine.

Her face was so expressive—her eyes full of wonder and emotion. I felt humbled, like I needed to tell her something, anything.

"Claudia, you feel so amazing." My voice cracked. I felt near losing it, overcome with a rush of unexpected emotion. "Thank you," I whispered.

The words seemed so stupidly formal, but they were all I had.

Holding my gaze, she said softly, "No, thank you." And then, stroking my face, she whispered, "This is us. Us together, in love," before she lifted her mouth to mine.

I began to rock against her in careful strokes, watching her for cues. Closing her eyes, she wound her arms around my neck and gave her body over to me. She was mine now.

Caught up in the moment, I pressed into her harder and faster. She gasped, a strangled cry of pain, and I stopped.

I kissed her temple.

"Sorry, baby, sorry." Berating myself, I attempted to pull back, but her fingers dug into my back, urging me to stay.

"I'm okay. Don't stop. Just love me."

My head spun. "Yes," I whispered, dipping my mouth to hers. Our tongues danced during a hot, endless kiss. I didn't want to leave this place—ever. I wanted to stay in the perfect warmth of her body, but the urge to finish was strong. With my control slipping, I fought the rush off until she arched her back and murmured my name in a breathless whisper. Lost in the silkiness of her body and the honeyed sound of her voice, I had no choice but to let go. Gasping, I bore down upon her and came so hard my whole body shuddered. With a sigh of pleasure, Claudia clamped her trembling body around me and I collapsed atop her.

We lay still and quiet for a few moments as we caught our breaths. She stroked my back gently, between my shoulder blades, in a way I'd come to know as her caress. I burrowed my face into her hair.

"Baby, that was so good." I'd somehow always known being with her, even with her inexperience, would be totally different from others I'd been with before. I felt her chest contract with a sigh, and I shifted my weight to see her face.

Propped up on my elbow, I asked, "Was it okay for you?"

Her eyes were bright. Laying a hand across my cheek gently, she nodded her head, but her lack of words concerned me.

"I was a little nervous. I didn't want to hurt you. Next time, it'll feel better. A whole lot better," I hurried to explain.

She pressed a finger to my mouth.

"Stop. Believe me, it was perfect, really," she said and grinned, shyly. "I liked watching you get so excited."

I laughed and kissed her face. "I only wish I could explain how good it felt for me," I said, feeling insanely happy.

"Toby..." she started to say, then got quiet.

I twirled a strand of her hair around my finger. "What, baby?"

She looked up at me, and her eyes suddenly filled with tears. Stroking my cheek with a shaky hand, she whispered, "I love you."

For a moment, I couldn't breathe. My lungs filled with fiberglass. Even though I sensed this was coming, and I was both amazed and charged that she felt that way toward me, I also knew she would expect me to say the words back to her.

"Toby, please don't leave me hanging here all by myself." She pinned me with those watery blues. "I just told you I loved you. Please tell me you feel the same way."

I grew hot and then cold, and opening my mouth, I hoped a convincing "I love you" would fall off my tongue. But, *nada*.

Instead, I smiled lamely at her. "Of course, I do."

I thought she was satisfied with that until I inadvertently tasted the salty wetness of tears on her cheek. With a tight sob, she began to cry, really cry. I'd totally bailed on the love thing, and now our night was crashing down around us.

"Claudia, please don't cry. Don't you know how crazy I am about you, that being with you like this means so much to me?"

"I do know," she said. She ran her fingers through my hair. "I'm crying because I'm happy."

I heaved a sigh of relief. "Shit, if you're crying because you're happy, then I should be sobbing, 'cause I'm mad-happy. I just had sex with the girl of my dreams."

She pressed a kiss on my mouth and grinned. "No, you made love to the girl of your dreams."

"Yes, I did." I could at least give her that.

After we both cleaned up and straightened our clothes, I pulled her back to me and held her tightly. "I hate that you're leaving. Are you really, really sure you want to go?"

She lay there quiet in my arms, and I sensed that she didn't know what to say. We were supposed to talk about this last week, but I had been too preoccupied with Dev's threats and dealing with Ray. A small part of me hoped that after what had happened tonight, Claudia would change her mind about going.

She glanced back up at me, her eyes soft and thoughtful. "I know it might not sound like the best thing for us, considering where we are now, but I still want to go. I've never done anything for myself or been on my own. I need to do this, for me. Can you understand that?"

I said sure, but all I really understood was that she was leaving.

"I have to get up in a few hours. I really need to get some sleep." Despite her words, she snuggled in close to me. "I wish you could come upstairs and sleep with me."

"Okay. Let's go," I said. Before she could respond, I got up and pulled her to her feet.

She tipped her head to one side and eyed me. "You'd seriously risk going up to my room this late?"

"Felicia's at the house with Julia, and your father's in a self-induced coma. This is the best opportunity we'll ever have." I blew out the candle and unzipped the netting. "I can be out before he wakes up."

She hesitated. "You do realize it's just to sleep. With our eyes closed."

"Yes, just sleep," I nodded, and held my hand out to her. "Do you want me to stay or not?"

She glanced around nervously. The simple question was loaded. She risked her father finding out. But did she think staying with me was worth it? Finally, she laid her hand in mine.

"I want you to stay," she said, and led me into the house, up to her bedroom.

I awoke with a start, wondering where I was, but when I felt Claudia's warm body sleeping next to me, I relaxed. I'd been in her room a couple times over the past few months, always when *El Capitán* wasn't home. The first time I'd seen it, I was surprised at how much it looked like a little girl's room, with its bright yellow walls and matching set of white furniture, the shelves full of stuffed animals and school awards. Trophies, framed certificates, and dangling medals—all with words like honor, merit and scholar inscribed on them—things she'd been awarded, for her smarts. Though the little girl theme didn't fit the Claudia I knew, I was very impressed by all her awards, especially the photo she had of herself standing with Bill Clinton. She told me she had met him during some charity dinner, the event a fundraiser for some human rights organization she had been involved with.

The clock on her night table said 4:28, and the first hints of morning light began to filter through the sky. We'd only slept for a few hours, and she'd have to get up soon to go to the airport.

Her house had central air, and her room was cool. I pulled a blanket up over us and curled myself around her. The bed smelled like her, and now, me, too. Us. I inhaled deeply.

I heard footsteps coming down the hall. Quickly releasing Claudia, I rolled as silently as I could to the edge of the bed and dropped to the floor just as the big guy tried the doorknob. I breathed a sigh of relief when the door only rattled in the doorframe and refused to open. Claudia had locked it.

He gave the door several loud raps.

"Claudia, time to get up," *El Capitán's* voice came from the other side. It was calm and gentle. Claudia was probably the only one he talked that way to.

"What?" The mattress shifted as Claudia shot off the bed. She looked around, her eyes wide with worry. Motioning for me to stay down, she went to the door. Opening it, she peeked out.

"I'm up, Dad."

"Okay. I'm going to make coffee. You want me to make you a cup?" he asked.

"Yes. Thanks," Claudia said, and closed the door as his footsteps moved away.

I crawled up and sat on the edge of the bed, weighing my escape options.

"Oh, God. We need to get you out of here!" she whispered urgently. Switching on the light, she flicked on her iPod speaker. The room filled with soft piano music accompanied by snare drum—a jazz song. A woman's clear, soulful voice joined in.

"I'll go out the window," I told her.

"Romeo escaping from Juliet's balcony?" Claudia came and stood before me, stretching her arms up, over her head. Her sleep shirt rode up exposing her belly to me. I kissed it, and she giggled.

"Yeah, but in our version, no one dies, and I scored with Juliet."

She laughed and laid her hands on my shoulders. "Do I look different?"

"You look beautiful and sexy as hell," I answered, and whipped her around onto the bed. Her hair fanned out around her head as she gazed up at me. I could get lost in her eyes.

She stroked my face. "No, I mean, do I look less like a virgin?"

"It's hard to tell," I smirked. "I think we should do it again, just to make sure the transformation is complete." I slid my hand between her legs. She automatically arched her hips against me as her breath hissed.

"Oh, you're so bad," she said, and pushed my hand away. "My dad is downstairs. We'd go right to hell."

"I don't care, as long as I'm with you."

Her eyes held mine, her expression soft. "Why?" she asked.

I stared at her perfect face and traced a finger over the light freckles on her nose. The truth was, she deserved so much more than me, but I hoped she never realized it. If she pulled away and let go now, I would fall away, spinning without direction.

"'Cause I feel like more when I'm with you," I told her.

"Ohh, you are Romeo. You said exactly the right thing," she whispered, and, pulling my face to hers, she kissed me.

"Claude, if you couldn't leave, I'd stay for you."

The smile fell off her face. "Toby, please stop making this harder than it already is," she pleaded. "It's just a week. You'll blink, and I'll be back."

I sighed and rolled off her. She got up and went into the adjoining bathroom. A minute later, she came out fully dressed.

She sat on the edge of her bed to put her sandals on. "And promise me you'll just stay home this week. No dealing with any of the Devlin mess."

I told her not to worry. She joined me at her bedroom window as I pulled back the curtain and pushed the glass pane open. She said she'd call me once she hooked up with her mother, and then she touched my face and murmured, "I can't wait until we can make love again."

"Wow, you're turning into a regular little sex kitten."

"Meow," she purred.

I pulled her against me to kiss her once more. Her 'bad' kitty impersonation had me wanting to take her back to bed, but I couldn't stay any longer. I released her and put one leg out the window. "Hurry up and come back home."

"I will," she said.

Chapter 27

~TOBY~

IT WAS A TIGHT SQUEEZE out of her window, and we both laughed as I maneuvered myself like a contortionist to get through. Her window was above a covered porch, so I crawled out onto the roof. Moving quietly, I crossed to the edge, lowered myself over, and hanging from my arms, I dropped down onto the front lawn. No problem.

The humidity seemed to have intensified. The warm, damp air sucked the breath from my lungs, and I immediately began to sweat. When I looked up and saw her at the window, I didn't move. She put her hands over her heart and pointed to me. It made me feel like a giant, happy fool, and, as I jogged down the street, through the quiet, sleeping neighborhood, to where I'd discreetly parked my Jeep, I couldn't keep the smile off my face.

I had left the Jeep's canvas top off, and the seats were damp with morning condensation. I popped in through the driver's side, revved the engine, and started down the road.

In a way, I was relieved that Claude would be away for the week. There was a lot of shit going down, and I wouldn't have to worry about her safety as I tried to ride it out.

I hadn't told Claudia all the details, not about the knife, or about what Ray had revealed to me. I'd called him the night Devlin had tried to mow us down with his car. I wanted to know why Dev suddenly felt so threatened.

Over the phone, Ray had been quick to spill it. "I screwed up big time, man."

"How?"

"I got b-b-usted with a bag on me." Ray stumbled over his

words, more nervous than I'd ever heard him. Since it was his second drug possessions arrest, the court-appointed lawyer had recommended that he plea bargain using the information he had on Dev to get his own charges reduced. The situation was being forced to a head. Ray said a case was being built against Dev, and it would be just a matter of time before a warrant for his arrest was issued.

"Do you honestly think he can p-pin this on you?" Ray asked. "Even if I say you, say you weren't there?"

"The hell if I know. But I'd rather not hang around waiting to find out," I said. "I can't gamble with this. I have to get the knife."

Ray promised to help me look for it. Between the two of us, I hoped we would get it before the case blew open and the police came for Dev. Once that happened, Dev would scramble to cover his ass, or take me down with him.

No matter what Claudia said, her father's privately fueled task force against me meant I couldn't go to him for help. He'd be more than happy to let me take the rap for Velerio's murder—just to keep me away from his little girl.

I got in the house as quietly as possible, but Felicia was up already, sitting on the couch with Dylan asleep in her lap.

"Wow, you sure are getting in late. Or should I say early. Lucky girl."

I ignored the comment.

"Is Dylan okay?"

"Had to feed him, but he just fell back to sleep. Would you carry him upstairs for me?"

"Sure." I reached down and took my sleeping nephew from her. Like a warm rag doll, he melded into my shoulder. His little baby breaths tickled my neck.

"You going to have some kids of your own one day?" Felicia asked, following me up the stairs.

"I'm totally digging this little man, but I don't think I'm daddy material."

"That's bullshit. You're real good with Dylan," she said when we entered Al Junior's old bedroom. "In fact, I was thinking that once that girl goes off to college, you should consider coming back to Florida to help me take care of him. We can get a place together, to make it easier." She stood next to me and watched as I put Dylan in the crib. I tucked the little guy in and patted his back, thinking it would be cool to be around him all the time.

Felicia touched my arm. "Raising a kid alone is hard. I could use help."

I felt bad for Felicia. My brother had messed up—and not that I thought Al would play the dad role so well—but Felicia was taking care of their kid on her own. The idea of helping out with my nephew sounded fine, but I couldn't imagine putting myself any further away from Claudia.

When Claudia had breaks from school, she'd come here, to Sayville, to be with her dad, April and me. And Julia, too. If I got settled in Florida again, it might be difficult to get back up here, especially on the holidays when Claudia was most likely to come home.

Just the thought of going back to that humidity was enough to put me in a bad mood.

"I have a pretty good thing going with Claudia and—"

Felicia interrupted. "I don't know what you see in that girl. She's too highbrow. And weird. I mean, I was talking to her about you in the kitchen and she never even said you guys were together. If you were my guy, I would have said, 'Honey, you just back the hell off. He's with me.' But not her, she kept it zipped."

"Claudia's different. She doesn't act like that." I leaned against the crib and turned to face her. "I'm sorry, but I'm going to stay here. I need to be here when she comes back from school."

"Back? You think once she gets a taste of that California lifestyle she's going to come back here? To this?" She waved her hand around, including me in 'this.' "Toby, don't kid yourself. She'll find herself a Malibu Ken and never look back."

I didn't like what she was saying or how she was saying it. "She's coming back. She promised."

"Come on. You know yourself what happens when you leave the island. At first, you promise you'll come back—and you actually mean it. But then you tell yourself you're too busy or you can't afford it. And then before you know it, a year has passed, then two. Suddenly, it's easier not to look back, not to miss it. Any of it."

Her eyes met mine, and she pursed her lips. "Truth sucks. But here's your reality check: smart girls don't have happily-ever-afters with guys like you and your brother." She laid a hand on my arm like she was trying to comfort me. "You're more likely to end up with someone like me. Someone who doesn't expect much more than a steady paycheck and a really good lay."

I shoved her hand away. "Just shut up. Maybe that's your and Al's version of a dream life, but I'm not anything like my brother. And you don't know a damn thing about what I want."

Dylan wiggled about and made a little whimpering sound.

Felicia's eyes sparked. "Unless you want to rock him back to sleep, be quiet!" she hissed, pushing me away from the crib. "I didn't realize how whipped you were, you poor bastard. Well, don't say I didn't warn you." Clucking her tongue, she twisted away sharply. "I'm going out for a smoke."

I went to my room and tried to fall back to sleep, but I couldn't stop thinking about what Felicia had said. Even as I cursed her for it, I knew what she'd said was a real possibility. Claudia might not come back for me.

I'd never wanted a long-term relationship with any girl because everyone I'd been with wanted me to fill some missing part of their life. To make the world right for them. My own world was so far off-kilter, the best I could do for them was distract them from their own unhappiness for a few months. I was good at physical diversion, but eventually, they cut me loose because I couldn't provide what they really wanted. Love. I couldn't give what I didn't feel.

Love, to me, was a backhanded slap from my father, a chokehold from my brother, and my mother's shattered tears. Love opened you up to hurt. After the anger had spent itself and everyone concerned went back to ignoring each other, you might be fooled enough to think the punishment was over—only to get another beat down. Finally, you learned your lesson. You kept your distance, prepared for the next strike.

What Claudia and I had was different. She didn't need me to save her, but that was its own problem. Unlike me, she was on her way up in the world. Going away meant she'd be surrounded by smart college guys—guys who were going to be doctors and engineers. Guys who would be a better match for her.

Yeah, so I signed up for some bogus computer classes—the same classes I could have taken in high school. Had I been a little more motivated, I'd already be so much further ahead than just delivering shit for minimum wage and tips. Right now, the best I could hope for was old Abe promoting me to head stock boy. He'd probably rather stand before a firing squad than give me a raise.

Fact was, I needed Claudia more than she needed me.

It was the first time I worried I might lose a girl. Even though she said she loved me, I wasn't foolish enough to think it guaranteed anything.

I lay in my bed, alone and missing her. I missed Claudia like I'd never missed anyone before. I didn't realize I'd fallen asleep until I woke to Dylan crying from down the hallway.

I looked at the clock. Damn, I was already late for work. I called in and spoke to Abe, then went down to make coffee. Felicia was in the kitchen picking up all the baby stuff that somehow was scattered through every room in the house. She and the baby would be with us for another day before they left to visit one of Felicia's friends and fly back. I played with the little guy, but Felicia and I barely talked.

Claudia would still be in the air, almost to California by now. On my way to my room, I checked Claudia's flight status on my phone, but Julia stopped me atop the stairs.

"What?" I asked, annoyed at the interruption before I realized how tired she looked. I tried to squash my anger.

"Felicia seems upset. What happened between you two?"

"Nothing." I wiped my face on my shirt sleeve. I wished we had central air like the Chiamettis. The small bedroom a/c window units cooled only the sleeping areas. The rest of the house felt like an oven.

"Where were you last night?"

"Nowhere."

"Toby." She eyed me. "What's going on?"

"Christ, I just want to be left alone." The answer left my mouth before I could tame it.

"Don't use the Lord's name in vain," Julia scolded, and then looked at my cell screen and saw the airline website. "Claudia land yet?"

I looked down at my feet and exhaled. "Soon. I'm waiting to hear from her."

Julia patted my back just as Dylan squealed downstairs. She turned her head to listen.

"I love having family in the house again." A little smile hung on her lips. "I think my cancer was a blessing," she said.

"And just how do you figure that?"

"Our lives are full again. First, you came home, then Claudia joined us. And now," she continued, "Dylan is here."

The visit had been great. The little guy had warmed up to Julia, and she was eating him up. As I looked at Julia's tired but happy face, I wondered why this all had seemed impossible to do in the past. I knew the change had a lot to do with Claudia.

Suddenly Julia's eyes glossed over, and she got that far-away look. I squinted at her. "What're you thinking about?"

"I just wish your father had lived to see our grandchild, too."

That was not the answer I'd anticipated. As far as I was concerned, the kid was lucky my father wasn't around. Who needed him? She seemed to be thinking about Big Al a lot lately. The other day, I'd walked in on her talking to him, out loud, as if she were having a whole live conversation with him. She stopped when she saw me. I was kind of embarrassed for her and hadn't mentioned it. It wasn't hard to see she was more emotional than usual. That she wished Big Al was here slammed me back into a mood. Talking about family memories was like a trip on bad acid. Going to work was almost a relief.

Feeling tense, I considered stopping at the gas station to buy a pack of bogies. There was no traffic as I made the turn onto Railroad Avenue heading south towards Main Street, but a small import came flying over the railroad tracks and rode my tail up the road. Swearing, I braked in the middle of the street and stepped out of the Jeep. I clenched my fists and, fixing my glare on the young driver, started toward his little blue car to show him what I thought of his obnoxious driving.

The kid's eyes went wide. He hurried to shift the car into reverse, rounding into a sloppy three-point turn and then sped back north.

Denied that outlet for my foul mood, I wanted a cigarette even more, but since I was already late for work, I decided to skip it.

Chapter 28

~CLAUDIA~

IN THE CAR, ON THE way to the airport, I was still exhilarated over all that had happened the night before, right up to my Romeo and Juliet balcony scene with Toby escaping out my bedroom window earlier that morning.

Dad was somber when he hugged me goodbye. He wasn't used to having so little control over what I did—and it was easy to see that he didn't like it.

"I didn't originally want you to go, but I think being away will give you some much-needed breathing space from that guy," he said.

"That guy's name is Toby," I replied with a huff.

I thought a lot about Toby on the plane. First, I thought about how our long-distance relationship would work. But that was easy—as long as I threw myself into my studies, without any distractions, I would excel. Toby and I could still talk on the phone and over the Internet. I romanticized about him coming to visit me on weekends, and the two of us, along with my mother, sitting around the small bistro set in her apartment eating Chinese food with chopsticks. Him sleeping on my mother's sofa while I bunked in with her; and me sneaking out after she fell asleep to lie in his arms for a few hours. I daydreamed, too about how it would be when I came home on holidays and for the summer. I imagined the homecomings being great, starry-eyed reunions for us. I would have both my mind and heart's desire.

As soon as my plane touched down at the airport in Los Angeles, I called Toby.

"I'm here!" I announced. "My mother is picking me up, and

we're going directly to the campus."

"Good," he replied, with little excitement. When he didn't say anything more, I wondered if something had happened.

I rushed to fill in the silence. "How's Dylan? And your mom?"

"They're fine. Everybody is fine," he grumbled and then said, "I can't talk. I got into work late this morning, and Abe's on the warpath. Call me later."

"Yes, of course," I said. And more quietly, "I love you."

I heard something like 'okay' or 'sure.' He'd not actually said those three words to me yet.

"Say it back," I demanded.

"Claude, I'm at work," he reminded me, but then, in a small voice he said, "I miss you."

I'd hoped for more, but knowing how tense he'd been about work lately, I let it go. For now, it would have to be enough to know he felt more than he was willing to say.

"I miss you more," I whispered.

"Impossible," he remarked wryly. "No one here laughs at my jokes. When I tried to kiss Marie this morning, she smacked me."

"Serves you right for trying to kiss anyone but me," I told him. "Now practice saying the 'L' word while I'm gone, tough guy. I want to hear it when I get home."

"I'll try, Claude," he said, sounding relieved. "Talk to you tonight."

Twenty minutes later, suitcase in hand, I walked side-by-side with my mother out to the parking garage, hot L.A. air gusting off the cement structure. Some people said I looked like her. We had the same oval face, the same blue eyes. But that's where the similarities stopped. Her perfectly coiffed blonde bob versus my long dark waves was only the most obvious difference. Our relationship had been strained since the divorce. We were more courteously polite than close, but she had helped make USC a reality for me and for that, she had earned a slice of my forgiveness.

"I'm so glad you're here, sweetheart."

"Thanks, mom. Me, too. It was hit-or-miss there for a while. I'm half surprised Daddy didn't actually chain me to my bed."

I could tell she wanted to say something, but her lips tightened for a moment; then she smiled. "He'll get over it. And besides, you're here. Now all you can do is make the most of it."

Maybe our relationship wasn't anything to brag about—like she shifted her schedule to absorb my visit, incorporating me like a minor hiccup to her routine—but it was liberating to not have my every little move be the focus of her attention. And I could easily imagine myself building a new life here, one with more freedom and independence than my father would ever allow.

The sun was shining as I stepped onto a walkway leading up to Hahn Central Plaza at the University of Southern California's main campus. I stared at the scene before me. It was one of the most beautiful views ever—a myriad of architecturally inspiring brick buildings. The sense of being in a place completely immersed in classrooms, books, computers, professors, and all things scholarly, made me feel warm and fuzzy all over.

Academia. I loved school. Here I was, making this learning atmosphere my new home. A new adventure, written just for me.

The transfer student orientation kept me busy with group exercises, paperwork, tours, and faculty meet-and-greets. Though I made several new friends, there was little time to have a complete thought. The day's events left me seriously exhausted, but when I got back to the temporary dorm, the girls I was rooming with—Kate, Misha and Emily—we stayed up late talking. Something I hadn't done in ages. I didn't even remember falling asleep.

When I opened my eyes, it was morning, and I realized that I'd never called Toby. I grabbed my phone and saw I had missed several of his calls.

"Where were you?" he barked into the phone. "You said you'd call me last night before you went to bed. Remember?"

He'd never taken such a tone with me before.

"I'm sorry. It was such a busy day. Some of the girls and I were talking, and I guess I fell asleep."

"Well, I hope you had a good time," he snapped.

Annoyed, I replied flippantly, "I did."

He made a growling noise.

"Stuff like this is going to happen from time to time. You're going to have to learn how to deal with it." I staunchly refused to set myself up to routinely defend a harmless girls' night.

"Shit. Shit. Shit," he muttered under his breath.

"Why are you so angry?"

"Why? 'Cause you're there and I'm here. 'Cause I wanted to talk to you last night. 'Cause my job is shitty. 'Cause I feel like you're moving forward and I'm standing still." The long stream of annoyances rushed out on a breath. He paused to blow out, and then more calmly said, "I'm in a lousy mood. I don't want to be here anymore. I'm practically crawling the walls."

I chewed my lower lip, thinking how best to get him to swing over to optimistic thoughts.

"We'll spend as much time together as possible before I leave to start the semester," I said. "And then you'll start classes at Suffolk. We'll both be busy, and the time will fly by."

"Claude, I have an idea," he said. "Now that Julia's getting better, I could come out to L.A. I'll find a job, get an apartment, and then we can be together. You could stay with me on the weekends."

His suggestion hit me sideways. The whole point of going to California was to claim my independence.

"Oh, Toby, I don't know," I murmured, my emotions warring. "Please don't put me in this position."

"What position?" he asked, stiffly. "Having your stupid fucking boyfriend around?"

"Don't talk like that," I said. "I only meant I would have to divide my time between you and my college experience."

"College experience? Oh, now I get it. You want to fuck around and don't want me getting in your way."

"You're being completely unreasonable."

"Yeah, fuck me, I'm an asshole," he said, his voice like stone.

"God, Toby!" I loathed when he was crass.

The line went dead, and I stared blankly at my cell. I dialed him right back. Straight to voicemail.

Miserable, crass asshole, I thought—and still, I missed him anyway. I started to wonder if I could I really do this—be separated, so far away from the guy I loved and everything I knew—for two years?

When I thought about how much I'd gone through to get here, the only answer was yes. I'd wanted this for so long. Too long. I couldn't wimp out and throw away this opportunity. I had to be strong. Toby would have to be strong, too.

I quietly began my second day on campus. Toby just needed some time, time to see everything would be fine. I planned to call him later and hoped to find him in a better mood.

Two days later, with orientation out of the way, I went to stay with my mother at her apartment in downtown San Diego to spend the rest of the week.

Toby hadn't called me, not once, since he hung up on me. I'd left him a zillion messages and texts. I reasoned that he couldn't possibly be that angry with me. Something must have happened with Devlin, or worse, Toby's mother. I decided to call Mrs. Faye. At least if I got hold of her, I would feel a little better.

"Hi honey," she greeted me, cheerfully.

"Mrs. Faye, thank God!" Although nothing in her voice hinted at anything amiss, I couldn't keep the distress out of my own. "Is everything all right? I haven't heard from Toby in a few days. I've been so worried."

"We're fine," she insisted.

"I've left dozens of messages. Toby hasn't returned any of my calls."

"I'm sorry he's had you worried. I'd put him on the phone now, but he's not home." Mrs. Faye paused and then said, "Since you left, he seems a bit off. I imagine he's probably worried about you being away."

"Mrs. Faye, I love you both too much to stay away," I rushed out. "I need to be here—to do this, but I'll be back."

"Oh, honey, I'm not worried. But my son seems to lack the faith it takes to see how changes can open the doors to a world of new opportunities. Maybe if I'd given him more reassurance when he was younger," she considered out loud. "I suppose that's what happens when you let a boy fend for himself at such a young age."

"It was a bad time for you, too."

"But I need to right some of my past wrongs. I want very much to help him figure out where he's going in life and see him get there. If only he didn't seem so restless the last few days. It's like he's getting ready to go."

"Go?" Nervously, I clutched my throat. I remembered his words. *I don't want to be here anymore. I'm practically crawling the walls.*

"Don't worry. I'll make him call you when he comes in tonight. And once you talk, I'm sure he'll settle down. Distance does not divide people, honey. Fear does."

Inspired by my conversation with Mrs. Faye, I took a long walk. Toby and I had not even had a full week apart, and it was already affecting us, the distance stretching and testing us.

Mrs. Faye was so right about fear. Both Toby and I had responded in fear—he worried he was losing me, and me … I'd worried about losing my independence.

Now I saw my error. It'd been unreasonable to insist Toby hang back while I go off to have my own private adventure. What could I say? I'd become fiercely protective of my independence. No small wonder considering my father. I'd had to stand tall and make my voice heard to get to California. Never again would I let anyone steal my voice.

But Toby wasn't my father. The only thing he'd ever stolen from me was my heart.

Chapter 29

~TOBY~

I WAS IN THE PISSIEST OF moods. We'd tailed Dev around looking for an opportunity to lift the knife off of him, but we'd lost track of him.

Ray had gone with me to the Dirty Dog Pub, an old dive next to the train tracks. I couldn't see straight. Adrenalin pumped through me like fire. For the first time in a long while, I went looking for a fight. It didn't take more than two drinks before I'd started to mix it up with some asshole. Before I'd been able to land any blows, though, the mammoth bouncer threw us out.

Out of ideas, we'd gone back to Ray's. He got stewed while I chased beers with shots of *Jägermeister*.

"Did you check your messages?" I asked.

"Yeah, man. He didn't call." Ray pulled at his hair. "Dev's a lot of things, but he ain't st-stupid. He knows s-something's up."

Shit.

Ray was taking the plea bargain, agreeing to testify in court that he witnessed Dev stab the Dominican. In exchange, he would get probation and have to enter a drug rehabilitation program. His lawyer was working out the details with the authorities. Once a formal agreement was made, the police would go after Dev. Once that was set in motion, my fate was a crapshoot.

I rested my head on the damp resin table, not caring that it was coated with a thick layer of yellowy-green pollen spores. "I have to bounce out of town. As soon as I can. Before Dev is arrested."

"Where to? California?"

"No. I'm not sure where yet."

"But what about y-your girl?" Ray asked.

I sat up and wiped the pollen away with the back of my hand. "That's cooked. Time to shoot it and put it out of its misery."

Ray just nodded. "A-another one bites the d-dust," he said.

I'd gotten too close, and now I was getting burned. Any schmuck understood that when a girl said she wanted her space, it was over. Felicia was right. With Claudia on the other coast, it was just a matter of time before she let go completely. I wouldn't let it drag out. I had to cut it off now, before it got even uglier.

Ray had to work the late shift, manning the counter and making coffee at 7-Eleven to the wee hours of the morning. I moved to leave, but the dick took my car keys. I didn't want to crash at his house, so a little while later, on his way to work, he dropped me off at the corner of Tariff Street and Roosevelt. I walked up the block, alone with my thoughts.

My life was veering off course, once again, and I wasn't sure how to put it back on track. I couldn't see a way out of this situation with Dev other than leaving town. Julia was doing better, and if Claudia hadn't made it clear that I was invading her space, I could already be on my way to California.

After this, I knew all love was shit.

At the door of my house, I glanced over my shoulder looking for Dev, his car or anything out of the ordinary. The night was dead quiet. In my head, a monster headache was screaming at my brain. The racket was storming, and a thick, blistering meanness rolling in. Darkness gnashed its teeth. I needed to sleep. It was the only rational way to sooth the hostile monster.

Julia was sitting on the couch in the living room, her head low as she read from a book in her lap. The air in the house was breathless and stifling, worse than the humidity outside. She didn't even have a fan on.

"Good, you're home," she said.

All I could think about was going up to my room and cranking up the a/c unit in my window. Julia reached out her hand and stopped me.

"Toby, we need to talk."

Placing a marker inside the pages, she closed the thick, hardcover book with an empowered thump. Then I saw the bold, gold-lettered title, *The Holy Bible*.

I suspected she'd been reading verses in preparation to speak to me.

"Oh, great," I moaned under my breath.

She eyed me. "Have you been drinking?"

I shrugged. "I had a few beers with Ray."

"I thought you were done with those boys," she said, giving me her exasperated frown.

I pressed on my temples. "Ma, I have a really bad headache. Talk to me tomorrow."

"No, we'll talk now." She wagged a finger at me. "Claudia called."

By the rigid set of Julia's shoulders, I knew this was not going to be quick.

"Don't mention her name to me anymore. We're done."

Julia's mouth dropped open. "What are you talking about? That girl loves you."

I squinted at her, wondering how she knew that.

"And I happen to know, you love her, too," she said with an air of certainty.

My back stiffened. "No, Ma. You're wrong. I liked her a lot, much more than other girls. But love? No."

"Of course, you do. That's why you're so grumpy lately," she reasoned. "You just don't recognize it. I can't say it surprises me, because Lord knows we've been through some dreadful times in this house. But those are past us. And, past you. You're moving forward. With Claudia, God has opened a whole new path for you."

"Are you saying God is only now opening this path for me? Where was he through all the other shit—your sickness, Dad's accident, Al's conviction?" I shook my head, annoyed by her attempt to bring religion into this. Her devotion to God had never done her, or our family, any good. There were so many years of shit that I'd kept to myself, all because she'd always been too fragile. Despite all the time she spent asking the Almighty for strength, her prayers had plainly fallen on deaf ears.

Julia lifted her chin, her face set for a lecture. "Sometimes we need to fall before we can reach new heights. But He is always with you. He is the one that has given you strength to keep going. And, you might not believe it, but you have yet to see your best days."

"Don't preach your bullshit to me."

"You listen to me." Julia stood, eyes ignited. "I may not have been a perfect mother, but I'm doing my best to make up for that now. My friends and I are praying for you. If you stay here and keep your head up, God and I will see you through it. God will hear our prayers."

"Ma, stop it. Look at me. Look how we live. This is as good as it gets."

"No, no." She shook her head vehemently. "You will do more, lots more. I feel it. I know it. Don't you see? You're uncomfortable where you are. It means you're reaching the turning point. Everything is about to change. You only need to stay strong. Have faith that things will turn around. You will be rewarded."

Her persistence hammered at my head, sharpening my headache.

I pointed at her. "I came back here. I took care of you. I got a nice girl and even signed up for college classes. I did every fucking thing right," I shouted. "I was the best goddamn possible version of me that I could be. But what has that gotten me? Nothing! I'm not being rewarded—I'm fucking being punished!" Sweat dripped down my temples and armpits. I wanted to throw something. "Why the hell is this fucking house so damn hot!"

My voice boomed through the house, and resounded in my head like a noxious hiss, and turned up my stomach. Julia shrunk back.

"I do not like that language," she said. She wiped her forehead with her hand and seemed surprised to realize, just like me, she was also sweating. She inhaled a tight, short breath and lowered her voice. "Claudia's gone to college. She hasn't left you."

"She's across the freaking country. She might as well be in another country. And, she told me straight out, she doesn't want me there. I know you like her, but you need to get it through your head, Claudia and I—we're done."

Julia clasped her hands together over her chest. "No. She wants to be with you, but she needs to follow her dream. The distance won't change how she feels. That girl has so much faith and passion. But she also has a clear vision of what she wants. That's the only real difference between you and her."

"You're right. I don't have faith. Or vision. Why do you think that is? Why didn't I plan for my future when I was younger?" I said. "Lazy? Or possibly it's because I was too damn busy taking care of you and this house, trying to survive through the day, the week, the month?"

"Toby, I'm sorry—"

"No." I deflected her. I couldn't tolerate another tired apology. "Just understand, I will never be anything more than what I am right now. There's no point in trying to pretend."

"Oh, you are so stubborn!" Her little hands curled into fists. "When you talk like that, it makes me so... so..."

I had never seen my mother so angry, but her anger only intensified my own.

"Want to hit me, Ma?" I leaned in and offered her my chin. "Come on. Take a shot. Maybe it'll make you feel better. It always made Al feel better."

Gasping, Julia recoiled as if I'd burnt her, her eyes filling with tears.

"Yeah, Ma, you're so anxious to get me to reunite with Al, but the fact is, while you holed away refusing to face the world, my brother beat the shit out of me. Did you hear me?" Needing her to really grasp it, I said it again, "Al used to beat the shit out of me."

Her lips trembled, but still she shook her head.

"Yes, damn it! Al always hated me. Bruises fade, but scars don't. Here, let me show you the most memorable one." I yanked my right sleeve up and thrust my tattooed shoulder under her nose. "That spot there, that's where my big brother burnt me with a lit cigarette."

Julia covered her mouth with one hand and held up the other. "Stop. I mean it, Toby, please," she cried out. Turning her back to me, she reached shakily for the arm of the couch.

"Yeah, go pray to your god. Let him handle the truth for you, since you can't." I threw a hand out in frustration and tromped to the staircase. "I'm done with this."

I slammed my bedroom door shut as hard as I could and clicking on my laptop, I cranked up the volume. My skull pounded even more as the rock beat erupted, but I needed to separate myself from Julia and this house. I cranked up the a/c to the coolest setting and dug around the piles of crap in my room until I found my duffle bag. I opened a dresser drawer and began to toss my shit into it. Time to go.

I'd started on a second drawer when I felt a soft shimmying within the house. I don't know why I suspected something wrong, but I notched down the volume on the computer and poked my head out the bedroom door to listen.

I heard Julia's cry. I tossed the bag aside and wrenched the door the rest of the way open.

"Ma?" I called from my doorway.

Her answering moan came from below. I leaned over the hallway railing, and my heart stopped. Julia lie crumpled at the bottom of the steps, unmoving.

I flew down to her and folded her into my arms. Gray-faced, she stared up at me as incoherent words fell from her lips.

Chapter 30

~CLAUDIA~

I HAD NOT SLEPT WELL SINCE the night Toby and I had fought. After my talk with his mother, despite the time zone difference, I fully expected him to call that night. I waited, fighting the fatigue of the last few days.

Just as I began to doze, my cell chimed the familiar melody of "Something"—the ring tone I had set for Toby.

I answered, but apprehensive of his mood, I waited for him to speak first.

"Claude," he said my name, quick and went on. "Julia's in the hospital."

I fell back against the couch. "Why? What happened?"

He didn't answer right away, and then he cursed. "She fell on the steps in the house."

"Is... is she okay?"

"No, she had a heart attack," his voice faltered. "They don't think she's going to make it."

"Oh, no," I whispered, tears already falling.

"We had a fight, and she fell trying to come upstairs after it. The doctors can't tell if the fall caused the heart attack or the heart attack caused the fall." His breathing was heavy. "It's my fault. I said some terrible shit—I'm sure she was coming to talk to me when she fell."

"Don't blame yourself."

"You don't understand. What I said, I knew she wouldn't be able to handle it, but I let it fly. I didn't hold anything back." His voice hitched. "Jesus, Claude, I was awful."

I tried to refocus him. "I'm going to try to get on a flight right away, but I want you to stay at the hospital with Aunt Joan. As soon as I get in, I'll come directly to you."

At the airport, I was put on standby, but no seats were available until the next morning.

It was late afternoon on the East Coast when I finally arrived. Dad met me at the airport and drove me to the hospital. Standing with me at the entrance to the ICU, he grabbed my hand and said, "Breathe, Claudia, breathe."

"I'm scared," I told him.

"I know. This won't be easy," he said, and kissed my forehead.

I grabbed his arm. "You'll stay?"

"Of course," he said and patted my hand. "I'm not going anywhere. I'll be right in the waiting room if you need me."

I nodded, recognizing the unfailing constancy that was so much a part of who my father was, and now, how grateful I was for it. Leaving his side, I entered the ICU. Through the glass partition that faced the nurses' station, I could see Aunt Joan's figure.

I crossed the threshold into the room. The sterile atmosphere with the steady beeping and buzzing of monitors was intimidating. Mrs. Faye, with her eyes closed, looked so small on the oversized hospital bed. Tubes ran every which way from her body to various machines attached to the wall behind the bed.

Toby was not there.

Standing at her bedside, Aunt Joan looked up at me and attempted to smile, but it faded into a trembly frown. I rushed to her side, hugging her and whispering comforting words until finally, I turned to face Mrs. Faye. I reached for her hand as I leaned in to kiss her cheek. For an instant, her fingers stirred gently against my own as if she were greeting me, before she settled, motionless, once more.

"Where is he?" I asked, knowing Aunt Joan would know whom I meant.

Joan moved to the bedside and gently brushed the baby fine hair on her sister's forehead. "He came to the hospital with Julia. We were beside ourselves when we got the prognosis. But then I had to tell him that Julia had requested not to be resuscitated, too. He hadn't known and didn't take it well." Her fingers moved downwards, smoothing out the sheet over Mrs. Faye's stationary form. "'The last thing my sister said to us was that she was 'so tired.'" Joan inhaled a steadying breath.

"She has been ill more than half of her life and has had to rely heavily on others to help her do so much. Add in the heartbreak of losing her husband and seeing her oldest child imprisoned—you can understand her exhaustion." Joan shook her head, the hopelessness in her voice unmistakable. "My nephew left, justifiably devastated. To lose both parents ... I just couldn't go after him. I need to be here, for her."

I went out to report to my father and found him staring, uninterested, at a television screen in the quiet waiting room.

"It's bad?" he asked.

I nodded, and he stood to hug me. I allowed myself a moment to grieve over Mrs. Faye's condition before I gathered myself together.

"Toby left. He blames himself for what happened. Dad, what if she dies before he comes back? If it were me, I don't know if I'd ever forgive myself ... He needs to come back. He needs to be with her."

"Okay. Let's go get him." Dad seemed willing, but after years of conditioning, I automatically refused his help.

"*Mia bella figlia*, I won't let you do this alone."

His endearment, "my beautiful daughter," made me realize this wasn't a time for a power struggle between us. It was a time to rally. We would find Toby together.

Inside the car, Dad told me a warrant had been issued for Devlin Van Sloot's arrest.

"He tried to run us over with his car," I blurted out.

"What?" Despite his surprise, Dad kept the car steady.

"If you promise to stay calm, I'll tell you everything I know about that night."

Dad nodded, and I relayed all that Toby had told me about the stabbing incident.

"This is far more serious than I thought. You'll both need to be extra careful until he's apprehended," Dad said in warning.

Now that my father was aware of Devlin's threats, he would be more protective of me, but, for the first time since I was little, I was comforted by it. Mostly, I was relieved to be rid of the heavy secret.

We drove to the Fayes' house, but no one was home.

"There's one other place I want to check." I directed him to

Ray's street. We spotted Toby's Jeep in front of the little gray prefab house.

"I'll get him," Dad said, unbuckling his seat belt.

I caught his arm and stopped him. "No. I need to do this."

Dad nodded and stayed seated while I got out of the car.

Two other cars were parked on the lawn closer to the house. I could hear the steady hum of a television show with a laugh track from outside the door.

I rapped on the dirty screen door.

Someone shouted, "We're in the kitchen."

Hesitantly, I stepped inside. A guy who looked a lot like Ray, but younger, was sprawled out on a faux suede couch, fast asleep with the television on. Moving towards the sound of voices, I went to the left and found the kitchen.

I stepped into the dimly lit room, and it became ominously quiet. Toby was sitting at a small, round table next to an ashtray overflowing with cigarette butts. A collection of beer cans was scattered across the table surface. Next to Toby was an older woman wearing a ton of eye makeup—Ray's mother? Alongside her was his sloppy friend, Ray.

These were not people I'd ever imagine myself comfortable with. Ignoring Ray and the woman's stare, I fixed my eyes on Toby. His gray-blue eyes flashed a momentary expression of surprise before he lowered his head and blew out a heavy breath. I couldn't understand how they could just sit around so unaffected. Didn't they know about Mrs. Faye's condition?

"Is this your girlfriend?" the woman asked, her raspy voice thick and smoky.

Ray eyed me with a dopey grin. "Not anymore, she ain't."

"Shut up," Toby snapped, as he rose from his chair and moved toward me. Our eyes locked, and my view of the room was blocked by his looming figure. He grabbed my shoulders and pushed me backwards. I almost tripped over a case of Red Bull as he cornered me in a pantry alcove. Accosted by a thick smell of frying oil that permeated the area, my stomach rolled.

"What are you doing here?" he demanded, his voice low and edgy.

I was shocked at how he looked—bloodshot eyes, wrinkled clothes. It was obvious he hadn't touched a shaving razor in days.

"What are you doing here?" I shot back.

"I'm doing what I do best—nothing."

"Don't you think you should be at the hospital?" I spoke loudly, not caring if the others heard me.

Toby cupped a hand over my mouth, silencing me. Then I knew, the others didn't know about his mother.

I pulled his hand from my mouth. "Toby, please, let's get out of here."

Whether he heard me or not, he didn't react. With a bearish grunt, he lowered his hand to my neck. His eyes dipped down to watch his hand's movement over my body as he continued to drag a heavy palm down across my collarbone and then over the swell of my breast. Despite everything, my body warmed under his touch, but it was for him that I put my hand over his and pressed it to my breast. His mother was dying, and there wasn't anything I wouldn't do to make him go back to the hospital with me. This was the easiest way to get him to cooperate.

"Damn," he murmured, an inflection of awe in his husky voice. In his eyes, I could see how stirred up he was. Without another word, he pressed me backwards. The hard ridges of the pantry shelving dug into my back as he tugged a handful of my hair, forcing my head back and my face upwards. Holding me in place, his mouth closed over mine, and he kissed me hard.

His overgrown beard felt like gritty sandpaper on my face, but like magnets drawn forcefully together, my body was incapable of staying away from his. My response to his kiss came automatic.

"Yo, this ain't no Commack Motor Inn," Ray yelled, cackling.

Flushed, I hungered to continue our kiss but pulled back.

"Please, let's get out of here." I took his hand and started to move, and willingly, he followed me. I led him outside, to the back door of my car, hoping he'd just assume I wanted to crawl into the back seat with him. I slid in first, moving over to make room for him. He bounded in after me, but as soon as he saw my father, he jerked to a stop.

His accusatory stare turned on me. "What the hell is this?"

"Shut the door and buckle up," my father ordered and started the car.

I sensed Toby realized this was not open for debate, but I was surprised, as well as relieved, when he actually did as he was told.

As we got onto Sunrise Highway heading towards the hospital, it was obvious Toby was furious with me. I tried to hold his hand, but he shook me off. The entire trip he stared out the window, his whole body bristling with anger.

Dad dropped us off at the hospital's entrance and went to park the car.

I took both of Toby's hands in mine. "I know this is hard, but I'll stay with you."

Without another word, Toby followed me up to the ICU. At the entrance to his mother's room, he stopped, and his face lost all color.

Two nurses were attending to Mrs. Faye, who was noticeably struggling to catch even shallow, little breaths. I could feel there wasn't much time left.

Aunt Joan came forward and took Toby's hand. "I think she's been waiting for you," she said and led him over to the bed.

Toby slumped into the chair at Mrs. Faye's bedside. He laid his head near his mother's and pressed her limp hand to his face.

I moved behind him, a hand on his shoulder, a gentle reminder that he was not alone. Aunt Joan gave me a fleeting smile of gratitude.

Time ticked by. At some point, Toby's shoulders wilted under my hand. With eyes closed, he appeared to have fallen asleep. He looked completely wiped out, and I felt a pang at the cruel twist of fate that was stealing his mother from him. I decided that despite my own sadness, I would try very hard to be strong for Toby. I would be his rock.

I had no idea how long it was, an hour, maybe less, when the monitor over Mrs. Faye's bed flat lined. Toby's head snapped up, and a nurse who'd been keeping watch stepped over and flicked off the electronic device to stop the droning noise. Because of Mrs. Faye's DNR request, there would be no further medical attention. The nurse gave us a slight nod as if to acknowledge Mrs. Faye's departure from our world. Toby's face registered no emotion, but Aunt Joan bowed her head and began to cry.

I stood looking at Mrs. Faye's now lifeless body and Toby's blank expression. So shaken by my own sense of loss, I leaned weakly over Toby and hugged him from behind. His aunt shuffled closer and took one of his hands into her own.

I kissed his temple and whispered in a shaky voice, "It's going to be okay."

We remained motionless, all of us dazed in our grief, for several long moments, but within my arms, Toby's body began to shake violently. I held tight, rubbing his chest, and tried my best to calm him.

Suddenly he shook off his aunt's hand and hunched forward, away from me. I fought to hold onto him, but he growled, "Let go," and pushed my arms away.

"You made me watch her die. Are you happy now?"

The harsh words shredded what was left of my fragile composure, and I began to cry. He didn't seem to care, and left us sobbing at his mother's bedside. I could only watch as he rushed the ICU entrance door in the main hallway. Shouldering the large windowed door open, it protested his force with a screech. Visitors in other ICU areas turned to stare. I saw him clutch his stomach just before the door swung shut.

Chapter 31

~TOBY~

I THREW OPEN THE DOOR OF the nearest bathroom. It crashed against the tiled wall. My body was too heavy to keep upright. Feeling myself buckle, I gripped the metal handicap bar next to the toilet and dropped to my knees. Claudia came in and started to run water. Hiccupping through her tears, she pressed a wet paper towel to my face. My stomach rolled violently.

"Don't!" I swatted her away. My body shook with spasms as I threw up. It went on, over and over, until I was completely empty.

I gulped air as though fighting to keep my head above water. This is what it must feel like to drown—lungs burning, struggling for air—so afraid you were about to take your last breath you'd kick and claw at anyone trying to stop you. Somehow I managed to get back on my feet and though I was shaky, I took off blindly down the corridor.

The night was as black as my mind. I started walking east, towards home, but I wasn't going back there. I couldn't. I just had to keep moving. I'd suffocate if I didn't.

Houses were dark, neighborhoods silent, when I finally slowed. Exhausted, I forced myself up the last step to the door of the place I'd always gone when I couldn't go home—Ray's. His car wasn't out front, but I banged on the door anyway. After several minutes, a light came on, and Diane yanked open the door.

"Cripes, Toby. You know Ray's on late shift this week," she carped, but I guess she saw how fucked up I looked. "What's going on? You all right?"

"No," I managed to get out before all the walls closed in on me. I bent over, gasping for air. Diane opened the door and helped me inside.

"What the hell happened?" she'd returned from Ray's bedroom with the bottle of tequila he kept stashed there.

She poured out a liberal amount of the amber alcohol and pushed the glass into my hand. I downed the contents, in one gulp. It burned going down, but I tipped the glass at her, and signaled for another.

"My mother just died," I said and brought the tequila glass to my lips.

Diane replenished my glass a few more times before my tongue loosened, and once I started talking, it all spilled forth—the fight, the fall, and afterwards, the bone-chilling, deathly look on Julia's face.

"It's my fucking fault," I wailed, mashing my forehead on the table.

Diane stroked my hair.

"No, it isn't. Kids say shit that upsets their parents all the time. You couldn't help that she couldn't handle it."

I lost track of time, but at some point, Diane led me back to her bedroom and made me lay down. My shirt was wet, and despite the warm weather, I shivered. I tried to take it off, but my arms were useless. The room suddenly began to rock. With a hand on my chest, Diane stilled me.

"I'll do it," she said. "Just lie back."

I was too wasted to do anything but comply. After she pulled off my shirt, she removed my sneakers. And then I must have started to bawl. The next thing I knew, she was lying next to me, hugging me and rubbing my back. I couldn't seem to control myself. I pressed my face into her neck and closed my eyes.

"Don't leave me," I moaned, barely audible in my fucked-up state.

"Poor baby," she murmured. Her fingers ran over the back of my head, smoothing out my hair as she kissed my forehead. I burrowed in tighter, afraid that if I didn't keep touching her, I would disappear.

Chapter 32

~CLAUDIA~

"CLAUDIA, LET HIM BE," MY father tried to reason with me.

I tugged on his sleeve to make him move.

"Please, Dad, we have to go after him."

"Men deal with sadness in different ways," he said.

I was sure this wasn't a man/woman-way-of-dealing-with-sorrow thing. Toby didn't deal with the grief—he simply cut out. I knew Dad would never do that. Even under pressure, Dad remained rock-solid. It was he who held me while I cried.

Dad drove home from the hospital slowly so I could keep a lookout for the familiar lone figure walking the streets. But we never found him.

I called April, and she and Dario came over to my house. Dario had located Toby via text. He was at Ray's house. Like my dad, though, Dario opted for letting Toby be for the night. April put her arm around me and let me lean on her shoulder.

"I feel like I failed him. I fell apart," I sobbed.

"You're only human, *mami*. You cared about Mrs. Faye."

"He was angry at me for making him go back to the hospital."

"You did the right thing, chica. He may not see that now, but eventually he will." April squeezed my shoulders.

The next day, Dad watched me as I pushed my dinner around on the dish. I'd cried all night and most of the day. He'd come in to sit with me for an hour and rubbed my back like he used to do when I was younger.

"Your financial aid package came in the mail yesterday. Everything seems to be in order," he said, an obvious attempt to lift my spirits.

Any other time, the way he simply relayed the message, without taking a stance, would've made me happy. Right now, USC seemed so unimportant. All I could think of was that Mrs. Faye was gone. Really gone. In all the time I'd worked for her, it never occurred to me that she might actually die. I'd never allowed myself to even consider it.

I tried hard to refocus my thoughts of her. I wanted to remember how the skin around the deep blue eyes crinkled when she smiled and how she held my hand when she encouraged me to chase my dreams. In such a short time, she had become a big part of my life, a bright spot as I worked through my problems with my father. I remembered how happy she looked when she found out Toby and I were dating. I knew, too, that she was part of the reason I'd fallen in love with Toby. I had fallen in love with both of them—being around them, watching the two of them together. Mrs. Faye had let me in—she'd made me feel at home and part of her family.

It was difficult to accept it was over, that all I had left were a few months of memories. I thought about how horrible it would be to lose my own mother, and it pained me not to be with Toby while he grieved. Could he still fault me for bringing him back to the hospital? How long was I supposed to wait to see him?

The day passed without a call from Toby's. After I'd finished helping Dad with the dinner dishes that night, I realized he wasn't going to. I would have to go to him.

But my father didn't like the idea.

"It's late. I don't want you driving around with this Van Sloot kid on the loose. Wait until tomorrow and then I'll go with you," he said.

"All right, Dad." I smiled tightly at him, but as soon as he was tucked away, busy in another room, I grabbed my keys and left the house.

It was dusk when I rounded the corner near Ray's house. After I'd found the Faye house dark and empty, I naturally went to the next place I figured Toby would be. There was no sign of the Jeep out front of Ray's either, just his mother, sitting on the front stoop smoking a cigarette. She was wearing only a short, black silky robe with her bare legs extended out in front of her. I got out of the car and approached her.

Up close, I could see she was almost attractive if it weren't for the bad skin and wiry hair. She looked tired and her makeup slept in. Not that she seemed to care.

I said hello and asked her if Toby was inside.

"He was, but not now," she said. I watched her pick at her teeth with a long pinkie nail. "Shame about his mother. He came banging on the door, late. Ray was working an overnighter, so he stayed with me."

Instead of letting me take care of him, Toby had chosen to come here—chosen to be comforted by this woman over me. The knowledge cut me.

"Do you know where he went?" I asked.

She tightened the sash on her robe and nodded. "Yeah, he and Ray went back to his mother's house. You just missed them."

Chapter 33

~TOBY~

RAY FOUND ME IN THE bathtub when he came in from work. I had slithered into the bathroom, turned on the shower, and, too drained to remove my jeans, I crawled into the tub and let the hot spray soak me. Wearing his 7-Eleven work shirt, Ray smelled of coffee and grilled hot dogs as he helped me to my feet and moved me to his bed where I'd slept most of the day away.

Later, sobered up, I drove home. Ray followed me back, making sure I got there without incident before going on a food excursion.

I was sick to my stomach, reeling from the after-effects of last night's tequila binge, but still, I couldn't bring myself to sit inside the empty house. I went out to the back deck instead.

I had awoken with slits for eyes that morning, my head banging, and Diane sleeping next to me in her bed. Her hair was in disarray around her face, and she was wearing nothing more than a T-shirt and panties. My own jeans were down low around my hips as if I'd either tried to get them off, or back on, and had lost interest in doing either. Diane's hand lay over my bare stomach, not far from my unzipped fly, and I recalled the awful dead feeling I had inside me. Last night, it had been so horrible, I'd clung to her just to feel alive. It was the first time I had ever been too drunk to remember what I'd done, or if I'd even been fucking laid.

I used my cell twice before I shut it down. I had texted a stock guy at work about Julia's death and asked him to relay it to Abe. I then answered a call from Joan, who cried into the phone that she'd been worried about me.

"Come stay with me for a few days," she begged.

"I'm fine," I tried to reassure her, though it was a lie.

She reminded me we had to make funeral arrangements, and I promised to call her back tomorrow to talk about it.

Ray returned with sandwiches and a bottle of Jack Daniels.

"Let's make a toast to moms," he said opening the bottle.

Yeah, *I killed mine and screwed yours. Salute!*

"Let's not."

I swiped the bottle from him and cracked the seal. I was afraid if I didn't keep myself mellowed, I would grab something, twist it, tear it apart, decimate it—and really, nothing deserved the punishment I so desperately wanted to give. Except maybe Dev. About to take a mouthful, the sweet bite of liquor hit my nose, and my stomach lurched with a sickening reminder of last night.

I pushed the bottle away and lit another cigarette. Letting my head rest against the chair back, I blew out a ring of smoke. My family was gone. It didn't seem real. I spiraled further under the weight of the truth. I was alone.

I didn't even have Claudia anymore. Being with her had always been a pipe dream. It'd been a fluke that I'd managed to get her in the first place. Even if she had wanted to stay with me, once she found out what I'd done, she would wish we were burying me instead of Julia.

As I stared up at the night sky, I briefly considered what was next. Before Julia got sick, I had wanted to enlist in the Marine Corps. Now there was nothing stopping me. I welcomed the thought of being pushed to my physical limit. Let them beat the shit out me. I wanted it. I deserved it. Maybe they'd send me overseas where I could lose myself in someone else's fight.

Chapter 34

~CLAUDIA~

THERE WERE THREE CARS IN the driveway: Mrs. Faye's little compact, Toby's Jeep, and Ray's white sedan, but when I pushed through the front door, the house was dark. No one was inside, but I heard voices out back.

Before I even opened the slider door, I could smell the heady scent of pot. Ray and Toby were slouched in chairs at the outdoor table. The burning ember of rolled hemp flared brightly as Toby took a hit. Gritty eyed, both of them looked up at me as the door squealed open in its track.

Toby looked disturbing. Dangerous and wild. He eyed me as he flicked ashes on the deck, his scrubby face an unreadable mask surrounded by the random mess of his wavy hair. Unnerved, I remained silent, waiting for him to say something first.

"You don't need to be here anymore." He exhaled a mouthful of smoke. "Julia's gone, and you've made it pretty clear you'd rather be in California. So just turn around and go back there." With a finger, he motioned a circle and pointed to the door.

Wow. I hadn't expected a warm welcome, but that stung.

"I'm not going anywhere until we talk," I said.

Ray took the joint from Toby's fingers and got up. I was glad when he dropped off the deck and disappeared around to the side of the house. Toby, too, got up and stepped off the deck onto the grass.

I was unsure about how to cross the distance that separated us. He'd never drank much or smoked, at all, around me. Despite it all, I felt the need to protect him. I moved closer and put my hand on his back. The stench of pungent smoke and alcohol hovered over him.

Before I could say anything, in a voice that was suddenly small, Toby said, "You know the last thing Julia said to me? She said she was tired. I was so awful, she didn't want to deal with me anymore."

The one thing I knew for sure was that Mrs. Faye would've never given up on him.

"Your mother was a frail, sickly woman. She had to fight to stay alive." I grabbed his hand and forced him look at me. "She probably was tired—tired of trying to be brave and keep a smile on her face, but Toby, she was definitely not tired of you!"

He shook his head. "She told me I didn't try hard enough—that I had no plan for my future. I know she was only trying to get me to do better, to want more, but I fought her. I was tired, too. Tired of tiptoeing around her and always having to take care of her. I hated everything about her that night. And I destroyed her." He put his head back and let out a long, ragged sigh. "You're right to get the hell out of here and forget about me. You took a smart, easy out, Claude. You ran."

I grasped onto both his hands. "I'm sorry, Toby. I was selfish," I said. "Going to California means so much to me, but I'm not going to run away from you. I'd never do that. I love you."

With cool eyes, he pulled his hands from mine. "You picked the wrong guy to fall in love with. I never said it back to you because I can't feel it. I don't know how."

"But you do love me," I persisted.

Angling his chin defiantly, he said, "No. I don't."

I stepped back. A physical slap would have stung less.

"Are you trying to hurt me?"

"No, but it's unavoidable. You believe everything's going to be fine, but you don't have any experience with this. As soon as you tear off to school, it won't matter how you feel right now," he said. "Things change. We won't last. Might as well cut ourselves loose now."

I felt my temper flare. "Oh, so you're the expert?"

"I know more than you about relationships." He shrugged. "We got caught up, and it was good while it lasted. Let's just admit it, Claude. We both know you don't belong with me. I'll never be enough for you."

I stamped my foot. "Who are you to decide where I belong, and what's enough for me? You're acting a hell of a lot like my father!"

His eyes narrowed. "At least your father has always had my number—a broken guy from a bad family who'll never amount to anything. His worst nightmare."

"My father doesn't know you. If you give him some time—"

"I don't need his fucking approval," he growled.

"You don't need it, but maybe you should want it. When I told him what happened with Devlin, he was actually worried about you."

"You told him! How could you fucking do that? Christ, you really are daddy's little girl," he said with a venomous sneer.

I swallowed hard and held myself in check. "Since Devlin's about to be arrested, I didn't see the need to keep it secret."

His eyes grew wide. "A warrant was issued?"

I nodded. "Yes. Didn't you know?"

"I thought I had more time. Shit!"

"Whatever you're worried about, my father can help you."

"Yeah. He'll help me right into a fucking cell."

Toby turned then, dismissing me as he shouted over his shoulder, "Ray!"

At that moment, the way he was behaving, I wanted to do exactly what he was telling me and leave him, but I knew I couldn't. *Fear divides*, Mrs. Faye's words came to me. I wrapped my arms around his waist and held myself against his rigid frame.

"I won't give up on you," I said, fighting to hold onto him as he struggled to push me away.

"Claudia, you need to leave. Go home. Right now."

"No. I want to stay with you."

Making an irritated noise in the back of his throat, he peeled me off him and stepped away. "Can't you understand? I don't want to be loved."

"I don't care what you say. I'm still going to take care of you."

"I don't want your charity."

"My charity?" I repeated numbly. "My love isn't charity."

"Whatever the fuck it is, I don't want it." He clenched his fists and raised them up between us. "I don't want you, I don't want love. I don't want any of it!" The scary, feral glint in his eyes and the cutting words challenged my determination, but I stood my ground.

"Are you going to hit me, too?" I stepped closer, presenting myself, open to his strike.

Standing stock still, he glared at me, and finally lowered his fists. "No. Just get out of here. I don't feel like playing nice anymore."

"Is that what you've been doing with me, playing nice?"

"You're not going to like who I really am."

"I know who you really are."

His nostrils flared. "No, you haven't seen the real me yet. I drink and I fight. I fuck around."

"You aren't like that anymore."

"I still am. Will always be."

"You've been drinking, that's all—"

"That's not all I've done." The look in his eyes went cool. "I was with Ray's mother last night."

"I know. She said—"

"I fucked her."

His words whipped the air from my lungs, and a burn blazed the back of my throat. "You're ... you're lying," I stammered, unable to accept that as a truth.

"Believe whatever you want," he muttered.

I thought back to the front stoop—the bare legs sticking out from a short black robe and the smeared makeup. He stayed with me, she'd said. I stared at Toby, waiting for him to fidget or blink—anything that would tell me he was making it up. But he didn't.

Something sour churned in my stomach and began to creep up my throat.

"But why? How ... how could you do that ... to me?" I cried.

He shoved his hands in his pockets and shrugged. "I was hammered. She was there."

His indifference was the last nail in the coffin. An awful funnel of energy twisted and turned inside me like a tornado. Stepping forward, I slapped him across the face, as hard as I could. My hand stung, and the ruddy imprint of it stood out even on his unshaven face. He closed his eyes and took a steadying breath. When he opened them, he nodded, almost seeming satisfied by my response.

Horrified that I'd just struck him, the steam left me. I dropped my arms limply at my sides and stood there, shriveling, like a balloon losing air. The loss, all the stress and the hurt piled on me like an unbearable weight, and I felt as if I would crumble to the ground at his feet.

Instead of falling down, though, I started to laugh. Tears burst from my eyes as I struggled to breathe through my hysterical laughter. Like a lunatic, I couldn't stop it.

The sky had darkened, and the only light came from a naked, yellow bulb over the back door. As Toby turned and strode toward the house, the laughter slowly ebbed in my throat until it died.

Toby yanked open the sliding glass door and barked, "Ray!" once more, then disappeared inside.

Feeling wretched and drained, I dragged myself to my car, but looking back at the house, I saw Ray and Toby having a heated conversation by the front door. Toby's eyes lanced me once before he turned away. He made sure I had nothing to hold onto. I climbed in the car and started the engine.

A set of headlights was coming slowly up the road behind me, but I didn't want to wait for it. I couldn't bear to stay one second longer. I dropped the car into gear and floored the gas pedal. The tires screeched as I cut out in front of the other car and raced away.

The water had always been my sanctuary and I headed to the beach. The air was cooler at the bay, and the water was like glass, serene and gently lapping against the sand. I got out of my car but didn't get too far out onto the beach when I fell to my knees. My throat was parched and achy. I didn't think I had any moisture left in my body, but tears still managed to fill my eyes.

I stared out at the water, not really seeing it. Mrs. Faye was gone, and Toby had thrown me away. After sharing so much, I never would've imagined that he could snub and betray me so easily. Had I totally misread him?

Over and over, Toby's awful words replayed inside my head, and I wasn't aware of anything around me until a thick-built figure stopped beside me. I looked up with a start, straight into Devlin's face.

He glanced down at me, almost sympathetic. "You okay, Claudia?"

Fear flashed through me.

From my kneeling position, I trained my eyes on him and squirmed as far from him as I could. "Don't touch me."

He held up his hands. "Easy. You looked upset. I just wanted to see if you were all right."

I contemplated my chances of getting to my feet and running before he could catch me, but he was too close. Banking on him not knowing I was aware of his impending arrest, I decided to behave calmly until I had an opportunity to run.

"I'm fine. But I'd rather be alone."

Instead, he moved closer. My pulse quickened. His eyes turned toward the water, and without looking at me he said, "I've never been good with girls. But you were nice to me, and I sort of thought I had a chance with you." He let out a wistful laugh.

Staying low and with as little movement as possible, I planted my feet in the sand.

"It was a real fucking disappointment when you started messing around with Faye. But I'll give the guy one thing, he certainly gets around." Devlin turned back to me, and I froze. "I can't believe he got you *and* Ray's old lady."

Toby's infidelity was common knowledge. That awareness made the knot in my stomach twist tighter. The pain forced me to drop back down onto my knees. Wrapping my arms around my stomach, I rocked myself, trying to repress the sensation when I felt Devlin's hand on the back of my neck. My skin prickled.

"Let go of me!" I tried pulling away from him, but he clamped down roughly and held me immobile. Dread bloomed rapidly in my heart.

Devlin dropped down next to me, practically ripping my arm from the socket, and pulled me back against him. I opened my mouth to scream, but a meaty hand clamped tightly against my throat making it impossible for any words to pass. Only able to pull in thin slips of air, I began to gag.

"I'm sorry. I almost wish I didn't have to do this to you," he said. "But this is his fault. I warned him I'd come for you if he tipped off the cops."

I jabbed my elbow backwards, connecting briefly with his ribs, but he only applied more pressure. Coiled in his thick, muscled arm, I was helpless. Devlin easily shifted me into the shadows of the old concrete building that housed the rustic beach bathrooms. At the north interior wall, he lurched forward, throwing himself on top of me. His massive body forced me down, slamming me into the compacted sand. All the breath left my lungs, and, for a moment, my mind went blank. Struggling to refill my lungs, I scratched at the thick arm that held me.

"Bitch," he howled as I dug my nails into him. Spittle formed on his lips, and his eyes went dark just before he raised his arm. The back of his giant hand clapped my face. The force spun my head round and I tasted blood. Dazed, I could do little to stop his hand as it slid over my chest and moved to the button fly of my jean shorts. He released his hold on my neck to tug at them.

No, no, no, I screamed in my head. Innately, I understood if I didn't stop him now, I would be forever ruined. I inhaled a lungful of air and screamed as loudly as I could.

My voice, dampened by the humid air, was shrill and wild. At the same time, I grabbed handfuls of Devlin's hair, yanking and ripping at it. With his weight on my legs, knees digging painfully into my shins, he tried to recapture my arms, but I twisted wildly under him, hitting his face.

My next memory is of a sudden loud grunt, followed by a spray of sand on my face. Devlin was gone, and I was left striking air.

I scrambled to my feet, shocked and panting, and saw two bodies locked in combat a few feet to my right. Their muffled grunts and angry jeers cut through the quiet night air. Devlin was now fighting off an attacker of his own.

Toby was over him. He slammed Devlin's head with his fists, over and over. It seemed to go on endlessly until finally Devlin stopped moving. Huffing, Toby fell to his knees.

Unable to move, I stared at them until a shadow came over me. Crouched low, I turned quickly, ready to strike. Ray looked at me, his face shadowed.

From behind me, Toby yelled, "Take her home!" For some reason, he was still with Devlin's motionless body. I wanted to look back, but I kept my eyes on this new threat. I stood Ray down with my glare, silently warning him to keep his distance. Again, Toby yelled, "Ray, you fucking take her home. Now!"

"Come on, Claudia. It's al-all right," Ray coaxed, but I wasn't falling for that. Not again.

"Don't touch me!" I hissed.

"Toby wants me to t-take you home," he urged.

"I'm not going anywhere with you," I snarled. He tried to take my arm, and I punched him in the face.

Ray moaned as he stumbled backwards, a hand over his eye.

The beach was quiet once again. All I heard was Toby's heavy breathing as he came closer.

"S-s-she won't let me t-t-ake her," Ray stuttered.

Toby was next to me, kneeling down. "Claude, come here."

He reached for me, and I fell into his arms, burying my face into his neck. In the safety of his embrace, I unraveled and began to weep.

He pressed my head into his shoulder and stroked my hair. "Shh, it's okay now, baby. It's okay." Putting an arm under my legs, he cradled me against him, and rose to his feet.

Toby carried me to the parking lot and put me into the passenger seat of the Jeep. He slid in after me. Ray jumped into the driver's seat and started to drive us up the block, toward my house.

Toby slipped an arm around my waist and gently tugged my chin upwards to examine my face.

"Are you hurt bad?" he asked, his eyes scanning me.

I twisted my head away from him. "I just want to go home," I cried.

He tucked me into him, his chin on top of my head. Under my cheek, his heart beat in frenzy as he exchanged words with Ray.

"You got it?" Ray asked him.

"Yeah," Toby answered.

At my house, Toby held me tight to his side and guided me up the walkway. Before we even got to the front door, my father came storming out of the house.

"Dad!" I cried and twisted towards him.

"What the hell did you do to my daughter?" Dad roared, ripping me from Toby's arms. Shaking and dizzy, I leaned heavily on my father.

"Dad, no," I tried to interrupt him, but he wouldn't listen.

"When I'm through with you, you'll be sorry you ever existed," Dad barked.

Toby bowed his head and took my father's blast.

"You do whatever you need to do. Arrest me now, if you want," he said, and then reaching into his pocket, pulled out a palm-sized object and handed it to my father. "This will make it easier."

Toby stood and waited for my father's reaction, but Dad, apparently taken aback by Toby's quick surrender, shook his head. "That's not necessary. I know where you live."

Accepting that, Toby turned and walked back to his Jeep. He and Ray drove away. As the taillights on the Jeep disappeared up the road, I looked down at my father's hand.

"What is it?" I asked.

Dad held open his palm for me to see. "A knife."

Chapter 35

~CLAUDIA~

DAD PUT IN A CALL to the precinct to pick up Devlin and drove me to the emergency room at Good Samaritan Hospital. I didn't initially want to go, but I had several cuts on my face and could feel, as well as see, bruises beginning to bloom all over my body. If Toby hadn't shown up when he had, I would also be having an internal exam. It was too terrifying a thought to dwell on.

It was a grueling few hours at the hospital. Everything was documented and my statement taken by detectives. I had to relive all that had happened in full detail. While I withdrew under my father's protective wing, Dad was all over it; he took names and made phone calls, all the while, snapping at the hospital staff as well as his colleagues. He was determined to make Devlin pay for what he'd done.

We were finishing up with the petite, dark-haired woman detective when Dad's cell rung. I watched his expression for clues about the call. After a few 'yeahs' and 'uh-huhs,' he hung up.

"Is there news?"

"Devlin Van Sloot is in custody, but there's been another … er, development," my father said, quietly. "A small house fire was called in. At the Faye house." He held up his hand when I jumped. "The fire was contained, but Toby is being treated for smoke inhalation."

I sagged against a nearby counter. "Are they bringing him to the ER?"

Dad nodded. "We can wait."

When Toby's arrival was confirmed, I walked to the curtained area where he was being treated. A man nearby was moaning in pain. I took a steadying breath before I pushed through the curtain.

Bare-chested and wearing only jeans, Toby was lying on the hospital bed staring up at the ceiling. He had an oxygen mask over his face and an I.V. tube attached to one arm.

The roll of the curtain in its tracks drew his attention to me. He put his head back on the pillow and closed his eyes, but suddenly lifted the oxygen mask from his face. I steeled myself and waited for him to rant and object to my presence. Instead, he broke out into a wheezy, bark-like cough that lasted several minutes. The person in the next area groaned again. I seized the opportunity to move close to him.

He smelled like a campfire and looked even worse than earlier. Besides his unshaved face and unruly hair, he had swollen lips, a blackened eye, and a long, thin cut across his cheek.

I inhaled and tightened my resolve. "Don't worry. I'm not staying. I heard about the fire, and I wanted to make sure you were all right. What happened? How did it start?"

Without looking at me, in a croaky voice that was painful to listen to, he said, "I started it. I lit the stove and threw dishtowels on it. I wanted to burn it down."

"Your own house?"

"I know, it was a stupid thing to do. After I did it, I started to freak out." He stared at the ceiling, his coarse voice eerily calm. "I realized I was burning down the only thing I have left of Julia. Of us." He draped an arm over his eyes, drawing my eyes to his raw, scraped knuckles. "I went inside and tried to put it out, but the flames were too big. That's when the fire department came."

"You're lucky you weren't more seriously hurt." I focused on a neutral spot over his head because if I kept looking at him it would break me.

A long, awkward pause between us drew my notice and I peeked at him. He was staring hard at me, his eyes scouring my bruised arms, my neck, and finally my face.

"Oh, Jesus, Claude, your face! I can't believe what that fucking asshole did to you." He lifted a hand as if he were going to touch me, but pulled back and fisted his hair instead. "I saw him follow you away from my house. Ray and I took off after him, but it wasn't until I drove to your house that I realized you'd gone to the beach instead." He dropped his hands in his lap. "I never wanted you to get hurt."

"I'm fine. And I certainly don't blame you for what happened," I replied, eyes low. God how I hurt, but the hurt was much more than physical. That he couldn't bring himself to even touch me, the hurt seeped from my heart into my limbs, quickly weakening me. I edged near the curtain opening, unable to tolerate him looking at me anymore. Skimming the fabric with my fingers, I prepared to leave.

I stopped, though. I had one last question. "What about that knife? Why did you take it from Devlin?"

"It has my fingerprints on it," he said. Just as I opened my mouth to question him, he continued, "It's not how it sounds. I held it once, the day after Dev stabbed the guy."

"Why didn't you tell me?"

He shrugged. "I knew you'd worry."

I met his eyes. "Worry. I suppose it's unavoidable when you love someone."

He lowered his chin and let out a tired breath. He didn't want my love, or any love. He'd already told me that.

I pushed past my anger. "So you wiped the knife clean before you gave it to my father?" He shook his head and I stared at him blankly. "But that means…"

"It doesn't matter," he mumbled.

"Of course, it matters," I said. "You weren't there. You shouldn't be punished."

"I've done plenty wrong."

"I won't stand by and let you get arrested."

"Claude, just let it be," he said.

"No. I won't. And I'm not listening to you anymore because obviously you don't know what you're saying," I said, annoyed with his stupidity.

He swung his legs over the side of the mattress and slipped off the bed. He came towards me, only to be stopped by the end of his I.V. tube. I could only stare as he yanked the needle out of his arm and came right up to me. He didn't try to touch me, but his nearness finally broke me, and I had to cover my mouth to stifle the cry on my lips. My reaction seemed to make him angrier.

"Leave me alone," he ordered, and yanked open the curtain.

"Go."

I saw dark red flowing down his arm. Blood. A lot of it. "Your arm!" I shrieked.

He looked down at the blood pooling on the floor. I rushed into the main corridor and called a nurse. Immediately, a scrub-clad woman followed me to Toby's area. He sat impatiently on the bed as the nurse bandaged his arm and admonished him about removing the I.V.

We had nothing left to say, and I quickly slipped out the curtained area and headed back to my father.

Dad was chatting amiably with the woman detective. Upon seeing me, she nodded and turned to him.

"Don, I'll call you when I know anything new," she said, and patted my father's arm.

"Wait, Detective," I called to her retreating back, and she came back. "I just learned that my boyfriend—I mean, Toby Faye—handled the knife that killed Velerio. But I swear to you, he had nothing to do with the stabbing." I implored her to believe me. "He came home that night."

She looked at my dad as if seeking permission to respond. Dad nodded.

"Let's see what the crime lab report shows. You might advise him to hire a lawyer. Besides you, is there anyone who can attest to his whereabouts that night?"

"Other than Ray Rudack, I'm not sure."

"We'll ask around," Dad said. We said our goodbyes to the detective and started towards the parking lot.

"I think by handing over the knife, Toby hopes to be incriminated." I stared into the distance, at the long shadows the lot lights cast, as we walked.

Dad glanced at me. "Why would he do that?"

"As punishment. He blames himself for his mother's death. He had a fight with her, said some upsetting things before she had the heart attack."

"That's a hell of a thing to live with. A whole lot of guilt." Dad squeezed my shoulders. "Sometimes we're tougher and meaner to those we love the most. A tragic event usually makes you realize how much someone means to you—and that you really ought to treat them better."

We arrived at the car, and, as my father opened the door for me, I thought about all the awful things I'd done and said to him in the last few months. How hard I'd tried to push him away. How would I feel if he was not here with me anymore, if he were suddenly ripped away from me? It was too awful to imagine.

"Dad, I'm sorry I went against your advice and left the house tonight, and I'm sorry too, for keeping my application to USC a secret. I promise to try to communicate with you better."

"I appreciate that." He kissed the top of my head. "Now, let's go home."

Home. The word alone made me long for solitude, a safe zone where I could drop the weight of the last few days and pull inward.

Chapter 36

~CLAUDIA~

I SPENT THE NEXT FEW DAYS tackling my room. Since I was going away to school, organizing all of my stuff was a necessary job and also a purposeful distraction.

While I cleaned and sorted through my childhood bedroom, the criminal case was broadcast all over the local news. The county prosecutor claimed they had enough evidence to convict. I'd been summoned to give preliminary testimony. It looked like Ricardo Velerio's murder was finally solved, and it seemed certain that Devlin Van Sloot was going to prison.

I went through my closet and moved to my dresser. I sorted through each drawer deciding what would stay and what would come with me to USC, when I came across my favorite wool mittens. No use for those in sunny L.A.

I put them in a box and went to tuck the box into to the back of my closet, but stopped. They would stay there, ignored, until perhaps I came back and unearthed them from their dark, out-of-the-way space. It seemed too cruel a fate. I clutched them to my chest and slid to the floor.

Dad came into my room and saw me sitting on the floor, holding the mittens. He sat down on the bed facing me.

"Are you all right?"

"How can I leave?" I squeezed the mittens in my hands. "What happened to Toby, it's not fair. He'll needs someone to lean on. Maybe I can delay my start date."

"Listen, Claudia," he said calmly. "It's noble to want to help this guy, but you've been through a lot the last few days. You need to think of yourself for once."

"Dad, his mother just died. He has no one."

"He still has an aunt. And besides, what do you think you can do for him?"

A valid question.

"Maybe nothing more than just be here for him," I said. "I don't know if he'd even let me do that. He's ... he's not been quite himself since Mrs. Faye died."

Dad eyed me. "Claudia, be honest with me. Did he hurt you?"

I pressed my lips together. "He did something really awful, and it hurt me, but he never physically harmed me."

"What did he do?"

I shook my head. I would never tell him. "He broke my heart," was all I could manage to say before I crumbled.

My father pulled me onto the bed to sit beside him. "It's all right, baby girl. It's all right," he murmured and rubbed my back to sooth me. "What can I do to make it better for you?"

I didn't have to think about the answer.

"Be okay with letting me go to California," I said.

Dad stroked his mustache thoughtfully. "I don't know if I'll ever be okay with letting you go, but if this is what you really want, I'll support your decision."

I gave him a quick smile and then bit my lip.

"What else?" he asked.

"I want to leave as soon as I can, to stay with Mom, until the semester starts."

He visually stiffened.

"No—"

"Dad, I'll be miserable sitting around here. If I can't help Toby, I need to be somewhere else."

Dad blew out and nodded. "Okay."

I pressed my lips together, only marginally relieved.

"What? There's more?" he asked.

"No, it's just that..." I sighed, unable to meet his eyes. "You're going to think I'm crazy, but as much as I want to go, I'm also terrified to leave."

"Oh, *bella faccia*." He laughed in exasperation. Raising my chin to make me look him in the eye, he said, "Despite the constant waterworks, you're much tougher than you look. You have a way of digging in and getting it done. I've always been proud of that."

He smiled. "And really, you got this, kid."

Dad insisted on attending Mrs. Faye's wake with me and held my arm as I entered the funeral home. He gave me the strength I needed to face the death of the woman I'd come to love.

The room was crowded with beautiful flower arrangements, and many of the churchwomen I'd seen at the house were there. Toby stood at the front with his aunt. Despite the scabbed-over cut on his cheek and the yellowy remnants of a blackened left eye, he looked handsome in a black suit and white dress shirt. The blue-gray of his checked tie matched his eyes.

Dad went forward to pay his respects and left me to greet the women I knew. I embraced the warmth of the church ladies who seemed to understand how much Mrs. Faye had come to mean to me. Toby, on the other hand, stood stiffly, clearly uncomfortable accepting the touches, pats, and occasional hugs put upon him.

I stayed back, but from across the room, Toby's eyes met mine. Neither of us smiled, but I couldn't look away. His stance, the stiff tilt of chin was a distinct mark of his anger; warning signs for me to keep my distance. My father's hand on my shoulder made me break the staring match. Dad motioned for me to go up and pay my respects.

"I'm going," I whispered, more to myself than him.

By sheer force of will, I walked to the front of the room and knelt in front of Mrs. Faye's casket. Draped in a light blue dress, her slender hands folded over each other and wrapped with a string of rosary beads, she looked peaceful, like I could reach out and give her shoulder a little shake and she'd open her eyes and smile.

"I know you're in a better place, free of your sickly body, but selfishly, I miss you." I pressed my hands together in prayer. "I know, too, you'd want me to help Toby through this, through losing you, but—" The words caught in my throat. I swallowed hard and tried again. "I want to help him, so very much, but he won't let me. Please forgive me for not being able to do more." I kissed her cool, lifeless cheek. "Be happy in heaven and know I will remember our talks, always."

I bowed my head recited the Lord's Prayer and with finality, I stepped away from the casket.

I waited in the receiving line behind a few older people. They were talking, reminiscing about Mrs. Faye, but they were also murmuring about my attack.

They say he got there just in time.

Look at the bruises on her face.

When I reached Aunt Joan, I hugged her tight.

"I'm so sorry. She was a special woman, and I loved her," I whispered in her ear.

"I know you did." She pulled back and her gaze hovered on my face. "Oh, honey, your face. I can't believe what happened to you."

Shaking, I took her hand in mine. "I'm fine, really. Is there anything I can do to help?"

"The church ladies have it covered," she said, her expression stoic and very much like Mrs. Faye's. "But thank you, and thank you for taking such good care of my sister. Julia adored you." She hugged me again, her lips pressing a firm kiss on my temple.

I braced myself to move forward in the line, toward Toby, but a flurry of activity caught my eye. April and Dario had arrived and were swerving through the crowd to reach us.

Dario hugged me, and April coasted into Toby's arms. He burrowed his face into her shoulder, his grief evident, and April held him tightly, rubbing his back and whispering to him. Jealousy had no place here, but it rose in me like an evil beast.

First he'd gone to Ray's mother, had spent the night being consoled in her bed. Now he allowed my best friend to comfort him. It hurt that April could so easily do what I could not. It was blatantly apparent that it was me, and only me, Toby didn't want.

When April let go, Dario pulled him into a hug, and April took my hand.

"Come on, Toby needs a break," she said.

The four of us left the warm, crowded reception area and gathered in the foyer lounge.

"How are you holding up?" I heard Dario ask Toby.

He blinked slowly and shrugged. "I hate these things," he said, pulling at his collar. His face was drawn, and he looked worn out.

"Let's get you some water," April said. Dario followed her to the water cooler behind us. The two of them moved together effortlessly, and, again, I felt jealous of my friend. Toby and I would never get to that level.

April and I sat down on an overly embellished settee, and Dario handed me a little triangular paper cup with icy cold water in it. Toby perched on the edge of a matching embellished chair. He did not look at or talk to me.

April said to me, "We have to get together before you leave. When are you going?"

"Next week," I told her. "I decided to go early and spend some time with my mother."

Without saying anything, Toby stood up and walked away. We all watched as he went out the back entrance of the funeral home. I twisted my mouth, willing myself not to cry. "I could delay it, but I don't see the point."

April hugged me.

"Try not to worry. Dario and I will be here. We'll keep an eye on him," she said.

A moment later, Dad came out and asked if I was ready to go. I nodded, and he said he would get the car.

I hugged my friends goodbye and made my way toward the back entrance. Outside, the night air hadn't cooled much, but everything was wet from the humidity. Toby was leaning with his shoulder against a portico column, smoking a cigarette and staring out into the back parking lot.

I stepped behind him and pressed my hand to his back. His body tensed at my touch, and I choked back a cry of frustration.

"I just wanted to say goodbye," I said.

Without turning around, he mumbled, "Okay."

I squeezed my eyes shut. I hated his unrelenting stubbornness. After what he did, how did he justify being so horrible to me?

As I went to move away, he caught my forearm. Flexing his warm fingers over my skin, he whispered, "I'm sorry."

His voice had a subtle inflection of anguish. Though I suspected he really meant it, the rift between us felt like a continental divide. With all that had transpired between us in the last few days, there was no fixing it. We could never go back.

I bit my lip and nodded. "Yeah. I'm sorry, too."

And then I left.

Chapter 37

~TOBY~

THE DAYS FOLLOWING JULIA'S DEATH passed with me in a giant, silent bubble. Lots of people spoke to me, offered the typical condolences and stuff, but I didn't want to talk, not to anyone. My aunt had handled conversing, and buffered me from most of the happenings, handling details, telling me where to be and when to go.

It was sunny on the day of Julia's burial. The funeral service was quiet and respectful. She would've said it was nice. I tried my best to tolerate the kindness everyone offered, but I had to hold myself above it. When the small gathering sang "On Eagle's Wings" inside the church, I'd nearly lost my shit.

After the last few stragglers walked away from the burial site at the parish cemetery, Claudia's father came up to me. Claudia kept her distance, as I preferred.

"I'm sorry son. It's never easy to lose your mother," he said, his hand gripping my shoulder. "Why don't you stop by the house tomorrow, sometime after dinner. I'd like to discuss what's happening with the investigation."

The following evening, I did as he asked. I thought Claudia might be there, but it was just the old man and me at the kitchen table.

He made himself a cup of decaffeinated coffee and asked me if I wanted some.

I refused. I wondered if Claudia knew I was there.

He sat down across from me. "I spoke to your boss, Abe Bernbaum—who, by the way, spoke rather well of you," he said, sounding surprised by Abe's approval. I might not like the old codger, but I'd always given him a good day's work. "And, lucky for you, Mr. Bernbaum has an excellent memory. He remembered running into you on the street the night of the stabbing. It puts you away from the scene of the crime. Being that Bernbaum is a respected community member, I'd say your alibi is secure."

I'd steeled myself for the worse. This outcome was unexpected. I leaned forward hiding my face as relief washed over me.

The sound of his cup touching down onto the table made me look up.

"I've heard the whole story, and I'm aware Van Sloot was threatening you. But the fact is, you continued to put yourself, and more importantly, Claudia, at risk," he sighed. Suddenly, his chair scraped against the floor. He stood and paced the floor like a caged animal. "I understand you've been through a lot and that my daughter cares for you, but it's taking a lot of restraint on my part not to kick your ass."

My stomach coiled around his words, but he had every right to feel that way. I had let this happen. I hadn't been able to keep Dev from getting at Claudia. The image of Dev over her, touching her, haunted me every night. I had to respond, say something. I rubbed my forehead hard, so hard it hurt, but then I straightened my shoulders and met his eyes.

"Mr. Chiametti, I'm pissed at myself for letting Claudia get hurt. She didn't deserve what happened to her. None of this was her fault, and I take full responsibility for what happened," I said. "At the time this all went down, my mother was very sick, and I didn't want to get involved. I only took the knife from Van Sloot because he threatened to use it against me."

Claudia's father seemed to calm a little. He sat back down and reclaimed his coffee cup. "While those reasons may be all well and good, there can be legal ramifications. You could be indicted for obstruction of justice."

He pulled a business card out of his breast pocket and slid it across the table to me. It had the name of an attorney on it. "With Rudack's sworn testimony, you should be cleared of any involvement, but if you need legal counsel, he's a good guy."

I rubbed at a crick in my neck. I'd been so uptight, everything felt stiff.

"Thank you," I said and picked up the card. I rose to my feet and hesitantly held out my hand to him.

Mr. Chiametti eyed me briefly before he finally shook my hand. "You're welcome, son, but before I let you go, I want you to promise to talk to Claudia. She won't say what happened between you two, but it's obvious you wronged her. I think you need to straighten that out. You owe my daughter a debt of gratitude. She went to bat for you."

Not able to look at him, I lowered my eyes. "I will," I agreed. "Is she here? I'd like to see her now—if that's okay."

"Not tonight," he said. "She's resting. Another time. It's been a difficult week for all of us."

The door clicked shut behind me. On my way to my Jeep, I glanced over my shoulder up at Claudia's bedroom window, imagining what she was doing and what was going through her mind.

April had chastised me at the funeral home after Claudia had left. "Stop being so mean to Claudia. She loved your mom. Think about how difficult this is for her."

It was true. I'd known it in my heart, seen it as she leaned over Julia's body, crying, her face pale, when she'd said goodbye. But Claudia had made me look death in the face. I'd felt hurt and betrayed and I hadn't been able to soften myself to her.

Now that my world was quiet again, I could see the path of destruction that lie in my wake. I went after Claudia as if she had been responsible for all my pain. I shredded her and amputated the best part of me.

I needed to see her, to hear her voice, to hold her and tell her I was sorry, but until I worked out what happened with Diane, I couldn't expect her forgiveness.

I waited until I knew Ray had gone to work to stop in to see his mother.

She went to pour me a drink, but I shook my head.

"I need to know about the night I came here, after my mother died. I'm not sure what happened. It's all a blur. All I know is when I got up, my pants were unzipped."

She laughed. "I had to help you take a piss. That was quite an experience."

"But I was in bed with you. Did anything happen between us?" I pressed for details.

"It certainly had the potential to turn into something more."
Her eyes met mine. "But you were so sad and lost that night, I felt
bad. I just held you. Eventually you fell asleep."

We didn't. I hadn't.

I closed my eyes as a sense of relief once again washed over me.

"Sorry you had to put up with me," I mumbled.

"Ah, I'm no saint." She waved at me. "But I do have some scru-
ples."

"Thank you," I said and gave her a hug. "I have to go. I need to
talk to someone."

I stood in the Chiametti driveway again, barely an hour after I'd
left, staring up at Claudia's window. The light in her room was on.
Now that I'd spoken to Diane, I needed to see her, but I didn't
dare knock on the door after the old man had told me to come
back another night. I'd easily vaulted off the porch roof the morning after we'd been together. It wouldn't be hard to get back up.

I anchored my foot on the porch railing and hoisted myself up
onto the roof. Keeping low, I scaled the short distance to her window and rapped on the glass. Inside, the sound of muffled footsteps
came closer.

"Claude," I called loud enough for her to hear, but hopefully not
so loud her father overheard.

"Toby?" She pulled the curtain aside and concentrated on
unlocking and pulling open the window.

Not giving her a chance to stop me, I dove through the window,
Navy Seal-style, and rolled to my feet.

Claudia stepped back, her eyebrows furrowed. "What the hell
are you doing?"

"I came to see you."

"You're crazy," she said and pointed back at the window. "You
need to leave. Turn around and crawl right back out."

I shook my head. "No. I'm not leaving until we talk."

"My father's downstairs." She crossed her arms defensively. "I'll
call him up."

At the taunt, I lifted my eyes to hers, daring her to carry it out.
"Go ahead. I'm still not leaving, Claude. I have something important to tell you."

Impatient, she sighed, "Then say it and go."

"I spoke to Diane."

"Who the hell's Diane?"

"Ray's mother." Recognition lit her eyes, and they narrowed in anger.

"How nice. You talked for a change."

"Nothing happened between us."

She arched an eyebrow. "Then why would you say something did? Even Devlin seemed to think there was something going on between you two."

"Dev doesn't know shit," I snapped but pulled back. It wouldn't do any good to lose my temper. More calmly, I said, "I was upset. She only slept with me."

"So, you were in bed with her!"

"Yeah, but that was the only time and I wasn't with her. We didn't have sex. She consoled me. She said I fell asleep next to her. Actually, I passed out."

I wanted to touch her, to assure her Diane meant nothing, but as I moved closer, she stepped back.

"Oh, great, there is such a thing as a happy ending after all," she bit out. "Thanks for clarifying that. Now get out."

"I thought if you knew what really happened, it might somehow make a difference." I lowered my voice and took a tentative step closer. "Claude, I miss you."

She scowled and put her hands on her hips in answer to my confession.

"Are you trying to tell me if you hadn't passed out, you still wouldn't have done anything?"

"No, I don't think so," I told her.

"You don't *think* so?" she snorted. "By your own admission, you were hammered. I'd say we're both aware that being in that condition lowers inhibitions. I might be naïve about a lot of things, but I don't believe what happened in Diane's bedroom was as 'G-rated' as you claim."

I looked away. I wanted to focus on the fact that nothing had actually happened, but there was no denying it could've happened.

"Do you understand how much trust and faith it took for me to be intimate with you? Was I just another piece of ass to you? My virginity some kind of trophy?"

"Come on Claude, you know it was never like that."

"Why should I believe you? Since that night you've been mean, said terrible things, and held me at a distance. And you know what? I still could've forgiven you for everything. But running from me into the arms of another woman to ease your grief?" She shook her hands at me. "I can't get past that. I can't."

"I didn't have sex with her. And while I might've kept some things from you, I never lied to you," I persisted.

"How can you say that? That night out in my yard, I thought that was love. At least it was for me, but you don't love me. You never have." She choked back a sob, but her eyes reignited with anger. "It must be true, because you've never said it. Not once.

"You made me believe you were better than the guy who avoided me all last week, a guy who curses, smokes and drinks, and takes his hurt and anger out on others." Claudia clenched her hands into fists at her sides. "So apparently, you were right the other night, Toby. Until now I hadn't seen the real you. And being in love with the 'real' you hurts. I should've never agreed to go out with you in the first place. I'd rather be alone than be with the kind of guy you are." Once again, she pointed purposefully at the window. "Now get out!"

As I stood there, not making any motion to go, she suddenly lurched forward and shoved me, hard. Not expecting it, I stumbled back a step. A flash of heat rose up my neck.

"Go! Get out!" she yelled. Her voice cracked despite her fury, and tears streamed unchecked down her face. I could tell she wanted to hate me right then, but I knew she didn't.

I stared at her, our eyes held for a long, intense moment. I willed her to forgive me, to take me back, to love me again.

"Claudia," I whispered and reached for her.

She trapped her lip between her teeth and moved closer. For a second, I thought she was going to hug me, but her eyes were dark … and hard. Then I realized she was aiming to hit me. Bracing myself, I closed my eyes. She pummeled my chest with her balled fists.

"I said, go! Get out!" she yelled with each blow.

I didn't try to stop her, just let her hit me. She wanted to hurt me. She needed to. And I needed to let her. I would've let her continue, but the sound of her crying and spiraling so out of control tore me apart. Cursing under my breath, I captured her arms and pinned them at her sides.

I held her tightly to me.

"Stop it," I ordered. She tried to pull away, but after a few useless attempts, she stopped struggling. "Please, Claudia, I'm really trying here."

Closing her eyes, she stilled. With her body pressed against mine, my body heated up, and I was slammed with that familiar ache for her. Holding her with one arm, I pressed my mouth to her temple and stroked her back in an effort to calm her. But my touch set her off in a whole other round of squirming.

There was a loud, forceful knock at the bedroom door.

"Is everything all right in there?" Her father's voice threw me into a panic. I wasn't finished. I hadn't gotten to do what I'd come for.

Claudia glowered up at me obviously waiting for me to react. Her tight smile told me her father's interruption was welcomed. She would not defend me being there. I was on my own. My heart thundered in my chest. I looked at her face, but then the door swung open, and her father's broad-shouldered build filled the doorway.

Even as this guy, who never wanted his daughter to have anything to do with me, stood surveying the scene with a kick-ass expression on his face, I did not let her go.

Chapter 38

~CLAUDIA~

"SIR, I'M SORRY WE DISTURBED you," Toby said with a timorous respect. "I've only been trying to talk to Claudia. She's making it pretty damn hard."

"How the hell did you get back in?" Dad glared at him. "The window?"

Toby nodded, and Dad's eyes flew to the open window. Instead of his typical response, he actually smirked—like he found the situation amusing!

"Dad," I struggled in protest against Toby's restraint of me. "Make him leave."

Dad put his hands on his hips and eyed Toby. Instead of sending him packing, Dad shook his head.

"Well, now, baby, I don't believe you're in any real danger here, and since you've been telling me over and over again to let you take care of yourself—that's just what I'm going to let you do."

"What the...?" I almost cursed out loud. "Dad?"

"Claudia, you got this." Dad smiled and looked more seriously at my captor. "Toby, take it easy on my daughter. Don't give me an excuse to come back up here. When you two are done talking, you'll leave through the front door. Understood?"

"Yes, sir." Toby nodded, and my father, muttering about the window, pulled the door shut.

I didn't know whether to laugh or cry.

The silence between us was heavy until Toby loosened his hold on me. "I'll leave once we've finished talking, okay?"

"Fine. Talk." I pushed away from him and perched on the edge of my bed.

I chewed at my cuticles while he drifted over to a wall of shelves and browsed my dusty high school memorabilia, the only stuff I hadn't purged my room of.

"I don't know how to explain anything I've done other than to say, I didn't think. I just reacted," he said without looking at me.

I took several calming breaths, doing my best to cap my anger. We'd hit bottom; it wasn't possible to go any lower.

Twisting my fingers together, I finally spoke, "When you called me in California, and told me about your mother, all I could think about was coming home to be with you. I expected to mourn with you—to hold you, to cry with you. No one should have to go through the death of a loved one alone." Despite my resolve to remain detached, my voice quaked. "But what I came home to wasn't the guy who'd spent the night and crawled out my window a week earlier. You just walked off—you left me, Toby. You were so mean, it made me numb."

He spun around and wrung his hands. "I was already angry with you because you didn't want me in California with you, but then you tricked me into going to the hospital. It wrecked me to watch Julia die after saying what I did." His gazed dropped to his feet. "I shouldn't have blamed you. I shouldn't have left you, either. You have to understand, I've always dealt with this kind of stuff by myself. I never considered someone might need me."

"You didn't seem to want or need me, either." I choked on the last word and my eyes became awash with fresh tears.

His face fell.

"Claude." He knelt down before me and wrapped his arms around my waist. "I didn't know what I needed. I'm sorry I didn't stay with you." He crumbled into me, his head heavy in my lap.

It'd been a long time since he'd let me touch him, and I took comfort now in being able to do so. I folded over him and pressed my face into his broad back, letting the soft cotton of his T-shirt absorb my tears. We stayed together, woven in our awkward embrace, weakened by the loss that both held us together and tore us apart.

"I can't believe she's gone," he whispered as his warm tears trickled down my bare legs. I gently stroked his hair. I was mentally and physically fatigued, but he was finally sharing his pain with me, and it felt cathartic.

He wiped his face on his sleeve and sat up, to look at me. Only then did I see the dark shadows under his blue-gray eyes. He looked like a wounded warrior—tired and weary—and my heart twinged at the thought of what he was going through.

He searched my face before he reached up and put his palm on my cheek. "I hate that I was so mean to you," he said hoarsely. "This is hard for me. I've never felt this lost before."

"I know. Things will be different without your mom around. It'll take time to get used to, but you will. First though, you have to stop drinking and smoking," I said. "And your anger, Toby. You really have to learn to control it."

He leaned back against the bed, draping an arm over my leg, and looked up at me. "Claudia, help me. I can't do this without you."

Our shared grief and his admission of regret had softened me, but I had spent the last week counting down to my departure, trying not to think about him.

"I can delay my flight, for a week or two."

"No, don't go. Stay with me. I'll do whatever it takes to make this right between us."

My heart felt like it was being pulled from opposite directions. I wanted to help Toby, but for the past year, I'd put my energies into getting into USC, and I wanted that, too.

He saw my hesitation and rushed on.

"Claude, listen, the stuff I did and said, it doesn't mean anything. It's behind us now. Everything I do from now on will be about you and me." He moved to sit next to me on the bed and put his arms around me. "Being with you will make me better."

The weight of his need sat heavy on my chest. "Toby, I can't make you better."

"But being with you helps. I'm more focused around you."

"I'll help you with whatever you need. Anything, you name it," I said, struggling to get out from under the weight. "But I'll be doing it as your friend."

"My friend?" he snarled and snapped to his feet. "We're way past the fucking friend thing."

His anger startled me, and my back stiffened. "If you're going to get mean, you better leave right now."

He ran a hand through his hair and steadied himself. "You still love me. I know you do."

The yoke upon my shoulders grew heavier.

"Toby, I can't go back to where we were. I don't know how to move past what's happened. Honestly, I don't think I can."

"You won't even try?" The question came out strangled.

"I've lived my life playing it safe—you've always known that about me. Now that I've seen this other side of you, it won't be the same for me."

"I can go back to being the guy you know. I will. I promise," he pleaded, once again sinking to his knees and pulling me to him.

The wounded plea devastated me, but still, I knew myself— knew I could never feel the way I did a few weeks ago.

"It isn't as simple as making a promise." I wiped the wetness from my eyes and moved away from him. I needed to give him other reasons, concrete ones he could accept. "I'm leaving for California in a couple of days. I'll be in a new city, at a new school and taking on some pretty tough classes. I'll be stressed enough. Our relationship is too much to handle right now."

Without warning, he sprung from the bed and whirled around. His face was red and his eyes dark. "So that's it? You're just going to break up with me—when I need you most?" His words stung. I could only blink; my insides recoiled, ready for an outburst. "Then just forget it. Forget that I asked anything."

"Come on, Toby. Don't be that way. I'll still delay my flight and stay to help you," I stood up and went to him, but he yanked open my bedroom door.

"Don't bother. I don't need your help. I don't need anyone's help. Have a great life in California!" he roared, slamming the door shut behind him. The sounds of his footsteps were loud as he barreled down the stairs. When the front door wrenched closed, the house shook with the force of his anger. I ran to my window and watched as he strode to his Jeep, jumped in and tore out, tires screeching.

Letting him go wasn't easy, but I knew deep down inside I had to.

Even so, as the red Jeep drove out of sight, I felt broken all over again.

Chapter 39

~TOBY~

I STOPPED AFTER WORK TO GET a case of beer. My only plan for the night was to play my guitar and drink. I'd gone back to my job at the appliance store the week after the funeral. It wasn't like I was eager to get back to work, but I felt like I owed that much to Abe. The old guy had really come through for me.

I kept moving, going through the necessary motions. I got up, went to work, did my job, and when it was time to go home, I left. Each night, I came home to an empty house, a blatant reminder that Julia was gone, and I was on my own.

"If there's anything I can do, just call," the funeral folks said, one by one, as they left that day. As if I would call. As if I would ever ask for their help. And, as expected, I hadn't heard from any of them. They all faded back into their mediocre, Stepford lives, leaving me alone.

When I pulled up to the driveway that night, Claudia's car was in front of the house.

She was neither in her car nor in the house. I pulled out a bottle of beer and stashed the remainder of the case in the fridge. I saw her then, through the charred remains of the kitchen window. She was in Julia's garden—the project that had started it all. On her hands and knees, she was pulling weeds, her dark hair twisted in a tight ponytail.

My fingers twitched. I wanted to go over, set her hair free and watch it fall about her face. I wanted to trace the freckles that ran across the bridge of her nose. I wanted her to rise up on her toes to kiss me, like she used to.

Just as it had been back in school so long ago, she was out of my reach. Once again, unattainable. Emptiness washed over me.

I had tried to explain away my behavior, tried to pull her back to me, but the fallout was too much. She'd gotten a good look at the guy I'd camouflaged over the last few months, and she'd made it clear that loser wasn't for her.

Glued to my spot, I watched her like a voyeur, absorbing the sight of her like a junkie. She was my drug, and I was already starting to shake from withdrawal. I debated with myself about whether or not I should go out to her. Knowing her, after the way we left things last week, her conscience was probably bothering her, and I was sure her visit was a mission to make it right.

I could've left. She would never even know I'd been home, but like an addict, I needed to get closer. I needed a fix.

I moved through the back door and, without her noticing, stood silently nearby. She was absorbed in her work, oblivious to everything but what she was doing. I watched her for a few moments, remembering the day we'd started the garden and how cute her dirt-smudged face was when she realized I was checking her out.

"What's the matter, not enough weeds in your own yard to keep you busy?"

The spade in her hand jerked in surprise.

"Oh, hey." She stopped and glanced up.

The motion revealed the bruise on her opposite cheek. It seemed to have grown in size, seeping from under her eye to the corner of her lip. Seeing it again, I felt both angry and ashamed that I'd had a hand in letting it happen. But it was her look of uncertainty that slammed me.

"I was waiting for you and well … I just figured…," she said.

I had to look away from her face and eyed the flowerbed instead. All of the plants were shriveled. Some were dead.

"I let it go. I didn't keep it up."

"You've had other things to worry about." Claudia surveyed the garden, then looked back at me. "But it's not completely gone. With a little bit of attention and some care, it can be fixed."

I popped the top off my beer. "Are you talking about the garden? 'Cause it kind of sounds like you might be talking about me."

A tight smile flitted across her lips before she turned her attention back to the flowers.

I settled down at the top of the deck steps with my beer and

watched her. Didn't she know that when you broke up with someone, you were supposed to stay away from him? It would be easier
if she stayed away—at least easier for me. She seemed unaffected,
indifferent, while I was destroyed.

I didn't offer to help as she finished weeding. After a time, she
stood and went to the side of the house, reappearing again with
the hose and sprinkler. She moved about with a comfortable
knowledge of the yard that depressed me. I'd blown the best thing
I'd ever had—blown it big time. My head felt heavy, and unable to
look at her anymore, I let it drop onto my forearms.

I hadn't heard her come up to me, but suddenly she was sitting
down next to me. I took a sip of my beer and looked out into the
yard. She reached out and put her hand around the bottle. I don't
know why, but I let her take it from me. She put the beer down
on the other side of her and eyed the cigarette pack in my shirt
pocket.

"I hate that you're smoking again."

"What's it to you?" I didn't even attempt to hide my annoyance.

"But you quit."

"Yeah, well, I'm back to doing a lot of shit I stopped doing."
When she sighed, the flames continued to rise. "Why are you
here? What do you want?"

"I wanted to tell you I'm sorry for yelling at you the other day.
And for hitting you, too. You've been through a lot. It was …" she
faltered. "It was wrong. I don't usually go around hitting people.
Even when I'm angry."

I understood her anger and her need to hit me, but it couldn't
stop the little spur of hope that wiggled its way in, and I kept quiet.

"And," she continued, "I understand what you're going through.
I can't compare my situation to yours, but I know what it's like to
lose someone."

"If you think losing a grandparent compares to what I've gone
through, you are seriously mistaken," I said with a grunt. "You
couldn't possibly know anything about what it's like to be me. My
whole family is wiped out."

"Your brother…"

"As far as I'm concerned, I don't have a brother."

She hesitated, obviously picking her words carefully before continuing. "Um, well, it's true, my experiences with death probably

don't compare in your eyes, but it's the pain of losing someone that I empathize with," she said quietly. "And, though it's not death, my parents' divorce was like losing someone, too. What makes a difference is that I had someone to talk to. I had someone to lean on."

"I thought you were my someone. My bad."

I saw the quick intake of breath and knew my words hurt her, but I didn't care.

"I really wish I could be what you need me to be. I wish I could make you happy again," she choked.

I caught her hand and pressed it against my chest. "Claude, you can make me happy."

She bowed her head. "Toby, that's not fair. You're asking too much of me. It's too much to ask of anyone."

I dropped her hand. I wasn't even angry with her, just annoyed that I'd even gone there, opening myself up to the pain.

"You're right." Frustrated, I stood up and grabbed my beer from next to her. "Well, thanks for coming by."

I went in the house hoping she would leave, but she followed me inside.

"You—oh." She stopped mid-sentence and covered her mouth when she caught sight of the fire-damaged kitchen.

I'd forgotten she hadn't been in the house since the fire. I hadn't fixed anything. The flames had eaten through the interior wall and surfaces of the back part of the kitchen. I saw it now for the first time through someone else's eyes—the blackened stovetop, dull and sooty, the burned back wallboard up over the sink and around the window. The ceiling was scorched like a Rorschach test, an uneven inkblot fanning out overhead. The once yellow, checkered curtain that Julia had hung over the window, now an uneven curl of melted fibers. The harsh lingering smell of fire was inescapable.

The burn of embarrassment crept up my neck. I couldn't look at it. And I didn't want to witness Claudia's expression as she looked at it either. I escaped to the living room, away from the reminder of the spectacular feat I'd performed that day.

I dropped onto the couch and picked up the television remote. Claudia followed me, saying nothing about the kitchen and pulled out a folded piece of paper from her back pocket.

"My father gave me the name of a counselor. He comes highly recommended." She held the information out to me, but I didn't take it.

"So that's the real reason you're here."

"You need to talk to someone," she said.

"Claude, just stop. I don't believe in all that emotional, psycho-babble shit."

She sat down on the coffee table in front of me, her hand absently gliding over the smooth surface before she came to look into my eyes.

"Counseling can help you come to terms with your mother's death. It will help you sort out the guilt you seem to have. And the anger. Put your animosity aside and try it," she whispered softly and touched the back of my hand. "It will help you put your life back together."

I stared down at my worn work boots. "What life?"

"Toby, look at me," she said.

My heart punched against my chest. Her face was soft and full of emotion, and it weakened me. I closed my eyes and concentrated on her fingers touching my hand.

I had to ask. "If I go, will that change anything for us?"

She took a deep breath but remained quiet.

"Jesus, Claude. Can't you lie to me, just once?"

"I won't lie to you. After what's happened, I really don't see it changing anything for us," she said. "But I still care for you. I want to help you get back on your feet."

I pulled my hand away and ran it through my hair. "I'll think about it," I said, without conviction.

She stood. "I should go."

"No, don't." I grabbed her hand and kept her from moving away. As much as it hurt to have her there, it was worse for her to leave, to be alone. "Stay for a little longer. Please."

She heaved out a breath, but then straightened her shoulders. "Will you let me make you an appointment?"

"Sure," I said with a shrug.

She made the appointment, but she must have known I never intended to go.

Chapter 40

~CLAUDIA~

I SENT MOST OF MY STUFF on ahead to the campus, which only left two large suitcases for Dad to load in the car. I was nervous about leaving. Though I'd done everything I needed to do, I still felt things were unfinished here, but I was out of time. Mom was expecting me. I had promised to spend my last available week with her before I moved onto campus the following week.

I checked my bedroom over one last time. This room, in this house, was the only place I'd ever lived. Even though I was ready to go, somehow, I knew I'd miss it. Dad came up behind me and hugged my shoulders with one arm.

"Did you ever think this day would come?" he asked.

"I prayed for this day, and now that it's here, I'm sad." I turned and gave my dad a tremulous smile. "Daddy, I'm sorry I've been so impossible the past few months."

"Baby, you grew up a lot in those months, and you've stuck your neck out for what you believe in," he replied. "And now my little bird is leaving the nest."

My stomach rolled with nerves. He must have seen it on my face.

"You all right?" he asked.

Despite the nerves, I smiled and nodded. "Yeah, I got this."

I glanced around the house once more. I wouldn't be back for months if I even came back for the holidays. Dad and I were still trying to figure all that out.

"Christmas in California is nice, and if you came, it'd be the first time in years that I'd be able to share it with both of my parents," I'd said.

"I'll think about it," Dad had replied.

That was more than I'd expected.

Dario and April had seen me off the night before, but I'd not spoken to Toby since my visit to his house. Dario had told me he'd had a preliminary meeting with the D.A. on Devlin's case.

I'd texted Toby that morning to let him know I was leaving and that I hoped everything had went well. He hadn't responded, so I wasn't totally surprised to step outside and see the red Jeep at the curb. Toby was leaning against Dad's car with his arms crossed, wearing a pair of mirrored sunglasses. Dad said he'd forgotten something and disappeared back inside the house.

"I'm glad you came by," I said as I made my way over to him. "I'm anxious to know how you made out with the lawyer."

He removed his sunglasses. "They set a date for the trial. I'll have to testify, but I haven't been charged with anything."

I exhaled. "What a relief."

Toby nodded his agreement and then motioned towards my suitcases next to Dad's car.

"So, this is the big day?"

"Yep, the big day." The bare exchange left an awkward silence between us. Uncertain what to say next, I blurted out, "I'm sorry."

"Jesus, don't do that. I didn't come for an apology." He looked over my shoulder, his stance rigid. "I just wanted to say goodbye."

I almost apologized for apologizing, but caught myself. "Don't forget your appointment with the counselor next week."

"I'm not going."

"Toby, we went over this. You have to go! You need to talk to someone."

"Stop it, Claudia. You're leaving. You don't get a say in what I do any more."

He was pushing me away. I supposed it was inevitable, and he had every right to, but I didn't like it.

"I didn't mean to come on so forceful," I atoned. "I just worry about you."

"You don't need to worry about me. I made other plans."

I wrapped my arms around my midriff. "What other plans?"

"I joined the Marines."

"You enlisted?" The words came out rushed, critical.

He shrugged. "Yeah. Nothing stopping me anymore."

I hadn't seen this coming. I bit my bottom lip, quelling the need to say more.

"I should go," he said.

The finality of the moment, and of us, filled me with growing trepidation.

I met his eyes. "You'll stay in touch?"

He looked away.

"No. I probably won't."

"No?" I hadn't expected a complete severance.

With a forced smile, he patted my arm. "Go be great in California. It's what you really want."

Before I could prepare for it, he gave me the briefest of hugs, kissed my forehead, and left without looking back.

His departure was so immediate; I was stunned that he'd actually left and that I found myself alone.

There are moments in life that stay with you. As he drove away, I knew this was one of them. With vivid clarity, I would remember the day Toby Faye walked out of my life as much as the day he walked into it.

Chapter 41

~CLAUDIA~

THANKSGIVING NEARED. AND STUDENTS GREW frenzied with the reality that there were only a few more weeks of the term to get work finished. I didn't get caught up in that tidal wave. Other than visiting with Mom on odd weekends, I'd had no distractions. I was on schedule with all my classes.

Dating someone like Toby had been a complete departure from my sensible self. I'd moved through the months with him in a vaporous state where emotions, and a whole lot of hormones, ruled. With distance from it, I could see that now. His reaction to all that had happened shouldn't have been so surprising to me—really, it was only a rude and blistering reminder of our innate differences. Our families and upbringings were so dissimilar. I was raised to deal with problems in a more sensible and calculated way.

I would be lying if I said I didn't miss him, but my life was back on track and I was in control—neat and orderly, everything in its proper place. I liked it that way.

"My roommate, Misha, is nice, but such a slob," I complained to April during one of our weekly catch-up calls. I picked up an empty yogurt cup and chucked it into the dorm's garbage pail. "How's things with you?"

She told me about everything going on at the DeOro house as well as what Dario was up to, and, apparently tired of skating around the topic, she asked the question.

"Don't you want to know how Toby is?"

I lifted my index finger to my mouth and gnawed at a cuticle. During our calls, I consciously tried not to pay too much interest in what she said about Toby. I told myself I didn't want to know, but this time, April was bursting to tell me. Of course, I wanted to know. It made me crazy that school-wise everything was exactly as I wanted it, but no matter how much I tried to put him out of my mind, Toby Faye inevitably crept back in—his smile intruding on my concentration during a boring lecture, or the memory of his arms holding me keeping me awake at night. I hated that.

"You know how he planned on joining the Marines?" she asked.

"Yeah."

"It's not happening."

"He changed his mind?"

"No, he failed the physical entrance exam," she explained. "He has some kind of hearing-related, balance issue."

"Oh, no. He must be so disappointed," I said.

"He took it pretty hard. After he found out, he was desperate to get out of here. He quit AB's and took some of the insurance money from his mom's policy." As April explained Toby's situation, I listened, disquieted by the information. "Dario and I tried to talk him out of it, but he wouldn't change his mind. Yesterday, he took off."

"Where to?"

"He didn't really seem to know," she said, sounding slightly miffed. More calmly, she offered, "But don't worry. You know him, he always lands on his feet."

"I suppose so," I mumbled, gazing out the large window of the common area that overlooked my favorite studying spot. I was several hundreds of miles away from Toby. What would be the point of worrying? There was nothing I could do about it.

Like a true friend, April sensed my apprehension and changed the subject. "How're the guys out there?"

Talking about guys was of little interest to me. I spent my first week in California at my mother's apartment, nursing my broken heart and allowing myself to heal. I had decided that I would move on, make a point to talk to guys on campus, and possibly go out if asked. When school finally started, though, classes like the Psychology of Adult Development, Administrative Problems in Aging, and the Science of Adult Development, took up all my time. Not that I minded much—I was too engrossed in my studies. I told myself that eventually, when I had time for it, there would be other relationships—I would someday feel excited about getting close to someone, again. Right now, I just didn't. And that was okay.

I had a ton of studying to do and ended the call with April.

Although it was months later, talking to April about Toby reminded me of the ache I felt before. I pictured Toby off on his road trip with nothing holding him back. He was free to roam, unfettered by any commitments. I didn't want to acknowledge how much it hurt, the idea of him out there—moving on, meeting other girls—knowing we would never move forward, and how those emotions, the ones I tried to keep buried, still twisted my heart.

This news about Toby made me realize it was time to put my proverbial foot down. I needed to let go of that last tie—the one, until now, I was unaware I'd been holding onto. The hope of him contacting me. Wherever his journey was taking him, I was no longer a part of it.

I resolved to stop checking my text messages so often and looking for him online. I put him out of my mind, and I concentrated on a life immersed in classes, term papers, study groups, and cleaning up after my roommate.

Dad arranged for me to fly home for the Thanksgiving break. I complained about the expense and the little amount of time that I would actually have. He insisted, and I was secretly pleased about it. I spent the weekend before the holiday with Mom feeling a little guilty that I would be leaving her alone, but I think she felt she had won the bigger prize when we decided I would stay on the West Coast for Christmas and the New Year.

On campus, the Sunday before Thanksgiving, I found a sunny spot outside and lay with my laptop, writing a paper due before I headed out for the holiday. My cell vibrated in my back pocket. I reached for it just as the familiar musical ring tone "Something," started to play.

I froze, almost too anxious to answer it, but I was too curious not to.

"Claude?" The familiar deep voice crackled in my ear.

"Toby. April told me you left Long Island."

"Did she tell me you I flunked out of the Marine Corps, too?" Without waiting for me to reply, he added, "I have some hearing problem that messes with my equilibrium. Guess I took a crack to the head one too many times," he sort of laughed. "I'm useless. Damaged goods."

"Have you seen your doctor?" I asked, quickly coming up with plausible explanations. "Tinnitus is a symptom of Ménière's syndrome."

"It doesn't matter, I'm done. The Marines plan is shot to shit. I can't seem to do anything right."

I wasn't about to feed into his downward spiral. "Where are you now?"

"I'm in Wichita Falls, Texas."

"And what's there?"

He was quiet for a long pause before he said, "Who the hell knows. I heard about a job from a friend of a friend's, but it didn't work out. I needed to get out of that house—to leave all the crap behind. I figured once I got on the road, an opportunity was bound to come along and I'd be okay," he said with a sigh. "But it doesn't feel any better out here."

"Maybe you aren't meant to be there," I said softly. "Go back home."

"No. There's nothing left for me there, Claude," he said, his voice barely above a whisper. "I don't have a reason to be anywhere. That's a fact. And, shit, it's freaking brutal to know it. I honestly don't know what the hell to do with myself." He let out a quiet, sob-like moan, and it broke my heart.

"Oh, Toby," I whispered, feeling helpless.

"I'm sorry. I'm so goddamn tired," he mumbled. "I probably shouldn't have called, but I'm feeling pretty fucking low. I needed to talk to someone, and all I could think of was you. I miss talking to you. I miss it a lot."

"I'm glad you called me." I wished I could reach through the line and touch him. "I've missed talking to you, too."

The line went silent for a moment before he rushed in to fill it.

"Can I come see you? If I drive straight through, I can be there in a day or so." His voice held an edge of hope.

"You'd come here?" Part of me lifted with the idea, another part of me sunk. I rubbed my thumb over the nail beds of my fingers in search of protruding cuticles until I found one.

I heard him blow out. "Bad idea. I'm not thinking straight."

Hearing him so shattered dispelled any reservations. I resisted the jutting cuticle and dropped my hand.

"No, no, it's just that I'll be back in New York on Tuesday. Do you think you can get back home by then?"

"Yeah, I guess." He sounded hesitant, maybe even a little leery, but interested.

I surged ahead. "All right, listen to me—go home. I'm going to make some plans for us, and when I get there, I'll come get you."

"Okay."

"I'll see you in just a few days then." I tried to sound upbeat. "Drive safely, please?"

"Okay," he repeated, his response wooden just before he choked and the sounds of a whimper came over the line before it went quiet.

I had to close my eyes and take a steadying breath before I could continue. Once I regrouped, I knew exactly what I was going to do. I spent the next hour making phone calls and putting a plan into action.

Chapter 42

~TOBY~

I DROVE HOME, THE STATES ON the way nothing but a blur in my mind, all the while wondering what Claudia meant by "plans for us." I hoped that somehow, after hearing from me, she wanted me back. Made no sense, but I wanted to believe it. I was that damn desperate.

I got home in the early morning hours of Tuesday. I left my stuff in the car and barely made it through the door before I crashed on the couch.

I must have been dreaming—fighting off a faceless opponent. For some reason, I wasn't able to punch back, and I was getting the shit knocked out of me. I took blow after angry blow. Cornered, I begged him to stop. He smiled, cruel and evil—my brother's smile, one that said he knew I had no more fight left. But still, he came at me. With a grunt, I threw my arm out to deflect the blow and connected with him. The contact felt bizarre—physically real—and I was surprised by the soft, almost girlish gasp he emitted. I opened my eyes with a start. The house was dark, and I had no idea what time it was. I saw a small figure hunched back away from me on the floor.

"What the hell?" I tried to sit up, but my head spun. I sank back down and closed my eyes until the spinning stopped.

"It's me," Claudia's voice came through the shadows.

"Claudia? Oh, Jesus. I'm sorry. Are you okay?"

"Yes," she puffed. "I was trying to wake you, and you swung at me. Caught me off guard."

Would I ever stop inflicting pain on this girl? I was dying to look at her, but I felt so damn embarrassed at the pathetic shape I was in.

Still, I was relieved she was there, that she actually still cared about me. I pressed my palms into my eye sockets to stop the burning behind my eyeballs, fighting to keep myself together.

"I'm really sorry. I didn't mean to hurt you," I clamored.

There was a shuffling sound as she came forward and touched my knee.

"I know," she whispered, her voice gentle. "It's okay. Everything's going to be all right."

Soon after, Dario and April showed up with sandwiches. I was extremely grateful. I was starving, and there was nothing in the house remotely edible. They hugged me and patted my back with concern in their eyes, then dropped into seats around the kitchen table as I wolfed down the food.

"Tomorrow," Claude said sternly from the seat next to me, "I'm taking you to meet with a counselor."

After she made this statement, I looked around at each of them. No one said a word.

"No—" I started, but Claudia interrupted me.

"You've tried it your way. It didn't work out." She looked me square in the eye. "The appointment is tomorrow morning. And I'm driving you. End of story."

I looked down at my last piece of sandwich thinking of a way out of it without pissing her off. I didn't want to make her angry, but I wasn't going to see some shrink.

"Toby," April said my name with a hint of Spanish accent, and laid her hand over mine. "You can't run from what's hurting you."

"We'll get you through this, man," Dario offered.

Every eye was on me. My stomach turned. Pushing my food away, I dropped my head down onto my forearm.

There was an awful tightness in my chest and a stabbing, burning pain behind my eyes. I wanted to get up. I wanted to run—but then Claudia leaned over me from behind, pressing her warm face against my back. That gentle pressure kept me in my seat.

"We're all here for you," she whispered.

Chapter 43

~TOBY~

"THIS THERAPIST CAME HIGHLY RECOMMENDED, and he agreed to see you right away." Claudia explained, as she drove me to the appointment the next day in her Camry.

Last night April, Dario and she had all stayed the night with me, and I had felt calm then. Now as Claudia navigated the roads west through Oakdale into Islip, I had a difficult time sitting still. It felt like a squirrel was gnawing at my insides. I opened the window for some fresh air.

We pulled up in front of a private home in a nice neighborhood. The squirrel, now frantic, was trying to dig his way out.

"What did you tell him about me—that I'm a sad sack of shit?" I muttered, staring down at my fisted hands.

She grunted, exasperated. "I would never say anything like that about you."

I stole a quick look at her. No, she wouldn't. Feeling ashamed, I said, "I'm sorry. It's ridiculous, but I'm nervous."

She bit her lip. "It's not ridiculous, but it's going to be okay. Come on, let's go inside."

She stayed in the waiting room while I met with Robert McCauley. His office was in a converted garage in his home, and he was kind of a geek. Forty-ish, sweater vest, loafers and glasses with full beard—I almost expected him to take out a pipe and ask me, "Vat seems to be zee problem?"

Instead, he said, "Call me Bob," and motioned to a small leather couch below a window. "Have a seat."

"I'd rather stand."

"Okay, sitting is optional. As long as you're comfortable."

I stood beside the couch and pressed my hands deep inside my jean pockets.

He cleared his throat. "I don't usually take appointments without speaking to the potential client, but Claudia was insistent and actually, quite persuasive. What's your relationship with her?"

Looking down at my feet, I said, "We dated, but we're not together anymore. I messed up." I glanced at him. "I get angry. She's trying to help me. She thinks if I talk to you, I'll get better."

I expected him to say more about her, but Bob only nodded thoughtfully and murmured, "Okay." He took a few minutes to jot down some of my basic information, phone number and address, family members' names, and then he put his pen down and faced me. "Successful therapy is based solely on your desire to improve your life. Positive change doesn't just 'happen.' You have to want it. And thusly, you need to make it happen.

"I'm going to tell you now, looking inside one's self can be extremely difficult, and at times, you might want to give up." He leaned forward. "But, here's the silver lining: I promise you, if you see this through—let me work with you and assist you in sorting out what's going on in your mind—your therapy will help you understand why you've done the things you've done. You'll learn how to avoid making the same mistakes over again and make better choices for yourself."

"Okay," I mumbled, realizing that without deciding to do so, I'd sat down.

He sat across from me, and, with nothing separating us, asked about the events of my life and how I ended up here. I'll admit, I wanted to shock him so I threw it all out there. He listened, hands folded together with his index fingers straightened and pressed against his lips, never even blinking as I told him about the drinking, the fights, and the beatings I'd seen and endured, and Julia's sickness and unexpected death. I even told him all about Velerio, Devlin, and the legal case that followed.

"You've had a pretty rough time of it," he said. "Tell me how all of this makes you feel."

I pulled back. "I don't do the 'talking about my feelings' thing."

Bob hunched forward like we were discussing a football play, and said, "Growing up like you did, that's not uncommon, but it's important for you to open up. You've been holding onto your emotions. You have to let them out. Show them. Have a good cry."

I shot to my feet. "No. I won't do that."

"All right, then," he leaned back. "Tell me how you feel, physically."

"Physically?" The question seemed safe enough. Considering my answer, I moved to the corner, away from him and briefly scanned over his framed credentials. I didn't read them, only noticed that one was imprinted with Princeton University. I ran a hand through my hair and sighed. "I'm tired."

The words alone felt heavy. Too heavy. I knew Bob was looking at me, and though he didn't ask me to, I could sense he knew I would need to say more. I had to release the weight.

"I'm tired of everything. I'm tired of feeling like I should be somewhere, but not knowing where that is. Tired of losing everyone who's ever been important to me." Abruptly I felt restless, and I strode back towards the couch. As I stood there, the steam left me, and I sunk back down into the cushions and bowed my head.

"I'm tired of being alone."

It was then that I folded. A feeling so powerful crashed over me. The tears came forcefully, stealing my breath and strangling my words. I quaked under the weight, drowning in it, until finally, it began to subside and eventually, sputtering and winded, it released me.

"That was a good healthy cry," Bob nodded with approval as he handed me a box of tissues.

He sounded so goddamned proud, that even though snot was running down my face and I had a headache the size of Texas, I felt like I'd gotten something right. And weirdly, it somehow felt … better.

After I'd mopped my face with half a box of tissues, he gave me a homework assignment. I was to picture my life as I wanted it to be. He told me to spend the next week thinking about it and to write down some details so I would have a clear image of it in my head. We scheduled another meeting for the following week.

My face must have looked like I'd been exposed to shrapnel when I walked out of Bob's office, but Claudia didn't mention it. Instead she took me grocery shopping. As we picked out food to restock my house, she kept a light conversation going, mostly by herself. I expected her to ask me about my time with Bob. She didn't, and I was glad. I didn't feel much like talking, but I also didn't want to be alone.

For Thanksgiving, Claudia invited Aunt Joan and me for dinner. Joan made my favorite sweet potato pie, and we joined Claudia and her father at the Chiametti house, along with several aunts, uncles, and cousins.

El Capitán was in a generous mood. Joan's and my presence was easily accepted, and we felt welcomed at their family's holiday. Claudia's Italian relatives were an amusing bunch of characters, clashing one moment, laughing the next. Watching them interact was entertaining in itself.

Claudia and her father buzzed around like a well-rehearsed team, getting drinks and making sure everyone had what they needed. Before the food was served, we all sat and held hands around the table while Mr. Chiametti said a prayer for the meal.

"And, I'm thankful for all of you who are sharing this meal with us today," he said and glanced at everyone, his eyes coming to rest on me.

Claudia, sitting beside me and holding my hand during the prayer, gave my fingers a gentle squeeze. I felt out of place, but I wanted very much to belong here.

They put out a traditional spread, but that was after we'd run through a round of antipasto and a macaroni dish. All in all, way too much food, but after being on the road, everything tasted so good. I ate through every course.

Not long after dinner, Claudia and I went to April's house and met up with Dario for dessert with the DeOro family. Not such a different gathering from the Chiamettis, but if possible, the volume at the DeOros was even louder.

"Eat," April's mother and aunts said as they pushed plates of food and desserts at me. Though I was full, I kept plugging away. Claudia sat beside me, occasionally rubbing my back and smiling as she teased me about how much food I put away.

As I'd done at Claudia's house, I watched the large family interact—joking, hugging, and even arguing with each other. I'd never had a family holiday that was so loud, crazy and messy. And, man, was I envious.

I drove Claudia home after we left April's house.

"Come in," she said, inviting me back inside. It appeared that most of her extended family was still there, but I was feeling uncomfortably bloated and more emotional than I cared to admit.

"Go spend some time with your dad," I told her.

She hesitated to leave the Jeep.

"Are you sure?"

"Yeah. I'm so full—I think I need to lie down." I sighed and patted my distended stomach. "Or maybe throw up."

"Your stomach isn't bottomless after all," she said, laughing as she hopped out. "Try some peppermint tea."

A light snow flurry fell, and her long hair blew in the wind. Waving a mittened hand at me, she smiled. Her grin made me happy. As I watched her run to the house, I realized that until just now, I hadn't seen her smile in a long time. The thought made me feel guilty because making her laugh used to be one of my favorite things to do.

I grabbed my guitar and went into Julia's bedroom to lie on the bed. Joan had cleared the room of most of the personal items, but I still went there when I wanted to talk to Julia. I lay down for a few minutes and tried to feel her presence.

"Ma," I said out loud. "You said you'd see me through this. I could use some help right about now."

I thought about what Bob had asked me to do—picture my life, as I'd like it to be. Resting my guitar over my stomach, I plucked through chords as I thought about what would make me happy. What didn't make me happy was working random jobs. And, being alone.

I wanted to do something that interested me, and like the Chiamettis and DeOros, one day I wanted to be surrounded by people who had my back—like a family is supposed to.

Putting aside my guitar, I found a notepad and pen in Julia's night table. As I lifted the pad out of the drawer, a photo fell out from between the pages. I was surprised to see it was one of Claudia and me, with little Dylan. I was holding her possessively around the waist, staring at her with an intensely open infatuation. The picture was taken only hours before we'd been together.

Oh, that night—our one perfect night.

I flipped it over and noticed Julia's loopy handwriting on the back. She had written one word. *Family.*

I turned the photo back over and stared at it—anyone looking at it might assume we were a young family. Warmth crept through me as I imagined what it might be like to be part of Claudia's family. Being able to hold her hand and kiss her in front of everyone, and each night, being able to sleep with her, to touch her freely, like I'd done the night we'd slept together in her bedroom. Her body fit so perfectly against mine. It was the closest I'd ever felt to someone. I missed that. I missed her.

I choked back a wave of emotions as the now familiar burn of tears stung my eyes, but despite it, I laughed. That I'd found this picture at this particular moment didn't feel like a coincidence at all.

"You left this for me, didn't you, Ma?" I said quietly. "You would have liked me to stay with Claudia. I was better with her."

Until these last few days, I'd forgotten a lot of the small things, like how amazing the sound of Claudia's laughter made me feel. It didn't matter how much I missed her, though. The way she'd been looking at me since she'd walked in the door the other day, I could tell she only saw me as a broken guy who needed her sympathy. I wasn't someone who could take care of her. Hell, I was a freaking mess.

I knew then what I wanted my life to be like—what would really make me happy. Feeling a little more optimistic, I tucked the picture under the strings of my guitar neck where I could see it and began to scribble out a rough draft of my homework assignment.

Chapter 44

~CLAUDIA~

MY MOTHER ALWAYS BOUGHT A grave blanket, decorated pine branches, to lay over the top of my grandparents' grave at the holidays, so following tradition, I picked one up at the garden center before Toby drove me to the cemetery early Friday. I hadn't been to Mrs. Faye's gravesite since I'd left the East Coast and made it point to go since I wasn't likely to have the opportunity any time soon.

Toby was wearing a black leather bomber jacket with the collar up against the cold while I was bundled in my winter coat, scarf, and mittens. He was quiet that morning, watching me from under his thick lashes as he squatted on the cold, snow-dusted ground. I leaned over the grave and cleared away some leaves before placing the fresh pine blanket in front of the headstone.

"Julia Marie Faye, beloved wife, mother and sister," it said next to, "Alfonse Faye, Sr., beloved husband and father."

"I know you're at peace, but I miss our talks." I spoke aloud to Mrs. Faye, my words billowing out in soft warm puffs in the cold air. "Do you want to say something?" I asked Toby, but he shook his head. I touched the frosty, smooth tombstone, and my eyes watered. "Merry Christmas in heaven." I included a silent prayer that she would somehow make her presence known to Toby so he wouldn't feel so alone.

He stood as I walked over to him. Taking off my red wooly scarf, I wrapped it around his neck.

"I'm fine," he protested.

"Your mother said you need to wear it."

"Okay." He smiled and let me tuck it under his collar.

"She still watches over you," I whispered, when I was done.

He nodded and we started down the aisle.

"She likes when you talk to her," he said. "She told me last night."

"Oh, yeah?" Smiling, I glanced at him sideways. "What else did she say?"

"That you're going to happily have a bigger family someday."

I remembered the day Mrs. Faye had spoken to me. "Lots of babies," she'd said.

I flushed hard. "You overheard your mother talking to me about that?"

"No." He shook his head, and a slow grin cut across his face. "I told you, we talked last night," he repeated and took my hand in his.

Bemused by this, I continued to let him hold my hand as we walked back to his Jeep.

We met April and Dario for lunch, and, conscientious student that I am, I begged off to follow-up on a few teacher emails and do some course reading before I spent the rest of the evening with Dad.

On Saturday, I helped Dad do some early Christmas shopping for my aunt and cousins. Dad was silly, making me laugh as he picked out some hideous outfits, and again when he suggested boxing gloves to ward off the guys at USC since he couldn't be there to keep them away. I made him try on hats in every store we entered. Some were rather ridiculous, but he was a good sport. We finished our expedition in the food court—we both secretly relished the sublimely bad food there. Our time together was easy, and it felt like old times before everything got so difficult between us.

Since Dad had to work, I didn't feel guilty about spending my last night with Toby, April, and Dario. Everyone came over to my house, and we made popcorn and watched a movie. It was a good night.

Toby hesitated to go after April and Dario left, but I handed him his jacket.

"I'm sorry I have to ask you to go," I told him. "I booked a 7 a.m. flight to get the cheaper airfare, and I need to get some sleep."

We stood at the door as he pulled on his coat. It had not been an easy few days. While I had been eager to help him, and I was so glad that he had finally let me, it was complicated to be around him again. At times, it was difficult to separate my compassion for him apart from my love for him. I was aware of every touch, even the most minute, and I tried to be careful not to let any contact between us linger.

It would have been easier to move on and get over Toby Faye if only I stayed away from him. As things stood now, I couldn't separate myself from him, not entirely. I would continue to do whatever I could to help him, not just for Mrs. Faye's sake, but also because love didn't just end.

I was returning to California with a sense of relief. I had witnessed a shift in Toby's mood and felt confident that he was doing better. He'd even made us laugh by cracking a few jokes. It was a good omen.

"Oh, wait, I have something for you." I grabbed my bag and pulled out a small box wrapped in Christmas paper. "I want to give you this now since I won't see you for the holidays."

He took it from me and bowed his head. "I don't have anything for you."

"Stop it," I said. "It's just a little something. I saw it and thought of you. Open it."

He removed the paper slowly, until finally he revealed a black velvet box. He flicked his eyes to me before pulling the hinged cover up to reveal the silver oval pendant inside.

"St. Jude," he read the stamped words over the figurehead. "Is this guy like a saint of lost causes or something?"

Taking it from him, I smiled. "Sort of. St. Jude is the patron saint of lost hope," I proclaimed clasping it around his neck.

"Um, thanks," he murmured.

"Please, don't take it as an insult."

"How can I be insulted? It's an accurate description. I'm pretty desperate." He touched the pendant, now nestled against his T-shirt.

"I only meant to encourage you. And, really, you already seem so much better," I told him. "I think you're well on your way to being your old self again."

He looked at me, his expression deadpan. "That guy had a lot of issues."

I smiled. "No more cross-country road trips?"

He shook his head.

"No, I think the therapist will be more than enough adventure for me."

"Toby," I held his eyes. "You're going to be okay. I can feel it."

He stepped closer and reached up to hold my face.

"Claude…" He said my name in that achy way that made my pulse quicken.

The touch of his warm hands on my skin, and the smell of his leather jacket swarmed my senses. It was the first advance he had made towards me since I'd been back. I stood still, frozen, as we looked at each other for a charged instant until I pulled his hands away.

Shaking my head, I whispered, "Nooo, nooo. You can give me a hug. But that's all."

Letting out a breath, he wrapped his arms around me and held me tight, rocking me gently. "Thank you for the present and, mostly, for taking care of me," he said.

I pressed my cheek to his, feeling the slight stubble of his beard. "I'm glad you finally let me." Stepping back, I looked into his eyes so that he could see that I meant it.

He cleared his throat. "Would it be okay if I call you every once in a while?"

I knew how hard it was for him to ask.

"You'd better," I replied.

Chapter 45

~TOBY~

AT MY NEXT MEETING WITH Bob, I shared the vision of my life—a family, a great job and a life that included Claudia. While he listened attentively as I told him how I planned to improve myself and how I was going to win her back, Bob suggested that I let go of the Claudia-part of my vision for now and concentrate on other aspects of my life. He claimed that because Julia was gone, I was unconsciously placing my need for family onto Claudia.

"Let her go," he'd said. "We need to heal you and build you back up before you can fully love anyone else. You'll never have a healthy relationship until you first love yourself and feel good about who you are."

This was the opposite of how I saw this going.

"No, Bob," I refused. "If I let her go, I'll lose her. For good."

Bob was calm. "Toby, you want Claudia back for the wrong reasons."

I got what he was telling me, and I wanted to believe Bob knew what he was talking about. It felt like I'd just gotten her back, and now he was telling me to let her go. I was sure if I did, she would find someone else and be totally happy, forever—without me. I decided not to talk about Claudia to him anymore.

Bob suggested I reach out to my aunt and even Al Junior.

Joan, I knew, had lots of friends, but much like I'd not thought of Claudia and her pain, I hadn't really thought about how losing Julia had affected my aunt, either. She had lost her husband years ago, and she had no children. She and Al Junior were all that were left of my faded and splintered family—an old widow and a convicted murderer. Certainly, nothing to brag about, but they were mine.

Bob assigned me more homework—visiting Joan and having dinner or doing something with her at least every other week. I was to keep in mind that she, too, was alone. He felt that by reaching out to her, I would be surprised how good it would feel to support someone else instead of focusing on my own problems.

Joan was ecstatic when I called and asked if I could come to see her. She made a huge meal and fussed over me. Later, she wrapped up the leftovers for me to take home.

She lived in old condominium that she obviously couldn't keep up with. I made a mental list of the things that needed to be done, and the following Saturday I went back with supplies and some of Big Al's tools. Over the next few weeks, I fixed a leaky faucet, patched a hole in a wall, changed light bulbs in her ceiling fixtures, and got her computer working again. Each time she made dinner and told me stories about Julia. It was through these stories that I came to understand how much Julia loved my father.

"You must have the wrong woman," I laughed when Joan told me Julia had asked my father to marry her.

"Oh, yes, your mother, when she was younger, she was different. Before she immersed herself in faith, she drank socially and was an impulsive romantic."

My mother drank? My mother impulsive?

"We all knew Al wasn't the best choice, but your mother, how she loved that man," Joan said. "She thought he would change. And he did try hard to make it work and keep her happy. I had such hope in the beginning. He stopped drinking—even went to AA meetings. But the responsibility of being a parent and supporting a family proved to be more than he could handle. He turned back to the booze. And then that night happened."

Clenching my jaw, I remembered Julia crying. "Why the hell did he get behind the wheel of his truck in that condition?"

"You probably didn't understand how depressed he was." My aunt pursed her lips, and a nauseous feeling started to build in the pit of my stomach.

"It's about time you knew the truth." Joan sat down next to me with a soft grunt. "When your father took to turning the living room into a boxing ring, your mother gave him an ultimatum—

sober up or get out. The accident was his way out."

I stared, unable to believe it.

"Didn't anyone try to stop him?"

"Understanding the depths of depression isn't easy. And Al Faye wasn't open to letting people help him."

I closed my eyes and put my head in my hands. This was yet another thing to add to the list. Bob would be all over it. How was I supposed to keep up with all this crap?

"How could my mother keep that from me?"

"She thought you were too young. She tried to protect you from the truth."

Heat crept up my neck. "Protect me from the truth?" I snapped. "I started taking care of her, the house—everything, when I was twelve. But I was too young to know my own father killed himself?"

Bob had made me understand that, despite my grief at losing Julia, deep down inside, I was angry with her for always needing my help, for relying on me at such a young age. We were working on it, but the force of my anger still overwhelmed me.

Joan rested a hand on my shoulder. "My sister wasn't perfect, but she tried hard to be a good mother. And though she never apologized for loving your father, she didn't want you to be like him. She hoped that, by protecting you, it would give you a chance to become a man without the same weaknesses."

I went home that evening, grabbed a flashlight, and went out to the barn. The overhead light had burned out a while back, and no one had ever bothered to change it. I sat in the dark, aiming the beam of light over my father's work area. Over the years, Al Junior and I had used some of his tools. Some were gone for good, others dotted the worktop, carelessly thrown without any regard for our father's ordered system.

I flipped through the years in my mind, trying to recall a few good memories of Big Al. Back when I was a kid, I liked being with him, following him around like a shadow, stoked by any attention he'd give me. I remember him patiently showing me how to use the tools in his workshop. He'd been so proud of his work, and I had tried very hard to mimic his motions. But always later, he would drink. With slurred snarls, he became someone else, someone mean. I remembered the last time he'd spoken to me. It was after he and Al Junior had battled. Things were broken, and Al had stormed off. For the first time, Julia had reamed my father behind closed doors. She was careful to keep their conversation private, but whatever she'd said had silenced him. He had left their room without a word and retreated to the barn. I waited a while and then went out there.

Unless he granted permission, the barn was off limits to us as kids. It was the one place Big Al was fussy and meticulous about. The mix of sawdust and oily wood stain filled my nose. I loved the way it smelled in there.

My father wasn't working that night, though. I found him sitting in an old, decrepit lawn chair, staring vacantly at his workbench. He didn't seem to notice me, but all of a sudden, he spoke.

"Learn how to use these tools," he'd said, without looking at me. I remember feeling proud that he had put the order to me. Somehow that meant he preferred me over my brother. Then, in a strange, disembodied voice, he told me to get out.

Two weeks after that night in the barn, I woke up to Julia's crying. The police were at the door. Big Al was dead.

How could my mother think I wasn't strong enough to handle the truth, especially since a girl I'd dated in high school had overdosed? Hadn't I handled it and moved on?

Maybe she knew how the shadow of guilt remained with those who survived.

No, Julia wouldn't knowingly add to my daily struggles, not when she'd witnessed me struggle through school, get into fights, and plow through a pile of crummy jobs. I reinforced all her fears by running away and putting as much physical distance between us as I could, out there 'looking for my place.'

I avoided things that required too much effort or anything I had to invest myself in. She had been right when she told me I wouldn't just stumble upon my happiness out on the road.

Now, seeing a long, empty future staring me in the face, I was ready to make changes.

I picked up a hammer that was lying on the worktop area. Gripping the handle and liking the feel of the weight in my hand, I scanned the pegboard wall with the light beam until I found its permanent marker outline and put it back where it belonged. I walked back to the house feeling unsettled. It was useless to try sleeping. It would be after midnight West Coast time, but I texted Claudia anyway. A minute later, my cell rang.

"Hey. Is everything okay?" her voice was sleepy. I had woken her.

"I found out some stuff about my dad," I sighed.

"Want to talk about it?"

"Sorry, I know it's late, but yeah, I do."

"It's okay. I'm here."

I sunk down heavily into the couch, took a deep breath, and told her everything.

One by one, Bob had been going through each of my family members and making me think about the relationships I had with them and how they affected me.

When it came to Al Junior, I told Bob about the letters he had written me, but that I never read. I also told him how Julia tried to encourage me to visit him, but that I'd refused to go. I could not think of one good thing to say about my brother.

"I'm sure somewhere along the way, Al must have been nice to you," he said.

"I'm pretty damn sure that's not so," I replied.

Bob shuffled papers in his lap, and I sensed he was going to tell me something I wasn't ready to hear. I braced myself.

"You need to visit Al and give him a chance to make amends. And to reopen a relationship with you," he said.

"No way." I wasn't ready to see Al. I could picture him laughing at me and asking me why I'd bothered coming. "I won't bend over and let him stick it to me."

As usual, Bob refused to accept my resistance. "Toby, you don't need to be afraid of your brother. He isn't a physical threat to you anymore."

"I know that." I let out a nervous laugh. "I can't say why, but the thought of seeing him still makes me uncomfortable."

Bob leaned forward, and the motion inexplicably made me tense. "He was your big brother, and he should have been looking out for you, not hurting you. But I think you're reacting now, not so much to the physical pain, but to the way he made you feel, deep inside."

I hated when Bob hit me with crap like that. I didn't want the session to end in another embarrassing cry fest, but that familiar, telltale lump formed in my throat. I tried to clear it.

"When you see him, it's possible he might try to hurt you with his words, but you're in control. You choose whether to let him hurt you or not hurt you."

"Is this really necessary? I really don't see the point." I sighed, restless, barely holding myself together.

"To grow we have to endure some discomfort."

Facing Al Junior would be one of my most difficult hurdles, but I was climbing out of the hole. More than I saw the light above, I sensed it, and I wouldn't let Al block me from getting to it.

Chapter 46

~TOBY~

I PUT IT OFF FOR AS long as I could. Christmas came and went. The Sunday before the New Year, I drove upstate to the Otisville Correctional Facility.

The other visitors and I were given a number that corresponded to a labeled, laminate table inside the cafeteria-styled visiting room. The guards instructed us to wait at our assigned tables. The prisoners would come to us.

Inside, there was no sign of the holidays. The room had industrial stick tile and drab, off-white walls with high, barred windows. With armed guards posted on each wall and an additional two cruising a metal catwalk above, the room was a not-so-subtle reminder that we were among dangerous individuals.

I sat and watched for my brother while other visitors remained standing, eagerly awaiting the sight of a familiar face amongst the convicts as they shuffled through the door into the visiting area. That damn squirrel was back, once again shredding the lining of my stomach.

I saw the smiles, tears and heard brief shouts of joy. I wondered if Julia cried when she came. I imagined she did. In spite of his meanness and all his faults, Julia loved Al—just as she'd loved me in spite of my own.

And then, I saw him. Our eyes met, and, not knowing what else to do, I stood up. I was amazed at how happy he looked as he came towards me, but nothing prepared me for the shock of seeing him cry. Tears rolled shamelessly down his face, and when he got close enough, he pulled me into a rough embrace. His emotional display tore me up and had me bawling, too.

I pushed away from him. "Cut it out, you big fucking baby."

We both laughed awkwardly as we wiped the wetness from our faces and sat down across the table from one another.

People said I resembled him, but his face was fuller than mine and his body was thick with the bunchy muscles of an extreme weight lifter.

"Shit, you grew up. You're a man," he said in his deep gravelly voice, and looked me over. He looked older, too.

"You read my letters?"

Without looking at him, I shook my head. "I destroyed them."

"What the hell? I spent all that time writing to you, fucking pouring my heart out, and you trashed them? What kind of gratitude is that, man?"

"Gratitude? For what?" I gritted my teeth and arched forward. "Come off it, Al. You hate me. Why would I read your damn letters or come see you after the way you've always treated me? I didn't really care if I ever saw you again."

Al stared at me with no expression. Disheartened, I realized this 'brothers' reunion' was already a trainwreck. I didn't know what the meeting was supposed to do for me. Though we'd grown up in the same house, we'd never been much for talking. Now as I sat there, rigid in my seat, it was clear to me that Al and I had nothing to hold onto but our anger and resentment. This was no surprise. It was part of the reason I'd never come.

"I shouldn't be here." Pushing away from the table, I stood up, ready to leave.

Al grabbed my arm. "No."

A few feet away, a correctional officer motioned for us to break contact.

Al let me go, but leaned forward. "Don't go. Sit down and listen."

I stilled for a moment to look at him. Something in his face, a hint of anxiousness maybe, made me sit back down.

I held my breath and waited for him to talk.

"I had one screwed up relationship with our old man—and because of it, I blamed him as well as Mom, and even you, for everything that went wrong in my life." He looked down at his thick sausage fingers, pressing them together as if he were trying to still his shaking hands.

"But around here, I've got nothing but time to think. I've been reading and going to group therapy. I think a lot about everything that happened and all that I've done."

Al flicked his gaze back to me. "For months, day after day, I stare at the same damn four walls, and one day, like an epiphany, it came to me—blaming others for the way your life turned out isn't good."

I could hardly believe he was serious. A tickle spun in my throat, and with a snort, I said, "You're a fucking genius, Al."

He squinted at me, and, quite unexpectedly, he doubled over and let out a loud cackle. Actually relieved that he'd found my comment funny, I laughed along with him. For a few minutes, sitting there with him felt okay.

But then, all of a sudden, he covered his eyes with a large hand. "God, Toby, I was so awful to you—such a shithead with an ax to grind. I tried to explain it, in the letters." His mood changed so swiftly that I was startled when he choked back a sob and put his curled hand out on the table between us.

The sight of my older brother falling apart wigged me out. Embarrassed, I glanced out the barred window. He was stuck in here, alone, constantly reminded of the mistakes he'd made. I was alone, too. Though I'd made my own mistakes, I could walk out. I could still make something of my life—put my past behind me and get a fresh start. Al would never have that opportunity.

I looked at him, and became conscious that, even if it wasn't perfect, we'd had a conversation. Even shared a laugh. Maybe our first. We had to begin somewhere. I slid my fist across the table and nudged his. "It's okay, Al."

"You'll come see me again?" He looked up hopefully. "'Cause I got no one now that Mom's gone."

That was exactly how I'd felt. "Yeah, sure," I said. "Oh, here." I pulled out an envelope with two photos that security had allowed me to bring. I laid them out in front of him. "Pictures of Dylan."

He moved the photos closer. One of them was Dylan alone, but in the other, Julia was holding him. At the sight of it, I could see him getting choked up again. I looked down at my feet. I had more than exceeded my emotional quota.

"I'll try to bring more next time." I stood up and glanced at him. "See you, Al."

With the visit to Al finally checked off my list, the next thing I focused on was finding work. I tried to return to my old job at AB's, but Abe Bernbaum just frowned at me.

"You're too smart for this job," he said. "Time for you to move on and find something more suited to you."

While he meant to encourage me, I felt anything but. I didn't have a good list of credentials. I'd quit most of my jobs within a few months, and I hadn't been working at all in the last two. I filled out a lot of applications—wholesale, retail, stock, you name it—but I got nowhere. I found myself with a lot of time on my hands.

Out of boredom, I decided to fix the charred kitchen. Armed with my father's trade tools, I gutted the room. It felt good to have a project. With a fresh slate, I did a computer-aided sketch of the renovation: the same four walls, but with a different floor plan. The process of designing the layout and figuring out the details was interesting. When I started rebuilding it, I surprised even myself with how much I already knew about the construction aspect of it.

I stopped in at AB's to visit with Abe, and when I told him about the kitchen, he asked me to do some work around his house—odd jobs like putting up moldings and tiling his bathroom. Though it was piecemeal, he paid me pretty well, and I got turned on to the idea that I could make a living working as a handyman or a finish carpenter. Bob suggested I take drafting classes.

Reconstructing my life was harder than the kitchen. It was a long, grueling project, seeming without end. Despite the occasional setback, like the job issue, I felt a forward shift in momentum. Better days became better weeks. The New Year marked a new start.

Even though I'd been in counseling for months, Bob still didn't want me to date. He said I wasn't ready. That was okay with me because, other than talking with a girl here and there, I didn't want to hook up. Mostly, unknown to Bob, I still had my sights set on Claudia.

I stayed out of the bars, preferring to spend my weekends playing my guitar or hanging out with Dario and often with April, too.

I continued to have dinner with Joan once a week and planned to visit Al again. During the week, I worked on the kitchen. Sometimes Dario came over and helped me.

I spent a lot of time browsing the online classifieds. I found everything, from brake pads for my Jeep to an affordable granite countertop dealer. As I scrolled through pages on various sites' music sections, I found a local rock group looking for a guitarist to join their band and play gigs.

I met the lead singer, Dan, first. Not only were we close in age, but he also had a sense of humor like my own. We gelled right away. He heard me play and seemed pretty enthused. Later that week, I joined in on a band rehearsal in Dan's garage. The other guys were several years older, and each of them worked a day job unrelated to the music industry. Two of them had families. After we swapped some bullshit for a bit, we got to playing. There was some cutting up while we jammed, but one thing was for sure, those guys were serious about their sound. For me, it was musical ecstasy.

Chapter 47

~CLAUDIA~

B ECAUSE OF THE COST AND mostly the timeframe, I wasn't planning on going back to New York until the summer. There was plenty happening on campus to keep me busy. Toby and I talked regularly. He seemed to be well, despite the heaviness of the therapy that had him digging into his scarred past. He shared milestones with me, like seeing his brother. He also confided in me at times when he was shaken, as he was when he'd found out his father had committed suicide.

"Thank you," he said after the last time we talked. "You have a way of twisting things around and helping me see something positive even when it's all crashing down on me. Sometimes it's that alone that helps me hold it together."

He wanted to come for a visit. I kept putting him off, but I couldn't refuse, when in February, he said he was coming out to stay with a friend in Palm Springs and would stop by for a day or two to hang out with me.

He arrived on a Friday, late in the month. When he called to tell me he was outside my housing unit, I went tearing out of the building to greet him. We hugged, and I smiled until my face hurt. He seemed a little reserved and nervous. We went for a bite to eat, and as I spoke about school and visits with my mom, he seemed to relax. He told me more about his visit with his brother in prison.

"We need to do L.A. tourist-style," I said and whipped out my list of places to see. I planned to keep us busy with activities for his visit.

I navigated; Toby drove. We visited Griffith Observatory and did a walking tour of downtown. It was going really great, so much to see and talk about, until a middle-aged businessman in a hurry slammed into me and sent me stumbling. He didn't even acknowledge the slight. I could see a dark mask sliding over Toby's features, that residual anger raising its ugly head. He growled and lurched forward, but I stepped in front of him and physically held him back.

"It was an accident. Let it go."

Ignoring my objection, Toby yelled after the guy. "Learn some manners, asshole!" Thankfully, the man was oblivious and kept walking.

I got the okay from my roommate for Toby to stay on the couch in the living room of our apartment for the night, but when we got back from our day out, she left a note saying she was going to stay at her friend's place. I hadn't anticipated a night alone with him, but I was glad she at least cleaned the place up.

I stood Toby in the middle of the plain white common room and made him turn in one complete circle. My décor consisted of string lights crisscrossing the ceiling and a large poster of Van Gogh's "Starry Night."

"That's all of it." I smiled proudly at the tiny space and even smaller galley kitchen. "'Cept the bedroom. It's in there." I led him to the doorway, where two single raised beds were against opposite walls, on either side of a small window. Two unimpressive, light-stained wooden desks were at the foot of each of the beds, heavily adorned with memorabilia, task lists and piles of textbooks.

"It's small, but it smells like independence to me," he said, and my grin grew wider.

Toby changed into sweatpants and a T-shirt, and, seated on the room's small blue couch, he began to surf the web for funny, viral videos to show me. Sitting next to him, in my bulkiest sleep clothes, I kept a pillow stationed in front of me, a physical barrier preventing any accidental contact.

"Who are you visiting in Palm Springs?" I asked.

"Believe it or not, it's Abe Bernbaum."

"Why are you visiting your old boss?"

"I did some carpentry work at his house back in Sayville. He has a vacation home out here, in the desert somewhere, and now he wants me to do some work there." Toby shrugged. "He paid for my flight, and I'll stay with him and his family for the week. He said before I leave, he wants to take me golfing."

"But you don't play, do you?"

Toby laughed. "I once scaled the fence of the West Sayville Country Club to get tanked with my friends."

I shook my head and smiled. "Sounds like Abe has a soft spot for you."

"Maybe." He studied his hands for a moment and looked up at me. "He's a tough ol' fossil. Expects a lot. But after the court case and what he did for me, I appreciate the stand-up guy he is. And what's more surprising is, I kind of like hanging out with him."

He folded my laptop closed, and slipped it onto the nearby table. We continued to talk for a couple more hours. He listened patiently as I told him about my classes and the professors I had—which ones I liked, which ones I despised—until finally, somewhere around 2 a.m., I began having trouble stringing coherent words together.

He rubbed my knuckles with his and said, "Goodnight, Claude." I yawned a sleepy goodnight back, and, as I headed for the bedroom, he went into the bathroom. For a second, I thought about offering him my roommate's bed, but then nixed the idea. He'd find a way to get comfortable on the couch. Exhausted, I dove into bed and fell right asleep.

When I opened my eyes, it was morning and sunlight was filtering in through the blinds of the dorm window. I awoke to Toby's arm draped over me. His face was in my hair, and his steady breaths warmed the back of my neck.

In my sleep-muddled state, I wasn't sure how or why he was lying with me, but his nearness invoked vivid memories of us together and the way he used to touch me. I imagined his hand now, sliding slowly over my bare skin, teasing my hip and cupping my breast, his thumb stroking me to breathless agitation. Like a movie playing in my head, I saw myself turning over to see his face, the one I had once loved so much that I had given him all that I had. His pale eyes would flutter open in the morning light. My attention would be drawn to his mouth, the soft fullness of his bottom lip and the memory of kisses he once relished on my neck as he tasted my skin. I remembered, too, the weight of his body over me. A resounding hum pulsed through my core as I remembered his hips pressed into me and of the astonishing and strangely wonderful fullness I had felt while he was inside me. I could barely breathe for wanting him so much.

Toby's hand shifted, ever so slightly on my hip, and it startled me out of my reverie. This was a minefield. My heart had accelerated, and my skin had warmed almost to perspiration. I worried that if he woke now, he would sense my state of arousal. I had to change the channel in my head. For a moment, I mourned the loss of what we'd had, felt the dry ache in the back of my eyes where tears usually formed, but I shut it down. Tight. I wouldn't put myself in that soft, unbalanced place where I so easily lost footing. I wouldn't be weak, and I would never look back. Slipping out from our cuddle, I made for the bathroom.

Other than our proximity, there was nothing to suggest anything had happened, and I decided not to even mention it. To bring it up would only be admitting that it disturbed me and give it undue importance. After I showered and came back into the room fully dressed, Toby was awake. With hands behind his head, he was staring at the ceiling.

"Hey, I forgot to ask you how the kitchen renovation is going." I opened the blinds and threw the room into bright daylight.

He rolled up on his elbow. "Really good."

"How did you learn how to do that?" I asked, tossing him a granola bar and opening one for myself.

"Carpentry? It's genetic." His longish bangs fell into his eyes, and he grinned. "I figured the rest out with some online tutorials."

I felt the temptation to reach over and brush the hair away. With a shake of his head, though, the bangs shifted aside, alleviating my inclination to do so.

He popped a chunk of granola into his mouth. "I still have a lot to do."

"Any news on the job front?"

"Nothing steady. But I joined a band," he said, looking at me as if waiting for my reaction.

"Playing guitar?"

"Yeah. We call ourselves 'Young Cranky Old Guys."

"Interesting name."

"We've already played a few gigs just from word-of-mouth—a Sweet Sixteen and two small parties. Probably do the bar circuit soon," he said. "We do mostly cover stuff, but we might try working on our own music eventually."

"That's nice." I picked up a comb and ran it through my wet hair. "I'll bet you have lots of fans."

He made a low snorting noise. "Yeah, if you count all the sixteen-year-olds who follow us on our fan page, we're quite the celebrities."

"Why is it that I can totally picture a group of teeny boppers vying for your attention?"

He laughed. "Just what every guy wants, his own personal, underage harem."

"Oh, I'm sure more appropriately aged women are showing you attention, too. Being out there, in the public eye, you're bound to meet someone." I put on an air of teasing but stopped when Toby's lips tightened into a frown.

Bowing his head, he hopped off the bed and went to the window. His uneasy expression reflected in the glass as he looked outside.

"I think it's great that we can talk like friends, but I can't discuss meeting new people with you, Claude. Not after what we've been through." Turning to face me, he ran his hand through his hair. "I understand you want me to be happy. But I'm not in the same place as you. Even thinking about it puts me on edge."

"Okay." I nodded. "We'll talk about something else."

In spite of the promise to divert our conversation to a safer topic, I couldn't think of anything else to say. For a long moment, neither of us said anything. Thankfully, his cell beeped with an incoming text and broke the silence.

Glancing at it, he grimaced. "It's Bob reminding me about our next appointment." Toby said, but avoided looking at me. "He didn't want me to see you."

"But I was the one who brought you to meet with him."

He stole a quick glance at me. "It's because he knows how I feel."

My face burned with indignation, and for a moment, I was too livid to speak. Tight lipped, I asked, "You didn't come all this way thinking there was a chance of us getting back together, did you?"

"No." His quick reply was defensive, but he looked flustered. "But I was thinking over the summer, maybe we could talk."

I twisted away from him and turned his hopeless proposition over in my mind.

Glancing back at him, casually, I said, "I'm not coming home this summer."

His eyes narrowed. "Not at all?"

"No. My mother got me a job in her office, and I need the money." It wasn't the complete truth, but I would make it happen. He opened his mouth to say something, but I forged ahead. "It'll be better this way. I don't want to complicate things between us. And it will also give me a chance to spend some extra time with my mom."

He avoided looking at me. "When will you be back?"

"I don't know. Holidays?"

Frowning, he shoved his hands in his pockets.

"When I come back doesn't matter. We'll keep in touch." I put my hand on the bedpost, as close as I dared get. "All that matters is that you get the help you need."

Toby groaned. "Jesus, I know you think I overreacted yesterday, but that guy plowed into you."

"You can't go around fixing situations with your fists. And believe it or not, I can defend myself."

He stared at me for a tense moment and, remarkably, broke into a grin. "With the way you held me back, I don't doubt it. But Claude," he said, standing more erect. "I am getting better at controlling my anger."

"That's good." I tried to sound enthusiastic, but I wondered if his anger would be something he'd ever truly have control over.

"It's the truth. You'll see," he said. He stepped closer, his hand settling on top of mine on the bedpost. "Since you're not coming home, can you promise me something?"

I looked at his hand and then at him.

"Don't be with anyone over the summer."

Just like that, my temper flared again. "Just the summer? What about the fall and the winter?" I jerked my hand from under his. "Do you think I should never have another relationship and perhaps become celibate?"

He smiled sheepishly. "Too much to ask?"

I bristled. "Not only is it too much to ask, but you have no right to ask!"

"You're right. I'm sorry," he sighed. "But the thought of you being here with all these guys and now that you're not, you know ..."

"Are you afraid I'll go on a sexual rampage now that I'm freed of my virginal burden?"

He winced.

"You come here with your sad eyes, crawl into my bed while I'm sleeping, and expect me to forget everything that happened?" I snapped. "We are not together, and if I decide to screw around indiscriminately, I won't be discussing it with you!"

He leaned his head back and inhaled sharply. When he looked back at me, I saw anger in his eyes, tinged with uncertainty.

"This is hard for me."

I crossed my arms in front of me. "And what you did was hard for me."

"Claude, don't," he pleaded, lowering his eyes. After a nerve-racking moment of silence between us, he said, "I should go."

I felt a need to close the awkwardness that had opened between us. "Look, as long as you understand we're not getting back together, we'll be fine. What's done is done. Please call me when you get to Abe's so I know you got there safely."

"Sure," he said, and he opened his arms to me. "Hug?"

Done in by our squabbling, I let him pull me into his arms. I wanted it to feel different, but I fit right into him just as I had in the past, my cheek finding the once familiar place between his neck and shoulder. I always admired the unyielding firmness of his body, the toughness that was synonymous with his strength. The warmth of our bodies intermingled through our clothes, and the smell of him filled my senses. Nothing had changed for us physically, but emotionally, though the pain had dulled, a throng of old hurt left me feeling hollow inside.

He rubbed up and down my back twice and relinquished his hold on me.

"For whatever it's worth, I'm glad you followed your dream, that you're going to school here, Claude. I know how much it means to you."

His acknowledgement astounded me. He understood. My lips twitched with a flimsy, emotional smile. "Thank you. I'm exactly where I want to be."

He nodded, picked up his backpack, and waved before he left my room.

After his visit, I never mentioned anything to Toby that might remotely hint at the dating subject. I didn't do much socializing anyway. Occasionally, I agreed to have coffee with a guy, but it never went past that. I preferred simpler diversions—a good movie, cheering our Trojans to victory during a game, and volunteering time to campus events. These small outlets helped me recharge and stay focused.

With my nose to the grindstone, semesters tumbled from one into another.

Chapter 48

~CLAUDIA~

A Year Later…

MID-JANUARY IN NEW YORK WAS bitter cold. I parked my Camry in the lot of The Mad Monkey, the name of the bar April had given me. It amazed me how quickly I'd become used to the moderate temperatures of Southern California. I had barely stopped shivering since arriving home, but the snow on the ground made me feel nostalgic.

My life was hardly recognizable from the one I'd left in New York. The last year and a half away had changed me, irrevocably. I was sprinting toward graduation with a possible internship lined up and acceptance into two graduate programs for my master's in wellness management. I felt unstoppable.

I had taken advantage of cheap airfare to come home for an extended weekend. Dad and April were the only ones who knew I was home. Tonight, I had bailed on the get-together April and Dario were hosting when I'd heard Toby's band was playing nearby.

Through the still air of the night, I could hear the sounds of his band, Young Cranky Old Men, playing inside the building from the parking lot. The sound of the lively beat sent goose bumps down my arms. I would finally see Toby perform.

For the first time in a long while, I was nervous about seeing him, and, as I approached the entrance to the bar, I rehearsed things I could say to him. We had been apart longer than we had been together.

I made my way through the door, paid the cover, and found a place near the bar to watch the band. It took a few minutes for me to adjust to the darkened, vibrating atmosphere. A loose and sweaty crowd was on their feet dancing. I felt out of place, but I batted down my anxiety and found Toby, on the band platform, amongst the other band members.

I stayed back and assessed him from afar. The first thing I noticed was his beard. He'd let it grow out so much that it covered the whole lower part of his face and crept down onto his neck. His long, wavy brown hair stuck out from under a gray knit cap. He was dressed in fitted blue jeans and an untucked dark blue button-up shirt. With the sleeves rolled up, I could see his forearm muscles move as his fingers maneuvered quickly and confidently over the strings of his guitar. He tapped his foot in beat to the song, seeming oblivious to the crowd, even to the mix of women dancing and gazing up at him; it was clear he was caught up in his music.

When the set ended, I pulled out my cell and sent him a text.

Hey. Coming to see you.

I watched him check his phone, and seconds later my phone beeped with his reply.

Cool. When?

Rapid fire, I shot him an answer. *Now.*

Summoning up my courage, I approached the stage.

Toby, with his back to the room, held his cell out in front of him as he shrugged off the strap of his guitar.

He hit me back.

Where r u?

The band's lanky, short-haired blonde lead singer moved to the edge of the stage, and with a practiced smile, gave me the once over. "Hey there, gorgeous. How's about you tell me your name over a drink?"

Ignoring him, I texted Toby again,

Right behind you. Turn around.

But instead of turning around, Toby stared at the phone as if my message was cryptic.

"No, thanks," I told the singer and pointed at Toby. "But could you please get your guitar player's attention for me?"

Obliging me, he reached back to swat Toby's shoulder. "Hey, T, I believe this Betty here wants to rock your world."

Unsuspecting, Toby finally turned around.

"Holy shit," he swore. "You're here." He hopped down from the platform in front of me and lifted me up off the ground in an energetic hug.

After releasing me, he jacked a thumb over his shoulder, towards the stage. "You hear us play?"

"Yes, and I'm very impressed. You guys sound amazing."

"Ah, we're just having fun. But that people actually dance and sing along, it's virtually the best high I ever had." Practically giddy with energy, he did a little drum roll on his head and grinned.

"You seem to really be enjoying yourself."

"I am. I really am." His eyes were bright with an air of self-assurance I hadn't seen in a long while. "Jesus, I can't believe you're actually here. It's been forever since you've been home."

"You let your hair and beard grow. Long." I reached up to tug at the unruly mop at the back of his neck when a glimmer at his ear caught my eye.

"What is that?" I asked, letting my fingers slide over the small diamond stud in his ear.

"You don't like it?" He raised his eyebrows in question, and up close, I was reminded how dazzling his eyes were.

"No, it's … unexpected." My face heated. The change in appearance, the engaging smile, the exuberance—it all threw me. I hadn't expected to find him so changed. "Everything about you looks different. Do I still know you?"

"Other than I'm now a way-cool musician who's in dire need of a shave and a haircut, I'm still me, Claude." He took my hand and squeezed it, then motioned towards the bar. "I hope you'll stay for a while and meet the rest of the guys before we have to pack up the equipment. I'll even buy you a drink. I'm sure they have soda or something."

"Now that I've reached the age where it's legally permissible, I actually enjoy a glass of wine once in a while," I said.

He cocked an eyebrow and grinned. "Never mind me. Do I still know you?"

I returned the grin with a lighthearted shrug. "I suppose we've both changed some."

The band had converged around the bar where their friends, girlfriends, and even some fans were waiting for them.

"Good set." A guy reached out to shake Toby's hand as I hopped up on the last available stool at the bar. Toby thanked him, and waved to the bartender. At the same time, a tall girl with short, black hair came up alongside him. She was more solidly built than me, but also curvier, and sported a tattoo on her neck and a nose piercing. The girl touched his back with familiarity, and Toby turned toward to her, blocking her from my view. He leaned close and said something to her that I couldn't make out. The girl nodded and stepped away from him, but not before she looked me over with her dark assessing eyes. With a lump in my throat, I realized it was probably his girlfriend. Coming here, I never thought to consider he might be with someone else. It hadn't entered my head.

"Who was that?" I asked when Toby turned back to me.

He shifted uneasily. "Who?"

I snorted at his attempt to cover it. "That girl you were just talking to. Is she your girlfriend?"

He looked over his shoulder, but the girl had disappeared into the crowd. "She's no one."

This only made me want to know more, but he didn't owe me any details. He had a private life—one that didn't include me. I tried to forget the pretty, tattooed girl.

I ordered a white zinfandel, and Toby asked for a beer. It was only after I sipped it that I realized I'd become the focal point of the band members' curious stares. Toby called out to them, introducing me. There was Dan, the lead vocalist that I'd met on stage; R.J., another guitar player; and Keith, who played several instruments, but mostly keyboard.

An older guy I recognized as the drummer bounded up between us. He was built compactly with thick muscled arms and a tattoo sleeve that ran down his right arm. His dark and wild curly hair was just short enough to display the impish glint in his eye. Animated and unable to sit still, he grabbed the back of my seat and threw his elbow on the bar top.

"So, who we got here?"

"Bones, this is Claudia. Claudia, Bones."

"This is Claudia? *The Claudia*?" He took my hand and pumped it up and down with exaggerated enthusiasm. "How about that—she does exist!"

"All right, that's enough," Toby muttered, appearing somewhat uncomfortable. He pushed at the drummer to make him go away. But Bones, refusing to go, put his arm around Toby's neck.

"Were you here when he blew those cords during our first set?" he asked me.

I laughed. "I think I missed that."

Toby scoffed. "Dude, you're making me look bad."

"Just messing with you, bro." Bones winked at me. "This guy's aces." He patted his shirt pocket before pulling out a pack of cigarettes. "Damn, lost my lighter. Either of you got a light?"

Both Toby and I shook our heads. Bones shrugged, and, winking at me, he raised his beer glass. "Cheers Claudia. Nice to finally meet you." Then he turned yelling out to someone else for a lighter and pushed away into the crowd.

Before I had a chance to ask, Toby said, "I quit smoking again, about six months ago."

"That's terrific!"

He didn't mention how Bones knew my name, but I was too thrilled with the news to care.

Conversation and laughter with the band continued through another round of drinks. My presence made Toby the butt of much ribbing, the guys taking enjoyment in trying to embarrass him in front of me. Eventually, the band began to trickle back to the stage to dissemble and pack the equipment.

"Sorry you had to endure that," Toby said.

"I'm not. They're sweet, and they only tease you because they like you," I said. The band members were nothing like Devlin and Ray, who, from the beginning, had given off a bad vibe. But now, Toby surrounded himself with a close knit of decent guys.

"Yeah, they're cool." He looked back towards the stage. "I have to go pack up. It'll only take a little while. Will you wait?"

"Of course," I said. "I was hoping you could finally show me that kitchen of yours."

He smiled. "Definitely. Sit tight. I'll be back as soon as I can."

It was after midnight when the group finished loading all the equipment into Dan's truck and I followed Toby outside. It was flurrying, and a thin coat of snow had already settled over the cars in the parking lot.

As we ambled towards my car, Toby said, "I know L.A. has nice weather, but don't you miss the snow?"

The night air was quiet—the kind of wintry-night-quiet from my childhood. I took a moment to inhale the fresh air, but as I did, Toby scooped up a handful of snow and tossed it at me.

I laughed, dusting the flakes from my coat. "I do miss the snow, but not having it thrown at me!"

We giggled and flung the fluffy stuff around like little kids as we helped each other clear the snow from our car windows. He was playful and silly, his attitude infectious. I hadn't seen him this way since that first summer, before all hell broke loose.

When our cars were cleared and warmed, I followed the red Jeep to the Faye house.

Inside the kitchen, I spun around in awe. He had installed cherry wood cabinets, granite countertops, a new refrigerator, stove, and ceramic tile on the floor. The only thing missing was a curtain on the window.

"This is amazing." I ran my fingers over the new stone counter-top, stunned at the level of skill it must have taken to complete the renovation. "I can't believe you did this all yourself. You must have done this kind of work before."

Toby shrugged. "As a kid, I always liked to build stuff. When Big Al wasn't tanked, he was a good teacher." It was the first time he'd spoken of Mr. Faye in a positive way. "I guess somewhere between then and now, I forgot how much I liked it."

He glanced around, and I could sense the pride he had for his work. I was aware, too, that something in the way he thought about his father had changed.

"Yeah, I think this is what I'm meant to do. I want to be a carpenter."

I looked around the kitchen feeling happy, feeling proud. Yes, carpentry was his calling.

"When you apply to potential employers, you should include photos of the renovation with your resume."

He frowned. "That's a great idea, except I don't have a resume."

"That's easy. I'll make one for you." I noticed the time on the new stove. "I should get home. I told my father that I'd be home before he finished his shift, which ends soon." Toby nodded he understood. "But I want to talk more. Come back with me?"

Toby was more than agreeable about coming over to my house. We decided to have coffee, and just as I finished setting the coffeemaker to brew, my father came home.

Dad stood in the entryway of the kitchen surveying the scene with his perceptive eye. Toby was leaning back against the counter as I set out mugs and spoons for our coffee.

"Well, would you look what the cat dragged in," he said to Toby.

"Damn, I wish I knew I was going to see you." Toby moved toward my father. "I would have brought some donuts. I know how you cops like them."

I halted, watching for my father's reaction.

Dad eyed Toby's unshaven, scruffy appearance with distaste. "I'm surprised Claudia recognized you with that small animal growing on your face."

Toby stroked his overgrown beard. "You kill me, old man, but I missed you." Out of the blue, he held open his arms to my father. "Bring it in here."

My jaw practically hit the floor.

Dad waved him off. "Get out of here."

"Come on," Toby persisted. "Don't leave me hanging."

Dad shook his head, but to my amazement, he stepped forward and hugged Toby briefly, clapping his back with a few loud thwacks. "You're a nut," Dad grunted.

"Goodness gracious." I fanned myself in jest. "Is this truly joking banter between my father and Toby Faye?"

"Had the troublemaker over here to watch some football. Seems we're in agreement over the Giants. But baseball?" Dad paused to shake his head with ridiculous remorse. "The lines are drawn."

"Wait for the season to start," Toby taunted and turned to me. "Pops and I made a bet as to who'll have the better record, the Yanks or the Mets. Loser's team buys dinner."

"Dinner?" I balked.

"Only 'cause he'll be buying," Dad boasted. He looked at Toby. "You'd better have a job by then."

Toby chuckled.

The scene unfolding before me was truly ironic. "Jeez, go away for a while and all kinds of weird stuff happens."

My father shrugged. "You miss a lot when you're not around. You should take that offer Bill Ramsey made. Offers like that don't come around every day."

"Dad, drop it." I glared at him. He wasn't supposed to mention the job offer I'd received from the director of Sterling Senior Care. I hadn't told any of my friends yet. By the way Toby was tilting his head, I expected now he'd want to know what we were talking about.

When Dad left the kitchen to change out of his uniform, I poured two mugs of coffee and offered one to Toby.

"I can't believe you talked to my father like that. You're lucky 'Pops' didn't pop you."

"Once you get past his crusty outer shell, he's kind of soft on the inside," Toby shrugged. "We actually get along okay."

"Wonders will never cease." I led Toby into the living room and got comfortable on the couch. Feeling relaxed, I beckoned him to sit with me. "Park it, mister. I want to catch up on everything I've missed."

He plopped down next to me. "Tell me what I missed, first. What offer was your dad talking about?"

"It's just a work-study opportunity I was offered here in New York. You know my father, he always has to make his preference known." I carefully skirted a detailed explanation. "He's just upset because my mother is giving me a pretty spectacular birthday and graduation gift. My birthday is during spring break, so she booked me a week's stay at a hotel on the beach."

"I heard. April and Dario told me they're going to be out there with you for the week. Sounds great," he said with a casual air. Though his manner was offhand, I suspected he felt snubbed that I'd not asked him to join us.

I had purposely not included him in the plans because with our past, a whole week together seemed like asking for trouble. But tonight, remembering the girl at the bar, it felt safe to extend the offer to him. "You're welcome to come, too."

"Text me the dates. I'll look into it."

"Sure," I agreed, and took a sip of my coffee. "So, besides the kitchen and job searching, tell me how you're doing. Don't skip any details."

"What can I say? There are still moments when I want to throw my shit in the Jeep and take off." He waved a hand, motioning off and away from here. "But I squash it and for the most part, I'm doing real good. With the band, Dario and April, my aunt, Abe, and even your dad, I don't feel so alone anymore." He lifted his eyes to mine then. "It feels pretty good to be here, where I know people and actually have a life I like."

Toby was happy.

I blinked back tears, almost speechless in this knowledge. I knew Mrs. Faye would have been so excited to hear his words. She had wanted this for him. It's what I prayed for, too.

"I'm so happy for you."

"Yeah, things are finally coming together." He paused a moment. "Claude, when we were dating, I saw being with you as a way out of my life. I wanted you to make me a better person. I realize now that it was unfair to expect that from you. Changing my life is solely up to me. And, over the last year, I've been making a conscious decision to move toward my goals. Focusing on what I want, and what I need to do to get it, seems like such a small change in mindset, but it's made a huge difference. I feel almost … invincible."

"Toby, that small difference has made all the difference. Your life is better because of it. I'm so excited to see you like this."

"Thanks. Unfortunately, I still haven't found a job, but since I'm not working, we can hang out all week."

"Can't. I'm flying out tomorrow."

He gaped at me. "But you just got here."

"I have to get back. My required Gerontology Practicum work-study program just started last week," I explained. "And, I'm co-chairing the campus' Relay for Life."

"Damn, you're so busy all the time," he muttered. "We could have had more time if you'd told me you were coming home."

"I didn't want you to fuss over me."

"Really, Claude, you've hardly been back since you started USC. It's a major event when you come home."

"I bet your girlfriend wouldn't like you making such an event over my homecoming."

"My girlfriend?"

"That girl at the bar. You're seeing her, aren't you?"

He ran a hand through his hair. "You sound as if you hope she's my girlfriend."

"It might be a little weird for me, but I'd be, um, happy for you," I said in earnest. "And I think it would make things easier between us."

He made a project out of putting his mug down on the coffee table, sliding it one way, then the other. I could see he wasn't comfortable telling me, but finally he said, "Leah and I hang out sometimes."

"That's very vague."

"It falls into the category of, 'We don't talk about it.' So leave it alone."

That meant they were involved, and knowing him, probably sexually. My blood turned cold.

"Okay," I inhaled, trying to push past the sting. "Whatever it is that you have with Leah, I can't be the center of your attention. Things are different. We're long past that kind of relationship."

"I'm well aware of that, Claude. You really put me in my place the last time I saw you." He scooted forward to the edge of the couch, putting some distance between us. I remembered the harsh words I said to him and, in guilt, bowed my head.

Sighing, he leaned back. "The point is, I get it. We're friends and that's fine. Actually, it's great."

I stared at him trying to determine his truthfulness. "Seriously?"

"Yes, seriously." He grasped my hand and let out a woefully exaggerated sigh. "Please, don't walk a tightrope around me."

"O-okay," I faltered, surprised by his steadfast certainty.

Appearing somewhat pensive, he smiled. "Julia said if I had faith, I would be rewarded. Maybe our friendship is my reward."

I wrinkled my nose. "Wow, that's sweet. Saccharine sweet. But I hardly believe even my friendship is enough a reward for what you've had to deal with."

"After what I put you through when I lost Julia." He shook his head. "You didn't give up on me. And still, across the country, when I'm having a rotten day, I know I can call you, and you'll give me that—"

"Annoying pep talk?" I supplied.

He laughed. "Yeah, but really, it helps me keep going."

"You're doing it all on your own," I said. "I'm just the cheering section."

"Are you kidding?" Twisting to face me, he grabbed the silver chain around his neck and pulled the attached medallion out from under his shirt. Between his fingers, he held Saint Jude's silver carved image. "I wear this every day, Claude. You got me through that first Thanksgiving. And if you hadn't made that appointment and taken me to meet Bob, I'd probably still be driving around the country, lost and confused. Even now, you still help me just by listening—and being my 'cheering section.' Don't underestimate what you've done for me." Gently, he stroked the back of my hand with his thumb. "I don't."

I was surprised, overwhelmed, too, by his depth of gratitude.

"You just needed someone to lean on."

"Yeah," he agreed as he put a hand on my shoulder. "Hopefully, you'll never need the kind of help I needed, but I want you to know that I'm here for you if ever you need me. I owe you."

I warmed under the weight of his pledge. He was very different—calm, collected, and focused. He even looked different; that haunting sadness in his eyes was gone. It pleased me to realize that, without consciously attempting to do so, I had ultimately kept my promise to Mrs. Faye. I had helped Toby find what she'd always known he'd been looking for.

"You don't owe me anything," I insisted. I had to cover my mouth as a powerful yawn escaped me. "I'm sorry. The East Coast-West Coast time zone change is throwing me off. How about I lean on you right now … and sleep?"

"Sleep?" he laughed and shook his head. "Oh, hell. It's late. I should shut up and let you go to bed."

As he rose to his feet, I grabbed his hand. I really didn't want him to leave. "It's snowing bad. Hang out and wait for it to stop. We can check to see what's on television, and I think there's some cookies in the kitchen."

He raised his eyebrows. "You have cookies?"

For the first time since we'd broken up, I didn't worry about him blurring the lines of our friendship. He got it, and now that he had someone else in his life, I felt safe to really, truly relax with him. Knowing that, I set out a sleeve of chocolate chip cookies and turned on the television.

He draped an arm over me as I rested my head on his shoulder. It was the perfect end to my visit home.

Chapter 49

~TOBY~

THE HOUSE'S HEATING SYSTEM MADE gurgling noises as it kicked on. Claudia hadn't even made it through the first ten minutes of the show she'd put on before she fell asleep. From the Chiametti's living room couch, I could see the snow swirling around outside on the front lawn. It was sticking—a sign that the temperature outside had dropped to or below the freezing mark, but with Claudia tucked in under my arm, I didn't care what was happening out there.

Claudia was finally seeing me do well. I pressed my face against the top of her head and inhaled. With a sigh, I stared up at the ceiling. I could not act on my attraction to her. Instead, I thought about the trip out to California in March. It would be an opportunity to create some new and positive air between us.

The hallway light in the stairway went on, and I heard the old man's footsteps.

"You still here?" Mr. Chiametti asked, as he came into the room. He was wearing a rumpled long sleeve T-shirt with plaid lounge pants, and by his half-cocked eyes, he looked as if he'd been asleep. He still had the need to check on us.

Claudia stirred sleepily, yawned, and then stood up. Looking out the front window, she commented, "The snow is really piling up."

I stood up, too. "Mind if I crash here tonight?"

"You should," Claudia said, walking to the stairs and then glancing over her shoulder. "We can have breakfast before I go to the airport in the morning."

Her body was backlit by the hall light, making her appear unearthly. My body pulsed at the stirring thought of lying next to her sleep-warmed body. It had me itching to follow her up the stairs.

"Sleep on the couch, not with my daughter," Pops said, as if he were reading my mind.

"Dad," Claudia mumbled a drowsy complaint. "I wasn't offering him my bed."

"Yeah, she might not be able to keep her hands off of me, and then you'd end up with a grandkid with my face."

"Don't give me nightmares," Pops muttered.

I smiled. "We'd make beautiful kids."

"Keep it in your pants."

"I'm just saying."

Heavy-eyed, Claudia turned around on the stairs and pouted. "Stop talking as if I don't hear you."

"Go to bed," her father said.

"I'm going. Goodnight."

"Goodnight," we echoed. She disappeared up the stairs. Seconds later, the hallway went dark.

Pops went to the door, flicked off the porch light, and checked the door lock.

"She's a good girl, my daughter," he said with admiration.

I nodded. "She's pretty terrific."

Opening a closet next to the bathroom, he pulled out a blanket. "I hope she comes back to New York after graduation."

"I didn't know she was thinking about staying out there."

He handed me the blanket and shook his head, clearly not happy about it.

"Unfortunately, she seems to like it there, with her mother. My ex-wife booked her in some fancy hotel on the beach for a graduation present. I'm sure it's some tacit plan to sway Claudia to stay out there and get her master's degree at USC," he said, with a sneer. "But the senior residence she used to volunteer at offered her a tempting arrangement—a paid internship. She'd be able to work on her degree at Stony Brook University while working part time at the home. It's good work experience, and I'm pushing for it."

I dropped back down onto the couch and pulled off my shoes. "Can I give you some advice on Claudia?"

He snorted. "You're going to give me advice on my daughter?

This I gotta hear."

I overlooked his jab and made eye contact with him. "Let her make her own decision. She doesn't like being pushed into anything."

He opened his mouth to say something, but snapped it shut. He knew I was right.

"Damn, that kid is too much like me. Stubborn," he muttered. Turning to scrutinize me, he said, "Now, let me offer you some advice. No one's going to hire you looking like that." He waved a finger at my hairy face. "Clean yourself up."

Chapter 50

~TOBY~

THE WEATHER IN CARLSBAD, CALIFORNIA, was perfect for an early morning run. I did a few leg stretches before I stepped out from behind the palm trees that lined the covered stone walkway in front of our suite and headed to the beach. The resort was right on the shoreline, and it only took a minute to reach it.

I started with a light sprint to warm up. My toes dug into the soft sand, and the muscles in my calves started to fire up. I pushed myself to go faster. As I did most days in New York, I had run every morning since I'd hit the West Coast. The mild breeze carried the taste of the Pacific along with it. The ocean air felt good on my freshly shaved face. Right after Claudia's visit home, I'd cut my hair and shaved off the matted whiskers. Clean-shaven.

I welcomed the salty fresh air. It helped me focus and clear my head as well as discharge tension. It was not anger I needed to release, but the growing need for something I knew I couldn't have. I ran hard to drive the hunger away.

The place Claudia's mother had picked out was pretty freaking incredible. Luxury accommodations—a full kitchen and two bedrooms with queen-sized beds. Dario and April shared one room and the other bedroom, one overlooking the ocean, Claudia had to herself. I was stationed on a pullout couch in the common room, but I was fine with it. We spent our days laughing while we moved aimlessly through the streets of the city. Every night featured a table full of mouth-watering foods and plenty to drink. We were having a great time together.

It was good to be here and see Claudia happy. It gave me a

sense of satisfaction. I'd done the right thing by letting go. Without holding on and without really losing her, we had both been able to move forward. Over the course of the last year and half, I'd been able to define what I wanted out of my life—I'd amended and streamlined it until I was sure I was working towards the kind of life that I saw myself having. And now, for the most part, I had it in place. I had friends, family, and finally a job.

Claudia's resume did the trick.

I was now a full-time carpenter with Delfino Brothers, Incorporated. My new bosses, two *Pisans*, offered me a great package—benefits, holiday pay—the works. I was making more money than I'd ever made, doing work I honestly liked. I was fulfilled as I'd never been before. Still, it didn't stop there. I had more ideas, more plans. Claudia continued to be a part of that picture.

I didn't want to overwhelm Claudia with what I saw as our destiny—a future where we were together, but with us spending so much time in close proximity, I was getting impatient about keeping my hands to myself. I wasn't sure how long I could continue to hold back. Running was my only outlet. As a last ditch effort, I tried to purge it from my system.

We spent our last night in Carlsbad at a local club, The Lounge, a seedy little dance bar that we hit several nights during our stay. The drinks were watered-down, and the crowd noisy and rude, but we called it ours. It was Claudia's birthday, but she made us swear we wouldn't buy her any gifts. So instead, we scored a coveted booth near the dance floor and didn't allow her to pay for anything. We toasted her through several rounds of drinks, co-conspirators in our aim to get her drunk for the first time in her life.

Dario and Claudia were out on the dance floor dancing to some obnoxious techno remix. April stayed back with me to order another round. I stared off at Claudia dancing with Dario, admiring the way she moved. Sighing, I forced myself back to conversation with April.

She glanced at me with knowing eyes. "You still got it bad for Claudia."

I tapped my fingers on the table. "That obvious, huh?"

With a sly grin, she said, "*Papi*, you practically have moonbeams in your eyes."

"Moonbeams?" I grunted, and then laughed. "That sounds like

a serious condition."

"Yes. And contagious. Over the week, Claudia seems to have developed the same condition. I believe I saw the identical look in her eyes, too."

I rounded forward. "Really?"

She nodded and then smirked. "I think you should just grab her and lick her like you did the first time. That seemed to work."

I chuckled. "Tempting, but I can't."

"Because you're seeing someone else?"

"Come on, April. You know Claude just as well as me. I can't just throw myself on her, not after what happened between us. She'll freak."

"But you were hoping something would happen this week, weren't you?"

"Sure, but even though nothing did, it was still a great week," I said. "There's always hope that if she comes home, things will fall into place."

"Wait, so you don't have a girlfriend?" April cocked her head. "And what do you mean 'if' she comes home?"

Laughing and breathless, Claudia and Dario came bounding back to the booth.

Dario held out his hand to April. "Let's go, mama. Dance with me."

April's eyes lit up. Sliding out of the booth, she followed him onto the dance floor.

"Let's go. Your turn to dance with the birthday girl." Claudia put out her hand for mine.

I took her proffered hand without hesitating. On the dance floor, with all of us slightly buzzed, I entertained my friends with my off-the-cuff moves. With her arms loosely around my neck, Claudia was sweaty, and her natural smell intensified. I had to fight the impulse to pull her tighter to me.

"Thank you for coming out here to stay with me. The dinners, the beach, dancing—this week has been the best time I've had in years," she hollered over the grinding beat. Her gaze dropped to my hairless chin. "I'm glad you shaved. Not a fan of the full beard. Such a handsome face should never be covered."

Encouraged by her appreciation, I leaned down and rubbed my smooth cheek against hers.

"Nice," she purred, stroking my face with her hand.

I was further buoyed by her touch. "Mmm. You smell edible, like coconut."

Claudia angled her mouth to my ear, like she was telling a secret, and whispered, "That's the *piña coladas*. They go down easy."

Her breaths made my skin tingle.

I teased her. "You're so laminated."

"Am not!" She giggled, tightening her arms around my neck, and looking into my eyes. "I'm just having fun."

I appreciated that we had finally arrived back to being relaxed with each other, but as her hips swayed sexily under my hands in rhythm to the music, Claudia held my gaze. The invitation seemed transparent, but still, I wondered if she was conscious of how she made me burn for her.

For the first time all week, I didn't want to drive the hunger away. I wanted to feed it.

Chapter 51

~CLAUDIA~

"WOOO! LAST ONE IN THE pool is a rotten egg!"
I raised my arms in the air and ran for the door of our hotel unit. I chucked my sandals on the floor and zipped into the bedroom to put on my bikini.

Tired and sweaty from dancing, we were going to finish the night at the hotel's heated, kidney-shaped pool.

Because of the late hour, the pool area was empty. April, Toby, and I sat on the edge with our feet in the water. Dario began swimming a backstroke across the pool, belting out, "Volare," at the top of his lungs. With a complete lack of inhibition, he jumbled through the lesser known verses in awful, broken Italian, making April and I giggle.

"God, I had so much fun tonight, but my feet hurt from all that dancing," I groused.

Toby patted his lap. "Put 'em up here. I'll rub them."

I lifted my legs out of the water and swiveled on my butt until he caught my feet and cradled them in his big hands. Concentrating on one, he pressed his thumbs firmly down over the balls of my foot. It hurt so good, and, closing my eyes, I sighed, "Ah, that feels amazing."

Seemingly bolstered by my appreciation, he caressed my foot with more intensity, and, sliding his hand up the length my calf, he worked that, too. His touch blossomed like a warm vine curling around my senses. I leaned back on my elbows, one foot in Toby's hands, the other resting against his ribcage. Our eyes met, and for a long exhilarating moment, neither of us could look away, until April spoke.

"How soon after graduation are you coming home?" she asked.

Laying down made me conscious of how much I had to drink. My brain felt like it tilted to one side. I tried to order my thoughts. "Um, I'm not sure I'm coming home."

Toby's fingers rested on the instep of my foot. "If you're staying at USC, that means you turned down the internship at Sterling."

"You know about that?"

"Your dad told me."

"My dad? Jeez, I don't know if I like that you two are so friendly," I said, but then shrugged. "I think I'd like to go home, but I hate to leave my mom." I looked up at him. "It's crazy, but now my feelings are reversed—I want to go to Long Island, but now I worry about how my mother is going to handle it."

"Hey," Toby said, rubbing the arch of my foot soothingly. "You're twenty-two now. You can't worry about what makes your parents happy all the time. You have to start thinking about where your future lies, where you want to be."

April made an irritated sound. "I didn't know you were thinking about staying here. How come you didn't tell me anything about this?"

"I knew you'd try to talk me into coming back to New York." I made a pretense of adjusting my bikini top. "I was accepted into USC's as well as Stony Brook's graduate programs, and I haven't made a decision."

"Really, *mami*, there's nothing to decide. Your home is with us." April scowled, her opposition clear.

I bit my lip. I didn't want to do this with her. It would ruin the night, our last one together.

Toby nudged her. "Cool it, April. Claude doesn't need that kind of pressure from you."

"I'm not alone in wanting you to come home." Ignoring the warning, April turned to Toby. "Tell her you want her to come home, too. Now would be a good time to tell her why you came here." Without allowing him to answer, April blurted out, "He wants to get back together with you."

I stared from one to the other, speechless.

Danger lit Toby's eyes as he glowered at her. "April, what the fuck are you doing?"

"Don't yell at me," April pouted. "How will anything ever move forward between you two if she doesn't come home?"

Numbly, I pulled my foot out of Toby's hands and sat up. "Is this some kind of plan between you two?"

"No," Toby started to say, but I didn't hear much else. Water splashed noisily as April popped out of the pool and scampered to my side.

She wedged herself between Toby and me and hugged my neck. "Chica, chica," she cried, and squeezed my shoulders. "You're my best friend. I want you to come home."

By now, Dario had climbed out of the pool. Picking up a towel, he stepped up next to us. "Come on, my little trouble-maker," he said, wrapping the towel around April's shoulders. "I'm taking you inside to find some other way to keep your mouth occupied."

April stood up and turned into him. "Dar, I want them to be as happy as we are." Drawing her towards the walkway leading to our unit, Dario replied, "Yes, mama, but you need to let them find that happiness on their own."

Until then, I hadn't realized how trashed April was, but then I tried to stand and swayed too. I wasn't in any better shape than she was.

Toby rose up next to me and took hold of my elbow. "You okay?"

I swallowed hard. I wasn't okay. We had gotten through the week in a mostly relaxed atmosphere. He had been funny and easy to be with, but there were instances when a glance seemed to hold a beat too long or a touch lingered for more than was called for. Considering our history, it was hard to ignore the subtle implications, but unwilling to let it spoil our week, I did just that.

Tonight, however, something had shifted. The mood at the dance club seemed to have blown everything open, and now, as he stood shirtless before me, the expanse of his muscled shoulders and bare chest taunted me to distraction. I was swarmed with a heady awareness of him. But still, I stepped closer—close enough that I could feel the heat from his body without touching him. I raised my eyes to his.

"Is it true? Did you come here to try to start something up with me again?"

He inhaled noticeably and rubbed the back of his head, seemingly in distress. I took pleasure in knowing my nearness affected him like his did me.

"What if I said 'yes?'"

"But, our relationship … it's comfortable."

"Comfortable?" Reaching out, he yanked me up against him. The hardness of his masculine body pressed into me as he held me tightly to him. The warmth of his bare chest hit me like scorching furnace. "Does this feel comfortable?"

I drew a sharp, quick breath. This close to him, I couldn't think straight.

He didn't smile. "It's only comfortable as long as we're twenty-five hundred miles apart," he said roughly, his warm breath fanning my face. "Being here with you all week has been incredible, but comfortable? No, that's not how I'd describe it."

I struggled to remain calm. "What about your girlfriend, Leah?"

His eyes were intense; his lips drew into a thin line. "I haven't seen that girl since February. But she was never my girlfriend. I haven't had a girlfriend since you."

"You lied to me!" I wrenched away from him.

With his fists clenched, he stood there watching me. "You wanted to believe I had moved on. I let you."

Bristling with anger, I turned and ran up the walkway to our unit. It wasn't so much that I'd believed a fabrication that made me angry, it was the fact that he was right. I had wanted to believe he was off limits, for him as well as for me. It had given us a line to toe. It had felt safer knowing we couldn't go there. Now it was another dismissible barrier.

Our hotel unit was quiet; April and Dario's bedroom door was shut. I made a dash for my own bedroom, but as I tried to shut the door, Toby pushed his way through. It infuriated me how composed he appeared as he calmly closed the door and approached me in the darkness.

Feeling exposed and defenseless, I crossed my arms. "Get out," I ordered.

"Claude," he said, putting a finger to my lips to silence me. "Stop pushing me away. I can tell by your reaction, you didn't see this coming, but at least hear me out." It was a long moment before he continued. "When you first agreed to go out with me, being with you was almost intimidating. I was blown away that you wanted to be with me because I put you on such a pedestal." He picked up a strand of my hair. "You are so textbook perfect—the good girl with the big heart. I was so out of my element around you, but I worked hard to behave myself and be a decent guy. Even then, I always knew deep down inside, I'd never be enough, and that once you left for USC, you wouldn't come back for me."

"Coming here was never about getting away from you," I rushed out.

"I know. You were following your dream." A quick smile curved his lips. "I've always envied that 'get it done' mentality of yours. I needed someone like you in my life. I needed the push."

"You don't need me to motivate you anymore. You're doing great on your own."

"Yeah, it's true, and that's my point. Things are so much better for me now. I feel stronger than I ever have, but I still need you. Not to push me, but simply because I miss you when you're not around. I miss talking to you, kissing you ..." With his fingers, he gently stroked my bare shoulder, continuing up the column of my neck. Automatically, I lifted my chin to allow him to continue, my whole body reeling from this touch.

"Claudia ... I miss the way it feels inside me when I touch you." His words came out tattered, and I was startled by the blatant ache I heard in their tenor. His tone, coupled with the soft look in his eyes, only further teased my own yearning for him. "Tell me you don't miss me, and I'll leave you alone."

We stared at each other through a long, loaded silence. Unwilling to have him leave me, I wound my hands around his neck and pulled him to me until our mouths met. Our kiss was noisy, breathless and frantic—the result of the week's building attraction. As if we didn't need to breathe, our lips held to one another's. I pushed myself against his bare chest, reveling in his hardness, while he palmed my backside. His strong hands held my butt firmly, and he lifted me, pressing me into him before spinning us around to the bed. He lowered me down slowly, his erection grinding against my pelvis and then my stomach. When my feet touched the carpet, without pause, I crawled onto the bed to lie across the flowered bedspread. He followed, moving over me until his body covered mine.

"Are we going to regret this?" I whispered the question, but I had already moved past caring about the repercussions.

He slid his hands down my arms until both sets of our fingers were intertwined. His eyes locked on mine as he pressed my hands back into the mattress on either side my head. With the weight of him on top of me, and my hands restrained, I felt vulnerable. Instead of being fearful, though, my desire grew. He lowered his face to my neck, his shallow breaths like gentle strokes upon my skin.

"Never," he whispered.

With his teeth, he tugged at the strap of my bikini top, pulling at the stretchy material until he succeeded at exposing my right breast. A thrill licked hotly down my spine, and I quivered. Moonlight streamed over us from the room's large window, but even in the darkness, I could see the heated look in his eyes as he gazed down at me.

"I still dream about that night out in your backyard and the way it felt to be with you," he murmured, lowering his head until his nose and then his mouth pressed against the crest of my collarbone. "I miss the way you smell," he said softly, and his lips skimmed the sensitive skin just above my hardened nipple.

"Please," I begged him, arching my back so he would take me in his mouth.

"No, not yet," he whispered. "I'll get there, but first I want to kiss you again."

He let go of my hands, and I stayed still, mesmerized and more than a little eager, as he reached towards me to untie my bathing suit top and peel it off. His body was corded and tight with his arousal as he lay back over me, warming my skin with his. The sparse hairs of his chest tickled my breasts as he brought his lips back to mine. This time we kissed slowly, our mouths sipping and tasting each other's as if we couldn't get enough. His hands moved to cover my breasts, and I moaned my approval. He teased me, stroking me with his fingers as his mouth drifted down over my chin to my neck. As promised, he kissed my chest, paying attention to one side and then the other while I squirmed blissfully under him.

In our intimate twist, he lowered his hands to my bikini bottoms and began to pull them down my hips. I raised my knees up, hindering his efforts.

"No, we're not having sex. Not tonight."

"You sure? I have caps, in the other room. I'd be back in two seconds."

I shook my head. Things were moving at a scary pace. "If you leave the room, you're not coming back in."

My own resistance surprised me. I waited, fearing he would call my bluff, but then he smiled. "Okay, okay. Can I at least give you a birthday present?"

I bit my lip. "What kind of present?"

Still wearing his swimsuit, he knelt before me and applying pressure to my legs, he straightened them up, along his chest. "The kind that doesn't have a price tag but is sure to please," he said, and holding my gaze, he pulled my bottoms off, letting them drop carelessly to the floor.

He lowered my left leg onto the bed beside him, and holding my right leg up, he pressed a series of hot kisses behind my knee before he dragged his teeth back up my thigh. I hissed as a pleasurable ache shot through me. When he shifted lower on the bed, I knew beyond any doubt what he intended to do.

Reflexively, I tried to close my legs, but his strong fingers held them apart. He pressed his palm against my sex. The warmth startled me, and I let out a little moan.

"Don't fight me." The command was gentle. "I promise, you'll like it."

In a state of arousal, my heart beat at a frenzied pace. The sight of him over me—this sexy, handsome guy, the only guy I'd ever trusted to touch me so intimately—consumed me with physical need. It had been so long ago that I'd let anyone touch me, *that he'd touched me*, but it was the sudden conscious awareness that I still loved him that weakened me. I was so desperate to feel him, I didn't have the strength or desire to stop what was about to happen.

Without waiting for my spoken consent, he stroked me with his thumb. Leaning over my stomach, he kissed my belly as his fingers slid lower to pet me. I sighed with pleasure while he nipped sensuously at my hip and pelted me with kisses and licks down over my pelvis until he reached the top of my thigh.

"Claudia," he whispered, pausing his motion. "Open your eyes, baby. Look at me."

Flushed, I peered down at him. He hovered over me, just as tense with desire as I.

"You love me?" he asked.

I was too struck by our intimacy to hide it.

"Yes."

"Say it."

"I love you."

Leaning back over me, he kissed my lips. "Thank you, baby," he said softly.

He shifted his body lower, and as his fingers stirred and teased me, he said, "Say it again."

Faltering and breathless under his deft strokes, I repeated, "I love you."

With a contented sigh, he replaced his fingers with his mouth, kissing me softly between my legs. As his lips moved slow and gentle over the sensitive area, I gasped, shocked at how powerful the sensation was.

With darkened eyes, he gazed at me, a brief, triumphant smile on his handsome face before he kissed me again, and again, gradually increasing the pressure and the length of each kiss. I squirmed under him and shuddered when his tongue flicked over me. Clutching handfuls of his hair, I let my head fall back and became lost in sensation.

My legs began to shake as riotous seizure took hold of me and strung me out. It was so intense, I whimpered at the release. As my body trembled, Toby rose to lie beside me and hold me in his arms.

He pressed his face into my hair. "Did you like your birthday present?"

"Mmmm, nice," I murmured through a smile, as my body tingled with warm fuzziness. I was utterly sated.

"I'm glad I'm the first for that, too."

Wistful, I swished my fingers over his chest. "Will I ever be able to claim a first with you?"

He leaned back to look in my face, his eyes meeting mine. "Claudia, you love me," he whispered. "I never had that with anyone else. That outweighs anything and everything else."

His words, though sincere, were missing something. A seed of doubt began to take root, but too exhausted to dwell upon it, I curled myself around him, and fell asleep.

Chapter 52

~CLAUDIA~

FIGHTING THE MORNING SUN COMING through the bedroom window overlooking the Pacific Ocean, I opened my eyes slowly. With a groan, I noticed the bed was disheveled, and I was naked—a reminder of the night's spontaneous events. The only sign of Toby was the indent in the pillow where his head had been. I slipped on a T-shirt and panties and padded to the bathroom. I downed some painkillers for my headache and brushed the rancid sweetness from my mouth—both, no doubt the effect of the piña coladas I'd consumed so blithely the night before. Back in my bedroom, I engaged the lock on the door and sunk back down into bed. I needed to think about what had happened last night.

Before I could even attempt to rationalize anything, there was a tap at the door.

"Good morning, beautiful. I have coffee for you," Toby said through the door.

"Leave it on the table out there," I mumbled.

The doorknob rattled, and I heard him sigh. "Claude," his voice lost the easy tone. "Open the door."

"No."

Then gentler. "Let me in. Please. I just want to talk."

"I don't want to talk."

"Okay, then just let me in anyway," he said, but I didn't reply.

There were three hard raps against the door.

"Hear that?" he asked.

Of course I'd heard it, but still, I remained quiet.

"It's my head banging against the door."

I coughed out a laugh despite myself. "Well, stop doing that."

He banged again. Three times. "I'm going to keep it up until you either let me in or I knock myself out."

His cajoling insistence was distressing. It made me weepy. "Go away," I begged.

"Uh-uh. I'm not going anywhere," he said, then added, "Better figure out how you'll explain my unconscious body to April and Dario when they find me."

He hit the door three more times. "Starting to feel woozy."

His ridiculousness exasperated me, but I threw my legs over the side of the bed anyway. "Okay, already!"

Unlocking the door, I retreated to the bed, bowing my head so he wouldn't see the tears in my eyes. I saw him balancing two paper cups of coffee and a white, waxed bag as he came through the door. With his foot, he pushed the door shut behind him, gingerly placed everything on the night table and knelt on the floor next to the bed.

"Hey, what happened?" He looked up at me. "When I woke up, you were practically wrapped around me like a second skin. Guess I shouldn't have gone to get coffee, huh?"

I peeked at him. Despite the serious look on his face, he was charmingly disheveled; light stubble shadowed his chin, and though shorter, his wavy hair was errant and sleep-mussed. My body pulsed with the desire to touch him.

I dared not.

"Toby, last night was a mistake."

"Nothing has ever been so right as you and me," he insisted. "Claude, this was not some one-night stand." He took my hand in his. "I want to be with you."

Pulling my hand from his, I fell sideways, collapsing heavily on the bed and clutched a pillow to my chest. "How can we possibly think this will work between us?"

The bed creaked as he moved to lie down next to me, his face only inches from mine. "If you give me a chance, we will make it work."

I rubbed my eyes tiredly. "We tried this before. We don't fit in each other's lives."

"Didn't last night remind you how amazing we are together?"

"Yes, it did." Our eyes met, and I struggled to articulate the thing that scared me most. "But when things got tough, you were not only angry, you were cruel to me. In all my life, no one has ever been that mean to me before."

He exhaled gruffly and released my hands, backing up as if I'd taken a shot at him.

"Jesus, I was such a mess then. Dev was in my face, you were leaving, and then … and then Julia died," he whispered. "Claude, it got too difficult to be the guy I was trying to be for you. And I was sure it was the end of us, so before you could break up with me, I struck first." He glanced up at me, his expression solemn. "Bob said I pushed you away to protect myself. I've had a lot of hurt in my life. I was so afraid of getting hurt, again."

I remembered the boy he'd been, the kid in middle school with the sad eyes. "I know what you've been through. I would never add to it," I cried.

"I know that." He pulled the pillow away from me and moved closer. "I'm not looking for sympathy. I just need you to under-stand why I did what I did. Claudia, I know how much I hurt you, but I'm not that guy anymore. I swear I won't hurt you again."

He put his arms around me and stroked my hair. I closed my eyes. Even though I empathized with his story, and I did understand, I was still ambivalent about a future for us. But for the moment, in his arms, I was comforted, and I didn't attempt to move away.

He looked at me, seeming lost in thought as he swept the hair off my face and caressed my cheek. He leaned in and nuzzled my cheek. His lips skimmed my eyelashes to the tip of my nose, and, grazed my lips until he pressed them against my mouth more fully, eliciting an answering response from me. Giving in, I closed my eyes and wrapped my arms around his neck. We kissed over and over. Our lips met softly in kisses that were tender, yet unmistak-ably passionate.

Moments later, we heard April and Dario's voices in the kitchen. Toby stilled, and, with a sigh, he gave me another quick kiss before he pulled back and stood up.

"Everything's going to be fine. We'll hash out the details when you come home, all right?" Moving to the night table, he picked up one of the cups and handed it to me. "Coffee, just how you like it, and there's a blueberry muffin in the bag." He ran a hand through his hair. "Shit, I gotta get moving. We have to leave for the airport in a few minutes."

He took the other hot cup, and opening the door, moved to leave the bedroom.

"Toby," I called out, and he turned back around. "I haven't made a decision on where I want to go for my master's degree."

He leaned against the doorframe. "I'm the deciding factor, I guess. You'll come back to New York, for school and for me."

"What if I don't want to go to school in New York?"

His eyes narrowed as he came closer. "Claude, my life is in New York. I got a new job and my band … there's no other way."

I clutched the warm coffee cup between both my hands and raised my chin. "You want me to base an important decision on what you believe is good for us, but while you asked me to admit my love for you, you still haven't admitted your love for me."

Sighing, he shifted his weight from one foot to the other. "That's not fair. You know I don't have an easy time with that."

"What's not fair is that you expect me to drop everything I have here to run back to New York without any assurances."

"I meant everything I said this morning. I won't hurt you again."

"And I'm sure you believe that." I peered up at him through lowered lashes. "This week with you, it was so much fun. And last night … was incredible. But what forced us to an end that July was not only your anger—it was your inability to admit you loved me. How can I trust that you're honestly vested in our relationship?"

There was a motion behind him. "Sorry, man," I heard Dario say. "We got to get a move on. We have to turn in the rental car at the airport before the flight."

"Yeah, okay," Toby mumbled over his shoulder. Turning back to me, he ran a hand through his hair. "Claude, I don't know what to say."

I raised my eyes to him. "It's simple. Tell me you love me."

He blinked, but said nothing.

For a moment, I had to close my eyes and cover my mouth. I fought through the heartache and shook my head. "That's what I thought."

He shot forward, towards the bed, his arms open. "Claudia, I—"

"Oh, please don't." I threw out a hand to make him stop. "Don't try to pacify me by saying it now."

"But I can say it."

"I've no doubt you can pronounce the words. Most people can," I reproved. "But I won't believe you if you do."

"What do you expect me to do with that?"

"There's nothing you can do," I snapped with tears scorching my eyes. "You'd better go. You're going to miss your flight."

"Screw the flight. I can't leave like this."

"I can't do this with you," I argued. "Please, just go."

He came closer, his legs touching the bed as he leaned towards me. I took a breath, and wiping my eyes, I met his stare.

His expression was terse. "I'm not just going to let this go. We need to talk about this, Claudia."

"Fine," I swallowed hard. "But it will have to wait until after graduation."

Chapter 53

~CLAUDIA~

AFTER TWO YEARS, LAX TO JFK had become a routine plane ride. Now, with the final two years of college completed and graduation over, it felt anything but routine. A major part of my life had ended. Finished. While I had the next step in my education mapped out, I had a whole, unplanned summer ahead of me—one that involved going home to face Toby.

Despite my restlessness, Dad snored softly in the seat next to me. I smiled as I thought back to how happy he had been yesterday at my ceremony.

The weeks leading up to graduation had been tiresome. Between studying for finals and an incredible amount of tasks, rehearsals, exit interviews, sifting through loan documents, and other university forms, I spent so much time hunched over my computer, I was sure rigor mortis would set in. Despite all the work, the result was worth it. The commencement ceremony at the University of Southern California was exhilarating. It'd been a perfect seventy-five degrees, and it was with an incredible feeling of accomplishment that I marched to the platform to receive my bachelor's diploma, *magna cum laude*. Having my mother and father together, smiling proudly from the crowd, was one of the highlights of the day.

Even with the excitement and busyness of all that encompassed those weeks, I'd known once graduation was over I had to talk to Toby. That last day at the resort he'd told me if we were to move forward, he wanted me back in New York. It meant I wouldn't have a decision of where I'd be doing my graduate work. Though I was excited about the possibility of being with him again, I was also nervous about how we would reconstruct our once failed relationship. Coming home solely to try and work things out with him would mean taking a great leap of faith, one I wasn't sure I was ready to take. Because of this uncertainty, I knew my choice needed to be based on what I needed. And what I really wanted.

I liked to think that over the last few years I'd learned a lot about life and people. And about myself. Death and heartbreak had toughened me up, but it was my time away at school that gave me new perspective and taught me to appreciate all the blessings I had in my life. I was returning home a much more confident, strong, and fiercely independent person than the one who left Long Island two years ago. In the end, the decision I made was for me.

Toby was expecting to hear from me as soon as I got in so we could get together, but after Dad and I arrived home, I decided to wait to call him. I hopped in the shower to freshen up, and twisting my wet hair up in a knot, I put on the first thing in my suitcase that wasn't a wrinkled mess—a simple flouncy-skirted, floral print dress. Dad had my Camry gassed up and ready to go. I kissed my father's cheek, grabbed my keys, and headed out the door.

Nervous and fidgety about the impending conversation I needed to have with Toby, I decided to take the short drive up to St. Lawrence Cemetery and spend some quiet time with Mrs. Faye before I called and arranged to meet up with him. I drove through the familiar town streets to the memorial park.

Time was slipping towards the evening hour, but the sun, weeks from summer solstice, was not ready to surrender the sky to the moon. Beautiful splashes of orange and pink colored the horizon as I pulled into the small cemetery and navigated to the most northern end. There were two other cars parked along the narrow roads. One of them was a red Jeep. With an immediate twinge of nerves, I pulled up behind the Wrangler and turned off my car. I rechecked my appearance in the rearview mirror before I got out. Stepping onto the lush mat of grass sprouting from the rain-softened ground, I scanned the area for Toby's tawny-colored head, but I didn't see him.

I started toward the grave, and rounding the beginning of the row, I finally spotted him. He sat in front of his mother's grave, leaning back on his arms, a jacket clutched in one hand. There was seriousness in his disposition, his eyes trained on the headstone as if he were deeply absorbed in his thoughts. I stood for a moment noticing the long length of his jean-clad legs as they extended straight out in front of him, and the way his heather-gray rugby hugged his muscular shoulders. His hair was wavy and hit the collar of his shirt. A perfectly groomed goatee shadowed his mouth and chin. He seemed older, more mature, and more gorgeous now than when I'd first met him.

I approached quietly. "Hope I'm not interrupting."

Turning in surprise, he leaned his head back and squinted through the low-angled sunlight.

"Claudia," he murmured. Almost self-consciously, he ran a hand through his hair. "Just having a chat with *mi madre*." He twisted his upper body towards me. "I was telling her that you had your graduation yesterday. She would have been proud of you."

I glanced over at the headstone and smiled. "She always supported my decision to go."

"Well, you did it. You're officially a college graduate." He gave me the thumbs up. "How was the ceremony? Did you get my message?"

"It went well," I said. "And yes. I got your message. Thank you." He had left me a brief but sweet voicemail yesterday morning, wishing me a good day.

He looked down at his hands. It was easy to see he felt as nervous about this as I did. A gusty breeze whipped at the hem of my dress, and automatically, I pressed it down against my thighs to keep it from flying up.

Toby watched me wrestle the fabric until finally the wind let up. His eyes, lit with a palpable and all too familiar interest, leisurely made their way back up to my face. My whole body warmed.

"You'd better pop a squat." He nodded, motioning to the ground. "My mind will be in the gutter if the wind keeps lifting your dress like that. And since you didn't attempt to hug or kiss me hello, it's obvious that you have other things on your mind."

So focused on what needed to be said, I was flustered by the sudden sexual tension that emanated between us. Quickly, I bent my knees and sank down onto the soft, spring grass. "After what happened in Carlsbad, I don't think there's any question as to whether we're still attracted to each other. What we really need is to talk."

"Yeah, I know," he said, plucking out a handful of grass and letting it flutter away in the breeze. "Claude, I hate the way we left everything. I've done a lot of thinking about what I could have done and said that would have made it easier. What's kind of funny is, I told your father to let you make your own decision about where you wanted to go to school, and there I was pressuring you the same way."

His smile was tight as he shifted into a more upright position.

I bit at my lip and waited for him to continue.

"I called Bob when I got back. I told him we were trying to work things out." His eyes flicked to mine. "He wasn't surprised that I'd never told anyone how I felt. Hell, I never told Julia either," he murmured, glancing over at his parents' headstone. "I should have."

"She knew you loved her."

"But you don't know how I feel about you, and that's the problem."

Tense, I swallowed hard and nodded once.

"It's so frustrating to keep hitting walls. I've spent the last few weeks trying to understand what prevents me from getting close to anyone. Bob said I'd find a girl who'd be patient with me until I felt comfortable enough to admit my feelings." He lifted his hands in question. "The thing is, he's right. I could find plenty of girls out there willing to give me a chance."

I hadn't expected this, but raised my chin preparing to take the blow.

"But I told Bob, I'd already found a girl who'd been more than patient with me—a girl who'd gone through hell with me, but despite it all, never tossed me aside."

Suddenly, his blue-gray eyes brimmed with unshed tears, and seeing this show of emotion, my own eyes filled, too.

"That's because I love you."

A pained and strangled groan rumbled in his throat, and he bowed his head. With difficulty, I remained waiting for a cue from him.

All of a sudden, he reached for me.

"Come here. Please." His hoarse plea shattered my reservations, and I closed the distance between us, scurrying into his arms. I huddled close to him and pressed my cheek against his chest. The last few weeks, I had dreamed nonstop about being close to him again.

He hugged me tight to him and kissed the top of my head. "Claudia, if you'd rather go to USC, I promise not to make you feel bad about it. I just need to know you want to be with me…" his voice wavered. "Tell me you want me back and I'll wait. And when you're done with school, we'll figure it out, together, what comes next. California could work for me. I can look for a job—"

Not waiting for him to finish, I wrapped my arms around his neck and hugged him. Hard. It seemed to immobilize him. He fell silent.

"Thank you." I smiled up at him, loving him even more for being unselfish. "I know that wasn't easy for you to offer."

"No, it isn't hard. Because all I want is to be with you. But I won't be happy unless you're happy, too." He pressed me closer into him and rested his chin atop my head.

"I'm happy right now, right here," I said.

"But, I still haven't told you how I feel."

"It's okay. I suppose I expected too much, too soon," I whispered.

Suddenly he pulled back to look into my face. "No. It isn't too much to expect. Even from me."

I stared at him, afraid to hope.

"I don't think I ever had the kind of trust it takes to get close to anyone. And, I've done my best to keep everyone at a safe distance." His eyes held mine. "Except you. You're the only girl I ever wanted to cross over that line for."

Even though I was desperate to hear it, I wanted to hush him and tell him it didn't matter.

"Claudia, you're inside me. And, I like you there." He cupped my chin and stroked my cheek with his thumb. "After all we've been through, I know if there's anyone I can trust, it's you." The soft, vulnerable look in his eyes made my breath catch. "It knocks me out how much I feel about you."

Unable to move, I waited.

He whispered, "So, like, I do."

I leaned closer. "You do what?"

He momentarily squeezed his eyes closed and inhaled. "Love you," he finally said.

"Oh." I bit back my smile. "Think you can arrange those words into a cohesive statement?"

"I'm saying I love you. Okay?" The words came out with verve and yet, still had an air of uncertainty, as if he suspected I might not accept them.

I beamed through the tears that spilled down my cheeks. "So you actually can say it."

His arm tightened around my waist. "Yes. I can say it. And I mean it, Claudia. I love you."

He lowered his face towards mine, and our eyes held for a long, heated moment. With his mouth only inches from mine, I moved to close the distance, but as I angled my mouth upwards, he suddenly turned away.

Glancing over his shoulder at his mother's gravestone, he said, "What's that, Ma? You think I should hurry up and kiss her already?"

Giggling, I locked my arms around his neck. "You'd better do as your mother tells you."

Finally, he lowered his mouth to mine and kissed me. Sighing in contentment, I pressed myself into him, greedy for the kiss to deepen. I reveled in the feel of his large hands on my back as he held me possessively against him. A thrilling burn fired up inside me, strengthened by the knowledge that now, beyond a doubt, he loved me.

"Hey, I just realized something." He grinned and leaned his forehead to mine. "I've had my first, first with you. I've never told a girl that I loved her before—a huge first that you get to call yours. All yours."

"Yes!" I gloated, dotting his lips with another kiss. The sun, now considerably lower in the skyline, was not as warm as when I'd arrived. I shivered in my light sweater.

Toby picked up his jacket and put it around my shoulders. "Come on. Let's go back to my house. I'll warm you up with the 'official reunion' ceremony."

I laughed. "Is that anything like the 'official girlfriend' ceremony?"

"The girlfriend ceremony only required a kiss," he said. "The reunion ceremony is much more involved. We have to get naked for it."

"Jeez! I see there are some things about you that haven't changed.

All you think about, still, is sex."

"Claude," he groaned with theatrical exaggeration. "It's been a long time. I want to get you naked and under me as soon as possible. I'm going to show you how much I love you." He nuzzled my face, his breath warm on my cheek.

Smiling apprehensively, I slanted away from him. "Um, about that."

He raised an eyebrow. "About what?"

"Sex." I bit my lip. "I don't want to rush right back into having it."

"But, I thought after the resort…"

My face flamed as I remembered what he had done to me with his mouth and how I had enjoyed it.

"Yeah, well, things moved awfully fast that night." I traced the curve of his chin in an effort to soften my explanation. "I want to be with you, but I'd like us to be on solid footing before we move into such an intimate relationship again."

Letting out a loud breath, he looked away for a moment. I knew this was asking a lot, but I needed the time to adjust. To be sure.

His eyes returned to me. "I guess I can do that. But only because I know what I'm waiting for," he said and lifted my hand to press a kiss into my palm. "It's worth the wait."

I stroked his chin, enjoying the feel of his groomed stubble as it grazed against my fingertips. "Thank you."

I moved to stand up, but before I could, he wrapped his arms around my waist and held me fast to him. Leaning down to look into my eyes, his expression was serious.

"I'll do whatever I can to make you happy. Even if I have to follow you to California to finally get you naked."

"Thank you, baby," I said, the whispered endearment slipping naturally from my lips. "You might have to wait for the naked part, but you definitely don't have to follow me to California. I'm not going back."

His mouth opened and closed without words coming out, and I laughed.

"You're staying here? On the island?" he managed to ask at last.

I nodded. "I finalized my schedule at SBU, and I'm meeting with the director at Sterling to talk about my internship." I looked up at him. "I wanted to give us a chance, but I also miss being here.

This is my home."

He let out a breath of relief. "I'm so freaking happy right now. You have no idea," he said, smoothing my hair with his fingers. "Claudia Chiametti, I want to be with you forever."

I kissed his chin. "Wow, such an optimistic romantic."

"Maybe I am." He shrugged. "Optimism is potent stuff. I wouldn't let myself believe anything else but that we'd get to this very place. And now, here we are."

"But forever is a long time. And why put that kind of pressure on us? Let's just start with a month and work up from there."

"A month?" he balked.

"Well, what did you have in mind?"

Looking at me, he cocked his head to the side. "What I have in mind is forever."

Though the sentiment was sweet, 'forever' was a nonsensical word. "Nothing lasts forever."

He tsk-tsked me. "Oh, ye of little faith."

"Oh, please." I rolled my eyes at the archaic phrase. "I have a lot of faith."

"But not in us."

This time I opened and shut my mouth without a word.

Toby chuckled. "That's all right. I have enough faith for both of us. If it'll make you feel better, we'll say the summer to start with. But I plan on making you want me forever."

"I don't know how you can be so sure, but okay." I shrugged. "I'm certainly interested in seeing you pull that off."

Holding me immobile with his smoldering gaze, he slid the full expanse of his large hands slowly over my hips and pressed his palms against the fleshy anterior. The heated look matched with the provocative manipulation had an immediate effect.

A ripple of excitement swelled inside me.

I released a slow, tight breath. By his smile, I could tell he knew how it affected me.

"Mmm. It would be a helluva lot easier to do it with some mind-blowing sex. I guess I'm going to have to get creative until you give me the green light," he whispered. "But, oh, baby, when we finally do it, you're not going to be able to walk for days afterwards."

The promise had me practically panting. "Holy cow," I crowed and shook my head. "How can you talk to me like that in front of your mother? She's probably horrified."

Chuckling, Toby stood up and offered me his hand. "Julia's not listening anymore. She's too busy doing a happy dance up there in heaven. With my father."

"Because we're together?" I asked, as he pulled me to my feet. He nodded. Picturing Mrs. Faye swirling around with Mr. Faye, a big smile on her face, made me swallow back tears. "I really like that image."

We linked hands and strolled closer to the gravestone. "You know, your mother brought us together."

"I think it was her master plan, since day one," he said.

I turned to face him. "Her master plan was for you to be happy."

"She always knew I'd be happy here. But she was sure I'd be happiest if I were here, with you." He squeezed my hand within his and laid the other warmly on my cheek. "Turns out, she was right."

A Note from the Author

Hello reader! A big thank you for reading my novel, Saving Toby. I sincerely hope you enjoyed Toby and Claudia's heartfelt story. Their journey continues in sequel, "Keeping Claudia." Be sure to sign up for release updates at SuzanneMcKennaLink.com.

Public, online reviews are everything to an Indie author like myself. So if you enjoyed Saving Toby, please take a moment to leave an online review at your favorite book retailer. And by all means, feel free to contact me via any of the sites below.

Peace,

~ Suzanne

Crave more Toby and Claudia?

To read deleted scenes, hear Saving Toby's music playlist, and get author updates, visit *www.suzannemckennalink.com*

Like me on Facebook at *www.facebook.com/SuzanneMckennaLink*

Follow me on Twitter *@SuzMcKLink*

Check out my blog: *suzannemckennalink.blogspot.com*

Read on for a preview of
KEEPING CLAUDIA...

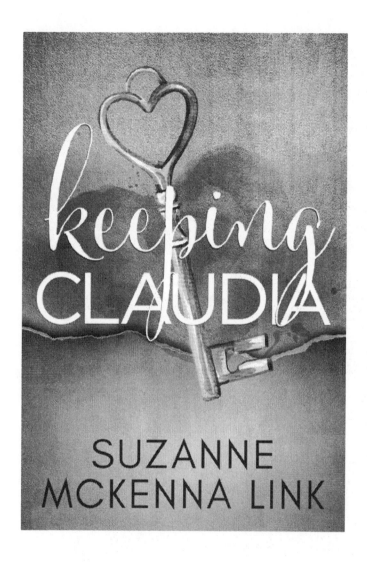

keeping
CLAUDIA

A Novel By
SUZANNE MCKENNA LINK

Chapter 1

~TOBY~

NIGHTCRAWLERS CREPT INTO AND FILLED every space of the Mad Monkey's cave-like barroom. Electronic music whirled in from overhead speakers, and the pulsing, driving beat blended with the vibration of alcohol-laden voices. A fast-moving current of energy rode the air with a palpable force. Typical of Fridays, impatient clubbers ringed the stage, waiting for the band to begin its performance.

Having finished up the sound check, I set my guitar down and absently scratched my week-old facial hair while scanning the crowd for Claudia.

"Hey, rock star."

I turned toward Leah's voice just as the tatted band groupie came up on stage. "Rock star? Yeah right." Unshaven and dressed in a T-shirt and jeans, I might've looked the part of a wannabe rock star, but it was just my normal, everyday look.

"Heard a couple of bands bailed on the Monkey's annual lineup. Some shit with the new owner. They're actively seeking hot new talent," she said, slipping her right arm, an intricate weave of flowers and flourishes etched into snow-white skin, around my waist. "This place isn't just another local dive; it's got a reputation."

For sure. A gig at the Mad Monkey substantially upped the chances of getting laid. It also laid claim to a successful start for two local bands, according to Dan. He'd done his research. Headlining nightly as a line cook over at Applebee's, he was good at organizing stuff. And, he'd made sure we all knew to treat tonight's performance like an audition.

"Yeah, whatever." I didn't care much one way or the other.

"Those old guys aren't much to look at, but they know their shit," she said nodding in the direction of middle-aged music teachers, Keith and RJ on keyboard and bass. "And Bones, he's a presence on his own."

At the back of the stage, the large-framed and heavily tatted, leather-clad Bones messed around with the drums.

"Dan's a little too in love with himself, but no denying he's got strong pipes. And you and him up front? Total eye-candy."

She kind of nailed it. On appearance, Young Cranky Old Guys looked like a mismatched, patched-together tribe.

"And I like candy." Leah pressed into me and smiled. "I'll buy after the show." She turned and dropped off the stage. On her back, feathery angel wings spanned the width of her shoulder blades.

I should've responded. Should've said something. I'd slept with her, but she knew the score. I'd not given her any reason to believe there was anything between us.

We'd met after a show last year. I couldn't stop staring at her. She reminded me a lot of a girl I once knew, the resemblance damn near eerie. I'd just gotten back from visiting Claudia at school, having failed at my attempts for a reunion. She'd turned me down, hard. Dark times. I looked up, and there was Leah with her striking likeness to Lacie. Self-medication. I didn't push, hadn't even been particularly nice, just told her that I wanted to see those wings. That's all it had taken.

Pushing those thoughts aside and getting anxious about seeing Claudia, I knelt on the floor to arrange the foot pedals for my amplifier.

Dan sauntered over and slapped my back. "Dude, pyromaniac playing with explosives. Watch your back. Your main squeeze is onsite, eleven o'clock."

I stood and looked out over the barroom. From the height of the stage, it only took a moment to spot her across the room. Long dark hair cascaded softly over bare shoulders, her smooth skin a shade of Mediterranean bronze. Though it might've been a trick of my memory, I could smell that skin across the distance— the soothing scent of honey warmed by the sun. In the darkened room, her white sleeveless dress was nearly fluorescent, making Claudia Chiametti stand out from the rest—too beautiful and too perfect for her surroundings. Moving carefully through the crowd,

Claudia looked up. The instant those sky-blue eyes connected with mine, her smile flashed brilliant against the warm caramel tone of her skin. An electric current ate up the distance between us, and for a moment, everything stilled except the staccato drumbeat of my heart.

Claudia, several yards back and at odds with the crowd that engulfed her, wasn't interested in popularity contests. She was the kind of girl who was more at home speaking in front of a crowd than pushing through one. She was the kind of girl you hoped you could get alone, away from the noise, so you could sit and listen to her because whatever she said would benefit you. She was the kind of girl you wanted on your side because no matter what shit you got yourself into, she would stick it out with you right till the end. After everything we'd been through, she was my rock. She was the reason I hadn't completely self-destructed.

No, Claudia wasn't tripping over star power, mine or anyone else's. I wouldn't have wanted it any other way. I joined Young Cranky Old Guys to show Claudia and everyone else that I had rejoined life, that I was no longer letting my mother's death hold my future hostage.

I watched some guy tap Claudia's shoulder, and my stomach clenched when she turned to talk to him. Even with our friends April and Dario at her side, I wasn't confident Claudia could handle guys full up on liquid courage and dogged to score. I was all about her coming tonight but had forgotten that while I was up on the stage, she would be down with the masses. And I would have to stand witness to all the shitheads hitting on her.

Now that she was home, it was an unspoken challenge for me to fold her into the life I'd created while she was away at school. I'd do it because I'd asked for this. No, fucking begged for it. After nearly two years apart and a long, uphill battle to get her back, I'd earned the right to be a bit territorial.

Dan whistled and circled two fingers over his head, rousing the group. "Let's get this show started."

It was go time. I slung my guitar strap over my shoulder and went back to tracking Claudia's movement. It was all I could do not to jump down and drag her back to the stage to stand in front of me.

As a last-minute ditch effort, I leaned toward Dan. "Do me a favor. Call Claudia up here."

He cupped his hands around the microphone and spoke in a droning voice. "Attention, shoppers. Paging the stunning Miss Claudia. Please report to the left-hand side of the stage. You are needed immediately for *debriefing*."

Claudia rolled her eyes but pushed her way through the crowd and came to stand at the edge of the platform.

"Hey," I said, squatting down to her level.

Our gazes met and held. A bubble of indefinable energy crackled between us.

"Hey," she returned, a warm flush creeping over her face. "Nice shirt."

The large white letters across my dark-blue T-shirt bragged: *Always in a Position to Score.*

I laughed. "Got a reputation to uphold. Can't let all these people know how long it's actually been."

"Sorry," she said with a smile.

She definitely wasn't.

In agreeing to start over, part of our deal was that I would not pressure her to move ahead too fast. Which plainly meant: no sex. Patience had never been my strong suit, and being patient for sex… Well, let's say it's not something I was used to, but one month in, I was practically a poster boy for patience. Claudia Chiametti was the only girl who made me want more of the same. She had given me a second chance, and I promised myself I wouldn't screw it up. I was keeping her no matter what it took.

Without looking away, I motioned towards the schlep she'd been talking with. "Who's the guy?"

"Don't know. Wanted to buy me a drink," she said with a shrug.

"Thought it might've been an old boyfriend."

"I dated one guy in college very briefly." She held up a finger. "The chances of finding him in this crowd are slim to none. Bet you can't boast the same about your old girlfriends, Romeo."

Girlfriends, probably not, but with Leah here, at least one bump and go. Could be more. Who could say? It was a big crowd. I had a long history. Of course, I'd never tell Claudia that. If it weren't for me, her father would be the only man in her life.

April and Dario's dark heads materialized, and wearing color-coordinated outfits, the couple bookended Claudia.

"When are you guys starting?" April asked.

I glanced over my shoulder at the rest of the band.

Dan raised his hands in question.

I grabbed Claudia's hand and kissed the back of her fingers. "We're starting now. Stay put where I can see you."

"Afraid I might wander off and get lost?" she asked, amused.

"Stop worrying." April pushed at me. "My *chica* is no delicate wallflower. Didn't you see her karate chop that guy back there? You probably can't see him because he's out cold on the floor."

Grinning, I shook my head. "I'm afraid Claudia will make a run for the door to get the hell outta here."

Claudia pulled at the front of my T-shirt and rose up on her toes. I tasted her berry-flavored lip balm when she kissed me.

"I'm not going anywhere, at least, not until I see you play."

"It's all good, *ese*," Dario said with a nod. "We won't let her abandon you. Now go make your mama proud."

Assured Claudia was secure with our friends, I stood and readjusted the strap of my Fender, then gave Dan the thumbs up. Dan signaled the rest of the group. The crowd hooted its approval.

With Claudia in front of me, I bowed my head and began to play.

Chapter 2

~CLAUDIA~

THE VOLUME OF THE CROWD had risen substantially since April, Dario, and I arrived. With the first notes played, whoops and cheers rose from the audience and, in the ensuing excitement of the show, there was a further melee of elbowing and pushing for a prime view of the stage. An overexuberant girl, probably drunk, stepped on my toes and knocked into me, jarring my expanding bladder.

Oh, the joys of bar etiquette. Or lack thereof.

What a difference a month made. Four weeks ago, I was tucked in a shoebox-sized dorm room at the University of Southern California, cramming for finals with graduation a beckoning light at the end of the tunnel.

Unlike the majority of the other undergrads I studied alongside, when I wasn't at the library, I was more likely to be found volunteering at campus blood drives or charity events than at places like the Mad Monkey. In the madness of the typical bar scene, I was the figurative square peg. It was difficult not to stare and cluck my tongue at girls whose clothing was so tight or minuscule that they left nothing to the imagination.

If it'd been any other night, I might've abandoned the place in annoyance, but tonight I exhaled a patient sigh. For this night, I would stay. It didn't matter if I was a square peg or unfamiliar with the music. For a night, I could try to assimilate and be one of the crowd—well, with a little more clothing on and a lot less alcohol—because tonight I was here for Toby. And that was all that mattered.

Despite the blasting air conditioner, the air was heavy and sticky.

346 SUZANNE MCKENNA LINK

Bartenders worked at a dizzying pace, popping bottle tops, clinking ice cubes into glasses, and pouring short and tall drinks.

I held firmly onto my glass of wine as hot, sweaty bodies swarmed around us. I lost my position at the front, but an opening between heads still allowed me to see my six-foot-one, lean-muscled guy with the high-gloss maroon electric guitar. By the looks he was amassing, I'd say there were more than a few women in the crowd who would enjoy exploring the dips and peaks obscured by his tight, dark T-shirt. I didn't blame them. His body was indeed nice to touch. Too bad for them, Toby was taken.

The music was energetic and catchy. April, Dario, and I danced, clapped, and hooted through several songs.

In between songs, April poked me in the arm. "See that girl with curly reddish hair and purple shirt over there? Toby went out with her in eleventh grade."

"I remember her," Dario said. "Hannah Hendricks. Still very pretty."

With Hannah's focus pinned on the stage, I stared openly. Dario was right. She was pretty, extremely so. Long copper tresses, slender but well-proportioned and, in a pair of minuscule, tight shorts, legs that went on for days.

"Messy breakup," April said.

"Why messy?" I asked, unable to take my eyes from her.

Toby had a formidable list of ex-girlfriends—common knowledge about our small town—but when I thought of the girls in his past, it was easy to imagine them all as harmless, faceless figures. I'd never actually seen any of them up close. Until recently, we hadn't really traveled in the same circles.

April cupped a hand around my ear. "She was super controlling, totally stalked Toby for like a year after their breakup."

High school already seemed like forever ago, but I still found myself troubled by the idea that Hannah had probably known Toby intimately. More intimately than I did.

A tall girl with a thick head of cropped black hair pushed her way in front of me to get closer to the stage. She was at least a head taller than me and wearing a red tank top and a pair of denim cutoffs that gave me and everyone in her wake an eyeful of her round butt. Her skin was more colorful than her clothes. Numerous, extravagant tats and piercings mocked the otherwise soft lines of her feminine figure. I couldn't help but stare. There was a certain beauty to it all, but I couldn't imagine why anyone would choose to do that kind of thing to their body.

Suddenly, the girl turned wide, catching me with dark and unblinking eyes. Blood-red lips parted, revealing unusually pointed eyeteeth. The teeth and the sunless white skin of a vampire.

"Take a fucking picture. It lasts longer."

I fell back a step, shocked at the unexpected vitriol.

"You got a problem?" April stepped closer.

The girl stared us down for a moment but thankfully, turned away.

When the set ended, Toby hopped down off the stage. Before he could reach us, Vampire Girl closed in on him. Her fingers curled around his forearm as she leaned in to whisper in his ear.

"Oh, hell no." April latched onto my arm and lurched forward with me in tow.

"Easy, April," Dario called, but she ignored him.

"Hands off, honey. He's already spoken for." April carted me forward as verification.

Vampire Girl pelted April with a frosty glare before turning it on me. Something in those bottomless brown eyes told me had there not been a roomful of pesky eyewitnesses, she would have bled me lifeless.

Toby pulled me from April's grasp to his side. "Leah—Claudia, April, and Dario," he shouted over the din, making informal introductions.

Leah. The name paired with the face rebooted my memory.

"Leah, sweetheart, there you are." Dan, the band's singer, broke into our cluster and hugged Leah from behind.

Leah hissed and chafed in Dan's hold, but just when it appeared she was about to do him bodily harm, she twisted around and kissed him. The smooch quickly escalated—hands grabbed, tongues flashed. We all stared, morbidly fascinated, as the lanky, blond-haired singer and Vampire Girl openly groped each other.

Except for Toby. Without a backward glance, he led us away, snaking through the crowd to the bar.

April pressed forward, confronting Toby before he could get the bartender's attention. "What the hell was that? How do you know that bitch?"

"Jesus, relax," Toby threw back at her. "Leah follows the band. Claudia knows about her."

April crossed her arms. "Well, she better watch that attitude."

"Who wants to watch her when there are two flawlessly coiffed, perfectly matched Latino lovers to look at?" Toby motioned to her and Dario. "Seriously, you two are just adorable."

April rolled her eyes and laughed. "After seeing that shirt, I'll bet Claudia wishes you had a smidge of our fashion sense."

"It takes time to look this good, *ese*." Dario smoothed the collar of his vivid blue shirt.

"Claude, we seriously need some *muy suave* matching outfits like them," Toby said and kissed the side of my face.

"We'll have to work on that. First, I need to hit the ladies' room." I grabbed April's hand because, social outcast that I was, even I knew girls didn't go to the bathroom alone.

"So, Leah?" April asked as we jumped into the quickly growing line of full-bladdered women.

"I came to see Toby play here, back in February. She was hanging out with him at the bar. She was just as charming back then. I'd assumed they were dating. Even told him I was happy for him, but you know, also really conflicted that he'd moved on. But when we celebrated my birthday in Carlsbad, he told me Leah had never been his girlfriend."

"She's into him," April said.

"Yeah, seems like a lot of girls are." I frowned and did a little tap dance to hold it in. "Is this line even moving?"

A blonde girl in a slinky, low-cut dress came out of a stall with the back of her dress hitched up awkwardly. She'd tucked the hem into her underwear.

April giggled, but I tapped her arm. "Hey, your dress."

"Omigosh. Thank you!" She laughed but blushed furiously as she fixed the wardrobe malfunction.

She was far too pretty for the heavy layer of makeup she wore. What's more, she looked too young to be in the bar in the first place.

Like the pretty blonde, the other women who hugged the wall waiting for a stall were all in costume with painted war faces and cleavage and butt cheeks on display.

"Is it me, or is everyone here selling it hard?"

April hooked her arm in mine. "Whatever. Dario and Toby see all these girls with their hoo-has and what-nots hanging out, and they only want us, 'cause we're their lobsters."

Obviously, April had been watching reruns of *Friends*, her all-time favorite sitcom.

"At least you and Dario come from similar backgrounds. Toby and I, we're like totally different species of crustaceans," I said.

"Right. He's a lobster. You're a crab," she said matter-of-factly.

"Shut up." With a smirk, I pinched her forearm.

"Then stop it," April said, leaning into me. "You're exactly what he wants. And needs. You guys are a perfect fit—his rough to your gentle, his relaxed nature to your exacting one."

I gave her a sidelong look. "The yin to his yang?"

"Milk to his cereal, bread to his butter," April said. "Cheese to his macaroni, shoes to his socks. I could do this all night."

"You always know how to show a girl a good time," I said, and we both laughed.

Exiting the bathroom, I looked up to find Toby's attention focused in my direction. Part of me really wanted to believe he and I were made for each other, but we were just so…different. His mouth crinkled upwards with that smile, the one that made me go all soft inside. And completely distracted me. The guy coming out of the men's room must've been distracted too because the two of us collided. My cell went flying.

"Oh my God, what a klutz. I'm so sorry." He quickly scrambled to retrieve my cell, continuing his apology.

April sighed with impatience behind me. Unlike the majority of guys there, he was a bit older and dressed nicely in a button-up shirt with belted shorts and tan designer leather skips. He was clearly as much a misfit at the Monkey as me.

"It doesn't appear to be damaged." He examined the phone, apologizing again before finally looking up at me. His mouth popped open and the ongoing loop of apology ended. "Well, hello," he said offering me his hand. "I'm Andrew."

April grabbed my cell and shoved it into my partially extended hand. "Have a nice night, Andrew."

Anything I might have wanted to say was nixed as she seized my elbow and drew me away.

"C'mon, Crabby. Our lobsters await."

"You just alienated me from one of my own species." I glanced over my shoulder to find Andrew's gaze following me. He was only one guy, but I had to admit I was the teeniest bit satisfied that Toby wasn't the only one with admirers.

⁂

To read more, get your copy of
KEEPING CLAUDIA at
Barnes & Noble or on Amazon.com

About the Author

Suzanne McKenna Link works for a local family of newspapers that covers events on the South Shore of Long Island, New York. She resides in the town of Sayville, New York with her husband and children.

Find out more at *www.SuzanneMcKennaLink.com/about*

Made in the USA
San Bernardino, CA
08 May 2020

71289038R00222